LONG SHOT

"I wish you guys would shut up before somebody hears us and comes over here and shoots our tails off," said Gerber. "Jeez. Anyone would think that you guys have never been in Indian country before. What do you think this is, some kind of Boy Scout picnic?"

Gerber's criticism was a bit harsh. None of the men had spoken above a whisper. But the rebuke did serve as a reminder of the seriousness of the situation they were in. None of the men took it personally, but all were quiet after that.

They waited until they were sure that no one was following the Pathet Lao patrol, and then moved on.

Ten minutes later, Bhang touched Krung lightly on the arm and held up a hand, then motioned the others forward.

"What is it?" Gerber asked anxiously. "Another patrol?"

"No, Captain," said Bhang. "It is the end of the journey. The camp lies just over the next ridge. We have arrived."

VIETNAM: GROUND ZERO®

SNIPER

ERIC HELM

A GOLD EAGLE BOOK FROM

W🌐RLDWIDE.

TORONTO • NEW YORK • LONDON • PARIS
AMSTERDAM • STOCKHOLM • HAMBURG
ATHENS • MILAN • TOKYO • SYDNEY

First edition November 1990

ISBN 0-373-60505-6

SNIPER

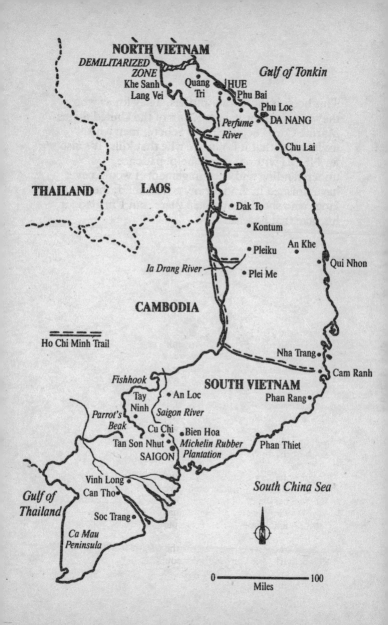

This book is for all the snuffies. They know who they are. And for the graduates of the United States Marine Corps Scout/Sniper School, men who understand that it is not the rifle that kills. It's also for NS7X, without whose help, patience, understanding and encouragement, I would never have finished it. And for my good friend, the Bush Hog, who should have been there, but I'm glad for his sake that he wasn't.

VIETNAM:GROUND ZERO®

SNIPER

PROLOGUE

**NORTHERN I CORPS,
RVN MAY, 1968**

United States Marine Corps Corporal Robert C. Corbett lay in the wet grass atop a little knoll overlooking a trail intersection northeast of the Rockpile and somewhere between Con Thien and Dong Ha, a few klicks north of Route 9 but still south of the Song Ngan Valley. It was between midnight and oh-dark-thirty in the morning, and his eyes burned from the strain of staring through the Starlite scope mounted on top of his heavy Remington bolt-action rifle.

Corbett would have liked to know what time it really was, but he didn't want to fight the black electrical tape covering the luminous dial of his self-winding wristwatch. Once you'd loosened the tape a few times, it refused to restick, and if you didn't keep the face of your watch covered, not only could the glow give away your position, but the brush and the thorn-covered vines would scratch away at the crystal until the watch was unreadable.

Besides, he was using the scope on his rifle to scan the surrounding countryside for targets, and he didn't want to look away for even the few moments it would take to check the time. Stingray Three One, a Marine recon team working just east of the Rockpile, had reported an NVA patrol heading in the direction of Corbett's team about an hour and a half ago, and it was time for them to show up in the vicinity if they followed their usual routine. A meter or so away, Sergeant Derek Erickson, Corbett's partner and the sniper-team leader, was using another Starlite scope, a hand-held model, to check his half of the curved area, roughly two-thirds of a circle, that made up their ROA. The other one-third was covered more or less by the five-man Marine security team deployed to their rear. In theory, the team would keep any enemy forces from sneaking up on the two snipers and serve as a fire-and-maneuver element should any unpleasant surprises occur.

For the umpteenth time Corbett wondered if he'd made a good career choice. It was something he had done about a dozen times a day since he arrived in-country. He could have been smart and joined the National Guard, or even gone to college and enrolled in one of the service branches' ROTC programs. His high school grades were good enough, and ROTC would have kept him out of the draft and given him a commission. He could have enrolled in the Navy ROTC, for instance, and if the war were to continue for another four years, he'd have found himself sitting safe and snug aboard the cruiser *St. Paul*, floating around in the South China Sea, the ship's one-eight-inch guns able to outdistance anything the VC or NVA could throw at it. The one thing he couldn't have done was run off to Canada. That option would simply never have occurred to him. Corbett came from a long line of small-town Midwestern patriots. His great-great-grandfather had fought in the Civil War, his great-grandfather in the

Spanish-American War, his grandfather in World War I and his father in World War II. An older brother had served in Korea. Except for the great-great-grandfather, who had purchased a cavalry captaincy, all Corbett's male ancestors had been NCOs in the U.S. Army. He had created quite enough stir by enlisting in the Marines. That he could have become a draft dodger was utterly unthinkable.

Corbett, who preferred the nickname, Bob, had been known to most of his fellow Marines in boot camp at Paris Island as the Professor, a swipe by his brethren at his preference for reading philosophy and science texts instead of *Playboy* or comic books. Later on, in sniper school, he had become known as One-Shot Corbett, a name that had as much to do with his approach to dating females as it did with his marksmanship. That nickname had stuck and had followed him to Vietnam.

Corbett was an oddity in the Marine Corps. Valedictorian of his high school class, he was smarter and more widely read than most of his mates. He also didn't look much like the Marines one always saw on the recruiting posters. Five feet six and a half inches tall, with brown hair already beginning to thin by the time he graduated from high school, he had a barrel-shaped chest and a slight potbelly that even Marine calisthenics had failed to cure, and had come out of boot camp weighing ten pounds more than the 135 he had started at. The efforts of numerous tailors notwithstanding, he always managed to look just a little bit rumpled in his dress blues, as though he had just gotten off a bus or a train. He smoked a pipe, or a Russian cigarette when he could find one, and had taken two years of Spanish and two years of French in high school. He could type fifty words a minute, had run cross-country track in school where his endurance had made up for his short legs, played the saxophone well and had sung in school and church choirs with a rich, deep bass. But, to the never-ending dismay of his father, who had been a well-known amateur and semiprofessional player, he couldn't hang on to a football with glue on his hands and was a dismal failure at baseball. He also had an innate revulsion from bugs, particularly spiders and insects that sting, and was squeamish about cleaning fish or dressing game. Perversely he was fascinated by snakes, lizards and birds and could identify more than one hundred different trees by their leaves, buds or bark. In short, he had a great love of the outdoors, despite the bugs. Back home he had a large collection of knives, but seemed incapable of sharpening them to a decent edge. It was hard to imagine a more improbable candidate for the Marines.

In fact, there were only three things about Bob Corbett that made him the perfect choice for the job he was doing now. One of the first merit badges he had earned as a Boy Scout was for orienteering, which meant he was an expert with map and compass. Second, he had a penchant for forcing himself to do things he didn't like to do or was afraid of doing. And, finally, he was an absolutely uncanny rifle shot.

In boot camp he had performed the unheard-of feat of shooting a possible on the rifle range. The DI, a gunnery sergeant with nineteen years in the Corps, had never seen anyone shoot a possible before. He had refused to believe it and insisted Corbett fire again. Corbett had complied, dropping three points to a score of 247 out of a possible 250. The sergeant had promptly chewed his ass, roaring, "Any Marine who can shoot that damn good has no excuse for ever missing."

It was the closest thing to a compliment Corbett ever got from the man, but he detected the subtle change. From then on the gunnery sergeant referred to Corbett as a Marine. The rest of the platoon were still "boots."

After boot camp and IRT, Corbett volunteered for Marine recon training. Even he couldn't say why he'd done it, any more than he could tell someone why he'd enlisted in the Marines. In high school he'd been something of a bookish weakling, the kind of student other boys liked to pick on. Maybe he'd been trying to prove something with both choices, but to whom? He didn't know. It had just seemed like the thing to do at the time.

He barely passed the swimming qualification, and the battalion commander called him in for a personal conference. There were two pipelines leading to a reconnaissance qualification—Recon Man-SCUBA and Recon Man-Paramarine. He recommended that Corbett consider the latter. The commander didn't think he'd make it as a swimmer.

Corbett thought it over and reluctantly agreed. The truth of the matter was that he was a lousy swimmer, and he knew it. But he also suffered from acrophobia. Flying in an airplane didn't bother him, but he couldn't climb a one-story house without a safety line and a supply of knuckle Band-Aids. He absolutely hated the towers on the infiltration and confidence courses. But he wanted his recon rating, and if the only way to get it was to jump out of a perfectly good airplane before the engine even stopped or the wings fell off, he'd do it. Being a poor swimmer wasn't something he could fix overnight, but he figured all he had to do about jumping out of airplanes was force himself to take that first step. He did it, and earned his recon wings.

In the meantime the Marine Corps hadn't lost sight of Corbett's marksmanship abilities. When he finished his recon training, he was given the opportunity to attend the two-week-long scout/sniper course. Although the program was normally reserved for combat-experienced riflemen, there was a shortage of snipers in Vietnam, and the Corps had no intention of wasting the talent of somebody who could shoot like Corbett by seasoning him for a year in a place where he might get killed walking point the first week.

It turned out to be one of the better bargains the Marine Corps ever made. By the end of his third week in Vietnam, Lance Corporal Bob Corbett had thirteen confirmed kills to his credit and a Combat Meritorious promotion to corporal. The 7.62 mm ammunition that Corbett's Remington sniper rifle fired cost the Marine Corps about fourteen cents a round. Few of them were ever wasted.

Corbett felt no pangs of conscience about his job, despite the fact that he didn't agree with the view taught at sniper school that his art was a sport, albeit a dirty one. He knew the people he killed were human beings, infantrymen like himself, but he also knew they were the enemy. If he didn't kill them, they would certainly kill Marines. Nor did he trouble himself over the increasingly popular view back home that there would be no killing on either side if America would simply leave Vietnam. Policy decisions regarding the employment of military forces were decisions he left to politicians. All Corbett knew was that he was in a war, no matter what civilians back home called it. The situation was simple—kill or be killed.

The night was cold, and Corbett shivered involuntarily. It never ceased to amaze him how Vietnam could be so swelteringly hot during the day and so cold at night. The climate was a miserable one to fight a war in, but then he couldn't think of any really good climate for fighting a war.

It had grown cloudy since dusk, and the Starlite scopes, which worked by greatly intensifying existing light, were now almost useless. The only thing that could be said for the Starlite scope on Corbett's rifle was that at least his vision wasn't any worse with it than without it. Right now he would gladly have traded the several-thousand-dollar technological wonder for an old, reliable, infrared weapons sight. With an active IR system a rifleman might be more noticeable to an enemy sniper, but at least the IR beam let a man look into the shadows, and the system worked no matter how dark it got. With the passive Starlite scope, anything in shadow remained shadowed, and when there wasn't any background light to be amplified, the scope didn't work at all.

As he pressed his eye against the rubber cup of the ocular, there was a sudden, brilliant flash of green in the scope, almost instantly washed out as the image intensifier overloaded and the momentary circuit breaker interrupted the power to keep the circuits from burning out. A wave of light swept over the countryside, turning the inky-black shadows into high noon as Corbett jerked instinctively away from the scope. Lightning.

Terrific, thought Corbett. That was all they needed. Rain. Thunder rolled over them like an artillery barrage, then it grew quiet again.

Corbett continued scanning with the scope, but the situation was hopeless. It was just too dark to see, and when the lightning arced through the sky, the intensifier, straining to find the least little bit of light and multiply it, overloaded and washed out.

Corbett finally gave up and lowered his rifle. He crawled a couple of feet to where he could whisper to Erickson and indicated that he wanted to trade rifles. For reasons only known to the Joint Chiefs of Staff, the Marine Corps had yet to issue a quick-change mount for the scopes on their rifles, so snipers, who always worked in two-man teams, kept one rifle fitted with a Starlite scope and the other with either the eight-power Unertl or the new Redfield three-to-nine-power variable optical telescopic sight, depending on what they'd been issued. In Marine sniper teams only one man fired at a time, anyway, the other man spotting targets for the shooter to engage. It was thought by the experts to be a more efficient system, but in fast action at relatively close ranges, say two hundred yards or less, the observer could wonder whether he was doing anything useful, or was just excess baggage. Toting a heavy rifle with the wrong kind of sight on it half the time didn't help one's confidence, either, but then the Marines had a long tradition of making do with equipment that was either second-best or discarded by the other services.

Since Erickson was the designated spotter right now, he didn't mind the trade. He knew that with the Unertl-scoped Remington Corbett would at least be able to see during the intermittent flashes when the lightning lit up the sky. He'd already switched from the hand-held Starlite to the 7×50 mm Bushnell binoculars for the same reason. He doubted whether they'd be able to spot any targets at all on a night like this, but then you never knew. It was certainly the kind of weather Charlie liked to move around in.

As they were making the trade, the heavens finally opened and somebody upstairs turned on a series of two-and-a-half-inch fire hoses. Both men dragged out their ponchos and pulled them on over their heads, more in an effort to protect their weapons and their expensive sights than for personal comfort. Erickson and Corbett were instantly soaked through and through.

The two Marines crouched beneath their ponchos, struggling not to shiver and trying their best to catch a glimpse of their respective trail intersections as they silently cursed the weather, Vietnam, the U.S. Marine Corps and life in general.

The downpour pounded them unrelentingly for forty-five minutes, then mercifully slackened to only a steady rain. The rocky dirt beneath them, never comfortable, turned into a sticky morass that, pressed down with their weight, allowed pools of water to form wherever their bodies contacted the ground. Both snipers were by now so wet and cold that their hands shook as if they had palsy.

Corbett's fingers felt almost numb inside his sodden gloves, and there was a nearly steady flow of water across his back. In order to get any use at all of the Unertl scope, he could only partially cover it and the rifle. He'd had to drape his poncho over himself like a blanket and tuck in the sides around him, leaving the end open for the barrel and forearm of the rifle and the objective of the scope to stick out. Every time the wind whipped around the loose hood in the center of his poncho, he got a shower right across the kidneys. The rest of the time the wind seemed to have an uncanny ability to blow the rain right under the open end of the poncho and into his face.

Erickson, at least, could wear his poncho in the manner intended and only had to contend with wet hands and a bit of water running down his arms and soaking his sleeves as he peered through the binoculars, his hood pulled down to an opening just barely large enough to accommodate the eyepieces. However, he was still cold, wet and miserable, and was just about ready to write the whole evening off as a waste of time when a flash of lightning illuminated the trail intersection he was trying to watch, revealing several men standing in it.

What he saw was so unexpected, so startling, that despite all his training and experience, Erickson instinctively jerked the binoculars away from his eyes for a better look and promptly lost sight of the intersection. Before he could recover, the flash of lightning died, plunging everything back into blackness.

Precious seconds had been lost. Erickson knew he would have to wait for another bolt of lightning before he could line up the binoculars on the intersection again, and then, probably, for a second flash before he could get a good look at who was standing on the trail. Certainly it was long past curfew, and no civilians should be out wandering around at this time of night, but they had to be absolutely certain before Corbett fired. It was a matter of pride among Marine snipers that they killed only the enemy, and the press coverage that would follow from the accidental shooting of a couple of local farmers was a horror to be avoided at all costs. By the time he could find the intersection again, ascertain that it was the enemy he had seen, direct Corbett's attention to the intersection and have him acquire a target, the odds were excellent that they would be long gone. And Erickson wasn't even sure he'd spotted the enemy yet. It might be anybody. It might even be just a couple of oddly shadowed tree stumps.

The lightning cracked again, and Erickson got lucky. He found the intersection just before the light faded, using a large tree with a broken overhanging branch near the crossroads as his marker. Taking a deep breath, he forced his hands still and held his gaze just to the right of the tree.

It seemed to take an eternity while he waited blind in the blackness, until finally another flash of lightning illuminated the scene. Not more than thirty-five or forty seconds could have passed, but it seemed ten or fifteen times as long. Abruptly the sky lit up, and there, clearly silhouetted in blue-black against the gray-green backdrop of jungle under the light of electrostatic discharge, were the shapes of three men, each bowed under the load of a heavy pack and each carrying something with the unmistakable curved magazine outline of an AK-47.

Erickson reached out with his left hand, feeling without looking for Corbett, wanting to let him know that he had a target, yet not wanting to take his own eyes off the intersection again. He found a corner of the other Marine's poncho, tugged on it and was about to risk a loud whisper amid the falling raindrops when the lightning flashed again, the thunder following almost immediately.

Before either lightning or thunder had died away, there was a second flash, golden-red in color, and a loud *kaboom*! The sound was a sharper version of the thunder, and Erickson knew that Corbett had fired, but didn't know what the target was. To his left he could hear the metallic *snick-snick* as Corbett worked the bolt of the heavy-barreled Remington.

Another flash of light broke the night, and Erickson could see that there were now perhaps as many as half a dozen men in the intersection, more or less evenly spaced, but with a curious gap between two of them. Corbett fired again, and a second gap appeared before darkness shut out the view.

Erickson didn't speak. There was no need. Corbett had found the range and was doing what he got paid for. Talking now would only serve to distract the man. The lightning flashed, and Corbett fired a third time. The line of men in the trail intersection had been reduced by nearly half.

Again the lightning flashed and again Erickson could hear the sounds of Corbett at work.

Kaboom! Snick-snick.

Flash.

Kaboom! Snick, a pause, and then, *snick.*

Erickson knew what had happened. The magazine of the Remington held only five rounds. Corbett was now reloading by hand, one round at a time.

As Corbett fired a sixth time, there was an unusually long flash of lightning, and Erickson could see the scene laid out starkly before him—the trail intersection littered with bodies; the sharp outlines of the NVA soldiers against the foliage of the trees; the sudden, wrenching spin of one of the NVA as the bullet smacked wetly into him, whirling him around before he dropped facefirst into the mud; the look of surprise, abject terror on the face of the man next to him as he came to the jarring, sickening realization of what was happening.

Snick. Pause. *Snick.*

Flash.

Kaboom!

The report of Corbett's rifle sounded almost simultaneously with the flash of lightning, and an NVA who had turned away pitched headlong into a tree, slid down the trunk and lay still.

Snick. Pause. *Snick.*

A flash of lightning.

Kaboom!

Then there was a brief image of one last man stumbling, then darkness and the sounds of Corbett reloading.

When the lightning turned the night into high noon again, the view had taken on the eerie quality of fantasy. Nothing moved in the trail intersection. Men lay sprawled in grotesque postures, arms and legs akimbo, necks bent at improbable angles, no longer quite supporting heads. Erickson even imagined he could see dark stains spreading across the uniforms of the slain men, although he knew that was impossible with the distance and the precipitation falling. There was only the sound of the rain.

For perhaps ten minutes they watched the scene of recent carnage, the only motion an occasional splash of mud and water stirred up by the raindrops. Erickson could see at least six bodies lying along the trail. There was no answering fire. The enemy had fled.

The two Marine snipers didn't sleep for the rest of the night. The rain ended sometime before dawn, and in the dirty gray twilight world of first light, Erickson pulled the team in and he and Corbett walked down the slope to the trail intersection to check the night's work.

The previous evening's kills lay twisted, sodden and muddy before them, bloodstains still masked by the wet uniforms, eyes fixed and staring, faces contorted into hideous masks. Erickson and Corbett collected the AK-47s and inspected the packs of the dead NVA soldiers. In addition to his rifle and personal equipment, each NVA carried a large quantify of ammunition and hand grenades. The backpack of one of the men contained five Czech Skorpion machine pistols and twenty magazines.

In total there were seven confirmed kills. An extra backpack and rifle, along with a trail through the mud, indicated at least one NVA had been dragged off by his comrades, making an eighth probable kill.

During the brief engagement, Corbett had fired his Remington eight times, with only the brief illumination of lightning flashes to sight by. At fourteen cents a shot the

Marine's investment in Bob Corbett's training had paid off once again. He had been in-country less than two months. His record now stood at twenty confirmed kills.

1

TAN SON NHUT SAIGON, RVN

With the end of the spring transition period and the beginning of the southwest monsoon, nearly all of Vietnam, both North and South, and a good portion of the rest of Southeast Asia, were subject to heavy rains that made air travel difficult, turned roads into quagmires and made it all but impossible to distinguish night from day except by the degree of blackness.

The new diving watch on the wrist of U.S. Army Special Forces Master Sergeant Anthony B. Fetterman assured him that it was only a little after three-thirty in the morning, as he prepared to step down the ramp from the Air Force C-141 StarLifter and face the wrath of a Vietnamese rainstorm.

The flight of the big Lockheed air freighter had originated at Clarke Air Force Base near Manila in the Philippines, but for Fetterman and his traveling companion, Special Forces Captain MacKenzie K. Gerber, the journey had begun in Sydney, Australia, twenty-four hours earlier. Looking back on it, Fetterman couldn't say he'd enjoyed the trip. To begin with, it had started too damn soon.

He and Gerber had been promised a week-long R and R in Australia, following a particularly distasteful operation that had left several of their men dead or wounded and given both Green Berets an ugly case of the Nasty Attitudes. It was one of the little pluses of working for MACV-SOG. Most troops doing a tour of duty in Vietnam got one R and R of from one to two weeks' duration. Gerber and Fetterman had been to Australia twice and Hong Kong twice during their first and second tours in Vietnam.

Usually they attempted to coordinate such trips with the vacation of Gerber's girlfriend, Robin Morrow, a journalist who worked out of the press office in Saigon, but who covered the war from the field, not from behind a desk. Fetterman seldom had trouble finding a lady to share his company wherever he was, and the group made up a nice foursome, each couple having the good sense to allow the other an appropriate amount of privacy.

This time, however, the schedules hadn't meshed, and Gerber and Fetterman had gone off to Australia by themselves. They had been two days and nights into the serious guzzling of Australian beer and the not too serious fending off of the advances of ladies of questionable virtue in the King's Cross district, just beginning to make some inroads on the Nasties, when the recall telegram had reached them from Colonel Alan Bates, head of MACV-SOG's Special Projects Unit.

The message hadn't been well received by either man. Gerber had shown his enthusiasm by shredding the telegram, setting fire to it and stomping on the ashes before abandoning his Foster's lager and smoothing himself into oblivion on overpriced Beam's Choice. He had managed to stay comfortably drunk until they'd reached the Philippines.

Fetterman, more pragmatically, had opted to throw virtue to the winds and utilized the opportunity to retire to his hotel room for the rest of the evening in the company of three ladies whose virtue was no longer open to question, but whose self-esteem was perhaps a bit dearly priced. Such an extravagant excess was unusual for Fetterman, but the master sergeant had rationalized it on the basis that round-eyed women were in short supply in Vietnam, and that he didn't think it fair that he and Gerber should be the only people to get screwed.

They had caught a commercial flight to Manila early the next afternoon, then hopped a MAC flight out of Clarke. It had been a mistake. The plane had been loaded with metal coffins bound for Graves Registration in Saigon. Fetterman considered the cargo an ill omen. A hideously hung-over Gerber spent most of the flight alternating between throwing up and trying hard not to.

Fetterman cinched the belt on his Army issue, olive-drab raincoat, buttoned up the collar and steeled himself to be greeted by a face full of rain. The downpour might not be all that bad, he told himself. He could certainly use a shower. He just hadn't planned on taking it with his coat on.

Fetterman and Gerber grabbed their bags and stepped out into the rain. It wasn't at all like taking a shower with their clothes on. It was more like stepping fully dressed into the South China Sea. Their government-supplied rain gear was absolutely useless. They might as well have protected themselves with paper towels.

The two men trudged over to the Military Air Passenger Terminal and processed in, their dripping clothes leaving giant puddles whenever they stopped moving.

There were few other travelers to complain about the mess they were making. By the time they had managed to get all the necessary papers stamped and had forced down a couple of cups of the most god-awful coffee in creation, the airfield had been closed due to the weather conditions. It was one of the worst storms Saigon had seen in the past twenty years.

Oddly, in a city that supposedly never slept, finding a taxi or any other form of ground transportation proved impossible now. But the telegram had ordered them to report at once. So they stuffed their bags into a couple of straining lockers, wrestled the doors shut and hurried to the MACV compound on foot. There a startled duty sergeant signed them in, and then startled them in return by reporting that Colonel Bates was in the building. Despite the telegram, neither man had expected Bates to actually be in his office at such an hour.

Gerber and Fetterman made their way down the corridors, leaving a small river in their wake, and found the door to Bates's outer office unlocked. Inside, at a battered gray steel desk, was Bates's administrative assistant and longtime friend, Sergeant Major Robert Taylor.

The expression on Taylor's face was that of a man who has seen too much and pushed too hard for too long. The lines in his weathered, leathery skin seemed to have deepened and doubled in number since Gerber and Fetterman had last seen him less than a week ago. He smiled thinly as he recognized them, then pushed back his chair, using both hands on the desk to lever himself up out of the seat.

"Captain Gerber, Master Sergeant. I reckon you two boys look like just about the sorriest drowned rats I've ever seen. Good to have you back. I'll tell the colonel you're in and then see if I can scare up a decent cup of coffee and a sandwich. I assume you guys are hungry?''

Both men nodded, peeling off their coats and hanging them on hooks behind the door.

The sergeant major leaned over the desk and picked up an ancient field telephone. He spun the crank briefly, and a bell could be heard faintly ringing behind the closed door to Bates's inner office. Taylor mumbled something into the cracked mouthpiece, listened for a second, then hung up the handset and said, "You can both go on in. I'll knock when the coffee's ready."

"Didn't you used to have a real intercom in here?" Gerber asked.

"Used to. Some new hotshot leg general stole it for his own office while the colonel and I were up in Nha Trang a couple of days ago. The colonel was mad as hell about it when he found out, but the general was a lieutenant general. Not even the colonel messes with lieutenant generals. At least not publicly."

Fetterman and Gerber nodded their agreement, wondering just how Bates planned to carry out the implied private revenge. With Gerber leading the way, they slipped past the desk but halted at the door. Gerber knocked, then waited until the muffled command, "Enter," could be heard from inside.

If Taylor appeared to have aged almost before their eyes, Colonel Alan Bates looked like death warmed over. His face was gaunt, with dark rings under the eyes. Bates was usually careful about his appearance, but his khaki shirt looked as if he had been using it for a sleeping bag for the past week. His formerly meticulous crew cut was tufted up on both sides, as though he had been pulling his hair. It reminded Gerber vaguely of a koala's ears, and would have been comical had not the remainder of the man's appearance seemed so ghastly. Bates needed a shave and, as Gerber and Fetterman watched, he pulled a large cigar from his shirt pocket, bit off the tip and lighted up with a paper match.

Gerber shot a sidelong glance at Fetterman, who shrugged. Try as he might, Gerber couldn't remember if he'd ever seen Bates smoke before. Then the captain came to attention and gave a reasonably crisp salute, considering the hour and how he felt. "Captain Gerber and Master Sergeant Fetterman reporting as ordered, sir."

Bates puffed briefly, holding the match to the end of the cigar to make sure he got it going, then shook out the match and, in the same gesture, made a wave of his hand, approximating a return salute. "That's enough of the formality crap," said Bates. "Pull up a chair and sit down, both of you. I won't say it's good to see you, because you were owed the vacation, and right now you probably hate my guts for cutting it short. I'm sorry as hell, but it couldn't be helped. That's the honest truth, whether you believe it or not. I also won't insult your intelligence by telling you guys that you're the only people who could do the job I've got for you. There are probably half a dozen guys in SOG who could do the job, maybe a whole dozen. The problem is, right now they're all on assignment, sick, wounded, injured or down with the clap. That also is the honest truth." Bates paused for a moment and looked at the two men. "Jesus! You guys look like hell. I thought I sent you on R and R. Didn't you get any rest?"

"Sure," said Gerber. "We slept on the plane to Sydney four days ago. If you don't mind my saying it, Colonel, you don't look so hot yourself."

A thin smile formed on Bates's face. "That's pretty funny coming from a man with a green face. What'd you do, start drinking the moment you got on the plane?"

"No, sir. Like I said, we slept. We didn't start drinking until we got to Sydney, and we didn't get really drunk
until we got your telegram," said Gerber truthfully.

"Humph!" said Bates. "Master Sergeant Fetterman
seems to have weathered the experience a bit better than
you did, Mack."

"I didn't get quite as drunk as the captain, sir," Fetterman offered helpfully. "I was preoccupied with other
matters."

"Blonde or brunette?"

"One of each, and a redhead, sir."

Bates snorted. "Well, it's probably just as well, providing you didn't bring anything back with you. The next
couple of weeks aren't going to be much fun. Either of you
guys want a cigar?"

Both men declined.

"You might want to reconsider," said Bates. "I don't
think either of you are going to be smoking much in the
next two weeks."

"In that case I'll have a cigar," said Gerber, not really
feeling like it, but knowing what was coming.

Fetterman fished in his pocket and pulled out a scarred,
old briar pipe. He had given up smoking some time ago,
but had reacquired the habit during their brief R and R.
He held out the pipe and looked questioningly at Bates,
who nodded his approval. Then he pulled out a leather
zippered pouch and stuffed the bowl full of tobacco before lighting it with a Zippo that, like its owner, had sur-
vived three wars and several peacetime police actions.

"I take it we're going out in the field," said Gerber. He
took a couple of puffs on the cigar, and amazed by the fla-
vor and smoothness, checked the label. It was Cuban. He
raised a questioning eyebrow at Bates.

"A long ways out," said the colonel. "But not that far. You won't need to brush up on your Spanish, although Master Sergeant Fetterman may wish to review his language file."

There was a knock on the door.

"Enter," Bates said.

It was Taylor with a tray of coffee and sandwiches.

"Captain Gerber and Master Sergeant Fetterman expressed an interest in some food, Colonel," he said. "Thought maybe you could do with a bite as well."

"Thanks, Bob. You get anything to eat?"

"Waiting on my desk, sir."

"Go ahead and eat and then see if you can find these two some ground transport."

"Yes, sir."

Taylor left the tray and started out. As he reached the door, Fetterman called after him. "Where'd you find the pastrami and Swiss?"

Taylor threw a knowing grin over his shoulder. "When you're a sergeant major, you have to know these things."

"I've booked you both rooms at the Continental Hotel," said Bates after Taylor had left. "I wasn't sure you'd get the opportunity to use them, but I figured it was the least I could do since I spoiled your vacation. The rooms and the meals are on me, but not the bar bills. Do everyone a favor and stay in the hotel. You'll be leaving as soon as I can get you manifested, probably sometime tomorrow if the weather lifts. I'll either be going up-country with you, or following shortly."

Bates took a bite of his sandwich and chewed for a moment before continuing. "I know it's customary to give you guys a chance to refuse an assignment like this one, but not this time. You have got to be it, because you're all

I've got. It's a shitty deal, and I'm sorry as hell, but that's just the way it is.''

Gerber, chewing rapidly, nodded and swallowed. ''Your word's always been good with us, Colonel. Do we get any clues at all? You keep saying we're all you've got. Are Master Sergeant Fetterman and I the whole team?''

Bates smiled. ''You pick up the rest of your team in Kontum. Does that give you any ideas?''

Gerber held up a hand. ''All right, sir. You want to play the mystery man, that's fine with us. I presume we'll get a mission briefing at some point. And considering some of the things we've discussed in this office in the past, I also presume you have your reasons for not telling us any more now.''

''You'll know all you need to know when the time comes,'' Bates assured them. ''Now get out of here and let me get some work done.''

It turned out that the best Taylor could manage in the way of transportation was to drive them over to the hotel himself in Bates's jeep. Fortunately the canvas top had been put up, so they weren't completely drowned by the time they arrived. As wet as Gerber and Fetterman already were, they hardly noticed the leaks.

The drive into Saigon from MACV Headquarters at Tan Son Nhut normally took about fifteen minutes, but the driving conditions created by the storm slowed them down despite the lack of traffic. After they had picked up their bags, it took nearly half an hour to reach the Cong Ly Street Bridge over the Thi Nghe Canal and actually enter the city. There was a traffic accident of some kind at Phan Than Gian. It appeared that an Army truck had hit an ambulance, although it might have been the other way around. It was hard to tell in the rain. They had to detour all the way up to Hai Ba Trung and take it down to Le Loi, then double back southwest to Tu Do Street.

Gerber was less than totally enthusiastic about the trip. It wasn't just the delays, or his exhaustion, or the fact that he had an absolutely splitting headache and his stomach was still doing flip-flops. It was the idea of being unarmed downtown and getting caught in the middle of some terrorist attack or a simple mugging. Troops weren't supposed to be armed downtown, of course, but as members of MACV-SOG, both he and Fetterman had been issued the so-called Get out of Jail Free card, authorizing them to dress in civilian clothes, carry unusual weapons and not be unduly delayed or detained by the authorities. The problem was, all their personal weapons were still locked up out at Tan Son Nhut. It hadn't seemed advisable to try to go through Australian customs packing an SMG or a .44 Magnum. The most dangerous thing Gerber was carrying was a Swiss Army knife, and that was packed in his suitcase.

Fetterman, he assumed, was somewhat better off. The master sergeant had purchased a new diver's knife in Sydney, along with his new watch, although Gerber doubted very much that Fetterman would actually need a knife to take care of a mugger. For someone who looked as if he should be selling pots and pans door-to-door, Gerber thought, Fetterman was probably the most dangerous man he had ever known. Short, skinny and balding, the master sergeant looked about as lethal as a scoutmaster. Until you looked into his bottomless eyes. Fetterman had crazy gunmetal eyes that could freeze water at a glance or stare down a king cobra. Gerber had once said there were probably two hundred ways to kill a man until Fetterman thought of five more, and the captain had seen the man in action enough to have witnessed most of them.

Neither Gerber nor Fetterman attempted to pump Taylor for information on the ride in. To begin with, both knew the sergeant major too well to try that. If Bates wasn't talking, Taylor wouldn't be, either. Second, Bates had always shot straight with them. They trusted him. When the time came, he'd tell them what they needed to know to do the job, and he'd have a good reason for being so closemouthed in the meantime. As for having their leaves cut short, while they weren't happy about it, they knew Bates wouldn't have recalled them if he'd had any choice. Lastly they were both just too damn tired to care very much.

The only comment Gerber made to Taylor was to remark how tired both he and Colonel Bates looked. "Is the war going badly?" Gerber asked half-seriously. "I thought maybe from the way you and the colonel looked, we were losing."

Taylor guffawed. "The war in the field is going just fine, Captain. As far as I can tell, we're still kicking ass and taking names. Old Mr. Charles hasn't been able to get his act back together since that licking we gave him at Tet. If we lose this war, it'll be the politicians and the press corps that lose it for us. It's just been a very busy week. The colonel's a bit tired, that's all."

Gerber let it go at that. There was no point pressing for something they'd know in a day or two.

When they arrived at the corner of Le Loi and Tu Do streets, Gerber and Fetterman thanked Taylor for the ride, took their bags and trudged through the rain into the hotel lobby where the streams of water dripping from them drew a disapproving frown from the night clerk at the registration desk. The rooms were waiting as Bates had promised, and they signed the register, collected their keys and slopped their way over to the elevator, their boots making squishing sounds.

As soon as the doors had closed, Gerber turned to Fetterman. "So what do you think, Tony?"

Fetterman shrugged. "Kontum could mean practically anything. It could be Laos, could be Cambodia, could even be somewhere farther up-country. Kontum could be just a stopping-off point."

Gerber shook his head. "Except for that crack about you brushing up on your languages. How many languages do you speak now, Tony?"

"You mean besides English and Vietnamese, sir?"

"Yes. I think we can take those as givens."

"Well, Captain, I sort of lose track. I mean, I'm not all that fluent in some of them. Just know enough to order a meal and a beer, get a bed to sleep in, that sort of thing."

"Come on, Tony. How many?"

"Well, Captain, besides English and Vietnamese, there's Spanish, Russian, German and French. Then there's a little Japanese, Lowland Lao, Cantonese, Hmong and Nung Tai. Also a bit of Khmer, Italian and Greek. I guess that makes about fourteen in all, but you could only say I'm reasonably knowledgeable in nine or ten."

Gerber, who could speak Vietnamese and Nung Tai, and considered himself pretty good in French, shook his head slightly in amazement. Most Special Forces officers and NCOs were fluent in two or three languages besides their native tongue, but Fetterman was a regular Berlitz Institute.

"I think we can safely rule out Italian, German and Greek," said Gerber. "And Colonel Bates pretty much told us we wouldn't need Spanish."

Fetterman grinned crookedly. "Maybe we're going to invade Paris and force the French to take back Indochina."

"It's a thought, at that," replied Gerber, "but I think we can reject French, as well, along with Nung and Vietnamese, since the colonel aimed his comments at *your* abilities and I speak those languages as well. And the last time I checked, we'd already won our war against the Japanese."

"I think you could get an argument on that in any camera or electronics store," said Fetterman. "Anyway, that's not much help, sir. Still leaves Cantonese, Lao, Hmong, Khmer and Russian."

"I don't imagine we're going to invade Moscow from Vietnam," said Gerber, "so we narrow it down to China, Laos or Cambodia. Cambodia could make a certain amount of sense, since we've both been there before, but not northern Cambodia. Besides, I don't speak more than half a dozen phrases in Khmer, and you said you don't speak it fluently. I figure if the target was China, we'd stage out of Da Nang, or maybe even Udorn in Thailand. Which leaves us with Laos. The target area has got to be Laos."

"Which still leaves us with one big question, Captain. What's the target?"

Gerber shrugged. "I didn't say my hypothesis was complete."

The elevator doors opened and they got off, checking their keys against the room numbers. They came to Gerber's first, but the lock was stubborn and he had to put down his suitcase, needing both hands to deal with opening the door. As he straightened up, Fetterman pressed something small, cold and hard into his empty hand. The shape of the object felt familiar. Gerber glanced quickly in both directions, making sure the hallway was empty before looking down. He held a .380-caliber Browning semiautomatic pistol, the pre-World War II hammerless model.

"Thought you might sleep better with this under your pillow, Captain," said Fetterman. "It's not exactly what you'd want to stop a charging rhinoceros, but against ordinary street scum it gives good service if you place your shots well."

Gerber checked that the safety was on, then slipped the pistol into his pocket before a housekeeper or a hotel guest came along and spotted it. "I'm not going to ask where you got this," said Gerber. "I assume you had to be carrying it through customs and I don't want to become an accessory after the fact if I'm right, even though I confess a certain curiosity about how you managed it. In the future, however, please remember that if you get arrested for smuggling, I've never seen you before in my life. Are we clear on that point, Master Sergeant?"

"Of course, sir," said Fetterman, smiling wickedly.

"Good night, Tony."

"Good night, Captain."

Fetterman made his way down the hall, and Gerber let himself into the room. It was small but comfortably furnished, with a full-size bed, a couple of chairs and a small writing table. He turned on the ceiling fan and walked over to the window to open it just enough to allow the air to circulate, but still keep most of the rain out.

Gerber looked at his watch and saw that it was nearly time for the hotel kitchen to open. He thought about breakfast, but decided he needed sleep more than he needed something to eat. He peeled off his wet clothes and draped them over the shower rail to dry, laid out some dry clothes next to the bed where he could find them in a hurry in the dark if he needed to, then brushed his teeth. The last thing he did before turning out the lights was to check under the bed and in the closet. He didn't think of it as paranoia, just healthy caution. Finally he put the pistol Fetterman had given him on the bedside table and collapsed on the bed. He was asleep almost before his head hit the pillow.

2

HEADQUARTERS, THIRD MARINES DONG HA, RVN

Corporal Bob Corbett sat on the canvas-and-wood folding cot and cleaned his rifle.

This is my rifle. There are many like it, but this one is mine. My rifle is my best friend. It is my life. I must master it as I master my life.

He remembered the words from boot camp, the Rifleman's Creed. Perhaps no Marine ever truly forgot the words. Yet he knew the words were lies. It wasn't his rifle. It belonged to the Marine Corps. He was merely being allowed to use it for a while. It wasn't a friend. It was a tool, plain and simple. And it wasn't his life, although his life and the lives of many Marines might depend on how well he used it. The deaths of twenty enemy soldiers had already depended upon that.

It is not the rifle that kills. It is the heart of stone of the man who squeezes the trigger.

The first enemy soldier Bob Corbett had killed was a VC pushing a bicycle loaded with weapons and ammunition for delivery to a local guerrilla unit. It had been a very long shot in poor light, and Corbett hadn't been able to see the target well, but he had been able to see well enough to identify the rifles hanging from the handlebars. That had been all the recognition required. Afterward, both Corbett's partner and the captain to whose company they were attached had complimented him on the fine shot.

Later they had walked down the hill to collect the weapons and confirm the kill. Marine snipers didn't consider a kill confirmed unless they could walk down and put their foot on the body, like a sportsman lording it over his kill. Corbett had been surprised at how small the body looked, sprawled facedown in the dirt with a big hole in the back of its black pajama shirt. He had been curious about the face and had rolled the body over and pulled off the floppy cloth hat for a better look. It had been a mistake. The VC had turned out to be a fifteen-year-old girl.

There was no question that she was VC. The road was littered with rifles and there were three packs of ammunition strapped to the bicycle. If Corbett hadn't killed her, the weapons she was pushing along on her bicycle would certainly have been used to kill American Marines or ARVN soldiers.

But she was still a fifteen-year-old girl.

Corbett had never forgotten that first kill. He supposed that all snipers remember their first touch. He had given no outward sign that it bothered him. He had killed without hesitation when the need arose next, and he had gone down from the hill later to confirm the kill. He had repeated the process eighteen times since. But he had never again looked those he had slain in the face.

Snipers had often been poorly deployed in Vietnam by unit commanders who didn't understand the capabilities and limitations of the sniper's craft. Too many commanders tried to use them the same way they used recon teams, or as forward observers for the artillery. Some commanders employed them almost exclusively to counter enemy snipers, when machine gun and mortar or artillery fire were much more effective countermeasures.

The worst thing you could do with a sniper was use him as a regular rifleman. Many officers, figuring snipers had greater leadership abilities than less highly trained Marines, put them in charge of line rifle squads, not understanding that snipers were essentially loners, no more skilled at command then the next grunt. Being forced to control a squad of riflemen on a sweep through dense brush or jungle, where contact with the enemy occurred at ranges measured in feet rather than hundreds of yards, wasted both the talent of the sniper and the capabilities of his telescopically sighted rifle.

A sniper could reconnoiter targets at long range, either with his telescopic sight or the twenty- to forty-power spotter scope his observer carried, but he couldn't, unless also recon-trained as Corbett was, conduct a close-in sneak-and-peek, BDA or prisoner snatch. Even if he could, his sniper's rifle was useless in such a situation. A sniper could serve as a very effective one-man blocking force for troops conducting a sweep, provided he was assigned to cover a stretch of open ground that the enemy might feel compelled to cross to avoid pursuing infantry. In that role a Marine sniper team could deny the enemy safe transit over a strip of ground a couple of hundred meters wide and up to a thousand meters long, but the team was totally ineffective if used in jungle where the foliage restricted the visual range of the telescopic sights. A sniper could disrupt the enemy chain of command by eliminating officers and senior NCOs behind the front ranks of a battle, but a sniper couldn't stand alone against a machine gun at ranges under a hundred meters. A sniper could provide a very effective long-range ambush where the field of view permitted coverage of roads or trails at long distance, but he was virtually useless in a close-in ambush or counterambush situation.

The current assignment had gone well for Corbett. The area contained a lot of grassland spotted with sparse woods. It provided good cover for a sniper, yet regularly exposed the enemy in situations where they could be observed and neutralized. Captain Hargreeves, to whose company Corbett and Erickson had been attached, seemed to have a good grasp of sniper deployment. Usually they would be inserted into the AO as part of a reconnaissance or ambush patrol, which would drop them off at a predetermined site. The patrol would then move on through the area, later withdrawing in a manner likely to draw the attention of enemy observers. The sniper team, with its four- or five-man security detachment, would lie low for twelve to twenty-four hours, move to a new site, establish their ambush and go to work, remaining in the field for two or three days at a time.

Things weren't entirely smooth, though. For one thing, Corbett wasn't getting along well with his partner. It wasn't that Erickson was incompetent. He knew his job and did it fairly well. It was a question of personalities. The two men got on each other's nerves.

Erickson was a boastful type who enjoyed the reputation of being a killer and spent all his spare time regaling the grunts with fanciful tales of his daring, embellishing each victory until a good shot made at three hundred yards on an easy target became a fantastic piece of shooting accomplished at seven, eight or nine hundred yards in poor light on a running target.

When he wasn't bragging to the rank and file, he was busy bragging to all the young Vietnamese women from town, telling them what a dangerous, evil killer of the VC he was, while trying to get them to drop their pajama bottoms for him. Evidently Erickson thought they should equate homicide with masculinity. It seemed to work, too, in a limited way, although this close to the UMZ, Corbett couldn't help wondering how many of Erickson's "girlfriends" were actually VC agents, pumping him both literally and figuratively for whatever information they could pick up of a military nature.

At the same time he was screwing their daughters, Erickson loudly trumpeted his lack of respect for their parents. Day or night he could be heard expounding upon how much he hated Vietnamese food, beer, weather, culture, language and politics. He couldn't understand why the United States didn't just bomb the hell out of the country and turn it into a parking lot, people and all.

And Erickson believed in practicing what he preached. There was nothing funnier to his warped sense of humor than knocking over some old mamasan pushing a heavily laden bicycle to market, or shooting the hoe out of the hands of some aged papasan working his field. Except, of course, shooting some VC right between the eyes. Funniest of all was giving a can of Sterno or delousing powder to some Vietnamese kid begging for C-rations.

To Corbett, that kind of attitude just didn't make any sense. How were you supposed to win the hearts and minds of the Vietnamese people when you had fellow Marines like Erickson treating them like dog shit?

He had tried to talk to Erickson about it after the bicycle incident. "Suppose that old mamasan goes home tonight and happens to mention to one of her sons or one of her nephews about how some big Marine pushed her off her bicycle and then laughed about it. And then the kid's uncle comes along and tells him about how he's out working in the field one day and a Marine shoots the hoe out of his hands, or about how some Marine in a helicopter flying over his rice paddy decided to do a little target practice on his water buffalo. So the kid grows up hating Americans and one day he joins the Vietcong and shoots a grunt. Christ, Erickson, every time you fuck with the locals like that, you just make it all that much tougher for the next Marine who comes along. You want to turn the whole goddamn country into VC?''

''Listen up, shitbird,'' Erickson had responded. ''Don't go giving me none of that hearts-and-minds crap. When you got 'em by their fucking balls, their hearts and minds'll follow. I been here nine months. You ain't been here six weeks yet. You don't have the least fucking idea what it's all about. You listen to me. Over here the papasan who cuts your hair in the morning cuts your throat at night. The kid who shines your shoes is the kid who throws a grenade in the back of a truckload of Marines. The old mamasan who gives you a pineapple and a cold drink when you're hot and tired puts ground glass in your Coke. The pretty young *co* who smiles at you when she brings your laundry in from town is the Co Cong you find hanging in the wire some morning after a sapper attack. They're all VC to me, kid. You want to try sorting out the good gooks from the bad gooks? I say kill 'em all. Let God sort 'em out.''

''Look,'' Corbett had said, ''all I'm saying is that alienating the population doesn't help matters any. They can't all be VC, so why make them that way? If they're all VC, then who in hell are we over here trying to help?''

''Help? We ain't here to help anyone, pal. We're here to kill gooks. Didn't they teach you nothing at sniper school?''

"At sniper school they taught me to kill the enemy," Corbett had answered quietly. "The South Vietnamese aren't our enemies."

"The VC are South Vietnamese, you jarhead. If that don't make 'em the enemy, then who is?"

Corbett had suppressed the desire to say that he was beginning to wonder exactly that, along with several other things that might have escalated the argument into a fist-fight. He didn't have to like Erickson, but he did have to work with him. And Erickson was a three-striper. At the time Corbett had only been a lance corporal. He'd kept his mouth shut and walked away. They'd continued to work together after that, but otherwise each man did his own thing. Except for when they went into the field, they hadn't spoken more than fifty words to each other since.

Now, in the big squad tent, it was hot. Even when the sides were rolled up it was still stifling because most of the breeze got blocked by the four-foot-high wall of rubber-ized sandbags stacked around the tent to give its occu-pants some protection from mortar fire. This morning, though, the flaps were down to block out the rain, which would probably stop later on, turning the tent into a steam bath.

Corbett finished cleaning his rifle, then slid the bolt back into place. He was just putting away his cleaning kit when Captain Hargreeves stuck his poncho-covered head into the tent, the rest of his dripping form following. Cor-bett stood as the officer entered.

"Corbett, you in some kind of trouble?" asked Har-greeves.

The question took Corbett by surprise. "None that I know of, sir," he answered truthfully. "Is anything the matter?"

"Battalion CO wants to see you right away. You're to bring your gear."

"Aye, aye, sir. I'll get right on it."

Hargreeves eyed him speculatively. "You sure you're not in any trouble? Maybe I could help if I knew what it was."

"Honestly, sir, I can't think of anything. Maybe the team's being reassigned."

"I don't think so," said the captain. "The CO didn't say anything about any reassignment to me, and he didn't ask for Erickson."

"Well, thank you, sir. I guess I'd better pack."

Hargreeves nodded. "Well, whatever it is, good luck. You're a good shooter, Corbett. One of the best I've ever seen. The Marines need more men like you."

"Thank you, sir. You're a good man to work for."

When Hargreeves left, Corbett gathered up all his belongings, stuffed them into his duffel bag and put on his pack. Then he slung his rifle over his shoulder, put on his poncho over that, picked up his duffel bag and slogged through the mud to the battalion commander's hootch.

The battalion commander's hootch was a wooden frame structure with a plywood floor and a galvanized metal roof. The walls were screened with a fine mesh wire, and plastic ponchos had been nailed along the tops of the sides and anchored by ropes and tent pegs at their lower edges to make a fly for the windows but still let a breeze in. The building measured about forty feet square and had a screen door with a canopy over it and a red sign lettered in yellow paint proclaiming, Commander 2nd BN 3rd Marines. It wasn't lost on Corbett that evidently there were advantages to being a battalion commander.

Immediately inside the door were two desks, one of which was empty. Seated at the other was a lance corporal, typing away at a steady twenty words a minute on a battered old typewriter. Farther on, toward the back, were a couple of metal bunks, some filing cabinets, a wall locker and two more desks. Three of the four desks had field telephones on them.

The lance corporal finished a sentence and finally deigned to notice Corbett. "Yeah, what do you want?"

"Corporal Robert C. Corbett to see the battalion commander."

"Yeah, what about?"

"Captain Hargreeves said the battalion CO wanted to see me."

Corbett set his duffel bag near the door and drew a disapproving look from the lance corporal.

"Hey, you're gettin' my deck all wet," complained the clerk.

Corbett was amazed at the man's attitude. He thought that a Marine with a cushy soft job filling out forms for the battalion CO would want to protect it, and thus would be nice to people. But the guy seemed to be going out of his way to offend people. Corbett pulled off his poncho and dropped it on top of his duffel bag. Then he shrugged out of his pack, set it next to the duffel bag and carefully laid his rifle on top.

"Maybe you could just tell the CO I'm here. That way we could get this over with and I could get my gear off your deck," Corbett said wearily.

The lance corporal opened his mouth to say something else, changed his mind and instead shouted back through the filing cabinets, "Hey, Colonel! That sniper guy you wanted to see is here."

Corbett was appalled. He couldn't believe the battalion CO would have an administrative assistant who behaved in such a manner.

The lieutenant colonel looked up from the papers on his desk and called, "Well, send him back, then, Wysoski. I can't very well talk to the man if we have to shout back and forth at each other."

"The colonel will see you now," the lance corporal said unnecessarily.

Corbett ignored him and made his way through the maze of filing cabinets, bunks and lockers to the back of the hootch. He stood in front of the CO's desk, came to attention and saluted. "Sir, Corporal Corbett reporting to the battalion commander as ordered."

The lieutenant colonel returned Corbett's salute. "Stand at ease, Corbett. Are you in some kind of trouble?"

"None that I know of, sir. Captain Hargreeves asked me the same question just a little while ago. Why? Is something wrong?"

The battalion CO shook his crew-cut head. "Damned if I know, son. I got an order here says you're supposed to report to the personnel officer, headquarters, Third Marine Amphibious Force by the first available means of transport. It specifies that you bring all gear and personal belongings with you, so I guess you won't be coming back. You sure you don't know anything about it?"

"No, sir. I've no idea what it's about."

"Well," said the colonel, "at least it doesn't say you're under arrest. That's always a good sign. Regiment has a convoy going down to Da Nang in about an hour to pick up some supplies. You can hitch a ride with them. You'll find the trucks over by the mess hall. Whatever it is, good luck." He handed Corbett the copies of his travel orders, and they exchanged salutes.

Corbett tucked the orders inside his shirt, then picked up his equipment, dripping all over the lance corporal's floor in the process. He picked up his duffel bag, squished back out into the rain and slopped through the mud to the chow hall. Once there, he found a staff sergeant who seemed to be in charge in the absence of any officer and explained that the Second Battalion commander had told him he could hitch a ride to Da Nang with the convoy. The staff sergeant insisted on seeing his orders, so Corbett put all his gear down in the mud and dug out the papers.

"Kinda odd," said the staff sergeant, after squinting at the orders just long enough to get them thoroughly wet. "You in some kinda trouble? You lie about your age to get in maybe? You kill somebody maybe?"

"Staff, I'm old enough, I'm not in any trouble that I know of, and I kill people every day. I'm a sniper," Corbett told him. He was beginning to get a bit tired of people who kept asking him if he'd done something wrong.

"Yeah, I heard about you. You're the guy who dinged those eight Charlies last week. Pretty good shootin'."

"It was seven, Staff. The eighth guy wasn't confirmed."

"Seven, eight, what's the difference whether he was confirmed or not? You got the bastard, right?"

"Yeah, sure. I got him," answered Corbett.

He didn't know how to tell the staff sergeant that the difference was he didn't enjoy the reputation of being a killer. He didn't want credit for killing any more people than had to be attributed to him. Corbett operated by a strange set of personal rules, a sort of private code of ethics he'd developed hunting deer with his father. You didn't leave a wounded animal to suffer in the field. The deer had given you a good hunt, and you owed it to the animal to kill it quickly and cleanly with one shot. If you didn't, you weren't doing your job as a hunter. Corbett had a similar feeling about his job as a sniper. It was what worked for him. It was the only thing that let him sleep nights.

"Well, there it is, then," said the staff sergeant. "You can ride in that truck over there. The driver's name is Sanchez. He hasn't got a passenger, so you can probably stuff your gear in the cab if you like. We'll be leaving in about forty-five minutes, as soon as our escort and the supply officer show up."

Corbett looked at his muddy, rain-soaked gear, then threw it into the back, except for his rifle and webgear. Highway One wasn't always a secure road, and if they ran into any trouble, he wanted something to shoot back with. His gear stowed away, he climbed into the cab and settled down to wait.

Sanchez showed up ten minutes later, and Corbett introduced himself and explained that the staff had given him permission to hitch a ride. Twenty minutes later the supply officer turned up, and Corbett had to go through the whole routine with the orders once more. The escort, a couple of machine gun jeeps and a mortar truck, finally made an appearance, and the convoy got under way.

At Third Marine Amphibious Force Headquarters Corbett received two surprises. First, for his actions in the night ambush, he received a second Combat Meritorious promotion. He was now a Marine Corps sergeant. Second, he was out of the Marine Corps, at least physically, if not administratively. He was now detached from III MAF and was to turn in his weapon and report at once to the commander of the interservice MACV-SOG Maritime Studies Group in Da Nang for further orders. He did so and was told that he had been seconded to the MACV-SOG Ground Studies Group. However, he wasn't to report to their headquarters in Saigon, but instead would report directly to the GSG Command and Control Central in Kontum. The weather was clearing, and he had been manifested aboard a C-130 flight due to depart in an hour. If he hurried, he would have just enough time to make his plane. In effect, the Marine Corps had loaned him to the Army.

Corbett barely made it. The C-130 was crammed full of boxes of ammunition, and there were no passenger seats. Corbett sat on the floor, and the Air Force loadmaster secured a cargo strap across his legs. For fifteen minutes Corbett sat and wondered how he was supposed to get out if the plane crashed. Then, just as they were starting to pull up the tail ramp, a second passenger stumbled aboard.

He was a stocky fellow about Corbett's height with a scraggly reddish-brown beard and a shaggy mop of light brown hair topped by a dark blue beret with an ARVN Ranger crest pinned to it. He was dressed in tiger-striped jungle fatigues, the pockets of which sagged with lumpy-looking, apparently heavy objects. He wore a MACV patch and had the Vietnamese rank of captain pinned to one pocket and a set of cloth Army parachutist's jump wings over the other pocket. The man had an M-2 carbine with a folding paratrooper-type stock slung over his shoulder. He carried his webgear and a jungle rucksack by the straps in one hand and had two open bottles of Miller beer clenched by the necks in the other. From his gait and smell, he had apparently been drinking heavily for some time.

He collapsed on the floor of the plane near Corbett, stuck out the hand with the bottles in it and belched. "Here. Have a beer. You look thirsty, Corporal."

"Uh, no thanks, uh, Captain, is it? I don't think we're supposed to drink on the plane."

"Nonsense," the man said, belching again. "If we don't drink up all this beer, it might fall into enemy hands. It's our patriotic duty to keep it from the VC. *Giang le*, my friend. Drink up."

"I really don't think we should, sir."

The stranger belched again and forced a Miller into Corbett's hands. "Ah, come on, man. Have a beer. That's an order now, Corporal."

"Actually, it's sergeant, sir. Sergeant Bob Corbett, United States Marine Corps."

The stranger reached out and plucked at the insignia on Corbett's OD jungle fatigues. "You Marines sure got a funny-looking insignia for sergeant." He belched again and guzzled down half of his beer.

"I just got promoted," Corbett explained. "I haven't had time to pick up my new rank yet."

"Well, then, congratulations. This calls for a celebration. Drink up. Drink up. You're falling behind, Sergeant." He drained the rest of the beer, belched, set the bottle down carefully between his legs, then opened one of the bulging pockets of his fatigues and pulled out a can. "You need another beer? Sorry. The rest of this stuff is all Budweiser. They didn't have Miller in cans. Can't get the bottles to fit in my pockets."

Corbett stared at the man. He'd seen some pretty unmilitary types in some of the Marine infantry units, but never anything like this. "Sir, if you don't mind my asking, what are you?"

"Why, I'm drunk. Isn't it obvious?" Then he grinned. "Captain Rick Bunnell, U.S. Army Special Forces. Friends call me Bush Hog. But you won't be my friend if you don't drink your beer. And you don't want me for an enemy because I'm a really nice guy and I brought lots of beer. Lots and lots of beer."

Corbett stared even harder at the man. He'd heard many strange stories about Army Special Forces personnel, but he hadn't believed most of them. He was going to have to reconsider that skepticism. "Meaning no disrespect, sir, but isn't your cover the wrong color?" asked Corbett.

"Cover? Oh, you mean the beret. I've got a green one somewhere in my pack. This one's village militia. Spent the past five months advising a bunch of Ruff-Puffs. On my last tour I worked five months setting up A-camps down in Three and Four Corps and six months with an A-team working out near Dak To. Also did about a month with a team of advisers attached to an ARVN Ranger unit. I really am who I say I am. See." Bunnell pulled out his dog tags and waved them in Corbett's general direction.

The loadmaster walked back through, wearing a headset and trailing wires behind him. He noticed the new passenger, checked his clipboard and said with a certain air of distaste, "You must be Captain Bunnell."

"That I am. I'm also wonderfully intoxicated. Would you like a beer, Master Sergeant?"

"A beer? Thanks, Captain, but I'll have to take a rain check. Can't drink while flying." The loadmaster drew a cargo strap across Bunnell's legs.

"What's that for?" Bunnell asked.

"Don't want you to fall and get hurt, sir. We're about to take off." He cinched the strap, looked around the cargo bay, then walked over to check some of the pallets. Finally he walked back up front toward the cabin.

As the plane started to roll, Bunnell stared at the wide nylon webbing across his thighs, then looked at Corbett. "Gee," he said, "I sure hope we don't crash."

Corbett studied his fellow passenger. Bunnell looked about ten years his senior, maybe in his late twenties. He hardly seemed old enough to be on his second tour in Vietnam, but it was possible. At least part of his story must be true, though. There was practically no other way to explain the man's mode of dress and appearance.

"Are you going to Kontum, too?" Corbett finally asked. It wasn't really a stupid question. The plane was headed for Kontum, but Corbett had no idea where it was going afterward, or where else it might be scheduled to stop. Perhaps Bunnell was returning to Dak To. It was nearly on the way, and he had said he'd been stationed there before.

"Yep. New assignment. Got pulled out of my village on eight hours' notice. Been in transit for a day and a half."

Corbett could appreciate how the man felt. His head was still spinning from all the changes he'd been through in the past ten hours.

The big transport lumbered down the runway and leaped into the air with a sickening lurch, but they stayed airborne. Corbett let out a great sigh of relief. "Well, at least we didn't crash on takeoff."

"That's always a good sign," agreed Bunnell. "Say, aren't those recon wings you're wearing? I went through jump school with some recon types. They were one crazy bunch of motherfuckers. Real motivated, but, well, you know, crazy."

"I went through recon training, but I haven't been posted to a recon unit. I've been working with Third Marines up near the DMZ."

"So what are you going to Kontum for?"

"I wish I knew. This morning the company commander tells me the battalion CO wants to see me. The battalion CO tells me I'm supposed to report to the personnel officer at Third Marine Amphibious Force Headquarters. I spend six hours bouncing around in a deuce-and-a-half getting there, and then they tell me I've been detached to something called the Maritime Studies Group. I report in there and they tell me I'm seconded to Ground Studies Group, and put me on a plane for Kontum. I'm supposed to go to something called Command and Control Central, whatever that is, and ask for either a Colonel Alan Bates or a Captain Gerber when I get there. And that's absolutely all I know about it."

"Hmm. Now that's interesting," said Bunnell. He fished out another beer and opened it.

Corbett took note that in spite of the rate at which he'd been absorbing alcohol, Bunnell suddenly appeared to have become sober.

Bunnell looked thoughtful for a moment—at least he looked as thoughtful as any man can with an open beer in his hand and a couple of empties held between his legs. "You don't happen to speak any foreign languages, do you?" he asked Corbett.

The Marine shook his head. "Not with any fluency. I had two years of Spanish and two years of French in high school."

"Hmm. Very odd indeed. I speak Vietnamese, French and Lao."

"I'm impressed," said Corbett, meaning it.

"I wasn't trying to impress you. I was just thinking out loud."

"Why's that?"

"Because, Sergeant, I've got orders to report to either Colonel Bates or Captain Gerber, too. I know both of them slightly from my first tour. It kind of makes me wonder where we'll be going."

"I thought we were going to Kontum."

"I mean, after that. Kontum's just the jump-off point."

"I'm sorry. I don't know what you're talking about."

"Command and Control Central, among other things, conducts clandestine cross-border ops into Laos and Cambodia for MACV-SOG," Bunnell explained. "Gerber's been to both places, if I recall correctly. I've visited the scenic Ho Chi Minh Trail in Laos. Yet you don't speak any foreign languages, although you do know some French. You're recon-trained, yet you haven't been assigned to a recon unit. I imagine you've never been to Kontum before and that you're pretty green."

"About two months," said Corbett. "All of it in I Corps and mostly near the DMZ."

Bunnell suddenly leaned forward and stared at Corbett intensely. "Aren't you kind of young to be a sergeant in the Marine Corps?"

"I got two Combat Meritorious promotions since I've been here."

"Hmm. The plot thickens. I think I'm going to need another beer to figure this one out. You ready for another brewski?"

Corbett shook his head. He hadn't even touched the Miller yet, but now he took a sip, decided it tasted good and took another.

Bunnell belched, set down his empty and popped open another can. "You got any medals?" he asked suddenly. "A Silver Star maybe, a Bronze Star for valor, something like that?"

Corbett looked embarrassed and shook his head. "No, sir, nothing like that."

"Then what did you get two Combat Meritorious promotions for? Two promotions in two months at that."

Corbett shrugged. "I guess for doing my job well."

"Very well indeed, it seems." Bunnell took another large swig of beer, leaned back on one arm and stared right through Corbett as though the Marine weren't even there. "Two men. One a Special Forces officer on his second tour in Vietnam who speaks three languages besides English and has already done cross-border work. The other a young Marine recon specialist with no language skills and barely two months in-country. Both are suddenly pulled from their current assignments and ordered to report to a third man, another Special Forces officer with extensive cross-border experience, at a known MACV-SOG staging site for operations into Laos and Cambodia. That sure sounds like a trip in the making to me, a trip into Laos, since I have no Cambodian experience and can't see any other reason why they would want me along."

Corbett wasn't at all sure he liked the sound of what he was hearing.

Bunnell scratched his belly and burped. "That part of it makes sense. What doesn't make any sense is you. Why pick you? Recon training, but no experience. No foreign language skills. No experience in the probable target area. No cross-border experience at all. You're not even Army. Yet you've been promoted twice after only two months in-country. There must be something special about you. What is it? Just exactly what did you do while you were with the Third Marines to earn two Combat Meritorious promotions in two months, Sergeant?"

Corbett looked away as though embarrassed, then looked back. He took a big drink of his beer. "I'm afraid I know the answer to that one, Captain. I'm a sniper. There it is. You wanted to know what I did that was so special that it earned me two Combat Meritorious promotions in two months. Twenty confirmed kills and one probable. That's what it takes for a lance corporal to make sergeant in two months on the DMZ."

Bunnell whistled. "There it is, indeed."

3

MACV-SOG COMMAND
AND CONTROL
CENTRAL KONTUM,
RVN

The camouflaged Lockheed Hercules C-130 transport aircraft from Saigon bounced down hard, rattling the perforated steel-plate planking covering the runway and sending up countless little geysers of mud and water through the holes in the PSP's surface. The big airplane swerved a couple of times to avoid craters caused by enemy 140 mm rocket fire, reversed the thrust of its props and, with a great groaning, shuddering whir, came to a full stop before running out of landing space. The pilot, using the rudder and steerable nose gear, turned the plane in its own length and taxied over to the air operations control center to disgorge his load of cargo and passengers. As the tail ramp came down, Gerber and Fetterman picked up their bags and stepped out into the sweltering heat of a Vietnam midafternoon during the monsoon season.

"Jesus, this place stinks!" said Gerber, stepping down the ramp to the taxiway.

Fetterman sniffed the air and made a face. "Ah, yes, the unforgettable aroma of roasting excrement. Notice, please, the subtle fragrance of kerosene, the faint hint of decaying toilet tissue, the tiniest whisper of a trace of barbecued bacteria. It's almost enough to bring tears to your eyes."

"It's all of that," responded Gerber. "How about we get inside before it brings bile to the back of our throats?"

"You think that'll help?" asked Fetterman.

"No," said Gerber, "but it couldn't hurt. If I have to stand out here and smell burning shit, I'd rather go inside. That way when the time comes to puke, I can at least be sitting down. Christ! You'd think by now they'd have come up with a better way of getting rid of the stuff."

"We could always leave a message for Bates, telling him we've gone into town, and go check into a hotel room," said Fetterman, not really meaning it.

"It's a thought at that," Gerber admitted. "But with our luck the rooms wouldn't have air-conditioning and we'd still have to sit in front of an open window and smell burning shit. If we're going to be nauseated, there's no sense paying for the privilege. Besides, I'm curious to see if any of the rest of the team has shown up."

"Still playing detective, Captain?" asked Fetterman.

"Just curious, Tony, that's all. This whole thing is just a little bit too rushed, a little bit too hush-hush for my liking. Also I don't like not having any say-so in the composition of the team. If we're going on some kind of sneaky cross-border op, I'd like to know the people our lives are going to be depending on, or at least have a chance to look over their 201 files. The last thing I want is for us to find ourselves in the middle of a battalion of Pathet Lao guerrillas with a bunch of flakes we can't depend on covering our rear."

"I guess there's not a whole lot we can do about that, Captain," said Fetterman. "Except watch our own tails. It's not exactly like we've been given a choice in the matter."

"Yeah," said Gerber. "And if we complain, Bates will just remind us that we knew the job was dangerous when we took it."

"I didn't think we had a choice," said Fetterman. "Is it too late to change our minds?"

"I meant the Army," said Gerber.

"Damnation!" said Fetterman. "I knew I should never have gotten drunk with the boys and walked into that tattoo parlor."

Gerber glared at the master sergeant and then smiled. Fetterman, he knew, had lied about his age and enlisted in the Army when he was seventeen, fighting in France and Germany during World War II, and later working behind enemy lines with the United Nations Partisan Forces in Korea. His whole history was the Army. The man lived and breathed it. And he had never been in a tattoo parlor in his life.

They showed their IDs to the Nung corporal at the gate. He studied the cards carefully, scrutinizing Gerber and Fetterman closely, and checked their names against those on his clipboard, while two more Nungs kept a watchful eye on the visitors, their M-16 rifles held ready. Finally satisfied that the two Green Berets were who they claimed to be, the corporal nodded curtly, and one of the guards slung his rifle and unlocked the gate, admitting them to the MACV-SOG compound. Once inside, the corporal pointed to a jeep and indicated that one of the gate guards would drive them directly to the isolation compound, an ultrasecure area within the SOG compound itself.

Gerber wasn't sure he liked that. The isolation compound was where SOG personnel were quartered for briefing and training prior to classified missions, and where personnel and prisoners were held upon return until they had been debriefed or interrogated. As the name implied, it was isolated even from the rest of the SOG compound, and once inside, troops weren't allowed to leave or have any contact with the outside world except for such area studies specialists who might come in to brief them on the mission.

It was SOP for classified operations, especially for clandestine cross-border ops, and Gerber had been through it at least a dozen times. But he hadn't been able to reach Robin Morrow, his girlfriend, before leaving Saigon and had hoped to be able to at least telephone her before departing on the mission. She'd been irritated enough about his going on leave to Australia without her, and she was going to be really mad when she found out he had come back into the country and gone off on a mission without looking her up. She understood that such things happened in their relationship, and sometimes she didn't have any idea where Gerber was for weeks at a time, but she didn't like it one bit and never hesitated to tell him so. It was out of his hands now, however. This time she would just have to be mad.

At the gate to the isolation compound, the scene at the front gate was repeated with only a couple of exceptions. The security guards this time were even less friendly than the others. They had an M-60 machine gun bunker set up next to their gate, which was the first of two gates, both secured with a chain and padlock. After the proper ID check had been completed, the Nung guards opened the first gate and allowed Gerber and Fetterman to enter the area between the two barbed wire fences. The first gate was then relocked behind them and the second gate opened to allow the two Green Berets to pass alone into the compound. Not even the guards were permitted inside the isolation compound itself.

Gerber and Fetterman approached a long, low, concrete building, painted white with a tin roof and ringed by sandbags—the team house. Entering through the combination recreation/briefing room and chow hall, they found a few familiar faces.

Seated at a table, drinking beer and playing pitch, were Sergeant First Class Galvin Bocker and Sergeant First Class Justin Tyme. Both men had been on the same A-team with Gerber and Fetterman during their first tour of duty in Vietnam and had worked with them on several occasions since. Bocker was a communications specialist, an electronics wizard who could probably make a radio from a couple of seashells if the need arose. Tyme, on the other hand, was a light-weapons expert.

There were two other men at the table with them. The small man with Oriental features dealing the cards was unknown to Gerber, although his uniform indicated that, like Bocker and Tyme, he, too, was Special Forces. A fourth man, wearing what looked like a Vietnamese village militia uniform, seemed vaguely familiar, although Gerber couldn't place him. He didn't seem to be playing cards, but he was drinking a lot of beer. Bocker greeted them as they came in.

"Captain Gerber, Master Sergeant. Good to see you again. I take it this isn't a social call."

Gerber stuck out a hand. "Good to see you, too, Galvin. Justin. When you see the wife and kids, Galvin, tell them not to hate me for this one. I didn't request you. In fact, I didn't request anyone. I got drafted just like everybody else."

"You won't be leading the team, then, sir?" Bocker asked seriously.

"I've no idea who'll be leading the team," Gerber answered. "I haven't been briefed yet."

"That *is* a bit odd," said Bocker. "Here, let me finish the introductions. Our inscrutable Oriental winning all the money is Staff Sergeant Biff Yoon, and the officer and alleged gentleman who won't play cards with us, but keeps drinking up all our beer, says his name is Bush Hog. Claims he's an SF captain, but we've only got his word for that. If you ask me, he drinks more like an NCO."

The name stirred a memory somewhere in Gerber's brain, and he made the connection. "I've got some bad news for you guys," said Gerber. "This man really is a captain. Bunnell, isn't it? You were on Dave Henderson's team during my first tour."

Bunnell burped slightly and looked pleased with himself. "Aye, aye, Captain Gerber. His XO. I was a first looie back then."

"I'll be a son of a gun," said Bocker. "I never in all my days saw an officer could drink like that." He looked in Gerber's direction. "Well, not beer, anyway."

"I see your drinking habits haven't changed any," commented Gerber.

"I'm never dry if I can help it," said Bunnell, "except in the field." He seemed suddenly sober, as if a switch had been thrown. "Don't worry about me, Captain. I like a beer. In fact, I like a lot of beer, but it doesn't follow me into the field."

"I'm not worried," Gerber replied. "If it was a problem, Dave Henderson would have eighty-sixed you long ago. He said you were a good man, and I take Dave's word on things like that."

Bunnell looked uncomfortable. "You don't know, then, about Henderson? He came back for a third tour and didn't fill his calendar. Made it all the way down to a single-digit midget, I heard, then got shot down in a helicopter bringing him to Saigon for outprocessing. Were you friends? I understand he had a wife and two kids."

"Three," said Gerber. "Two boys and a girl. The boys ought to be just about high school age by now. I knew Dave from the old days with the Tenth in Bad Tolz. Any idea what happened to Martha?"

"His widow? I heard she was with her folks back in Massachusetts. Can't say for sure."

Gerber only nodded. He felt sick. Dave Henderson had been an old and close friend. Gerber didn't have many of those left anymore.

Fetterman broke the silence, stepping forward to grab Tyme's hand and biceps with both hands in the Montagnard handshake the Green Berets had long ago adopted. "It's good to see your sorry face again, Boom-Boom." He inclined his head toward the others. "You, too, Galvin, Captain Bunnell." Fetterman faced Yoon with a quizzical look. "Biff, was it?"

The young moon-faced sergeant nodded. "I'm from the Valley," he said, as if that explained everything. "You know, San Bernardino, California. Actually my name's Bernard, but you know, how you gonna hang ten with a name like Bernard?"

Fetterman had no idea what he was talking about, but figured it either had something to do with Hula-Hoops or girls. He couldn't keep up with all these fads and phases the kids went through back in the States.

"Is this all the team?" Gerber asked after a moment.

"Not quite, sir," Tyme told him. "There's two more racked out in yonder. One of them you might even recognize. Wiry little guy with big biceps and the largest trophy board this side of the '68 Olympics."

Gerber wrinkled his brow. "Krung?"

"Staff Sergeant Krung now. It's Strike Force equivalency rank, of course, but he's real proud of the promotion. Doesn't seem to have mellowed him out any, though. Did you know he started a second board when Lieutenant Bao got zapped?"

Gerber nodded. The man under discussion was a Nung striker, part of the original Strike Force at Gerber's old Camp A-555, down in the Mekong River Delta region, just south of the Plain of Reeds in Kien Phong Province near the Cambodian border.

Known to the Green Berets only as Krung, he told them his entire family had been massacred by the Vietcong, with the exception of a younger sister, who had been brutally gang-raped and left alive to serve as a living example of what happened to families who supported the Saigon government. Not yet fourteen years old, she had committed suicide a short time later rather than live with the memory of what had happened. Krung had escaped the carnage only by the good fortune of being away from his village when the VC came.

When he learned what had happened to his family, Krung had sworn a blood oath not to rest until he killed ten Vietcong for every one of his family who had suffered. He kept score by nailing the genitals of those VC he personally killed to a sheet of plywood in his hootch, and he had had a very large family.

Krung had proved himself a fierce, ruthless fighter in combat against the Vietcong and NVA, rising quickly to the rank of sergeant in the Strike Force, although he preferred to kill at close range with a knife. He was an excellent scout and tracker, but occasionally had to be reminded that the mission came first and personal vendettas second.

Krung's only close friend had been Lieutenant Bao, who had commanded the Independent Nung Tai Strike Companies at Camp A-555. Krung's grisly scoreboard had been nearly full when Bao was killed in an ambush led by a VC agent who had infiltrated the Strike Force. Following the death of his friend, Krung had once again embarked on a journey of vengeance.

"Who's the other guy?" Gerber asked.

"He's a Marine," offered Bunnell.

"You're kidding."

"I kid you not, Captain Gerber. His name's Bob Corbett. He's recon-trained but never posted. He's been serving with the Third Marines up on the Ultramilitarized Zone. He just made sergeant with less than three months in-country, closer to two, I believe. I don't think he's seen his twentieth birthday yet."

"Christ," said Gerber. "What's he doing here?"

Bunnell swallowed some more beer and shrugged. "I thought maybe you'd know the answer to that. Up on the DMZ he was a sniper."

"A sniper?"

"He's got twenty confirmed kills, and only one probable."

"Christ," said Gerber again.

"Captain," said Fetterman, "I've heard of this guy. It took me a minute to place the name, but I remember reading an article about him in the paper last time we were in the States. He got written up because he'd won an NRA small-bore rifle competition and a large-bore military competition both in the same week. One of his Marine instructors was quoted as saying the guy was the best shot he'd ever seen."

"It does kind of make you wonder, doesn't it?" observed Bunnell with a belch.

Assassination. Gerber hesitated to even think of the word. It was frowned upon almost as much by the Army as it was by the press, but it did occur. The CIA-run Phoenix program was one example, although it supposedly operated only district Provisional Reconnaissance Units. Phoenix undoubtedly did fulfill some reconnaissance and intelligence-gathering functions, but it was also a good way of eliminating someone you knew was part of the Vietcong infrastructure, but couldn't get enough evidence on for an arrest. Gerber had been involved in at least two assassination attempts himself: the effort to kill the Communist Chinese adviser to the Vietcong units that had plagued Camp A-555, and the unsuccessful attempt to eliminate Giap at Khe Sanh earlier that year. For some reason, though, the word still made him feel a bit uncomfortable.

Both Gerber and Fetterman had limited sniping experience, although it was neither man's specialty. The addition to the team of an outsider to clandestine operations, whose specific skill lay in long-range sniping, seemed to point clearly at an individual human target. But who? And why stage the operation out of Kontum unless the AO was going to be Laos or Cambodia? And which country was it? Gerber and Fetterman had been to both countries. Bocker, Krung and Tyme had only been to Cambodia. Bunnell had only been to Laos. Corbett and Yoon had never been been outside of Vietnam. Gerber was beginning to think the operation had been staged from Kontum just to confuse them.

4

A SHAU VALLEY, RVN

Sergeant Duc Van Co of the People's Army of Vietnam lay quietly in the tall wet grass, listening to the sounds of jungle birds and insects and feeling the warmth of the sun beat down on him.

This morning the sun felt very good to Duc. It had been cold during the night and had, of course, rained. In time the heat would transform the soggy ground and chilly air into a vast steam bath, but for the moment it was good to bask in the sun filtering through the gap in the leaves of the trees overhanging his position. It reminded him, however, that he wasn't perfectly concealed from aerial observation. Good though the sun felt, Duc made a mental note to be more careful in selecting his cover and concealment in the future.

The odds of an American observation airplane or helicopter passing over the precise spot and one of its crew members picking that exact moment to look down were terrifically small, and it would be almost impossible to pick out any detail through the hole in the foliage during the brief instant when one could look down through the branches, especially since Duc was wearing his new

Chinese-made camouflage suit. But it was exactly inattention to such little details that cost men their lives in combat. For the moment, though, Duc remained where he was. He had selected the best possible site for the task at hand and had no intention of abandoning it because of such a slight risk. The benefits to be gained were too great.

A slight breeze wafted through the valley, stirring the leaves and grass. The wind carried the sound of helicopters, a noise Duc had been listening to all morning. From the heavy sound of the rotors, he knew they were either Chinooks or the similar big twin-engined helicopters used by the U.S. Marines. He had counted the engines as often as possible and knew that a major operation, battalion-sized at least, was occurring south of his position. He was much more interested, however, in what had happened to another group of men.

About an hour earlier a flight of ten Huey helicopters had passed up the valley and landed nearby. Duc assumed they had off-loaded a company-sized blocking force in the area, which would eventually work its way into a position a bit farther down the valley where they could command good fields of fire and trap the Vietcong and NVA soldiers they hoped would be pushed up the valley toward them. The Americans were going to be disappointed today, however, because the unit that had been there, a battalion of the NVA's 324th Regiment, had moved out last night. What the Americans would find when they came to occupy their blocking position was Duc and his men.

Duc waited. The day grew hot, and the shadows cast by the trees shortened as the sun, a blazing golden ball, climbed ever higher into the sky. The warmth of its radiance, which he had at first found so welcome, grew uncomfortable, and he could feel the sweat beading slowly across his back and shoulders, then finally running down his sides.

He wanted a drink of water, but didn't reach for his canteen. This was the waiting game, and Duc excelled at it. The Americans, he knew, would be along shortly. The best position for the blocking force was perhaps eight hundred meters south of him, and the nature of the terrain was such that it virtually ensured the Americans would have to pass where he could see them. He would be ready when they came. It couldn't be much longer. The Americans wouldn't delay. They had no patience when it came to warfare.

Someone once wrote that combat was mostly sheer boredom interspersed with moments of stark terror. To Duc, the Americans always seemed in a hurry to rush toward the terror. He had seen many of them fight bravely once the battle began, but they were always impatient for the fight to start. Indeed, they seemed to fear the boredom more than they did the battle. To Duc this seemed curious behavior. Why rush headlong into a nightmare? Surely it was better to wait calmly for the unpleasantness to come to you and meet it on familiar ground. There was no point in hurrying the fear and horror that was sure to arrive soon enough, anyway.

Duc had trained himself to ignore discomfort during the wait. He could squat unmoving for hours if need be. He could lie motionless for an entire day. He would be aware of his thirst, of the sweat pouring from his body, of the oppressive heat in his camouflage suit, but he wouldn't yield to them. They were small things of no importance, like the chirp of a cricket lost in a storm. The torment of flies and mosquitoes, sometimes enough to drive a weaker man mad, were but the passing of the wind, the sting of their bites only grains of sand upon the beach. The hours that passed in an endless stretch were but tenths of seconds on the face of the cosmic clock. The Americans sought to end the war in months and complained when it took them hours to travel the length and breadth of the country. Duc was fully prepared for it to take decades to win the war, centuries if need be. Unlike the Occidental, the Oriental didn't count time in years, but in generations.

The one thing Duc hadn't been able to master completely, although he exercised great control over it, was the internal functioning of his own body. He had learned to ignore hunger and thirst when eating or drinking was impossible or inconvenient. He refused to pay attention to tired or sore muscles when he needed them to walk, lift or carry. To a large extent he had mastered the ability to disregard even the pain of wounds. What he hadn't been able to do was train his body not to urinate or defecate when his bladder or bowels were full. The time before elimination became a necessity he could prolong, but not indefinitely.

Now was such a time. At last unable to resist the pressure of his own weight against his groin, he was faced with the choice of either relieving or fouling himself. Had it been absolutely necessary he would have urinated in his pants, but as the Americans were nowhere to be seen yet, he rolled slowly onto his left hip, and using only his right hand, loosened the drawstring of his trousers and pulled down their top far enough to allow freedom to his penis. Even in relieving himself he exercised control, allowing the urine to escape only slowly and quietly and but a short distance into the grass beside him. When he had finished, he drew up his trousers with the same careful deliberateness and cinched up the drawstring. It took perhaps five minutes for his hand to return to the stock of his rifle, and another three for him to roll back off his hip and return to the prone position. He hadn't had breakfast and wouldn't eat or defecate until evening.

As Duc waited for the Americans, he was acutely aware of his surroundings. The slightest sound in the grass was immediately identifiable by the type of animal that had made it, the faintest rustling of leaves marked by the species of bird responsible. He could describe in detail the bark of the tree at his elbow or that of one a hundred meters distant. With equal accuracy he could identify by its markings each and every butterfly that had fluttered into his view in the past seven hours. The passage of nothing larger than a mosquito escaped his notice, and not even that within a range of half a dozen meters. When the Americans finally came, he would be ready for them.

Duc didn't observe all these things consciously. Such was his skill in the practice of his craft that his surroundings and any intrusion into his environment was automatically noted and cataloged by his subconscious mind. The input was filtered and weighed for interest or threat value, and if of sufficient importance was passed along to the conscious mind for further examination. It was an art that came only with experience, and Duc had nearly five years of that.

Somewhere in Duc's brain a tiny chemical messenger delivered its content, and he focused on an area of grass about four hundred meters distant where a gap occurred between two large teak trees. At first there was nothing, then just the tiniest hint of movement, and finally a shadow resolved itself into the head and shoulders of an American GI. The outline of his helmet was distinctive.

Moving with the same infinite care and patience he had exhibited in relieving himself, Duc fitted the stock of his rifle, an SVD Dragunov, to his shoulder and raised it ever so slightly to point in the American's direction. He fitted the padded cheek piece of the skeletonized stock to the side of his face, pressed his eye against the rubber cup of the four-power PSO-1 telescopic sight, centered the cross hairs on the soldier's head and read the distance off the integral range finder.

He could see the man quite clearly now. The soldier was young, perhaps nineteen or twenty years old, with a clean-shaven face and an expression of wary alertness mixed with a trace of fear. There was a peace symbol inked on the camouflage cover of his helmet, and the expression, We Kill for Peace, was lettered next to it. He was heavily burdened with a pack and equipment, and ammunition in cloth bandoliers crisscrossed his flak vest. The vest, Duc knew, was designed to protect the wearer from low-velocity grenade and mortar fragments and weighted about five kilograms. It wouldn't protect him from the heavy 7.62×54 mm rimmed round of Duc's sniper rifle.

Duc continued to watch as the American approached his position, the black M-16 rifle waving back and forth as he tried to cover the thick vegetation on either side of him. He walked slowly but steadily, occasionally stumbling slightly beneath the weight of his heavy pack. But he should have walked a few steps and then knelt to examine the terrain ahead and around him, then walked a few more steps and crouched again. Had he done so he might have had some small chance of spotting the movement of an enemy lying in ambush or of noticing a trip wire strung across his path. Even so he wouldn't have seen Duc.

It would be very simple to ease the safety off his rifle and put a bullet into the bridge of the American's nose, thought Duc. But not today. Not this particular American. This GI was walking point for the Americans coming down to set up the blocking force. He would be allowed to live and pass unhindered through this area so that his comrades, following fifty or a hundred meters behind, wouldn't be alerted to Duc's presence. They would feel safe because they had heard no shots. They would be careless because they felt safe, and they would die.

Duc followed the progress through his telescopic sight as the American walked past him and on down the valley, never aware of the cross hairs resting upon his head, or that today he had been only the pressure of a finger away from death. When the point man had vanished from view, Duc returned his rifle to the spot where he had first seen the man, and eased off the safety. The other Americans would not be far behind.

Duc was very pleased with his rifle. When he had first become a sniper, he had used the old Mosin-Nagant Model 1891/30 bolt action rifle with the PU telescopic sight. It was a heavy, awkward weapon, unpleasant to shoot, and slow between shots and to reload. The SVD weighed slightly less than an AK-47, fired semiautomatically, and was loaded from a ten round detachable magazine. The muzzle had a flash suppressor and a recoil compensator designed to help hold the barrel near the target for follow-up shots, and the PSO-1 sight had a battery powered reticle illuminator, a built-in range finder, and infrared sighting for use at night. It was accurate against man-sized targets up to eight hundred meters, and was relatively pleasing to shoot. Duc had little doubt that if he had started his career as a sniper with such a weapon, he would have killed over a hundred Americans by now.

The sudden appearance of the American patrol broke into Duc's thoughts. The column appeared precisely where anticipated. They were shuffling along, each man pointing his weapon in the direction opposite to that of the man preceding him, with about three to five meters separating each individual. There seemed to be a steady stream of them, increasing in number, and Duc suspected that the entire platoon was following the point man. It was even possible that the whole blocking force, probably a company, judging from the number of helicopters that had brought them, was moving down the valley in column formation.

Duc tightened his grip on the rifle. To steady his aim, he rested the forearm of the Dragunov across his pack, which lay in front of him. He put the cross hairs on the face of the first man in the line and tracked him as he came nearer, but didn't fire. Behind the American more and more GIs appeared. Duc's target was now close enough for him to see that this American had also written a saying on his helmet cover: Peace through Superior Firepower. It was a sentiment Duc heartily agreed with.

When the big-nosed soldier was only 250 meters away, Duc took up the slack in the trigger and fired. The blast sounded like a cannon in the peaceful morning air. Duc felt the rifle buck back against his shoulder, but it wasn't an unpleasant sensation, more bounce than recoil. The soldier's head was momentarily lost from view due to the movement of the recoiling rifle and scope, then reappeared only to vanish in a spray of red mist and gray matter.

Duc moved the rifle slightly, found the second man in the scope and fired immediately, hitting him in the chest. The man bent abruptly forward, then fell to the rear, as though he had suddenly decided to sit down. Quickly Duc moved the rifle slightly up and to the left, finding a third target, then fired. The bullet, going wide of its intended mark, struck the soldier in the shoulder, spinning him to the ground.

The GIs began to dive for cover, but Duc found a fourth target. There was no time for a slow and steady squeeze, though. The Dragunov bucked, and the man went down, clawing at his throat.

The enemy were firing now, and bullets whined through the trees and grass, M-16s crackling on full-auto and an M-60 hammering away. The round whistled in all directions. The Americans had no idea yet where the sniper was. They were merely putting out rounds, hoping to get lucky, or at least keep their attacker's head down.

Duc saw another man moving in the grass more than three hundred meters away and shot him through the side of the chest. The American officers and NCOs shouted orders to their men. Nearly four hundred meters distant a group of five soldiers got up and tried to run into the trees to Duc's right. He shot two of them in the back, and both men pitched headlong into the grass before they reached the trees. The other three made it to cover.

Farther back, toward the end of the column, a man carrying a bag, presumably the medic, hurried forward, crouching as he ran. The range was more than five hundred meters when Duc's bullet caught the man in the abdomen.

Duc hugged the ground when he heard the characteristic sound of grenades leaving M-79s. The detonations threw up dirt and shredded leaves, leaving Duc untouched. The enemy had his general location, but not the range yet, and he had the advantage. The grenadiers were firing at nearly their maximum range, and their accuracy was suffering. The grenadiers, however, were well within range of Duc's rifle. There was time for one more shot.

Duc found one of the grenadiers, sighted on his center of mass and pulled the trigger. The round hit the man's M-79, driving the grenade launcher back into his chest and knocking him off his feet. It was impossible to tell if he had been hit, or only struck by his weapon. And then Duc heard the sustained firing of his security team's RPD machine gun as a squad of Americans tried to flank his position. It was time to move.

Duc flattened again as a second salvo of grenades, only two this time, landed near his position. Cautiously he slithered backward into deeper cover. When he had crawled far enough for the trees to screen him from the Americans, he got up and ran. There was no need to attempt to pass a signal to his security team. It was understood that contact would be broken as soon as the enemy encountered them. They would try to delay the enemy only long enough for Duc to have a chance to escape, then withdraw themselves.

Dud had to wait only about fifteen minutes for the security team to show up. They had suffered no casualties and were jubilant. "What shooting!" exclaimed Corporal Tho. "Comrade Duc killed nine of the big noses! Did you ever see such shooting in all your lives, Comrades? Our cause is invincible with marksmen like Comrade Duc on our side."

"I *hit* nine of them, Comrade," Duc corrected softly. "It's impossible to say how many of them are dead. We weren't able to confirm the kills."

"What does it matter that we couldn't touch the bodies?" continued Tho, his joy not in the least restrained. "I saw them go down. We all saw them. We confirm your kills for you visually. They're all dead Americans. Today is a great day for the Revolution. It will be remembered for generations as your greatest triumph. The day Comrade Duc Van Co killed nine Americans in a single engagement by himself! And not only that, it's the day your record exceeded eighty-five kills. You're now the greatest sniper in the People's Army, in all of Vietnam, perhaps in the entire world! This day will be known as Comrade Duc Van Co Day.''

Duc started to protest that he had done nothing so incredible that it couldn't have been equaled by any other comrade dedicated to the cause of liberating the South, and then the impact of Tho's words hit him. Before today his record had stood at seventy-nine confirmed kills, six kills away from the record of Chan Vinh Minh, North Vietnam's greatest sniper. Today, in one single action, he had exceeded that record by three.

Duc smiled shyly. "I thank you for your endorsement, Comrade Tho, but perhaps the higher authorities won't recognize today's victories as confirmed."

"Impossible!" Tho shouted. "We all saw it happen. We'll all swear to it. Chan wasn't required to touch all the bodies, so long as the shootings were witnessed by at least two other comrades. You have six witnesses who can testify to the truth of your glorious victory. You are now the highest-ranked sniper in the People's Army. Why deny it? The honor is yours alone."

Duc smiled again, more confidently. "The greatest sniper in the People's Army. Yes. Yes, perhaps you're right. I'm the greatest sniper in the People's Army. And you, Comrades, are the greatest sniper security team. It's your diligent work protecting me that has allowed me to accomplish this great victory. But before we congratulate ourselves too much, I think it would be best if we left the area before the Americans reorganize and come to cut our celebration short."

"Ha! Let them find us," jeered Tho. "They will find only death. We have with us the greatest killer in the war. No American patrol can match Duc Van Co, the world's greatest sniper!"

Duc could hardly blame the men for being happy. It had indeed been a very good day. Nine Americans killed or wounded without a single casualty on their side. That alone was cause enough for celebration, never mind the record that had been broken. But the day wouldn't be over, and they wouldn't truly be safe, until they had returned to their base, a sprawling tunnel and bunker complex a few kilometers distant.

"Again, Comrades, I thank you for the accolades," said Duc, "but I must remind you all that not even the greatest sniper in the world is a match for American fighter-bombers and helicopter gunships. It's time for us to leave."

5

MACV-SOG ISOLATION COMPOUND COMMAND AND CONTROL CENTRAL KONTUM, RVN

Corbett had spent a fitful night, trying to sleep on the steel bunk in the squad bay of the team house. It wasn't a lumpy mattress. In fact, the facilities weren't at all bad. He'd slept in much worse—rat-infested bunkers, mud-filled foxholes, to name just a few. This place had a reasonably comfortable bed with clean sheets and blankets and, wonder of wonders, even a pillow. He could have done better, he supposed, but not on the DMZ.

It was the damn dream. He'd had it a couple of times, and it always started out the same way, with him shooting the fifteen-year-old girl. Except when he turned the body over to look at it, it wasn't a Co Cong at all. It was a blond-haired, blue-eyed American girl who stared up at him and demanded to know why he had killed her. Corbett didn't think he knew the girl, but somehow, in the dream, she always seemed familiar to him. He wasn't sure what it meant, except that he didn't like shooting fifteen-year-old girls.

After that the dream varied. Some nights he would dream about people he didn't know, other nights people he did. One night he'd dreamed about the twenty-two-year-old French teacher he'd had in high school, who had taught him a new meaning for the word *French* just before he enlisted in the Marines.

Last week, after he dreamed he'd shot the Co Cong, he'd dreamed he was back home hunting white-tailed deer with his father. He'd made the shot, a good clean kill at nearly four hundred yards with open sights, but when he walked over to cut the deer's throat and gut it, the animal had turned into a VC. He turned over the body, and it was an aged papasan with a thin, wispy beard, like Ho Chi Minh's. Then, while he watched, the face had melted into that of his grandfather.

And then there was last night. First, as always, he'd dreamed about shooting the girl. And then he'd dreamed about going out on a long patrol with a bunch of Marines he didn't know. It was miserable trudging through heavy brush and the day was hot as only a day in Indochina can be hot. They had slogged on all through the day without rest, the straps of his pack cutting into his shoulders. Finally, at sunset, the point had spotted a single VC crossing an open field at long distance, and the word had been passed back to send the sniper forward. Corbett had made the shot clean at six hundred yards, and the patrol had marched on down to claim the body. When they turned it over, the sight had been so unsettling that Corbett had awakened and sat up straight in bed, his mouth open in a scream that fortunately had remained silent. The face of the dead VC had been his own.

Corbett didn't think he was developing any psychological problems about doing his job, but he was beginning to wonder about the dreams. He didn't know whom to talk to about it. Not some sky pilot from the chaplain's office, that much was sure. The sky pilot wouldn't have any understanding of what he was talking about. He would just give him a blessing and exhort him to kill the enemy in God's name. He couldn't very well talk to his commanding officer, either, not without risking a Section Eight. Besides, he wasn't all that sure who his commanding officer was. And he certainly couldn't write home about it. His folks wouldn't understand any better than the chaplain. His dad still hadn't forgiven him for enlisting in the Marines, and his mother hadn't forgiven him for enlisting period.

He supposed he could try to talk to Bunnell, or one of the other Green Beret types about it, but what good would that do? They killed people in the heat of battle. He killed people in cold blood. Maybe they'd just laugh it off and think him silly. Then again, maybe they'd lose confidence in his ability to perform his part of the upcoming mission, whatever it might be. If that happened, they'd have to talk to Gerber, and then he'd be right back to the Section Eight discharge. No thanks.

Corbett knew he wasn't cracking up. He could do the job when the time came. He always had, and he knew he still could. He just couldn't think of it as a sport or a game. Maybe that was why he had the dreams. But they didn't bother him all the time. Most of the time he slept just fine, so maybe they didn't really amount to anything. He just wished they'd stop. He didn't like the direction they'd been taking lately.

Corbett looked at his watch, saw that it was seven-thirty in the morning and pushed himself upright on the bunk.

He'd slept in his pants in case of attack, but his T-shirt and OD jungle jacket were draped over the end of the bunk. He retrieved them and put them on.

Corbett didn't know what he would have done in case of an attack, anyway. He'd had to turn in his rifle at Da Nang, and nobody had issued him anything else yet. Bocker and Yoon had been carrying M-16s when they arrived, and Tyme had a shotgun. Corbett had been a little surprised at that. He'd thought shotguns were outlawed by the Geneva Convention. Bunnell had a carbine and a pistol, as did Krung, but neither Gerber or Fetterman had seemed armed or worried about it. Maybe this place was considered secure, although experience had taught him there was no such thing as a really secure place in Vietnam, at least not in I Corps.

Corbett found his boots, remembering to pick them up by the toe and bang the heel against the floor a couple of times in case any scorpions or spiders had taken up residence. That done, he pulled them on and laced them up. Then he pushed himself off the bunk and headed for the rec room and kitchen area. Most of the team members were already up, or hadn't gone to bed yet. The card game was in progress, still or again, and Bunnell was having his breakfast beer with some scrambled powdered eggs and bacon he'd cooked in the tiny kitchen.

Corbett rummaged around in the shelves until he found a can of peaches. Then, after putting a pan of water on the Coleman stove to boil, he made himself a cup of tea, opened the can of peaches with the can opener he carried on his dog tag chain and used the juice from the can to wash down his daily multivitamin. When he finished his tea, he took the can of peaches outside to eat them in the sun before the day got too hot.

It had rained during the night, and most of the compound was a mass of red mud. Here and there pools of water stood in mortar or rocket craters that dispelled the notion that the compound was completely secure. The wiry little master sergeant who had arrived yesterday with Captain Gerber was sitting atop the sandbags of a countermortar bunker near the end of the team house. He had his shirt off to catch the morning sun and appeared to be working on something. Corbett walked over and asked if he could sit down.

"It's a free country," said Fetterman, squinting up at him. "Leastways, this small little part of it is. Take a pew."

Corbett looked at the man a little uncertainly. His deeply tanned back, shoulders and chest were covered with scars of various shapes and sizes. The Marine decided that, having asked, he might offend the man by going elsewhere, so he sat.

For a few minutes both men said nothing while Fetterman finished reassembling a small pistol and Corbett ate his peaches. They hadn't been pitted very well and were a bit on the gritty side, but Corbett hadn't had peaches since leaving the States and hardly noticed the bits of pit stuck to the fruit. To his taste buds, it was the best breakfast he'd had in nearly three months.

Fetterman slipped a magazine into the little semiautomatic, chambered a round and set the safety. Then he extracted the magazine, loaded it with another round and reinserted the magazine into the butt. He tucked the pistol, ready for use, into his belt over a kidney, then put on his jungle jacket.

"I didn't think we were supposed to keep personal weapons loaded in the compound area," Corbett observed.

Fetterman shrugged. "We're not. You ever try to shoot a VC with an unloaded weapon? Silly rules are made to be ignored."

"Does Charlie ever get inside the wire here?" asked Corbett.

Fetterman shrugged again. "He got inside the main compound during Tet. Who's to say he won't get clear in here next time?"

"I wish I had a weapon," said Corbett. "They made me turn in my rifle at Da Nang."

"You're out here unarmed?" asked Fetterman, aghast. He pulled up a trouser leg and peeled off a Velcro calf holster containing a Walther PPK prewar model. "Here. Take this. You can give it back to me when the mission's over. It's sterile."

"Sterile?"

"Not made in America. Not registered to anyone. Can't be traced."

"Thanks," said Corbett. He slipped the pistol out and examined it to make sure he knew how it worked. The little leg holster also held a cleaning rod and two spare magazines, all retained by little Velcro straps. The bullets were half-jacketed hollowpoints. "I thought these things were illegal."

"Like I said, silly rules. I figure if Charlie can use punji stakes dipped in shit, I can use hollowpoint bullets. Just don't get caught with it, either by the MPs or by the VC. In fact, I'd recommend you don't let yourself get captured by the VC at all. I did once. It wasn't a pleasant experience."

"You were a prisoner of the Vietcong?"

"For about a week."

"What happened?"

"I escaped," said Fetterman matter-of-factly.

"How?"

"Simple," said Fetterman. "I killed the guards and walked away one night."

"It couldn't have been that easy."

"Son," said Fetterman, "killing a man is never easy. Oh, it's not hard to do, the act I mean, but making up your mind to do it, being ready to do it, keeping yourself trained so you won't hesitate when the time comes, that can be a real bear."

"I don't think any amount of training can really prepare you to kill somebody," said Corbett.

"I'm not talking about practicing with your rifle or working out on the hand-to-hand course," said Fetterman. "I'm talking about training yourself mentally. Knowing in your head that you can do it, knowing when to do it, knowing when to go along with the bastard that's got the drop on you, and when the time comes that you've got to act right then, completely ruthlessly, without any mercy or hesitation. That's the kind of training I mean."

"I still don't see how you could have done it without a weapon of some kind."

"Your mind is your primary weapon, son. Never forget that. You're never completely unarmed if you've got a brain and the ability to think with it. Besides, once I'd killed a couple of the guards I had all the weapons I needed."

"It is not the rifle that kills. It is the heart of stone of the man who pulls the trigger," Corbett whispered softly.

"How's that?" asked Fetterman.

"Nothing, Master Sergeant. Just something Gunny Anderson told me once. He was my DI back on Paris Island."

Fetterman leaned back and stared at Corbett for a moment. "You got something on your mind, Sergeant?" he finally asked.

Corbett looked uncertain. "Master Sergeant, do you ever have dreams? About combat, I mean? What I really mean is, do you ever dream about people you've killed?"

"No," said Fetterman honestly. "I like to think I never killed a man who didn't need killing. Sure, some of them were just scared grunts like me, but if I didn't kill them, they were going to kill me or some of my buddies. I figured that made them worth killing."

"But you never thought about it afterward?"

"I said I never dreamed about it. I didn't say I never thought about it."

"I have dreams," said Corbett. "About the first person I ever killed. I'd been in-country one week. It was a Vietcong mule pushing a bicycle loaded with arms and ammunition. It was almost an eight-hundred-yard shot, and I made it clean. When we went down to check the body, I found out it was a fifteen-year-old girl. I know it was something that had to be done, but I just can't get it out of my mind."

"I don't reckon you ever do," said Fetterman. "I remember my first. I haven't thought about it for a long time, but I remember it as clear as if it were yesterday. We dropped into the Cherbourg Peninsula just prior to D Day. It was a night jump and everybody got scattered all over hell's half acre. There I was, crashing through the brush like a blind bull, just trying to find my unit, when I came around a hedgerow the same time a German soldier did. It took us both a moment to recognize each other, and then he started to bring his gun up, a machine pistol.

"Well, I got my rifle up first and tried to fire, but it was jammed. I bayoneted him instead and got the hell out of there. I can still see the surprised look on his face. Didn't have time to dwell on it. I was just scared and wanted to find my unit before I ran into any more Germans. Didn't even give it any thought until the next morning. Then I got to shaking so bad I had to sit down and have a smoke.

"Later still I got to wondering who he was. Whether or not he'd had a family, that kind of thing. It wasn't very productive, of course, and for a while I wondered if I'd be able to kill the next German I came across. In the meantime I lost a couple of buddies to German artillery. When I did finally meet up with another German soldier, I found it was no trouble at all to squeeze the trigger."

"I guess you were pretty lucky," said Corbett.

"Lucky, hell," said Fetterman. "I was faster, that's all. That German boy hesitated and I didn't. That's why I had the time to bayonet him. That's what it all comes down to, son. Not hesitating when you have to kill. Some men never learn that. If they don't, and they're soldiers, they die."

"That's not what I meant," said Corbett. "You were face-to-face with the man. You had no choice but to kill him. It's different with a sniper. Most of the time the enemy doesn't even know you're there until he's dead. That's not being brave or lucky or fast. That's just plain murder."

"I've killed men that way, too," said Fetterman. "They're just as dead."

"You're saying it doesn't make any difference, then, how you do it?"

"Difference to whom? To the dead? To their families? To the man who pulls the trigger or the outcome of the war?"

"Dead is dead, right?" said Corbett with a halfhearted smile.

"There it is," said Fetterman.

"Thanks, Master Sergeant. I'm glad we had this little talk," said Corbett. He lifted the PPK in its fancy holster. "And thanks for the loan. I'll try to make sure you get it back in one piece."

"Anytime."

Corbett got up and walked back to the team house. Fetterman followed him with his eyes.

"Is he going to be a problem?" said Gerber, stepping around the corner.

"Still playing detective, I see," said Fetterman. "Eavesdropping, Captain?"

"Just happened to be stretching my legs and overheard the conversation. Didn't want to interrupt," said Gerber. "I'll ask again, is Corbett going to be a problem?"

"If you're asking me to read his mind, I can't. What we've got there is one troubled young man. He's very good at his business, which happens to be killing people from quite a long ways away, and it doesn't sit well with him. He's trying to cope with it as best he can, but he isn't totally sold on his own arguments, and he's looking for someone to convince him that he's doing the right thing."

"Did you?"

"Captain, you know better than that. The only person who can ever convince him of anything is himself. I just told the boy a story that I thought might make it easier for him to convince himself of what he really wants to believe, anyway."

"Do you think it helped?"

Fetterman scratched his nose. "Can't honestly say, sir. It'll depend on what he does with it. He's a bright boy. I'm sure that given enough time, he'll work things out for himself."

"Tony," Gerber pressed, "we may not have much time. If Corbett's problems are going to be a threat to the mission or the safety of the team, I need to know it now, so we can ask Bates for a replacement."

"I don't really think we've got much chance of getting one of those, do you, sir? The way this team has been scraped together, I mean. Would Bates have gone out and dug up a Marine sniper if there'd been an Army one available? Just think of all the red tape he had to cut through. Everybody on this team was pulled from some other assignment. This isn't a mission. It's a boondoggle. It's been thrown together at the last second because somebody waited too long to make a decision, or because some new intelligence suddenly came to light that demanded immediate action. I doubt very much that the colonel could find a suitable replacement in time."

"Then we go without him," said Gerber. "If Corbett isn't up to it, we leave him behind. I won't risk the team or the mission by carrying along as baggage some guy who can't hump his own load."

"If we do that, then who's going to do the shooting, sir? You? Me? Boom-Boom? Tyme's a good shot, but he's not a marksman. If you'll pardon my saying so, you aren't, either. And while I sometimes get lucky, I'm basically a close-in fighter like Krung. Young Corbett, he's lucky every time he shoots. He makes his own luck."

"Come on, Tony," said Gerber. "No one man is that important. You've shot Expert before. Plenty of times. If we have to, we can do the job without Corbett."

Fetterman shook his head. "No, sir, Captain. I'm sorry, but I think you're wrong this time. Plenty of guys have shot Expert. Probably everybody we've got here is qualified Expert. Corbett isn't just an Expert. He's a Distinguished Marksman. The rest of us aren't even in the same league with the man. It takes more than just good equipment to make a shot at more than a thousand yards. Maybe I could do it at five, even six hundred, with a good rifle on a good day. I might even be able to do it at eight hundred under ideal conditions with two or three shots. Corbett is the kind of guy who'll do it at twelve hundred yards in light rain at dusk if that's what it takes, and he'll do it with one shot. He's a natural-born rifleman. All I've got working for me is years of training and experience. I could probably take him in under three seconds in hand-to-hand in some dark alley, but put us a thousand yards apart with an M-21 apiece, and I'll be the one they ship home in a body bag."

"He's really that good?" said Gerber.

"From what I've read and heard about him he's probably better. After only two months in-country, he had twenty confirmed kills, one probable and no misses. And Marine snipers don't count a kill confirmed unless they touch the body. I don't think Colonel Bates would have gone to all the trouble he did to find such a man if he thought you or I could do the job."

"The question remains," said Gerber coldly, "will he do it?"

"That's not the real question, Captain," said Fetterman. "Judging from the young man's record, my hunch is that he'll do just fine when the time comes. The question is, how well is he going to handle living with it afterward? Not everybody is cut out to be a sniper, even if they can shoot like Annie Oakley and Wild Bill Hickock combined. It takes a certain kind of attitude to be able to kill repeatedly, dispassionately, in cold blood. It's not like killing a man in open combat."

"I thought you just told Corbett it didn't make any difference how you killed someone," said Gerber.

"It doesn't," said Fetterman. "Except to the man who does the killing."

"And what happens when it starts to matter too much? When the day comes that you say, all right, I've killed enough. No more killing. What if it happens to Corbett this time out?"

"It happens to everybody sooner or later, Captain. When it does, the lucky ones go home to their wives or girlfriends and open up a bar or sell insurance or become stockbrokers or teachers or writers or paramedics. You want to know when Corbett's time will come, and I can't tell you that. It might be twenty years from now, and it *might* be the next time he goes out. I can't tell you. Corbett can't tell you. And if you can find a psychiatrist who claims *he* can tell you, you'd better sue the man for malpractice. Each time a man goes out, it's a new test. Nobody knows for sure if he'll be able to drop the hammer until he pulls the trigger."

Gerber tugged off his beret and ran a hand through dark hair graying at the temples. It seemed to him that he was beginning to get thinner on top, too, but it might have just been his imagination. Gerber had seen plenty of combat, and he knew that what Fetterman had said was right. He didn't like it, but it was still right.

Gerber fished in a pocket of his jungle fatigues, brought out a pack of gum and offered a stick to Fetterman, taking one for himself. It was his way of chewing over a problem when there wasn't an easy solution in sight or a bottle of Beam's Choice handy.

"Tell me, Tony," he said after a while. "That story you were telling Corbett about your first kill, the German in France. Was that the truth?"

Fetterman grinned lopsidedly. "Part of it was. I told Corbett a story I thought he'd like to hear. Thought it might make it easier for him to make up his own mind that what he's doing is okay.''

"What part wasn't true?" asked Gerber.

"The part about my rifle jamming and my having to bayonet the guy," said Fetterman, a distant look creeping into his eyes. "The truth of the matter is, it was a carbine, and it didn't really jam, either. I was so damn scared I didn't realize I hadn't taken the safety off. I beat the guy to death with it. It probably took five minutes to kill him, although it seemed like five years. He wasn't much bigger than me, but he was strong, and he wasn't any more eager to die than I was. I broke the damn carbine in the process and spent the rest of the night wandering around without a weapon until I picked up another from a dead paratrooper the next morning.

"All the time I kept beating the guy, he kept shouting something at me, and I was afraid some other Germans would hear him and come to see what all the ruckus was about, so the more he shouted, the harder I hit him. I just kept hitting him and hitting him until he was quiet. I didn't run right off, either, although that probably would have been the smart thing to do. My carbine was broken and I needed a weapon, so I took the guy's machine pistol. That's when I found out it was empty. He didn't have a cartridge anywhere on him.

"And do you know what the guy was saying, Captain? He was saying, *'Bitte. Bitte.'* I asked one of the guys in my outfit who spoke a little German what it meant, and he said it meant 'Please.' That's when I decided I'd better learn to speak the enemy's language. You see, Captain, I killed a man I didn't have to kill, because I was scared, and I panicked, and because I didn't understand enough of his language to know he was trying to surrender. And that, Captain, is the dying truth.''

"And afterward?" asked Gerber softly.

"Afterward? Afterward," said Fetterman, "I learned to live with it."

6

A SHAU VALLEY, RVN

The general atmosphere at Heroes of Political Solidarity Camp Number 5 was one of restrained jubilation. It had been a good day for the Revolution, but a bad month.

A few weeks earlier the American First Cavalry Division (Airmobile), the 101st Airborne Division (Airmobile) and elements of the 196th Infantry Brigade, along with the ARVN First Division and the ARVN Airborne Task Force Bravo, had begun Operation Delaware/Lam Son 216, a major sweep of the A Shau Valley to preempt preparations of the NVA and the Vietcong for a repeat attack on Hue.

Since then bitter fighting had raged throughout the valley, the positions of the opposing forces seesawing back and forth on an almost daily basis. Casualties had been heavy on both sides. Eight hundred new heroes had been martyred fighting for the Revolution.

However, not even high casualties or the loss of many tons of arms and ammunition to the Americans, a loss that would prove a crippling blow to the planned strike against Hue, could dim the exuberance caused by the shooting down of several American helicopters. In the implacable logic of the National Liberation Front the loss of a thousand, or even ten thousand rifles, was more than offset by the destruction of a single half-million-dollar Huey.

The Americans had succeeded in disrupting the plans of the Front to strike Hue, but it had cost them dearly, and despite the high casualties suffered by the Front, most of the NVA and VC soldiers had successfully slipped away to bunker complexes and base camps in the hills. In the final analysis the battle for the A Shau Valley was a decisive defeat for neither side, and for the Front, fighting a guerrilla war, not losing decisively was the equivalent of victory.

There had been many individual successes. Each of the gunners whose murderously heavy antiaircraft fire had accounted for the downing of an American helicopter had been decorated. Other awards had gone to comrades who had fought bravely against the Americans, or who had sprung successful ambushes. And, of course, there was the great personal triumph of Sergeant Duc Van Co.

For his splendid shooting Comrade Duc had been appointed to the rank equivalent of staff sergeant and made a Hero of the Revolution for the third time. He had also been granted a day's exemption from duties and was spending it drinking *ruou nep* with his security team comrades and eating carp fried with celery and onions. There was even a bowl of tiny dried popcorn shrimp, served with leeks and hot sauce. To men used to a diet of rice balls with an occasional bit of dried mackerel and a few hot peppers thrown in, it was positively a banquet. It was intended to be; it wasn't every day that a man became the greatest killer in the People's Army.

Duc Van Co, current Greatest Hero of the Revolution by popular acclaim, sat in the shade of a broad-leaved hardwood tree, smoking his pipe and occasionally sipping his rice wine. His belly was pleasantly stuffed with good food. His rifle had been cleaned and put away. And his brain was comfortably fuzzy from the alcohol. The Americans were kilometers away, chasing one another's shadow through the rain forest, and one of the men from the security team had switched on his transistor radio, although he had been careful to keep the volume low. When the political cadre approached, the man tuned his set to Radio Hanoi, and when the political officer went away again, he turned the dial back to the rock and roll music emanating from AFVN in Saigon. Duc reflected that it would have been an almost idyllic setting if only he had had some decent tobacco for his pipe. The stuff available locally might as well have been water buffalo dung.

It was a warm day, but not yet unpleasantly so, and the combination of the warmth of the sun and that of the alcohol in his stomach made him comfortably drowsy. Across the valley fog hung in patches that sparkled in the sunlight and added to the dreamlike quality of the landscape. Duc was just considering how profitable it might be to spend the rest of the afternoon taking a nap when the battalion commander approached. The sniper was about to get to his feet as a sign of respect for the other man's rank, but the battalion commander waved at him to sit still, then squatted beside him.

"This is a glorious day, isn't it?" said the battalion commander.

"It's a very fine day, Comrade Major," agreed Duc, struggling to force his alcohol-fogged brain to concentrate on what the battalion commander was saying.

"I was speaking of your promotion and your recognition as the new top-ranked sniper in the People's Army," said the major.

The confirmation of both had come by radio message from Hanoi only that morning.

"Thank you, Comrade Major," said Duc carefully. "It's a privilege to be able to serve the cause of the Revolution."

"Of course it is," said the battalion commander, "but it's also nice to have one's contribution to the cause recognized, isn't it?"

Duc chose his words even more carefully. "I'm pleased that the Front has recognized my commitment to the liberation of the South and its reunification with the North." He had the uneasy feeling that his political reliability was being subtly questioned.

"You don't view it as a victory of competition over the record of Comrade Chan, then? I would have thought there was a competitive spirit among snipers," said the battalion commander.

"I compete only against myself, Comrade Major, that I may improve my inadequate skills and more effectively serve the Revolution."

Duc was now sure that he was being gently probed to determine if his views adhered to the Party dogma of subordinating individual importance to the needs of the Revolution. It was a test of some sort, but why?

"You're a modest man, Comrade Duc, but surely you must feel some sort of pride at your achievement."

"I've done only what any other soldier of the Front would do to the best of his abilities," said Duc. "There's no room for false pride in the people's struggle for freedom."

"Yes. We must all make sacrifices for the Front to prevail in the liberation of our repressed brothers in the South," observed the battalion commander. "Comrade Duc," he continued, "are you aware that an achievement such as yours would normally merit an extended leave, perhaps even a triumphal parade in Hanoi?''

For just a moment Duc's spirits soared. It would be wonderful to be able to visit Hanoi again. Hell, it would be great just to have a few weeks' leave. He didn't care where as long as it was someplace not being constantly bombed or shelled by the Americans. Then the exact meaning of the battalion commander's words sank in and he got a grip on himself. His commanding officer had said it would *normally* merit a leave. Fighting down a bitter taste in his mouth, he framed an appropriate response.

''I couldn't possibly consider accepting such a leave, Comrade Major, when our southern brothers in the struggle for freedom haven't been liberated yet.''

''Excellent, Comrade,'' said the battalion commander. ''I was sure that would be your attitude. You are indeed a loyal soldier of the Revolution. It's my duty and privilege to inform you that you'll be leaving us. You're to receive a new assignment.''

Duc was surprised. He had expected to remain in the A Shau Valley. ''May I ask the nature of my new assignment, Comrade Major?''

''You may ask, but I can't answer. In its wisdom the Front has seen fit to keep that information secret for now. I know only that you're to leave us. You're to be conducted out of the A Shau. A guide and escort will see you safely through the American troop areas and hand you off to comrades who will further convey you toward your destination. That's all I've been told.''

''What about my security team?'' asked Duc. ''I've worked with most of them for more than two years now. Are they going also?''

''They'll be given new assignments here,'' the battalion commander said abruptly.

Duc didn't like this at all. The men on his team were more than just political comrades and fellow soldiers. They were his friends. They depended upon one another for their lives. They worked so well together that in combat against the enemy they could act to protect one another by instinct alone. Without them, Duc felt sure he would never have achieved his incredible record of eighty-eight confirmed kills. Now the team was to be dissolved. There was nothing he could do about it. It was the decision of the Front.

"When am I to leave?" Duc asked.

"Tonight," said the battalion commander, rising to his feet. "Be ready by sunset. Again, Comrade, my congratulations. May your new assignment bring you even greater opportunities to add to the glory of the Front."

May the Front attempt aerial intercourse with a revolving pastry, thought Duc as the major walked away. Yet he prudently said nothing.

Duc was a member of the Party, committed to the liberation of the South and its reunification with the North, but he wasn't a dogmatist. He frequently had doubts about the wisdom of the leaders of the Front, although he wasn't foolish enough to publicly express them. As he sat there silently stewing about what he had just been told, he could see the political officer approaching again. The music from the transistor radio changed abruptly from rock and roll to martial drums.

THEY WALKED until nearly midnight, Duc and three soldiers he barely knew, following paths and trails known only to their local Vietcong guide. Twice they passed through areas controlled by other NVA or Vietcong units and received additional guides who took them through the area, avoiding booby traps and mines set out to catch the

Americans and ARVN. Three times they were close enough to American positions to hear the GIs talking or smell their cigarettes and after-shave, but they didn't see any and their passage went unnoticed by the enemy.

Duc carried with him all that he truly owned: his NVA helmet with the old World War II-style camouflage netting, his pack, his rice roll, his canteen, his knife, his hammock, his medicine bottle lamp, his flashlight, his American Bushnell binoculars, his compass, his plastic poncho, his groundsheet, his blanket and, of course, his beloved SVD rifle.

They would have made a strange sight, thought Duc, had anyone been around to see them. With broad-leaved branches tied to their equipment and uniforms to enhance their camouflage, they must have looked like a bunch of ambulatory bushes, striding silently through the night.

At last Duc's escort left him, returning to their camp in the A Shau Valley, while a new escort took him on for several more hours until they reached a small clearing. There they sat down to wait. No one knew for whom or why. They had simply been told to take Duc there and wait until someone else came to collect him.

At four-thirty in the morning a pair of black-pajama-clad guerrillas from the local District Mobile Company arrived and took Duc to their operating base, a small tunnel complex. There Duc spent the day sleeping, and that night another pair of guerrillas took him a couple of kilometers away to a large grassy field.

The field had been covered by logs cut from nearby trees to make it suitable as a landing zone for American helicopters, but as Duc and his guides approached, it became obvious that several guerrillas and a somewhat larger force of locally conscripted laborers were engaged in industriously moving the logs to the sides of the field. A short time later the sound of an engine was heard, and five signal fires, in the shape of an arrowhead, were lighted.

Duc didn't think this at all wise. It appeared as though the soldiers of the Front were actually attempting to signal to an American aircraft. Surely the pilot of the plane would see the fires and call for artillery or bombers to blast the area. If the signal was some sort of trap to lure the aircraft close enough to shoot at it, the plan seemed foolish to Duc.

He could tell that the aircraft was a fairly large single engined airplane, perhaps a Skyraider, one of the large propeller-driven fighter-bombers the Americans called Sandy. They carried four 20 mm automatic cannons, as well as a staggering amount of bombs, napalm or rockets, and not to mention miniguns, which were small six-barreled machine guns that could fire as many as six thousand rounds per minute. Duc couldn't think of any greater act of stupidity than to try to attract such an airplane.

He looked around for a hiding place, but there were no bunkers that he could readily see. Then he heard the pitch of the engine change and realized the aircraft was about to descend. The sound, however, wasn't the addition of power to the engine that preceded an attack dive, but a throttling back. Puzzled, he realized the airplane was attempting to land in the field.

The night grew almost quiet as the noise of the engine diminished. Then, suddenly, a rushing sound could be heard as the air turbulence flowed over the wings of a plane close to the ground. Briefly a brilliant white glare of light stabbed out, illuminating the landing strip. An airplane the like of which Duc had never seen before settled onto the grass and rolled to a stop before killing its landing light.

Duc had only a quick impression of a stubby, thick-bodied biplane before the light went out. There was no way he could have known it, but he had just witnessed the landing of an Antonov An-2 Colt, a light transport and cargo aircraft of Soviet design, intended specifically for operations from short, rough airfields. He knew the Americans didn't fly such an airplane, and slowly he came to the only possible conclusion. It was almost too much to comprehend. He was stunned. In the entire time he had been in South Vietnam, Duc had never before seen a North Vietnamese airplane.

"Come, Comrade," said one of his VC guides, materializing suddenly out of the blackness. "Your ride is here. It's time to go."

"My ride?" asked Duc dumbly.

"Yes. Yes," said the man excitedly. "Now hurry, please. The airplane can't wait. It must go quickly before the Americans realize it's here and send planes of their own to shoot it down. You must depart at once."

"Depart to where?" asked Duc, rising slowly to his feet. "I'm not going anywhere."

"Now is not the time for humor, Comrade," said the VC. "The brave pilots have risked much to come for you. You must leave at once. There's little time."

The man grabbed Duc by the sleeve and started dragging him toward the end of the field. In the darkness the plane's engine could be heard revving and dying as the pilot periodically gunned it, taxiing back toward them over the bumpy field so that he could take off into the wind.

"But what's this all about?" Duc asked, stumbling along as he tried to keep up with the VC. "I haven't been told anything about an airplane coming to get me. There must be some mistake.''

"There's no mistake," hissed the VC in exasperation. "You're Duc Van Co, the greatest sniper in the People's Army, aren't you? The plane has come for you. It'll take you to your new assignment.''

Before Duc could protest further, the airplane lurched to a stop. A small door opened in the side of the plane, and Duc was pushed toward it. Someone grabbed his arms and pulled him into the fuselage as the VC guide pushed and lifted from below. His rifle was shoved in after him, and the door slammed shut. Before he could even get up off the floor, the pilot gunned the engine and spun the plane around. Duc was pushed hurriedly into a seat mounted to the wall of the fuselage and a belt was fastened across his lap. The engine roared and the airplane bounced forward and bumped across the rutted field, rapidly gathering speed. Without warning they leaped into the air.

Instinctively Duc gripped the armrests of his seat with both hands. For an instant he was afraid that the airplane had hit something and was about to flip over. He had never flown before and had no idea what it was like to make a short takeoff. With each sway and dip of the airplane his stomach lurched. He was afraid he was going to be sick. Gradually, as he realized they were flying and in no immediate danger of crashing, he relaxed his grip and sat back in the seat. His breathing was rapid and shallow and he could feel the sweat of fear beading on his forehead. He swallowed hard and tried to relax.

Duc's eyes began to adjust to the dim interior of the cabin. Then he realized he had company. He was about to speak when the aircraft lurched again, and once more he sat bolt upright in the seat and gripped the armrests. He held himself there woodenly, panic-stricken, waiting for the sound of wrenching, tortured metal and tearing fabric that would signal his impending death as the plane came apart under the stress. He almost cried out, but didn't know what to say or to whom. The pilot would surely be aware of the peril they were in and would do everything he could to avert disaster.

After a moment the plane leveled out again, and he heard a soft click as a switch was thrown, bathing the interior of the plane in a soft white light.

"Try to relax, Comrade," said his companion. "The pilot has everything under control. I take it you're not used to travelling by air."

The man who had spoken was sitting a couple of seats away in a chair similar to Duc's. He was dressed in gray coveralls, high-topped black boots and a close-fitting gray cloth helmet.

"It's my first flight," Duc confessed.

"Well, as I said, you can relax. It's not the pilot's first."

The aircraft swayed sickeningly, and Duc gripped the armrests tighter and closed his eyes.

"Don't be alarmed, Comrade," said Duc's fellow passenger. "It's only turbulence. I'm afraid it'll get worse, but it's really nothing to worry about. Normally the air's very smooth at night, and it's pleasant to fly then, but we're on the leading edge of a storm front and may well be forced to fly through a rain shower or two before we reach our destination. There's a great deal of weather disturbance in the atmosphere this evening. There always is during the monsoon."

Duc forced himself to loosen his grip on the armrests, even though he was less than totally reassured by the man's words. "I take it you've flown before, Comrade," he said.

"Ho! And well you might, Comrade," replied the other. "I've flown many, many times." There was more than a hint of pride in his voice as he said, "I'm the mechanic. My name's Thieu."

Duc didn't know whether to feel relieved that the plane had its own mechanic aboard or not. On the one hand, he supposed the man would be able to fix things if something got broken, but on the other hand, he wondered about the advisability of traveling aboard any sort of conveyance that was so unreliable that it was necessary to send a mechanic along to repair it in the course of its normal operations.

"I'm Duc Van Co," said Duc. "I'm a staff sergeant in the People's Army."

"You must be a very important staff sergeant for them to send an airplane for you," said Thieu. "Usually only officers ride with us. Indeed, I once flew with General Giap."

"I'm no one," said Duc. "I'm only a soldier."

"I can't believe they'd send us on such a dangerous flight for only a soldier," Thieu said. "Perhaps you're an important political officer traveling in disguise?"

"Only a soldier," insisted Duc.

"Well, then, what sort of soldier are you?" asked Thieu.

"I'm a sniper," Duc told him.

"Really? A sniper? Have you killed any Americans?"

"Yes," Duc replied. "I've killed many Americans."

"How interesting. Have you ever met Comrade Chan? He's our greatest sniper."

"Not anymore," said Duc.

"I'm told Chan has killed eighty-five of the enemy. If he's not our greatest sniper, kindly tell me who is, Comrade."

"I am," said Duc. "I've killed eighty-eight."

"But Chan's kills are all confirmed," said Thieu with a smile.

"So are mine," said Duc flatly.

Thieu looked at Duc with an expression that said he didn't altogether believe him but had no wish to offend by calling him an exaggerator of the truth. The man apparently was a sniper, judging from his rifle, and besides, there was something important enough about him for them to be ordered to risk a night flight into South Vietnam. He decided to humor his passenger.

"In that case, Comrade, I congratulate you heartily. You must be a great warrior, very brave."

Thieu didn't think his charge looked much like a great warrior at the moment. Duc's face had a pasty, slightly greenish look about it, and the man grabbed for the armrests of his chair every time the plane hit an air pocket and bounced a little bit. He didn't seem to be enjoying his first airplane ride much, and Thieu had a hunch that by the time they landed, he was going to enjoy it even less.

"I'm going to have to turn out the lights now, Comrade," said Thieu. "We can use them for only a short time because of the danger of being spotted by an American patrol plane. Is there anything I can get you before I shut them off? Some tea perhaps? I have some good hot tea in a thermos."

Duc could have used a cup of tea, but he decided that at the moment his stomach probably couldn't. The almost constant movement of the aircraft was most unsettling, both to his stomach and his nerves. He didn't see how he could drink it, anyway, without spilling it all over himself, the way the plane was bouncing around in the sky. He declined the offer, and Thieu switched out the lights.

In the darkness, with only the drone of the engine to listen to, every movement of the aircraft seemed magnified. Duc leaned uneasily back in his seat, closed his eyes, tried not to think about his stomach and gripped the armrests until his hands hurt. It was the most miserable trip he could ever recall having made, including the long shuttle march by truck and on foot down the Ho Chi Minh Trail from North Vietnam.

He wondered where, exactly, they were going and thought about asking Thieu, but was unsure if the aircraft's mechanic would have that information. Their destination would certainly be known to the pilot, but since the mechanic only had to fix the aircraft if it broke, not fly it, he wasn't sure that navigation would fall under his duties, and everything else about this new assignment had been kept so secret that the mechanic might not be considered important enough to know their destination. Duc figured he'd know the answer soon enough, anyway. When they landed, he'd be there, wherever *there* was.

Through the small round window in the door opposite his seat, Duc could see an occasional flash of light. He didn't know if it was lightning or artillery. He hoped that if it was artillery, it was their artillery shelling some Americans or ARVN base as they had done at Khe Sanh.

Duc couldn't imagine where the Front was sending him. What could be so important that they would go to such lengths to move him there? If it were only some new offensive, surely there were other snipers capable of filling the job. And would the Front really risk an airplane to move him from one area of battle to another in South Vietnam? He didn't think so. Perhaps the battalion commander had been wrong, or Duc had misunderstood him, and he was being flown to Hanoi for that triumphal parade after all. Yet, if that was the case, why did the aircraft mechanic not know who he was? Why all the secrecy?

And then he knew the answer. A man. A very important man. A man so important that only the very best sniper in the entire North Vietnamese army would suffice. A man who needed to be killed.

Duc wondered who the target could be. The president of South Vietnam perhaps? The head of American forces in Vietnam, General Westmoreland? Some visiting American dignitary like the secretary of defense or the secretary of state? Perhaps even the American vice president? *That* would certainly bring the war home to the American people. But would that be a good thing? Perhaps it would strengthen their resolve to win, not weaken it.

A sudden buffeting of the aircraft brought Duc back to an acute awareness of his present situation. His stomach, which had almost grown calm, flip-flopped and his pulse quickened. The adrenaline released into his bloodstream dilated his pupils, and he could almost see Thieu sitting on the other side of the airplane.

"Is anything the matter with the aircraft?" asked Duc nervously.

"It's nothing, Comrade," came the other man's sedate reply. "Only some more turbulence. I warned you that it would probably get worse. The air's very rough tonight. Don't worry. We have an excellent pilot and this is a good airplane. A very good airplane. I know it inside and out the way I know my own wife. It will get us where we're going."

"Thank you, Comrade," said Duc weakly. His mouth felt dry. "It's just that when a man's not used to traveling by air, all these sudden movements are a bit unsettling. I don't mean to complain. I'm sure the pilot's doing everything he can."

"I'm sure of that also," said Thieu. "But really, Comrade, don't trouble yourself. The situation's not at all uncommon when flying in bad weather. We're actually much safer than we'd be on the ground, because in the air there's nothing for us to hit if the wind blows us around a bit."

"You've flown in weather like this before?"

"Oh, yes. Many times. And as you can plainly see, I'm still alive."

Duc didn't find the reassurance at all reassuring. He wanted to tell Thieu that not only could he not plainly see, he could barely see him at all. The fact that one had never been killed climbing a mountain didn't make the prospect of falling off the mountain any less real or frightening a danger.

For his part, Thieu wasn't completely honest with Duc, either. He had flown in bad weather, it was true, but never in anything quite so bad as they had encountered tonight. Flying in marginal weather was something that good pilots avoided whenever possible, and this weather wasn't just marginal; it was terrible. There were just too many things that could go wrong. But there was no point in telling his airsick comrade that.

They flew in the darkness, the inky blackness broken only by intermittent flashes of lightning outside the windows. The turbulence grew steadily worse, and Thieu could hear the spatter of rain on the fuselage. The plane bucked and twisted like an enraged beast. It was like being on some horrible roller coaster. Then, finally, Thieu heard what he had been waiting for but had hoped wouldn't come.

"Comrade Thieu," gasped Duc weakly. "I'm very sorry, but I must ask if you have a container of any kind. I'm afraid that I'm going to be ill."

Thieu timed his movements as best he could to coincide with the erratic lurching of the aircraft. Releasing his safety belt and holding on to an armrest with one hand, he slid quickly across the aisle of the airplane, grabbed hold of another armrest and dropped into a seat one away from Duc just as the cushion came up to hit him in the back of the pants. He found the safety belt and buckled himself in before the plane could plummet again.

Reaching into a pocket of his coveralls, Thieu pulled out a heavy paper bag and opened it, then stretched across the empty seat between them and pressed it into Duc's hands. "Here, Comrade, take this. When you're finished, roll the top tightly closed and hang on to it, or we'll have an airplane whose inside is covered with something neither of us wants to clean up."

"Thank you, Comrade," said Duc gratefully, his voice little more than a hoarse whisper. He barely managed to press the bag to his face in time.

For the next hour and a half Thieu sat in the darkness, listening to the sound of a man vomiting at regular intervals and wishing that he had a second bag for himself. Thieu was made of sterner stuff, however, and had much more experience with this sort of thing. He managed to hold off until the Antonov biplane bounced itself to three bumpy landings, finally staying on the ground on the third try. When the plane at last rolled to a complete stop and the pilot cut the engine, Thieu promptly threw open the door, hopped out into a light rain and, sinking to his knees on the wet earth, proceeded to decorate the surrounding countryside with the semidigested remains of his supper.

When he finished, he got shakily to his feet and found a deathly pale Duc hanging weakly to the side of the open door for support, the bag containing his regurgitated dinner held in the other hand. Nearby, a small group of men in raincoats and ponchos stood and stared at them.

After a moment one of the men stepped toward the airplane. Thanks to a flash of lightning, both Duc and Thieu could see that the man was a Chinese officer in the People's Liberation Army.

"Greetings, Comrades," said the Chinese. "And welcome to liberated Laos."

7

"All right, if I can have everyone's attention, we're ready to begin," said Colonel Alan Bates.

They were assembled in the rec room of the team house, an armed Nung guard posted outside each door. Bates had arrived about twenty minutes earlier by helicopter, bringing with him a Green Beret intelligence NCO and another person most accurately if somewhat unflatteringly described in intel jargon as a human intelligence resource. The HUMINT stood about four foot ten in new tiger-striped jungle fatigues and boonie hat, had dark brown eyes, nut-brown skin and jet-black hair that hung almost to her waist.

"I believe several of you are acquainted with Staff Sergeant Santini of the intel section at SFOB, Nha Trang," said Bates. "He'll be delivering the majority of the premission briefing today. The young lady with us is Bhangsang Souphonaphouma. I suggest you call her Bhang. It'll save a lot of time and you won't run the risk of dislocating your tongue. Bhang is responsible for getting a lot of the information Staff Sergeant Santini will be talking about to us, a task that wasn't accomplished without some cost to Bhang personally, as well as the loss of two of her friends.''

It was Bates's way of telling them that two people had died in order to get the intelligence information out of wherever it came from. Presumably Laos, judging from Bhang's name.

"I need hardly remind any of you, I hope," Bates continued, "that today's briefing is considered secret and is not to be discussed with anyone outside this room. I don't want to waste a lot of time, but I do want to give you a little background information on Bhang," said Bates. "Up until two weeks ago she was one of the CIA's most highly placed agents in the Pathet Lao Communist guerrilla movement, which controls nearly half of that country. She's a native Laotian but was educated at a rather exclusive boarding school in Paris and speaks French fluently. She's a bit short on English, but since all of you here speak either French or Lao or both, communication shouldn't be much of a problem. I realize Sergeant Corbett's French is pretty weak, but he'll just have to muddle through as best he can.

"Finally," Bates went on, "I don't want to belabor this point, but I want you to understand just how difficult this information was to obtain and the time frames involved. It may help you to understand why you were pulled from your duty assignments or leaves on such short notice. For now suffice it to say that we've been presented with a unique opportunity that will be lost if we don't act upon it within the next few days. Suffice it also to say that in order for Bhang to get the information out to us without blowing her cover and tipping off the enemy, it was necessary for her to arrange the fiction of her own death, which I'm told was convincingly accomplished. Of course, the CIA isn't very happy about all this, according to Jerry Maxwell. It took them more than four years to get Bhang into position, and they haven't got anybody waiting in the wings to replace her, not at the level of information she was able to provide."

Gerber shifted uncomfortably in his chair. He wasn't sure he was very happy about this, either. He and Fetterman had been involved with Maxwell and the CIA many times in the past, and the experiences had frequently been unpleasant and sometimes downright deadly. He had to give Maxwell credit on two counts, however. Number one, his intelligence data was usually good, and number two, Maxwell seemed to have a real knack for building a stable of some of the best-looking female agents in Indochina. In the past they had worked with a beautiful French-Vietnamese woman named Brouchard Bien Soo Ta Emilie, and this woman was nearly as good-looking. It was hard to believe, though, that Bhang was old enough to have spent four years worming her way into the upper echelons of the Pathet Lao. Back in the States she could easily have been mistaken for a freshman college coed.

"I'll tell you now that the target area is in Laos and that this operation has been approved at the highest levels of authorization," said Bates. "I need hardly point out that on a mission of this sort you'll be operating in enemy territory without benefit of air or artillery supporting fires. Your best chance for success will depend upon stealth and surprise, and upon a thorough knowledge of the target area and the mission profile. I suggest you listen attentively to everything Sergeant Santini has to say and save your questions for the end. Feel free to make notes of any questions you may have during his briefing, but remember that they're not to leave this room and must be destroyed before you depart on your assignment. You'll be issued appropriate weapons and equipment after the briefing, along with detailed area studies material. You will then have seventy-two hours to familiarize yourself with the material and equipment and conduct whatever training you deem suitable. Most of you are familiar with clandestine operations. For those of you who aren't, I recommend that you view this mission as you would any other mission and act accordingly to accomplish it within the constraints of the mission profile. Are there any questions at this point?''

Fetterman held up a finger and waited for Bates to recognize him. "Colonel, am I to understand that we go in three days? That's an awfully short preparatory period for a clandestine op, if you don't mind my saying so, sir.''

"Nevertheless, you leave in seventy-two hours. I'm sorry, gentlemen, but it can't be helped. Our intelligence indicates that the mission opportunity is highly perishable, with only a very narrow launch window. If you fail to launch within seventy-two hours, you won't be in position to conduct the strike at the necessary time. Ideally you would be inserted tonight. I'm giving you as much time as possible because I realize the kinds of problems you'll be up against. Also, the planning staff felt, after much discussion, that minimizing your time in the AO would make premature discovery by the enemy less likely. Lastly the marginal weather we've been experiencing has created its own set of constraints for the mission. Meteorological projections have pretty well indicated that the weather over the target area should be suitable for insertion in seventy-two to ninety hours. If you don't go then, the weather's likely to close down on us and you probably won't be going at all. Anything else?''

"Is Bhang part of the briefing team for today, Colonel?'' asked Gerber pointedly. He wasn't trying to be nasty, but if Santini was conducting the briefing, no one without a need to know the details had any business being present while the particulars of the mission profile were discussed.

"I'm sorry I didn't make myself clear,'' said Bates. "Bhang's here as part of the audience. She knows the target area intimately and she'll be joining the team as your guide.''

Gerber exploded. "Christ, Colonel! That's all we need. Dragging a woman along on a half-baked secret mission into a supposedly neutral country where we've got no support and apparently only the smallest margin for error. Have the people who thought this one up gone mad?''

Bates's voice turned hard, but his face didn't flush. "I can assure you, Captain Gerber, that *I* have not, as you put it, gone mad. It's precisely because the margin for error is so small that Bhang has agreed to go along. I might add that if there had been any choice in the matter, any choice at all, I most emphatically would *not* have asked her to accompany the team on this mission.''

"Excuse, please, Colonel,'' said Bhang softly, "but I think this man worry I not able to hold up. I understand his concern, but he wrong.'' She addressed the rest of her comments directly to Gerber. "Before I get information out, Captain, my network blown and two of my people killed. I exposed to Pathet Lao counterintelligence. They interrogate me three day before I escape, but I no tell.''

Without warning she unbuttoned her jungle jacket and held it open, revealing a pair of delicately formed breasts that had been mutilated and a chest and belly covered with scars, not all of which looked completely healed. "They do this me, Captain. For three day they do this me, and still I no tell. When escape, I make look I dead so they no follow and no change big plans. Then I walk to Vietnam. Sometime maybe I have to crawl, but I bring out information. You no worry about Bhang, Captain. I take care of self okay-fine."

Gerber sat there dumbfounded as the girl slowly refastened the buttons of her jacket. "I'm sorry," he said at last. "Please accept my humblest apology. It was stupid of me to say such a thing without knowing the details."

"Yes, it was," said Bates. "Now, if there are no more questions, I'll let Sergeant Santini get on with it."

The rec room of the team house was absolutely silent, except for a slight gagging sound coming from Corbett in the corner. Santini replaced Bates at the front of the group, standing behind a little plywood lectern. Before the briefing he had set up a small folding easel with flip charts and a map covered with a canvas cloth. For the moment he ignored them.

"Good morning, gentlemen. I remind you that today's briefing is classified as secret and is not to be discussed outside this room. We'll begin with a brief overview of the area of operations, then move on to the immediate target area and the target itself. Then we'll discuss specifics of the mission profile, including infiltration of the target area, operational time frames, communications, logistics, the actual conduct of the operation and exfiltration procedures. At the conclusion I'll be happy to handle any questions you may have."

Santini moved to the easel and flipped back the canvas cover, revealing a map of Indochina showing Laos, Cambodia and both Vietnams. The map was shaded to show areas under the control of Communist forces. The approximate route of the Ho Chi Minh Trail, running from China down through North Vietnam, Laos and Cambodia and cutting into South Vietnam at several locations below the Seventeenth Parallel, was marked in red.

"As you probably know," Santini began, "Laos is a country with an area of about 89,320 square miles and a population approaching one and a half million. The population is made up of approximately forty-two tribal groups, the actual number depending on how one draws the distinctions between them. Most of these groups have long histories of mutual animosity. The country has never been effectively ruled by any political group from one center, including the French. Laos is somewhat primitive, even by underdeveloped agrarian socioeconomic standards. There's virtually no industrial base in the few urban areas, and many of the once rich farming areas of the countryside have been all but destroyed by the war there. Since the early 1950s, on average, imports have exceeded exports by about fourteen hundred percent, the trade deficit being largely ameliorated by massive infusions of foreign aid, principally from the United States.

"Again, in the early 1950s, the Pathet Lao and their political organization, the Neo Lao Hak Xat, were formed in opposition to the French effort to reimpose colonial rule. The Pathet Lao has been very successful in organizing or subjugating the rural populace in the central and eastern part of the country, which feels little affinity for the urban class or the Lowland Lao inhabiting the area along the Mekong River Valley. The Pathet Lao now controls slightly more than fifty percent of the landmass, roughly the eastern half of the country.

"In 1957 an agreement among the various factions, including the Pathet Lao, to unite in a neutralist Government of National Unity was spoiled by a right-wing coup, and in 1959 an attempt to take over the administrative capital of Vientiane by a small group of civil servants and Royal Laotian Army officers resulted in the outbreak of open armed rebellion by leftist and neutralist factions alike. Other coup attempts followed in 1960 and 1964. Another attempt at a coalition government, following the neutrality agreements signed in Geneva in 1962, broke down when the Pathet Lao walked out of the coalition government in April 1963 after the assassination of two of their left-of-center supporters in the government by right-wing death squads.

"In May 1964 open warfare once again erupted between Pathet Lao forces and the Royal Laotian Army on the Plain of Jars, following the right-wing coup that had occurred a month earlier and the placement of control of the army under the leadership of an antineutralist and antileftist right-wing leadership. That warfare has since intensified, resulting in perhaps as high as twenty percent of the population becoming refugees. The Plain of Jars, once a fertile cattle raising area with a population of around 150,000, is now virtually a deserted wasteland."

Santini took out a telescopic pocket pointer, extended it and used it to trace a route on the map. "The Pathet Lao has, of course, been receiving considerable military and financial assistance from North Vietnam and other Communist countries in exchange for permitting the North Vietnamese to bring supplies down the Ho Chi Minh Trail, an extensive network of roads and footpaths running through the southern half of the territory controlled by the Pathet Lao, but actually originating inside North Vietnam and following the paths of National Routes 6, 7, 8 and 12 in the northeast part of Laos.

"Since the country is still *officially* recognized as neutral because of the Geneva and coalition agreements, the

United States is prevented from taking any direct action against the Pathet Lao. We do maintain a strong advisory presence to the Royal Lao government and have done so despite the frequent changes in administration. We also support the Meo or Hmong army of General Vang Pao, which is fighting the Pathet Lao in northeastern Laos.''

Santini drew a breath and rubbed the back of his neck before continuing. "Obviously we're interested in doing whatever we can to limit the flow of supplies down the Ho Chi Minh Trail, and the enemy is interested in doing whatever they can to increase the flow, particularly following the beating they took during the recent Tet offensive.

"Since Tet we estimate the enemy have lost approximately one-fifth of their total manpower with only about two-thirds of their combat units still having sufficient strength to conduct offensive combat operations. Especially in the heavily populated coastal lowlands of South Vietnam, the offensive proved a disaster for the VC and NVA, with estimates running to forty thousand killed, three thousand prisoners captured and perhaps as many as another five thousand disabled or dead of wounds out of a total commitment of eighty-four thousand combat maneuver forces and impressed labor or conscripts.

"If the enemy's going to continue the struggle to subjugate South Vietnam," said Santini, "it's vital to their interests that they rebuild an effective, large combat fighting force as soon as possible. It appears at present that the only way they'll be able to accomplish this is with a massive influx of regular NVA forces. Since a direct assault across the DMZ would undoubtedly be met with sustained retaliatory bombing by American and RVN air forces, we feel the enemy will instead embark on a gigantic program of infiltration of NVA units down the Ho Chi Minh Trail on a scale hitherto unequaled.''

Santini walked back over to the lectern and leaned on it. ''We now come to the most disquieting part of this situation. Intelligence has recently learned that the enemy will be assisted in their efforts in a very big way by the People's Republic of China.'' Santini smiled lopsidedly with grim satisfaction. The Red Chinese providing assistance to the NVA and VC in the form of arms, matériel and advisers was nothing new, but his carefully chosen words indicated a major increase in that effort had gotten the attention of the man in front of him.

''Solid intelligence,'' said Santini. ''Let me repeat that, *solid* intelligence, indicates the Chinese leadership and the PLA are giving very serious consideration to providing an advisory force of one hundred thousand volunteers. This force would be composed of engineer specialists and their associated heavy machinery for expanding and improving the road network of the Ho Chi Minh Trail, as well as security forces, including antiaircraft guided missile technicians, armored personnel carriers and T-54 tanks.'' Santini could see the looks of utter disbelief on their faces.

''You're joking,'' Gerber finally choked out.

''We thought the Chinese were at first,'' said Santini. ''We couldn't believe they'd want to escalate their involvement to that level. Of course, a hundred thousand men is a fairly minor investment for the PLA. We also had a hard time believing the North Vietnamese would want that many Chinese soldiers crossing through their country and protecting their supply routes. They don't exactly trust each other, you know. However, when you figure that Uncle Ho lost about seventy-five thousand troops in all four corps areas during Tet, he's got to make up the difference somehow. An influx of one hundred thousand Chinese volunteers taking over responsibility for the security and maintenance of the Ho Chi Minh Trail would go a long way toward loosening up the commitments of a lot of NVA soldiers.

"What it comes down to is this," said Santini. "*If* the Chinese do move into Laos, and we expose the move, they can always claim they were invited in by the Pathet Lao, who could forward a pretty good claim for being the legitimate government of Laos, since they control more than half the country, anyway. I think we could expect that such a declaration of independence would be solidly supported in the United Nations by all of the Communist countries. Once the Chinese are in place, they figure we won't take any direct action because we wouldn't want to risk expanding the war to include direct confrontation with Red China. That kind of war could only be won by the United States by resorting to nuclear weapons, and nobody wants to do *that*. The U.S. would then be faced with the prospect of a long, continuing war in Southeast Asia with no end in sight due to the increase in men and matériel Hanoi could move down an expanded and protected Ho Chi Minh Trail. In fact, we wouldn't even be able to bomb the Trail without risking killing Chinese and starting a war with Peking. The Administration would have no choice but to pour another half million men down the rat hole and prepare for an extended war of attrition, or tuck our tails between our legs and withdraw from South Vietnam, leaving all of Southeast Asia open to the Communists. Those Chinese volunteers might just win the war for Hanoi without firing a single shot."

"This is incredible," said Gerber. "Just utterly fantastic."

"Yes, isn't it?" said Santini. "And it'll work, too, unless we can convince the Chinese that sending all those volunteers down south is a very bad idea. That, gentlemen, is where you come into the picture.''

Santini walked back to the easel and flipped the map over, displaying a second map underneath. This one showed only the southern tip of Laos, the northeast corner of Cambodia and a bit of South Vietnam. He put the tip of his pointer on the map and said, ''Ban Tasseng, Laos. Only about fifteen kilometers from the South Vietnamese border. Major crossroads and southern Laotian terminus of the Ho Chi Minh Trail. Everything coming into South Vietnam through the southern end of the Annamese Cordillera passes through here. Everything going on south through Cambodia and coming in through the Mekong River Delta and the Plain of Reeds passes through here. Despite the Royal Lao airfields at Attopeu and Saravane, one less than eighty kilometers away, the other only about eighty, Ban Tasseng is the major switchyard for the Ho Chi Minh human railroad. It's easily the most strategically important part of the entire Trail network outside of North Vietnam itself.''

''Which is precisely why it's the most heavily defended,'' observed Fetterman sourly. ''What are we supposed to do, take nine people in there and ask them politely to hand it over to us?''

Santini showed no sign of being ruffled. ''Nothing quite that melodramatic, Master Sergeant. But we do want you to send a clear and unambiguous message to the Red Chinese that their interference in the area won't be appreciated or tolerated.''

Santini put down his pointer and walked back to the lectern. ''Some of you will recall a situation when greater involvement of Soviet Russian advisers threatened to become a problem in our prosecution of the war effort. We were able to send Moscow a clear message that such involvement wouldn't be tolerated, and the Kremlin backed off. We're now going to send a similar message to Peking."

Santini left the details of the Soviet affair unspoken. Several of the men in the rec room had been a part of it, taking a raiding force into North Vietnam to destroy a Russian Special Forces advisory camp just north of the DMZ. It wasn't the sort of operation to be talked about or even admitted to in the company of personnel not directly involved, not even the other MACV-SOG personnel in the room.

"We've learned," said Santini, "that in four days' time a delegation of Communist Chinese officers will conduct an on-site inspection of the Trail network at Ban Tasseng in order to determine the precise operational requirements for making the area impregnable to American air or ground assault. The Chinese delegation will be accompanied on the trip by a group of high-ranking dignitaries of the North Vietnamese government and the Vietcong. It's our belief that at the conclusion of the trip they'll sign a protocol document pledging increased Chinese support for the NVA and VC, leading to a formal agreement to be signed by Ho Chi Minh and the Red Chinese leadership at a later date, which will guarantee the commitment of PLA troops to protect the Ho Chi Minh Trail. It's our intention that you should disrupt this meeting by assassinating the Red Chinese officers."

The rec room in the team house had grown suddenly, utterly quiet. Santini returned to the easel. "You'll be inserted by night parachute drop five kilometers west of Ban Tasseng at precisely 2100 hours three days from now. It'll be a low-altitude drop from a C-123 flown by Nationalist Chinese pilots from the Ninetieth Special Operations Wing of Air Studies Group. The drop will be coordinated with a series of night bombing attacks on the Ho Chi Minh Trail north of Ban Tasseng to cover your infiltration. You'll be supplied with ComBloc weapons and sterile clothing and equipment insofar as we have been able to provide them. For certain items we had no choice but to use American equipment. Any American equipment is to be destroyed if in danger of capture. Once you've cleared the drop zone, you'll proceed overland to the target area and conduct your reconnaissance.''

Santini flipped the page again. The new one showed aerial recon photos and ground shots of a Pathet Lao base camp in the Laotian jungle. Gerber wondered if Bhang was responsible for the ground photographs. Someone had risked a lot just taking them, and even more to bring the film out.

''We believe the signing ceremony will take place in this open-sided structure near the center of the camp late in the afternoon five days from now,'' said Santini, using the pointer. Once you've completed your recon of the target area, you'll lie low and hide throughout the fourth day. You must be in position before dawn on day five and will have to remain in position until the signing ceremony begins. Then you'll eliminate your targets and escape and evade overland to the east.''

Santini flipped to another map.

''Once you've neutralized your targets, Sergeant Bocker will transmit the CW signal, Confirm Kills. If you're unable to complete your mission for any reason, the signal will be Unconfirmed Kills. If something goes wrong and you're forced to get out early, the signal is to read Opportunity Missed. In any event, you must make your way to one of the landing zones designated on this map. You'll find a smaller copy in your area studies briefing packets at the end of the briefing. You'll transmit the five-letter code designator group of the appropriate landing zone and will be exfiltrated by helicopter with gunship cover, again from the Ninetieth Special Operations Wing.''

Santini paused and looked at the men. ''In the unlikely event that the meeting doesn't take place on day five, you'll remain on-station through day six. In that case, Sergeant Bocker will use a tape delay transmitter carried aloft by balloon after dark to signal Visitors Delayed. Under no circumstances will you remain in the target area beyond day six. If the Chinese haven't shown by then, they won't be coming. In any case, we can't leave a team in the field in that area indefinitely. No Chinese on day six, make your way to one of the LZs that night and signal its identifier and the message No Visitors. You'll be picked up at dawn on day seven. Is everything clear so far?''

Fetterman held up a hand. ''Just one little detail. With a meeting like this, that place is going to be swarming with Pathet Lao and VC. How the hell are we supposed to take out the targets and get out with our skins intact?''

''You, Corbett and Tyme will each be using the M-21 sniper system with Sionics sound suppressor and ART sights. You should be able to get close enough to make the shots without bumping noses with any security guards. Anything else?''

Corbett held up a hand. ''Sergeant Santini, I've never used the M-21 system.''

''We realize that,'' said Santini. ''You'll have three days to practice with it.''

Fetterman spoke again. ''I hate to bring this up, but what's the nearest cover like around there? Neither Boom-Boom or myself are snipers, although we've done some fairly long-range work.''

"The nearest cover is about six hundred meters," said Santini, "but you won't want to use that because it'll probably be occupied by pickets. The sites we've selected as the most likely for your use are between eight hundred and a thousand meters, although the actual firing position selection is up to you once you've seen the place."

"Christ!" said Fetterman. "At that range we won't even be able to see the guys. How are we supposed to know who we're shooting at?"

"You'll be provided with sixty-power spotting scopes for target identification," said Santini. "We're also aware that you and Sergeant Tyme aren't experts in this field, however talented you may be. That's why the primary targets will be the responsibility of Sergeant Corbett. You and Sergeant Tyme will take the secondary targets. You each have two targets. Once they're eliminated, you're free to engage targets of opportunity at your own discretion. If you're ready, we'll proceed to the targets themselves. I apologize for the quality of some of the photographs. It's the best we could do."

Santini flipped the page again, revealing two grainy photographs that looked as though they might have been reproduced from newspaper photos. One showed a Chinese man who appeared to be in his early fifties; the other was older, possibly in his late sixties. Both wore officer's uniforms of the People's Liberation Army. Santini touched each photo in turn with the tip of his pointer.

"Corbett, these are your pigeons. Lieutenant General Fan Song Huynh and Colonel General Quai Chi Lim. Study them. Know their faces. Kill them. You'll find copies of their photos in your pack."

Santini turned the page again. "Sergeant Tyme, these are for you. Senior Colonel Chow Ping Lai of the PLA and

Major General Phan Van Phouc of the North Vietnamese Army. Phouc should be fairly easy to recognize. He wears an eye patch over the right eye."

Santini left the pictures up for a minute, then flipped to another set. "I think you'll appreciate these, Master Sergeant," said Santini. "Major General Le Shao Quan, chief of the political section of the Canton Military Region of the People's Republic of China. And, finally, a target so tempting that we couldn't resist the opportunity—General Nguyen Chi Thon, political officer and head of the entire Communist army in South Vietnam."

"My God," said Fetterman. "It'll be like shooting Westmoreland."

"You might want to rethink that particular metaphor," said Santini with a grin. "I'm not sure General Westmoreland would appreciate it."

"You know what I mean," said Fetterman. "Are you guys sure this is a good idea?"

"Was it a good idea to go after Giap at Khe Sanh? Right or wrong the decision's been made."

"I'm not saying we shouldn't do it," said Fetterman. "I just hope the boys in the Puzzle Palace have thoroughly thought out the potential retaliatory strikes this kind of thing could trigger."

"Well, gentleman, I think that's about all there is to it," said Santini. "If you can manage to take care of these six men, you'll have more than done your job. If you can only manage the four Chinese, we'll be quite happy, and if you can only get one or two of them, it'll probably be enough to break up the meeting and send the kind of strong warning we have in mind to Peking. Indeed, if the only person killed is General Nguyen Chi Thon, the mission will be considered a huge success, even though it will have failed in its original intent. Please study one another's targets carefully, as well as your own, in the event substitutions have to be made in the field. In fact, each member of the team should study the photos of the six targets in case anything unfortunate should happen to the primary shooters.''

"You mentioned targets of opportunity," said Bunnell. "Is there anyone in particular the rest of us should be looking for, or are we just along for the ride?''

"Your primary mission is getting the shooters into position to make their kills," said Santini, "and providing covering fire for their withdrawal. I doubt you'll see anyone in particular close enough to recognize him, although you may well have to deal with a roving patrol. There will undoubtedly be some other North Vietnamese officials, as well as Pathet Lao officers present. We don't have a complete list, but it's chiefly the Chinese we're interested in. Phan and Nguyen are considered nice bonuses if there's time to get them.''

Santini opened his olive drab canvas briefcase and dug out some papers and photographs covered in acetate. "The only other Chinese we've reason to suspect will be there is a fellow named Rhee Ming Wong," said Santini, shuffling through his stack of photos. "He's apparently in charge of security arrangements for the Chinese delegation and may very well be at the target site already. We don't know much about him. It's reported that he's an airborne officer, but some reports indicate he's an infantry officer. One report indicates that he's served as an instructor/observer with the Vietcong, but that's not confirmed. Bit of a mystery man, really. We think he's probably a senior captain or maybe a major. It's hard to get much information on these lower-ranking officers, and the only photo we have of him isn't in uniform. Here's his picture.'' Santini put the photograph, an eight-by-ten black-and-white glossy, on the easel and stepped back so that they could see it.

"Goddamn it! That's him!" yelled Fetterman, leaping to his feet. "I knew the son of a bitch wasn't dead. Down deep in my gut I knew it. I didn't get to touch the damn body, and the bastard is still alive."

"What's all this about?" asked Bates.

"Colonel Bates, Captain Gerber, it's him. It's the damn Chinese guy or I'll eat Captain Bunnell's shorts," said Fetterman. He was no longer yelling, but his voice was still fairly loud, and very angry.

"Tony," said Gerber, "take it easy, will you? You're still chasing ghosts. It couldn't be the same man."

Fetterman snatched the photograph off the easel. "The hell it isn't, sir. Just look at his picture, will you? I tell you, sir, it's him."

"Tony," said Gerber more sharply, "get a grip on yourself. It can't be him. You shot him, remember? He fell into the reservoir and never came up. He's dead. Drowned."

"Captain, I never got to confirm the kill. I never got to touch the body. I tell you, sir, this is him. He's still alive."

"Tony . . ." said Gerber.

Fetterman's voice turned cold. He extended the photo to Gerber. "Just take a look at the picture, Captain. Then you tell me if it could be anybody else. You saw him as well as I did. You and Miss Morrow spent a couple of hours with him."

Gerber got to his feet, a sinking feeling beginning to form in the pit of his stomach. Slowly he walked over to Fetterman and took the photograph from him. He stared at it and felt like throwing up. There was no mistaking that face. It would haunt him for the rest of his life.

"Will somebody please tell me what the hell this is all about?" demanded Bates.

Gerber showed the photo to Bates and stabbed at the face with the index finger of his left hand. "Something's screwy with your intelligence, Colonel, because this man is dead. He was an adviser to a VC unit operating down in Kien Phong Province, where Camp A-555 was located. He was responsible for the death of Ian McMillan, my senior medical specialist, and for the capture and torture of Master Sergeant Fetterman and Sergeant Tyme. He may have been implicated in the execution of a Special Forces officer and an NCO who were prisoners in the same camp where Fetterman and Tyme were held, and who were shot by the Vietcong. The only problem is, we bumped into the bastard while we were on that R and R you made us take when we extended our first tour, and he tried to kill us. Only he didn't quite get the job done. Master Sergeant Fetterman shot him, and he fell into the water and drowned. The body was never recovered. This man died in Hong Kong three years ago, which means your intelligence on this whole operation ain't worth shit."

"Impossible," said Santini. "That photo is less than a month old."

"Oh, yeah?" said Gerber. "Just how reliable is your photographer?"

Santini didn't say anything. He just pointed at Bhang.

"You wrong, Captain," said Bhang. "You wrong about me and you wrong about this. I see this man in Ban Tasseng. He come look at camp for big meeting, maybe four, five weeks ago. Not wear uniform, but all know why there. I take picture before arrest by Pathet Lao. This man no dead. He alive."

Gerber didn't want to admit it. He wanted the man to be dead, to stay dead. Fetterman had killed him. He'd shot him at least twice, and the Chinese had fallen into the water and never come back up. That was the way things should have stayed. But just like something out of a B horror flick, the guy wouldn't stay dead. He just kept coming back to life. He'd been harder to kill than a vampire, and Fetterman had never been convinced they'd gotten the job done. Every time he saw a Chinese male, Fetterman thought it was the man. Gerber had almost decided the master sergeant was obsessed with the guy, and now it turned out Fetterman was right. The man who had killed McMillan and put Fetterman, Tyme and Washington in a cage, the bastard who had taken such delight in torturing Robin Morrow and taunting Gerber, was alive.

"All right," said Gerber, "so the SOB is still alive. He didn't drown, after all. Well, we're going to fix that little problem. This time we're going to make sure. Santini, add another name to your hit list. This bastard is mine, and he's toast."

"Mack," said Bates. "I can appreciate how you must feel, but we can't allow personal vendettas to get in the way of the mission."

"There's nothing personal about it," snapped Gerber. "This time it's going to be strictly professional. We'll shoot your fancy officers for you, Colonel. We'll send your message to Peking. But if this guy shows his face at the meeting, if I so much as see somebody I think looks like him, he's history. He's going to be buried in the archives filed under Extinct Species of Red Chinese Officers. He's going to be sleeping with the dinosaurs. And that's the only way it'll be, or you can just throw a court-martial at me and go find yourself somebody else for this mission."

Bates considered the situation and decided not to press the issue. "All right, Mack, this man gets in the way, you have my permission to take him out, just so it doesn't interfere with the execution of the rest of the mission. Are we clear on that point?''

"Yes, sir!" said Gerber. "We shoot the big shots first, then we can waste this guy."

"Is that clear with you, too, Master Sergeant?" asked Bates.

"Absolutely, Colonel," replied Fetterman. "I've waited this long to put my foot on the son of a bitch's throat. I don't reckon four or five seconds more is going to matter all that much."

"And how about you, Sergeant Tyme? You've apparently got an interest in seeing this man dead, too," said Bates. "Do you understand that I mean it when I say the mission has got to come first? If it doesn't, I'll have all your balls on a platter."

Tyme shrugged. "Hell, Colonel, I thought he *was* dead. Now it turns out he's alive. So what? We got another crack at him. I'm not obsessed with killing him, Colonel. All he cost me was a lot of pain and suffering and the death of a good friend. All I want to do is cost him his life. Hell, I don't even care if he suffers or not."

Bates wasn't sure he could trust any of them to put the mission first if they saw Rhee, but he was smart enough to know that he was outvoted if he went against them. And it wouldn't matter one damn bit that the Army wasn't a democratic society once they were out in the field.

"All right, then," said Bates. "So long as everybody understands the mission comes first, then the man, as Captain Gerber put it, is toast."

8

PATHET LAO BASE CAMP ON THE HO CHI MINH TRAIL BAN TASSENG, LAOS

Now that the sniper had arrived, thought Rhee, the arrangements were complete. Perhaps he was just being overcautious, but he had learned through the years that the best way to guarantee one's own survival was to leave nothing to chance.

It was almost inconceivable that the American enemy could have learned of the forthcoming meeting, but not impossible. The affair of the three spies had proved that the American Central Intelligence Agency had succeeded in infiltrating agents into the highest levels of the Pathet Lao army. Although only General Kang Mang's underage mistress had been in a position to have access to knowledge of the meeting and she and her two coconspirators were dead, it was possible she could have passed the information on to someone else before her capture. Where one found three spies, it was quite possible there was a fourth.

Rhee was slightly disappointed that he hadn't had an opportunity to know Bhangsang Souphonaphouma better. She was a remarkable woman for her age. While spying for the CIA, she had managed to completely mesmerize a lover old enough to be her grandfather. She had endured three days of the most persuasive interrogation imaginable without divulging any useful information. And, finally, she had escaped from her bonds and cage, killed her guards and then blown herself up, along with half a dozen Pathet Lao soldiers, in an ammunition bunker rather than be recaptured alive.

It was only this last item that made Rhee feel a bit uneasy. The destruction of the ammunition bunker had been complete, and he hadn't been able to view Bhang's dead body. There had been only a smoldering crater surrounded by debris and bits and pieces of several human beings, both male and female. Yet there was no one else, it seemed, who could have been responsible for the explosion, and the Pathet Lao security team that sifted through the dirt and rubble had found the scorched remains of her watch and locket, both gifts from the general, and more tellingly, the gold-capped tooth a French dentist had given her.

Still, he hadn't been able to view her body, and Rhee had learned the lesson that comes from underestimating one's enemy. He had made that mistake twice before. Once with an American POW, a Special Forces NCO, and again with the same man and his commanding officer when he had accidentally bumped into them while on leave in Hong Kong. His underestimating the resourcefulness of both men had very nearly gotten him killed. He still had a stiff shoulder and walked with a slight limp.

There was really no reason to believe Bhang had been able to pass information to the Americans about the meeting, Rhee told himself, and even if she had, so what? What was there that the White Devils could do about it? There was plenty.

They could protest the meeting to Peking and Hanoi, which would be useless. They could entreat the Vientiane government to launch an offensive into the area to disrupt the meeting, then sit idly by, twiddling their thumbs while the Royal Laotian Army did nothing. They could raise the question of the meeting before the Security Council of the United Nations, where everything would be denied because the United States would only have evidence of a planned meeting, not of its content or actual occurrence, and the Americans would only wind up looking foolish. Or they could take more direct action.

Rhee pondered the possibilities. A massive air strike by high-flying B-52 bombers perhaps? Possible, but not probable. American aircraft of various types flew as many as twenty thousand sorties a month in support of the Royal Lao Army forces and the Montagnard army of General Vang Pao fighting the Pathet Lao, as well as interdiction strikes against the Ho Chi Minh Trail, particularly in the northeastern part of Laos. But saturation bombing of a region around a population center like Ban Tasseng wouldn't look good in the Western press, especially with the American insistence that they were always careful to bomb only targets of a military nature. And how would they justify it to the world? By saying, "We're sorry we killed all those civilians, but we didn't want the Red Chinese sitting down to tea with the North Vietnamese and the Laotian Communists?" Such an outrage would itself provide the perfect excuse for large-scale Chinese involvement, and the Americans had stated repeatedly that they didn't want to widen the war. Besides, it would require a precise knowledge of the exact time of the meeting.

Another option would be some sort of commando raid. To be effective, this again would require precise timing and an exact knowledge of the moment of the protocol signing, the hour of which had yet to be positively fixed. It would require at least a battalion of men, and it would be very difficult to support them. They would have to be extracted under fire. And it would mark a direct attack on the Pathet Lao by American ground forces, once again widening the war in the manner that President Johnson seemed so determined to avoid. It was for that same critical reason that the American politicians had resisted the advice of their generals to invade Cambodia and southern Laos.

No, it was unlikely that the Americans would do anything at all, assuming they were even aware of the meeting, despite the fact that there was plenty they could do. And if they were aware, they would be far more interested in trying to find out what occurred than in keeping the meeting from taking place.

Unless they knew the real purpose of the meeting already, and that seemed an impossibility.

So there was no reason to suspect the Americans knew of the impending meeting since the spies had been captured and were all dead. And if they were aware of the meeting, there was no reason to believe they knew its purpose. And even if they knew of the meeting and its importance, there was nothing they would do about it, anyway.

Except for one thing.

There was one thing they could do, and one thing alone. And if they knew and they did it, Rhee knew it would be enough.

A single man could ruin the meeting and destroy the planned agreement. All he had to do was shoot a couple of the signatories before the documents were signed. It would disrupt the meeting and delay the signing, perhaps indefinitely. While new protocols were being drawn up for others to sign, the incident would be discussed, analyzed and criticized by the leaders of the various countries and parties involved. Perhaps one of them would waver in its resolve and withdraw support. If that happened, the whole agreement could collapse. A single man might conceivably accomplish all this with a single bullet, and it was possible that a single man could slip into the area unobserved and lie in wait undiscovered for several days, waiting for the precise moment when the signing would occur. It would take a good man with a good rifle to do the job, Rhee knew, and it would take a good man with a good rifle to stop him.

That was why Rhee had sent for Duc Van Co. There were, of course, snipers in the Chinese People's Liberation Army, but none had Duc's expertise or experience and none could match his record. Except for occasional potshots at personnel on Nationalist Chinese offshore outposts, there had been no opportunity for PLA snipers to sharpen their skills since Korea.

Rhee didn't really believe Duc would be needed, because he didn't really believe the Americans knew about the meeting, its purpose or its exact location. And he didn't really believe the Americans would try such an action if they did know. But they might. Rhee wasn't prepared to face the consequences of failure if they did.

To catch a thief, one must use a thief, Rhee reasoned. And to catch a sniper, he needed the very best sniper available.

Rhee also had another reason for requesting Duc Van Co. Rhee believed that one could tell a lot about a man by the way he talked, by his political beliefs and by the way he performed his duties. Therefore he knew he had to meet the man. He also believed there was no truer test of a man's character than to observe the way he did his job under stress, and short of accompanying Duc on a combat sniping patrol, he could think of no better way to study the man under stressful conditions than what had been arranged now.

Duc's great personal triumph of achieving eighty-eight confirmed kills had been only barely recognized by Hanoi. He had received a promotion, a medal and a day off and that was all. Instead of a parade through the streets of Hanoi and a well-earned leave before receiving a new assignment, all of which had been heaped upon his countryman Chan, Duc had been suddenly shuffled off to a late-night rendezvous at a clandestine airstrip and flown through foul weather to a secret base outside his homeland, all without any idea of what it was about. Now he was about to be assigned a virtually impossible task, and it would be expected that he carry it out brilliantly, or disaster could befall his country's war efforts. It would be a good test of Duc's mettle.

And the purpose of bringing Duc to Ban Tasseng was as much to test his mettle as it was to help provide security.

Rhee paused in the shade beneath the overhanging roof of the open-sided assembly hall where the signing would take place. He took off his gray cloth-covered sun helmet and mopped the perspiration from his brow with a dark blue handkerchief. The air was sultry and still. There wasn't even the hint of a breeze. To the southwest dark clouds gathering on the horizon threatened rain before evening.

In all his years in Indochina Rhee had never grown completely used to the heat and humidity. He was a native of Sinkiang Uighur and came from a small town near the Tibetan border, the land the Chinese people called the Top of the World. It was a harsh, inhospitable land with long, bitter winters, more suited to the yak and the muskox than to humans, but it was his home, and he had grown used to the ways of its people and its weather. He didn't exactly cherish its memory, but he did miss it. On days like this in Indochina he especially missed its short, cool summers.

Rhee sat down on one of the folding metal chairs beneath the tin roof and marveled at the foolishness of it all. Ban Tasseng was a miserable location for holding the signing ceremony. They should have done it in Peking or Hanoi, where adequate security could have been provided for all those concerned. At the very least they should have held it in town, where there would be no danger whatsoever of an American air attack and where they could have been in one of the comfortable, concrete villas left behind by the French.

But, no, the Party political experts had chosen to do it at this camp on the Ho Chi Minh Trail itself in order to demonstrate their solidarity of opposition to the American involvement in Vietnam and Laos and as a symbolic gesture of the Chinese support to come. In some ways, being in the middle of a military camp enhanced the security aspect. But in others, security was diminished. In any event, holding the signing in an open-air assembly hall in front of several hundred Pathet Lao, Vietcong and NVA soldiers was ludicrous, particularly in this weather, the opportunities for political propaganda, backed up by photographs, notwithstanding.

Rhee had sent his interpreter off to fetch the NVA sniper and bring him to the assembly hall. It was time to acquaint him with the situation and the part he was to play in it.

Rhee chose his position carefully. He got up from the folding chair, moved to the front of the open-air hall, fanning himself with his sun helmet as he went, and sat down on one of the tables that had been set up for the signing ceremony, so that the table would be between himself and the Vietnamese. It was a psychological move, designed to reinforce the notion that he was in charge and that Duc Van Co was expected to obey his orders. When he could see the two men starting across the compound toward him, he carefully used the handkerchief to dry his face as thoroughly as possible, then replaced his sun helmet, straightened his Sam Browne belt and put on his best military countenance.

Although Rhee normally wore the black two-piece pajama costume favored by the Vietcong and Pathet Lao, he had dressed for the occasion in the dark green silk trousers and black boots of his summer service uniform, omitting the uncomfortably warm, high-necked, four-pocket coat in favor of a khaki shirt displaying his ribbons above the left breast pocket. His red-trimmed, gold shoulder boards, holding the four silver stars denoting his rank, but not the airborne branch insignia that was worn only on the collar tabs of his jacket, had been attached to the epaulets of his shirt. The uniform, like his position at the table, was carefully calculated to give him a psychological advantage.

When the two Vietnamese arrived, Rhee dismissed the interpreter and waited until the man had walked away. He didn't offer the sniper a seat. "Tell me, Comrade Duc," Rhee began, "how do you like Laos so far?"

It wasn't the sort of question Duc had expected, although in Southeast Asia it was common to begin any conversation with some general topic like family or the weather and gradually work your way around to whatever was actually the issue of concern. The technique could be infuriating to the Western mind, but was a natural enough way of doing things in the Orient.

"It's a bit warmer than where I came from," said Duc, "but today is much more pleasant than my arrival."

Rhee smiled fleetingly. "Yes. It must have been an arduous journey with the weather so uncooperative. How do you find your quarters? Are they satisfactory?"

"Very satisfactory, Comrade. I'm used to a life in the field. It's good to be able to use a sleeping platform again."

Duc was careful not to look directly at the Chinese officer as he spoke. This didn't mean he was embarrassed or afraid of the man. It was simply a polite expression of respect for the greater understanding of a superior officer, another small nuance of Oriental behavior, like a Vietnamese doctor or lawyer who couldn't be expected to wash his own car or tend his garden because he had risen above that level of work. For an Oriental to look a superior in the eye was considered either impolite or insubordinate.

"And the food? Are our Pathet Lao allies in the struggle for freedom feeding you well?"

"Very well, Comrade. Breakfast was excellent."

"Good," said Rhee. "Tell me, Comrade Duc, would you like to stay in Laos?"

Now it was time to get down to business. Duc framed his answer with great care. "I would prefer to return to Vietnam, Comrade, because I feel my talents can be of greater use to the Front in the struggle there. I am, of course, prepared to go wherever the Front sends me and stay as long as I'm needed. I don't question the wisdom of the Front, but I am curious about why the Front has sent me to Laos.''

"The Front hasn't sent you to Laos," said Rhee. "You're here because I wanted you, and the Front couldn't refuse my request."

Duc almost forgot and stared at the Chinese. He didn't think anybody had so much power that they could make demands of the Front.

Rhee noted the startled reaction of the other man. He had made his point. "Don't concern yourself, Comrade. You'll be returned to Vietnam very soon. In the meantime, you'll serve me as you would serve the Front. It's the wish of the Front that this is so. You understand?''

"I understand," said Duc, lying.

"Good," continued Rhee. "In a few days an important meeting will take place here. Members of the Front from both South Vietnam and Hanoi will be present, as will representatives from the People's Republic of China and the Pathet Lao. They'll be here to make an inspection of certain facilities on the Ho Chi Minh Trail and to sign an important agreement pledging greater cooperation between all our peoples in the continuing struggle to reunite Vietnam. It's my duty to ensure that nothing happens to disrupt this meeting, and nothing *shall* happen. You understand this also?''

"I understand, Comrade," Duc replied again. By now he understood nothing at all and wondered what the Chinese comrade was driving at.

"I'm told you're the best sniper the Front has to offer," said Rhee. "I wish to know the maximum range at which you can kill a man with your rifle."

"The maximum effective range of the Dragunov SVD sniper's rifle is 800 meters, Comrade, although the longest range at which I personally have ever killed a man is seven hundred and twenty meters," said Duc. "It's possible to kill a man at a range greater than eight hundred meters, but this can't be done reliably. Beyond eight hundred meters the rifle isn't sufficiently accurate to guarantee a one-shot kill. To ensure a one-shot kill, it's best if the range is six hundred meters or less."

"I see," said Rhee. "Comrade Duc, I want you to look around carefully and tell me, if you were going to shoot one of the visiting dignitaries who is seated where I am now, where would you do it from?"

What was going on? Duc wondered silently to himself. Did Rhee want him to shoot one of the visitors?

Duc looked around carefully, turning slowly in a small circle. When he was facing the Chinese officer again, he spoke.

"I would have to personally inspect the sites to speak with certainty, Comrade, but it appears there are a limited number of locations from which a shot could be made with a reasonably high degree of confidence in success. There's the small knoll about five hundred meters to your left, a tree line at the edge of the fields about six hundred meters behind you, and the edge of the jungle at six hundred and fifty to seven hundred meters in front of you. A sniper couldn't hope to fire from the knoll on your left and escape without considerable risk, however, if a patrol with automatic weapons were situated in the grove of trees to his right. They would be in too good a position to fire upon his retreat."

"You wouldn't choose such a position yourself?" asked Rhee.

"No, Comrade. Not without certain knowledge that a friendly patrol occupied the trees on my right. If that were so, then there would be time to withdraw to the jungle farther on, but it would still entail some risk for the sniper, since he would have to cross nearly two hundred meters of open ground where he would be exposed to mortar and machine gunfire."

"Then I will see to it that both the grove and the tree line are occupied by our patrols," said Rhee. "And that the jungle to our front is cut back another hundred meters. Is there anywhere else that an extremely good sniper, a sniper of your caliber, could hope to fire from with success?"

Duc looked around again. "Not with certainty, Comrade, although an extremely good sniper might try a shot from the hill to your far right. The range is quite long, nearly eight hundred meters I should think, but if the man were interested only in disrupting the meeting, it might be possible. He couldn't be assured of a clean kill, however, but with luck, and a rifle as good as the Dragunov, he might be able to hit his target."

"And if you wished to prevent this, how would you do it?"

Duc considered a moment. "The best spot to shoot from would be that small group of boulders about three-quarters of the way up the hill. You will note that it appears it could be observed from atop the next hill, perhaps six hundred meters farther on to the northeast. If I wished to prevent a sniper from occupying the boulders, I'd place myself atop the second hill. From there I should be able to see him and kill him before he shoots."

"Excellent," said Rhee. "Comrade Duc, conduct a reconnaissance of the two hills and select your shooting position to cover the boulders. If we're visited during the

meeting by any uninvited guests, you'll kill the enemy
before he can fire. The responsibility for ensuring that a
sniper doesn't fire from the boulders is yours. You're dismissed.''

Duc saluted and left.

As he watched the Vietnamese sniper walk away, Rhee
felt a renewed sense of confidence that he had chosen the
right man for the job. Duc could not only pick the best
spots for a sniper to fire from, he could easily see what
moves could be taken to counter a sniper firing from such
locations. It was small wonder that he had lived long
enough to amass a record of eighty-eight confirmed kills.

A man capable of that, a man who could contemplate a
killing from near the maximum range of his weapon and
also see what action the enemy might take to counter such
a threat, would be the perfect choice for the assignment
being contemplated for execution after the meeting.

The opportunity to assassinate the American secretary
of defense, Robert S. McNamara, a few years earlier had
failed because the man chosen for the job hadn't been
sufficiently cautious and had allowed himself to be discovered before he could get into position. But Duc wasn't
the sort of man to make such a mistake.

Rhee mopped his brow again and silently cursed the
heat of Laos during the monsoon season. Years of work
had gone into the planning of the operation contemplated. The supporting elements who would create the
diversion necessary to accomplish the task had already
been carefully infiltrated into Saigon, their weapons well
hidden with backups in three separate locations in case
any of the weapons caches should be discovered. There
was even a complete backup team with its own weapons
caches, totally unknown to the first team.

Now the perfect man to pull the trigger had been found. There was nothing that could stand in the way of the plan.

The target was no longer McNamara, of course. He had left the Johnson Administration in March, shortly before the American President had announced he wouldn't seek another term of office in the face of mounting political opposition within his own party to the progress of war in Southeast Asia. Both Eugene McCarthy and Robert Kennedy had announced themselves candidates for the presidency and had indicated their intention to seek a negotiated solution to the war.

American political resolve in continuing the war effort appeared to be crumbling. President Johnson had ordered a halt in the bombing of North Vietnam in a desperate ploy to get Hanoi to the conference table and begin peace talks, and General Westmoreland had been recalled to Washington to become chief of staff of the American Army.

Despite all their military victories on the battlefields of Vietnam, the Americans had grown weary of the war. With a few good pushes designed to show that the resolve of the Front hadn't weakened, the American political will would collapse and Hanoi would be able to deal from a position of strength at the peace talks suggested for Paris.

One of those pushes would be the addition of a hundred thousand Chinese volunteers to protect the Ho Chi Minh Trail. The other would be when Duc Van Co was sent to Saigon to kill General Creighton Abrams, Westmoreland's replacement.

9

MACV-SOG ISOLATION COMPOUND COMMAND AND CONTROL CENTRAL KONTUM, RVN

The remainder of the briefing was spent going over maps and photographs of the countryside in the AO and immediate target area, covering the Black Mission SOI to be used and making sure everyone understood the emergency extraction and escape-and-evasion procedures to be followed if the team became compromised before they could reach the target site and get into position to make the hit on the Chinese and Vietnamese officers.

The aerial photographs were amazingly detailed sectional blowups of large areas, and Gerber assumed they had been taken by sophisticated cameras aboard a high-flying U-2 or SR-71 reconnaissance aircraft. They were all high-angle stills; if any of them had been taken from an RF-101 or RF-4, he would have expected low-angle shots and some movie footage. The pictures had been carefully gone over by photo interpreters, and even well-camouflaged structures were clearly identified and labeled.

The maps were another matter. Although some additional details had been filled in using the aerial photographs and other sources of information not specified in the briefing packets, they were essentially redrawn versions of maps done by the French Cartographical Service anywhere from fifteen to twenty years ago. Gerber knew from previous experience that such maps were often inaccurate, and even when they were well drawn originally, it was possible for a lot of detail to have changed during a course of decades. Streams could alter their courses, lightly wooded areas could become thick jungle, brushland could be burned off and cleared for fields, and villages could die off and be abandoned when the land was worked out and the people had to move elsewhere to start a new settlement. The lack of good maps was always a problem for the American and Free World Military Forces fighting the war in Vietnam, and on a clandestine mission where you couldn't call up a nearby artillery fire base for a marker round, poor maps could make moving through thick jungle not just difficult but truly impossible.

When the briefing was finished, a group of Nung strikers carried in sealed cartons of the equipment and weapons that the team would use on the mission. Bates and Santini had brought the material from the Special Forces sterile equipment warehouse at Nha Trang.

Although the Nung were fierce fighters and loyal soldiers, devoutly anti-Communist and often more than just a bit anti-Vietnamese, the security was so tight that Gerber and the others had to sit in the separate barracks room until the boxes had all been left in the rec room and the strikers had departed. As unlikely as it was that any of the

Nung were VC spies, no one wanted to chance the possibility and allow one of them to get an accurate head count or description of the team members.

The boots were green canvas lace-up affairs with two-buckle strapped tops and cleated rubber soles used by the French Foreign Legion. The uniforms were camouflaged two-piece jumpsuits with padded knees and elbows and a preponderance of pockets used by Belgian paratroopers. The rubberized ponchos were tiger-striped Portuguese colonial forces models, and the two high-frequency continuous wave radios were British-made. The webgear and packs were captured North Vietnamese, the binoculars and spotting scopes had been made by the West German firm of Zeiss, and the parachutes were Czechoslovakian sport parachute models similar to the U.S.-manufactured T-10 steerable canopy military chutes. The rations, lightweight, freeze-dried and dehydrated stuff, were the same sort of commercially available food that Abercrombie and Fitch sold to upscale campers and backpackers. The medicines and supplies for Yoon's field medical kit were Japanese or Canadian. The limited amount of explosives, to be used for preventing the capture of equipment by destroying it, were French plastique.

Only the weapons had a familiar look about them. There was a Soviet-made RPD light machine gun, a collection of ComBloc AK-47 assault rifles and an M-79 grenade launcher.

"We figured the M-79 would be lighter and more versatile than an RPG-7," explained Bates, "and there are enough of them floating around Southeast Asia on both sides of the conflict that if you do have to leave it behind, it'll prove nothing. The hand grenades are all M-26s, which might be a bit iffy I suppose, but the same is true of them as the M-79. Charlie has captured so many of them that they don't really prove anything, and if you do have to use them, there won't be enough left for an identification. I hope you don't. The smoke grenades and flares for signaling the pickup choppers are British. All of this is stuff we had on hand. The only thing we couldn't do anything about was the rifles. There just wasn't anything on short notice that could do the job as well as the M-21.''

''We'll need an opportunity to zero and test the weapons before the mission,'' Tyme reminded them.

''There's a range here,'' said Bates. ''MACV-SOG fires enough captured weapons that a few AKs and an RPD being zeroed in shouldn't attract any excessive amount of attention. I'll arrange for a few of you at a time to have access, with appropriate security on hand. We don't want some local Charlie counting heads.''

''Colonel Bates,'' said Corbett, ''what's the length of the range? If we're going to be sniping from the kinds of distances you've been talking about, we're going to need to practice long-range.''

''That could be a problem for the M-21s,'' said Bates. ''I'll find out, and if the distance isn't long enough, we'll figure out something else for you and Fetterman and Tyme to practice. Anything else?''

''Just that I've never used the M-21 before,'' said Corbett. ''I may need a lot of practice.''

''Take all the practice you need for three days,'' Bates told him. ''Ammo's no problem.''

''I have question,'' said Sergeant Krung softly. It was the first time the Nung scout had said anything at all.

''What's that?'' asked Bates.

''Where are knives? We must have knives.''

"We thought of that, too," said Bates, handing him a shoe box sealed with duct tape. "There's an assortment of them in here, Finnish and Spanish hunting knives, I believe. Take what you want."

"Good," said Krung, taking the box and retiring to a corner to examine its contents. He was a man of few words.

"What about side arms?" asked Bunnell. "I really like to have a pistol in case things turn ugly at close range. Do we take our own or what? A good handgun beats hell out of a knife in hand-to-hand combat."

Krung stopped sorting through his box of knives and glared at the man.

"I thought some of you might feel that way," said Bates. "That box over there has half a dozen Belgian Browning P-35s in it. I'm sorry it's not enough to go around, but it's all that was available."

Fetterman looked meaningfully at Corbett and Gerber. "Don't worry, Colonel. It'll be enough."

"All right, then," said Bates. "I've got other work to do, and you people have plenty to think about during the next three days. Study your briefing packets and don't forget that all items of a personal nature, including dog tags, are to be left here. In an emergency the Special Forces camp commander knows how to get a message to me. Otherwise I'll see you all in three days before you leave."

When Bates and Santini departed, Gerber went over to speak with the young Laotian woman who was to be their guide through Pathet Lao territory. "Bhang, I just wanted to apologize again for doubting you earlier," said Gerber. "I'm sorry if I offended you in any way and want you to know that I have every confidence in your ability to work well as a part of the team."

"Thank you, Captain," she answered, "but I think this not entirely true. I think you prefer I not go. But also thank you for concern about my feeling. You are . . ." She searched for the words. "You are very considerate liar."

Gerber had to admit she had him pegged. "Okay," he said. "The truth is, I'd rather you didn't go along. A woman on a combat mission almost invariably is a bad thing. You can't carry as much as a man, you may slow us down, and timing is critical on this operation. And you've been captured and tortured by the Pathet Lao once already. What if it happens again? How do I know how you'll react, or what you might tell them? How do you even know? How are you going to react if it even just looks like they might grab you again?

"Besides that, there are the interpersonal problems. There'll be no privacy. Living conditions will be hard. Men get confused in their thinking when there's a woman along. There's a natural tendency to be overly protective of a woman, which can cause a soldier not to do his job properly because he's thinking about taking care of the female when he ought to be thinking about doing his job and looking out for the enemy. If you're wounded or can't keep up, we'll have to leave you behind, the same as any man. Have you thought about that? What if you get caught and raped? You're a good-looking girl. Suppose one of the team decides he'd like to get into your pants. I don't think that'll happen with any of these men, but have you considered what will happen if it does? Having a woman along on a patrol brings up a whole host of problems I'd rather not have to deal with. It just makes the whole mess that much more complicated, and this job is going to be tough enough without adding problems to it."

"All right, Captain. I listen to your objections. Now you please listen to me," said Bhang. There was no trace of anger in her voice. "It true I cannot carry as much as man, but I can carry as much as woman. That give you one more back for equipment, yes? I strong and not slow you down. I keep up and I carry own load. If wounded, I expect to be left behind like any soldier. I walk out of Laos on own before. Sometime I have to crawl. I do it again if need. You worry I tell Pathet Lao about team if capture. I no tell. Before Pathet Lao torture me three day and I tell nothing. I still tell nothing. Anyway, I kill self before I permit capture again. As to rape, I have been rape before, and worse. It bad, but it not kill one. No difference between rape and what General Kang Mang do me every day for last two and half year. I used to hard life, Captain. Bad living condition no bother me. No privacy no bother me. If men on team want to protect, would they not also protect other men on team who are friend? You worry men get too friendly with me. I give word I not encourage same. Anyway, it your duty to keep men in line, yes? Finally you need someone show you way, someone take you through Pathet Lao patrols, yes? I that someone. There no one else. Therefore, I must go. You no see reason in this? I am woman by birth, Captain. This I no can change. But I soldier by choice. First I fight Pathet Lao by spying for CIA. Now I fight this way. I do more, suffer more, than most soldier. Laos my home, Captain, and Pathet Lao my enemy. You no worry I no act like soldier. On this I give solemn word."

Gerber shrugged. "All right, Bhang. I suppose it's an academic issue now, anyway."

He turned to Fetterman. "Master Sergeant, see if you can rig up a blanket or poncho or something in the bunkhouse so that Ms. Bhang can have some sort of privacy, will you?"

"Yes, sir. Right away, Captain," said Fetterman.

Before he could move, Bhang stripped down stark naked, except for her jungle boots, dropped her clothes to the floor and calmly walked over to the table where the uniforms were piled.

Everyone else stopped whatever he was doing and watched. It wasn't every day that a young woman suddenly decided to undress in front of a bunch of men. Not even in Vietnam.

Bhang patiently sorted through the uniforms, selecting the smallest paratrooper jacket she could find, and slipped it on. It was still a pretty big jacket for her diminutive frame and fitted her more like a very short, long-sleeved dress. Seemingly oblivious to her audience, she rolled up the cuffs so that they wouldn't hang over her hands, then found a pair of baggy trousers and pulled them on over her boots, rolling up the cuffs. When she was finished, she turned to Gerber.

"I tell you, Captain, no privacy no bother me. Maybe you not hear too good." Then she looked at the expression on Gerber's face and said, "But I think no privacy bother you."

"I think maybe you're right about that," said Gerber, feeling himself flush. "Master Sergeant, get working on that curtain, will you?" Unable to think of anything else to do or say, he turned and walked out of the team house.

SOME TIME LATER, after he had curtained off one of the bunks in the sleeping quarters for Bhang by rigging a couple of blankets over some clothesline with safety pins, Fetterman hunted up Corbett. He found the young Marine seated on a poncho out near the countermortar bunker, a rifle, telescopic sight, Starlite scope and various accessories spread out on the poncho near him. He was studying a small technical pamphlet and would periodically test-fit a piece of equipment onto the rifle, then shake his head and remove it.

Fetterman walked over and sat down on a sandbag. "You don't look like a particularly happy man," he observed. "Having problems?"

"What? Oh, hello, Master Sergeant," said Corbett, looking up. "It's not that anything's really wrong," he continued. "It's just that this is so different from what the Marines use, different from anything I've ever used. Not that I'm complaining, you understand. If it's only half as good as the technical specifications in this little booklet indicate, it ought to be a very fine rifle. Less than a minute of arc accuracy. I should be able to cover my shots with a quarter at four hundred yards all day long. Of course we'll be shooting from at least double that distance.

"Basically it's an M-14 with a heavier match-grade barrel and a reamed flash suppressor. The action is glass-bedded, though, so you don't want to try fieldstripping it to clean it. And this scope is wonderful. Just crank it up until you've got a man framed from throat to belt buckle between the two little stadia wires at the bottom, then put the cross hairs on him and you're bang on target. No more estimating distances and figuring hold over. Not at all like the old Unertl.

"This quick-change mount that's supposed to hold its zero, now that's really nice. Lets you switch from the Automatic Ranging Telescope to the Starlite scope and back again without having to rezero the rifle. Wish I'd had something like that on the DMZ. I don't think I'd want to trust it completely on a really long shot, though. Probably better to zero the ART beforehand and stick with it.

"The really amazing thing, though, is this Sionics suppressor. Both reduces the noise and diffuses it, so even if the enemy's close enough to hear it, they can't tell where the shots are coming from. Helps keep down the muzzle-flash, too. And it's not supposed to reduce the velocity of the bullet. Of course, being an Army sniper, I guess you know all about that.''

"I guess you weren't listening closely enough during the briefing. I'm not an Army sniper,'' Fetterman told him. "I've used the M-21 sniper system before and I'm a pretty fair shot on a good day, but I'm out of practice at long-range work.''

Corbett looked confused. "I'm sorry. I guess I don't understand. I thought that you and Sergeant Tyme were both—''

"Sergeant Tyme isn't a sniper, either,'' said Fetterman, "although he's a pretty fair shot, too. And he's just plain handy with about any weapon you happen to have lying around at the moment.''

"Then why...?'' began Corbett.

"Because we're all that happened to be available at the moment, son,'' said Fetterman. "War's like that sometimes. Sometimes you don't have the luxury of having exactly the right man or the right piece of equipment for the job, so you have to make do with what you've got and hope it'll be good enough to get the job done.''

Corbett looked away. "Meaning me, too, I guess. And I thought I got picked because I was good.''

"You are good,'' Fetterman told him. "Assuming your record is accurate, of course. Hey, don't take it so hard. It's nothing personal. We both know there are other snipers out there with better records, more confirmed kills, but that doesn't mean there's anything wrong with you. You've been in-country what, a little over two months now? And you've already got twenty confirmed kills. That's pretty good shooting in anybody's book. You keep it up, by the time your tour is over you could break a hundred. Look at it this way. You got picked because you were the best they could get their hands on at the time. That's not a bad endorsement. Just think of all the strings Bates had to pull to borrow you from the Marines. If you weren't the best he could get his hands on, do you really think he'd have gone to all that trouble? Hell, Corbett, you're the expert here. Tyme and I are just talented amateurs. That's why you get to pop the Chinese bigwigs and we get stuck taking potshots at the small fry.''

"I hope I'm good enough to get the job done," said Corbett.

"You'd better be. Otherwise we're going to look awfully foolish out there. Boom-Boom and I'll probably be lucky if we can hit the damn camp.''

Corbett smiled. "I think you'll probably do a bit better than that. Otherwise Colonel Bates wouldn't have picked you, either.''

"Ah, the colonel just likes me," said Fetterman. "Besides, somebody had to come along to keep the captain out of trouble. You know how officers are. Can't do a thing without a good NCO to keep them pointed in the right direction.''

Corbett assumed that Fetterman was referring to Gerber, although at times he thought Bunnell could probably use a little guidance, too, at least in his drinking habits.

"Here," said Fetterman. "Got a little present for you.'' He reached over and dropped two small objects into Corbett's hand.

Corbett held them in his open palm and looked at them. Two small black metal collar rank insignia, each one representing the three stripes of a sergeant.

"I know it's not exactly Marine Corps issue," said Fetterman, "but I figured you might as well let people know you're not a corporal anymore. Made them for you by cutting the rockers off an old pair of mine with some wire cutters. It's a pity you'll only get to wear them three days."

"How's that?"

"No insignia on the mission. Sterile, remember?"

"Oh, yeah," said Corbett. "Say, Master Sergeant, what do you think of our newest team member?"

"You mean Bhang? She's got guts. I'll say that for her. That was quite a little performance she put on in there."

Corbett shook his head. "It must have been awful, going through what she did. And still she's willing to go back. I don't think I would be. Not after somebody had done to me what they did to her. I wouldn't ever want to go back after that."

"I don't think it's a question of wanting to go back," said Fetterman. "It's like the lady said, we need someone to guide us through the Pathet Lao patrols. Somebody who knows the area, knows the strong points and the patrol schedules. Only somebody who has been there can do that, and she's the only person we've got who's actually seen the place. She's going because no one else can do the job, and she knows the job has got to be done."

"Why do I get the feeling you've just given me a message?" said Corbett. "Like maybe I've got to do my job, because there's no one else available who can do it."

"There it is," said Fetterman. "You're a pretty smart boy for a Marine."

"Well," said Corbett, "you know what they say. If you've got half a mind to join the Marine Corps, that's enough."

"And I always thought they were talking about the Army," said Fetterman.

"It's all the same," said Corbett.

Fetterman bent forward. "Here, Sergeant, let me pin those stripes on for you." He took the insignia from Corbett's hand and pinned them to the Marine's shirt collar. "You have any dreams last night, Corbett?" asked Fetterman casually.

"You mean did I have *the* dream?" said Corbett.

"All right. *The* dream."

Corbett nodded.

"And?"

"It was different this time."

"How so?" asked Fetterman.

"When I went down to turn over the body, it didn't have any face."

"And what do you think that means?"

"I think it means I didn't kill anybody," said Corbett.

"You trying to tell me you're all used up?" asked Fetterman. "That you can't do the job anymore?"

Corbett grinned. "Hell, no, Master Sergeant. I'm trying to tell you I need practice. You about ready to go to the range? You can spot for me, then I'll spot for you."

"Outstanding," said Fetterman. "I'll get my rifle."

At the range Corbett set up the targets at a hundred, two hundred, three hundred and four hundred yards, the longest distances possible. Then he backed up fifty yards behind the firing line and set up the spotting scope. "It's not far enough," he explained to Fetterman, "but it's the best we can do with the range we've got. Tomorrow we've got to move outside the wire, security or not. If Santini's briefing was accurate, we won't get anything this close to shoot from."

"It's better that way anyhow," Fetterman told him. "Give us more of a head start when the bastards decide to come after us. Considering we're going to be a long way from any kind of help, the more distance we've got between the bad guys and us at the start, the better our chances are of making it to the pickup point.''

''I've been trying not to think too much about that sort of thing,'' said Corbett. ''What do you figure our chances are of getting in, doing the job and getting out with our skins still intact?''

Fetterman considered a moment before answering. ''Fair,'' he said. ''We've got a good team. A lot depends on Bhang. If she can get us through the Pathet Lao lines undetected, the odds get a little better in our favor. As to actually pulling off the hit, I don't know. There are just too many variables. We only know the approximate time of the ceremony. If they decide to hold the signing a day early, or a couple of days late, we could miss things completely. Then we just sit around until our time is up and leave quietly. If we do make show time and take out the targets, I think we can reasonably expect that things will get rough in a hurry. We'll need to vamoose instantly.''

''Fair, but not good,'' said Corbett.

''Like I said, there are just too many variables. You want a guarantee, you should have gone to work for Sears, Roebuck. It could be a cakewalk, or we could find ourselves in a world of shit.''

''I thought we were in a world of shit,'' said Corbett. ''What happens if we aren't able to just walk through the Pathet Lao lines? What if we run into trouble on the way in?''

''It'll depend on the trouble. If we blunder into the point for a Pathet Lao company, the mission will be screwed and we'll have to run like hell. If we stumble across some poor bastard out taking a leak in the bushes, well, then . . .'' Fetterman made a drawing motion across his throat. ''Then we hide the body where we hope it won't be found and go on with the mission.''

Corbett shook as though he were suddenly chilled. "I don't know if I could do it like that or not," he said. "I've often wondered about it. I mean, well, shooting a man is one thing, but I've never killed anyone with a knife before."

"Don't worry about it," said Fetterman. "I have. Besides, with Bhang to guide us, and Krung to scout ahead, I seriously doubt we'll run into anything we can't handle."

"Krung? The little Chinese guy? Is he good?"

"He's the best I've ever seen," said Fetterman. "At scouting or tracking. I wouldn't let him hear you call him Chinese if I were you, though. He's Nung Tai. They came down from China a long time ago, but they don't think of themselves as Chinese. He hates the Chinese almost as much as he hates the Vietcong."

"Have you worked with any of the others before?" asked Corbett.

"Bocker and Tyme were with Captain Gerber and me on our first tour," said Fetterman. "They're both good men. Bocker could probably build a radio out of a coat hanger and a plastic spoon and get it to work. Boom-Boom's a damn good light-weapons man."

"How come Boom-Boom?"

"It started because of that damn shotgun he likes to carry. We got in a little firefight one time and he started banging away with it, and that's what it sounded like. Boom-Boom. Boom-Boom. I started calling him Boom-Boom after that because I figured anybody with a name like Justin Tyme needed a nickname real bad. The others guys on the team thought it was real funny, though, and it stuck. Boom-Boom Tyme. Boom-boom time. It's what the hookers say in Saigon."

Corbett wisely decided not to mention to Fetterman that he'd been known as One-Shot.

"Bunnell I know by reputation. He's a hell of a beer drinker, but he's supposed to be a good man in the field," continued Fetterman.

"He's a beer drinker all right," said Corbett. "He must support half the brewery workers in Milwaukee. What about Yoon?"

"Him, I don't know, but he's supposed to be experienced, so I guess he'll be okay."

"Which leaves Captain Gerber," said Corbett.

"He's the best damn officer I ever worked for," said Fetterman. "I really mean that. He's not particularly charismatic, and I think he's a little bit frightened of the opposite sex, but he's a damn good field commander. He's smart. He listens to his NCOs but makes up his own mind. He isn't afraid to think unconventionally, and he was a Hat before being a Hat was cool."

"What's a Hat?" Corbett wanted to know.

"A Green Beanie. Special Forces. He wasn't one of the first, but he was an early one. He believes in counterinsurgency and guerrilla warfare as the war of the future. If he hadn't stayed in Special Forces, he'd probably be a major by now. A tour in SF is considered good for an officer's career, but anything over that is a detriment. The brass are afraid they'll get too unconventional in their thinking. It's probably why Bates hasn't got his star by now, too."

Corbett nodded. "Well, I guess with all this talent we can't lose, then. And here I was worrying about the team being thrown together just because we were what was available." He hefted the sniper rifle. "You ready to see if I can hit a bull in the ass with this thing?"

"Lead on, Macduff," quipped Fetterman. "It's your honor."

Corbett set the safety on his M-21, took a magazine loaded with twenty rounds of match-grade, boat-tailed ammunition out of his pocket and inserted it into the magazine well, sliding it in at an angle and snapping it back until the catch clicked. Then he settled down in a prone position with the forearm of the rifle lying across his pack. He didn't hold the forearm in his left hand, but used the hand to steady the stock against his shoulder. He checked his position a couple of times, then laid down the rifle and took a pair of white rubber earplugs from a little plastic bottle that he got out of his jacket pocket.

"You wear those things in combat?" asked Fetterman.

"Of course not. But we're not in combat right now and I'd like to save my hearing for when I need it." Corbett stuck in the earplugs and got back into shooting position. "Okay," he said. "First target."

He flipped up the plastic lens covers and put his eye to the scope, snapped off the safety and took a deep breath. He let the air back out, took another breath and let out half of it. Slowly he squeezed the trigger.

Blam!

The report, without the Sionics suppressor attached, was loud. The rifle bucked back against his shoulder, and the grass in front of him suddenly flattened in a fan-shaped pattern extending a couple of yards out from the muzzle before whipping back upright.

"About an inch high and half an inch out," said Fetterman.

"I see it."

Corbett went through the breathing routine and fired again.

"Either it went through the same hole, or you missed the whole target," said Fetterman, his eye to the spotting scope.

"I didn't miss the target," Corbett told him.

He unscrewed the protective caps over the adjusting dials on the scope and used a dime to move the cross hairs a couple of clicks before firing again.

"Half an inch high and a quarter inch out," said Fetterman.

Corbett adjusted the sights again and fired a fourth time.

"That one was right on the money."

"Okay," said Corbett. "Since two hundred is the lowest setting on the scope and we're shooting at a hundred and fifty yards, we'll want to move things just a little bit." He made the adjustments and said, "Let's move up to the line now and we'll see where we are at two hundred yards."

He snapped the rifle's safety on, picked up his pack, and they moved forward, Fetterman bringing the spotting scope. The first round was dead center at two hundred yards.

Corbett continued firing on out to four hundred yards, occasionally making minor adjustments to the scope. When he was satisfied that the rifle would shoot to point of aim at any distance out to four hundred yards, he repeated the entire procedure with the Sionics sound suppressor in place to see if it affected the point of impact of the bullets. It didn't, but it did make for much quieter target practice.

Corbett was amazed at the accuracy of the rifle. At four hundred yards he could shoot a three-round group and have all three holes touching one another. At two hundred yards the bullets all passed through the same hole.

After Corbett had finished sighting in the rifle, it was Fetterman's turn. Inside of an hour's time he was turning in groups almost as tight as Corbett's. Then Tyme, who had been inspecting the AK-47s, joined them to zero in his weapon. By late afternoon all three men could consistently cover a five-shot group with a half-dollar at four hundred yards.

The next morning, accompanied by a Nung security detachment, the three marksmen went outside the wire and set up targets at ranges of from two hundred yards all the way out to fifteen hundred yards. Taking turns firing and spotting for one another, they worked at it until shortly after noon.

By the time they broke for lunch, Fetterman and Tyme were consistently putting rounds in the kill zone of a man-size cardboard silhouette target at six hundred yards and consistently hitting the cardboard at eight hundred.

Corbett was shooting the heads off at those ranges, and killed it dead at twelve hundred yards.

10

ON THE HO CHI MINH
TRAIL BAN TASSENG

Duc Van Co stood on the second hill east of the camp and looked down at the pile of boulders on the first hill. It wouldn't be an easy shot, but it wouldn't be too difficult, either. He would have to improve the position slightly to give himself better cover and provide a better rest for his Dragunov sniper's rifle, but the range was perfectly within reason. If an enemy sniper tried to occupy the boulders for a shot at the dignitaries assembled in the open-sided hall below, that sniper would become a dead man.

Duc had no doubt about that. It wasn't a question of conceit; it was a question of faith. Faith in his rifle and faith in himself. Without a good rifle he wouldn't be able to make the shot, and without a good rifleman to squeeze the trigger, the rifle would be useless. Apart, neither had value. Together they became welded into a deadly weapon system that had accounted for eighty-eight enemy soldiers.

It was possible that some of those soldiers had lived, the grenadier from a few days ago in the A Shau Valley, for instance, but Duc didn't think their number large. Of eighty-eight men the vast majority, perhaps seventy-five or eighty, had been clean, one-shot kills. Only a handful had required a second round to finish them off and end their screaming. In two years of sniping he had never missed his mark. He had expended a total of ninety-three rounds in combat and had never failed to at least wound the target. Duc and his rifle were one. They were a great killing machine for the Front. Of this Duc was justifiably proud.

Duc wasn't a man who dwelt upon his work. He took pride in a job well done, and when it was over he made a little notation in the small notebook he carried and then put it behind him for the day. They were dispassionate, starkly factual entries that he wrote down in his little book with the stub of pencil he carried with it.

5.25.67—One American killed at 600 meters over open ground. One round of ammunition expended.

7.13.67—Two Americans killed departing from helicopter in landing zone, range 300 meters, two shots fired.

8.06.67—One American killed at 550 meters. Second American killed at 575 meters. Three shots needed. Second round was deflected by small tree branch and struck enemy in leg. Must be more careful to scout for such objects in killing zone.

Many of the engagements Duc recalled only vaguely, his memory of them hardly more detailed than the Spartan accounts in his notebook. The more difficult shots, and hence the more memorable ones, he recalled with the same sort of fondness a big-game hunter feels when recalling a trophy-class kill.

Duc occasionally had dreams about the war, but not about the men he had killed. He dreamed of being mortared, of being bombed, of the terrible shelling of American artillery. And he dreamed of death narrowly averted when American helicopter gunships had shown up unexpectedly, and of the face of death as seen on the countenances of comrades now martyred forever in the struggle for liberation. It was the faces of those he knew that bothered him in his sleep, not those of the men he had killed. When Duc Van Co didn't sleep well, it wasn't because of his job.

Duc had spent nearly two hours trying out different sites for their visibility, angle of fire and lack of intervening obstructions in the trajectory path of the bullet before finally selecting the spot from which he would shoot to cover the boulders on the nearby hill where a sniper might hide. Then he spent an additional three hours preparing the site.

First he arranged for the assistance of several Pathet Lao comrades in the cutting of two hardwood trees some distance away, the sectioning of their trunks into logs three meters long, and their transport up the hill to his shooting position. The logs were then carefully arranged and anchored with wooden stakes pounded into the earth, to form a low, three-sided box that would provide a barrier to enemy rifle fire from the opposite hill or from other sites below. Duc didn't intend that any enemy soldiers be given the opportunity to fire at him, and he also didn't intend to be unprotected from their fire if the unintended occurred.

When the logs were properly positioned and secured to prevent their rolling, Duc painstakingly chopped out a flat slot in one of them and then worked it down smooth, shaving away the wood with his knife. When finished, the rectangular slot was about half a meter long and twenty centimeters deep on the interior side of the box, sloping to twenty-eight centimeters on the outer face of the log.

It made a fairly smooth, solid rest for the forearm of his rifle, at the proper angle to shoot among the boulders.

Once he had completed the firing port, Duc carefully picked up all the wood chips and shavings so that there was no trace of any cutting having been done in the area. He then used mud to tone down and darken all the exposed areas of raw wood on the logs so that their whiteness wouldn't stand out against the background. Finally he prepared his position with camouflage.

From more than four hundred meters away he carefully selected fresh foliage to match the broad-leaved vegetation growing near his firing position, cut it and tied it to the logs with thin black thread. He also cut small saplings, pushing the pointed trunks deep into the soil and arranging the leafy branches so that they overhung the open top of the shooting box. Lastly he completed the concealment by digging up squares of sod containing long grasses that matched those growing on the hillside, then placed the squares of living camouflage around the outside of the cleared area where the log box had been erected.

When he had completed the shooting box to his satisfaction, Duc walked down the hill, across the valley floor and climbed up among the boulders of the second hill. Standing, sitting and lying in various positions, he checked the appearance of the shooting box from below, then returned to it to make minor adjustments in its camouflage. That done, he went back to the boulders and checked the appearance again. Satisfied that his firing position looked as innocuous as he could make it, he rechecked the angle of fire from the boulders to the assembly hall.

It wasn't, of course, a perfect location. The roof of the open-sided structure blocked part of the view from this height, as it would from any height. Depending on precisely where the delegates sat, a sniper, firing from the boulders, might be able to see all the dignitaries, some of them or none at all. He would, however, have a good, clear shot as the representatives either entered or left the assembly hall, regardless of their direction. It was as good a spot as a sniper could hope to find, with the exception of the small knoll to the west of the compound that he had pointed out earlier to Rhee. He didn't think a good sniper would choose that position because of the problems in withdrawing that he had pointed out to the Chinese comrade.

Duc realized that if a sniper did manage to occupy the position, it could present a problem. It had excellent observation of the target site, was close enough to present a fairly easy shot and had a good, clear, killing field on three sides, except for the small grove of trees. It would be almost impossible to fire from it and then withdraw without coming under fire from the patrol Comrade Rhee planned to station among the trees, but perhaps an extremely dedicated enemy who didn't care about withdrawing safely, an enemy so committed to the mission of disrupting the conference and killing the delegates that he would put the mission before his own life, perhaps such a man could manage to infiltrate the area under cover of darkness and establish himself on the knoll. If that happened, such a man might be able to kill the delegates, after all. He would have to commit suicide to do it, but it could be done.

Duc walked down the hill by a different route than the one he had taken up it, so as not to pack down the grass with his weight. The grass had been unavoidably compacted somewhat by his passage, but he knew that within a day the grass would straighten itself, leaving no indication of human footprints, something that might incur the suspicion of a sniper looking for a shooting position to occupy.

Duc strolled around the compound, checking his estimates of the firing angles from the boulders and the camouflage of his position on the second hill. He also searched for other likely spots for an enemy sniper that he might have overlooked before, but found none within what he considered reasonable shooting range. Finally he hunted up Rhee, finding him at work in his quarters.

Duc walked up the steps of the bamboo-and-thatch hut and paused respectfully in the doorway. The Chinese comrade was seated at a small wooden table. His shirt was partially unbuttoned and he was wearing wire-rimmed reading glasses. He appeared to be studying several papers and maps spread out on the desktop.

Duc waited patiently for about five minutes. If the Chinese was aware of his presence, he took no note of it. Duc used the time to look around. The one-room hut had a nearly empty, almost severe appearance. It contained only the tabletop desk, the single chair and a wooden sleeping platform with a bamboo mat rolled up at the foot. There were a few wooden pegs on the walls from which hung an AK-47, a pair of binoculars, a pack, webgear and a few additional items of clothing. There were no flags, no portraits of Mao Tse-tung or Ho Chi Minh and no political banners celebrating glories of the Front or exhorting comrades to greater efforts in the struggle for liberation. A single electric light bulb hung from a black cord over the makeshift desk.

At last Duc grew tired of waiting to be recognized and cleared his throat. "I'm sorry to interrupt your work, Comrade, but I wonder if I might trouble you for a moment of your time," he said.

The Chinese officer continued to ignore him for a moment, then abruptly folded his papers and placed them facedown on the table. He removed his reading glasses, folded them and put them in his pocket. From his other shirt pocket he removed a pack of American cigarettes, Marlboros, took one out and lighted it. He laid the lighter on top of his papers and took a long, slow drag on the cigarette. Only then did he motion Duc forward.

"Yes, Comrade Duc, what's on your mind?"

Duc walked across the wooden planking of the floor and stood before the desk. As usual, he didn't look directly at the superior officer as a sign of respect. As he lowered his eyes, two items on the desktop caught his attention. One was the corner of a folded map, labeled Saigon and Vicinity. The other was the lighter Rhee had used. It was an American Zippo with a United States Army Special Forces crest affixed to it and a name engraved above the crest. Duc was no expert with English, but he could speak and read a little of the language. The inscription read SFC Ian McMillan.

"Well, what is it?" asked Rhee.

"Comrade, I've been thinking about the security problem," Duc began.

"The security problem isn't your concern, Comrade. That's my concern. Your job is to make sure that an enemy sniper doesn't interrupt the conference."

"That's what I meant, Comrade," said Duc.

"You foresee a problem?" asked Rhee with more interest.

"A potential problem, yes, Comrade."

Rhee put his cigarette down in a tin can that held several butts and rested a hand on either side of the desk. "What's the nature of this problem?"

"It concerns the hill, Comrade."

"I thought you had made the necessary arrangements to deal with that. Haven't you spent nearly the entire day preparing your position to deal with any enemy snipers?"

"Yes, Comrade. That part's in readiness. I was speaking of the other hill. The small knoll to the west of the camp."

"I thought we'd agreed that a group of men in the trees just south of it would make it an untenable position for a sniper," said Rhee.

"It would make it impossible for him to escape, Comrade, and for that reason I didn't believe a thinking man would choose it as a site to shoot from. It has since occurred to me that if a man was prepared to give up his life in order to succeed, it might be possible for him to slip past the patrol in the trees under cover of night and occupy the knoll. It wouldn't be possible to do so during daylight, but at night it might be successfully attempted."

"But such a man couldn't hope to escape," said Rhee. "The signing will take place in late afternoon, but it will still be daylight. He would be cut down before he could get twenty meters across the open field."

"He might not have any intention of escape, Comrade," said Duc. "If this meeting is so important, perhaps they'll send a man to whom completion of the mission is more important than escape."

Rhee appeared to consider this. "Only a fanatic would attempt such a thing," he said at last.

"Or a man who believes in his cause above all else, Comrade. The Front has many such men. Are there none among our enemies?"

Rhee picked up the cigarette lighter from the desktop and rubbed it between his thumb and fingers. "Only a fanatic," he repeated. "Nevertheless, I'll make sure a guard is posted on the knoll. Is there anything else you wished to speak with me about, Comrade Duc?''

"No, Comrade. That's all."

"Then you may leave," said Rhee.

When Duc had gone, Rhee got up and paced nervously around his hut, absently rubbing the lighter and chain-smoking his beloved American cigarettes. The words of the Vietnamese sniper had disturbed him greatly. It wasn't that he was worried about some enemy sniper actually occupying the knoll west of camp. The posting of a guard there should eliminate the possibility of any trouble. What he found distressing was the notion that they might be confronted with an enemy who would put the success of his mission above his own safety. Only a fanatic would take unacceptable risks, but a calculated risk was another matter entirely. That required only a brave man with faith in his own abilities and a dedication to his job. It was the sort of task soldiers undertook daily, especially highly trained, motivated soldiers: commandos, Rangers, Marines, Green Berets. It made him ill at ease.

Rhee didn't think he had much to fear from the Royal Laotian Army or the ARVN, although some of their elite troops were quite good when well trained and led. But the prospect of a lightning strike by American Rangers or Green Berets chilled him to the bone. He knew only too well how terrifyingly efficient those troops could be. They were masters of the technique of the sudden, explosively violent raid. He had seen their handiwork before. Yet as his fingertips found the crest on the lighter in his hand, he reminded himself that they weren't infallible. They could be beaten. It was only a question of understanding their thought patterns and carefully preparing the trap.

Rhee considered how the Americans might launch such a raid. A sudden massive onslaught of troop-carrying helicopters and gunships was the most familiar scenario, striking hard and fast and then quickly withdrawing. But there were many problems with such a plan. Most important, it required that the enemy have knowledge of the exact timing of the signing ceremony, and that was impossible, even if the Americans had somehow been warned of the event. The precise time of the ceremony hadn't been set yet. It was unknown even to Rhee. Only the day and the approximate time had been finalized.

If the Americans came too early and destroyed the camp without killing the delegates, the location of the signing could simply be moved. If they came too late, the document would already be signed, the damage done and the visiting dignitaries departed. Furthermore, it would require a massive raid. This camp was headquarters for an entire Pathet Lao regiment. Although most of the troops were in the field at any given time, the Americans would need to use a battalion of crack assault troops at the very least. For an operation of that magnitude they would need time to coordinate activities and practice the assault on mock-ups of the camp itself, which required detailed intelligence of the camp. To time the raid precisely they would need to infiltrate a reconnaissance team beforehand, which would signal the raiding party at the crucial moment. There were altogether too many things that could go wrong in the execution of such a plan. Rhee dismissed it as unworkable, even for the Americans.

That left only the possibility of a much smaller attack. A small group of men might be able to work their way into the area unnoticed by patrols, and establish an observation post from which to study the camp compound, attacking at the crucial moment. Yet they would have to attack a structure near the center of the compound during daylight, with several companies of well-armed Pathet

Lao troops in the immediate area. They would be heavily outnumbered and couldn't hope to succeed or survive with a direct assault. The attack, then, could only be indirect. They could perhaps mortar the assembly hall, or snipe at the delegates, or both. A strike from outside the perimeter of the camp itself was the only way an enemy could hope to complete the mission and escape. And the Americans, Rhee knew, could be very good soldiers, but they weren't fanatics. He began to think that if any sort of threat to the meeting did occur, it would have to take the form of a sniper.

Rhee made his decision. He would speak with the Pathet Lao commander and double the number of outposts and roving patrols. He still considered the possibility of an actual attack on the ceremony remote, but it paid to be cautious when trying to second-guess the Americans. He suddenly felt very glad that he had brought Duc Van Co to this place. Being confronted by the top-ranked sniper in the North Vietnamese Army while on a mission to southern Laos wasn't a threat the Americans would anticipate. If the enemy did show their face, Duc Van Co might well turn out to be the secret weapon Rhee needed to give him just enough edge to turn the tables on the opposition. It was a pleasing thought.

There were few things in life Rhee enjoyed more than outwitting the Americans. After the disaster in Hong Kong that had nearly cost him his life, and that had required prolonged hospitalization and recuperation, he had been recalled to China and placed on light duty with the staff of the commander of the Canton Military Region. He had been afraid that his military career was over and that he would never again have the opportunity to match wits against the Americans. Only by force of will and dogged persistence had he overcome the handicaps of his injuries and become physically fit to return to regular duties. But obstacles had still remained.

He had been criticized for his handling of the Hong Kong affair. Even though the Americans had been careful never to mention it publicly, the presence of a large number of bodies and unusual weapons lying around could have proved a serious embarrassment to the Peking government. In the final analysis the Hong Kong police and Special Branch had convinced themselves that the killings were the result of a drug deal gone sour and not the expansion of the war from nearby Vietnam to the soil of the British Crown Colony, but Rhee's actions had still been considered politically incorrect. When he bumped into Fetterman and Gerber, he had mounted the operation personally without benefit of official sanction, and such activity was frowned upon by the Party political bureaucracy.

His knowledge of American operating procedures in Vietnam was what had ultimately saved Rhee from complete disgrace. He was considered too valuable an asset for the military, or the Party to dispose of completely. That was why they had given him the desk job rather than sack him outright. For a man like Rhee who craved the physical and intellectual challenges of the sting of combat, however, a desk job had been equivalent to slow death.

It had taken him three long years to rebuild his health and career. Three years of unflagging devotion and unquestioning obedience to the Party. Three years of dealing with endless mountains of the mindless paperwork that no bureaucracy can function without. Three long years of constantly making a spectacle of himself expressing both regret for his poor judgment and humble thanks for the Party's lenient treatment of his transgressions. Neither the regret nor the thanks was sincere.

In the end it had been enough. He had been cautiously forgiven and pronounced properly reeducated, and had been allowed to return to full active service, though not as an instructor/observer to the Vietcong. He had been granted a posting to the personnel security section of the General Political Department of the PLA, where his skills would be of some use and where a watchful eye could be kept on him for any deviance from official Party lines. Ironically it was because of that assignment that he now held his current job as chief of security for the Chinese delegation to the protocol signing. Even more ironically it was just possible, although the likelihood remained distant, that because of that he might once again find himself matching wits against the Americans.

Rhee stopped pacing and stood for a moment at the open window of his hut, idly smoking and staring out across the parade ground toward the open-sided assembly hall. The air was oppressively hot and humid and the sky was now a solid overcast of ugly, inky-black clouds. The scent of ozone was heavily present. Very soon now it would rain.

11

MACV-SOG ISOLATION COMPOUND COMMAND AND CONTROL CENTRAL KONTUM, RVN

Bates arrived in midafternoon via helicopter from Nha Trang. The air was heavy with the threat of rain and seemed almost charged with electricity. It was so sultry that it was almost like walking through a warm mist. Just breathing was an exercise best approximated by wrapping a wet towel around the nose and mouth and then doing push-ups in a sauna.

Bates showed his ID to the same Nung guard who had admitted him three days ago and waited while the man scrupulously checked it, compared Bates's photograph on the ID to his physical appearance and confirmed that Bates's name and serial number matched those listed on his clipboard. Finally satisfied that he was the same Colonel Bates who had been there three days before, and that he was still authorized entry to the compound, the Nung signaled his two fellow guards to open the gate and Bates was admitted to the isolation compound. He went directly to the team house and found Gerber cleaning an AK-47.

"It's confirmed," said Bates without preamble, pulling off his beret and tossing it onto one of the tables in the rec room. "You go in tonight."

Gerber raised a questioning eyebrow. "What about the weather?"

Bates ignored him for the moment. He walked over to the refrigerator, yanked open the door and pulled out a bottle of Miller, opening it with the bottle opener that hung from the refrigerator door by a dog tag chain. He guzzled down about half the bottle, then mopped at his forehead with the back of his hand. "Christ it's hot! Tell whoever this belonged to that I owe him a beer when he gets back."

He took another big swig, then walked over and sat next to Gerber. "I got the latest weather intel from Meteorological Services about two hours ago. The rain will probably hit here about takeoff time, but it should be dry over the drop zone until about 2130. It'll be overcast, which will make the ground harder to see, but it could work to your advantage. Less likely some Pathet Lao observer will spot your parachutes going in."

"If there are any Pathet Lao observers on the drop zone, this mission's going to be screwed before we ever get started," said Gerber dryly.

"There shouldn't be anybody near the DZ," Bates told him. "I was just thinking out loud. There's always the unexpected."

"There is that," said Gerber, "but this time there'd better not be. We're going to have a hard enough time spotting the drop zone as it is. Who's the reception committee? It wasn't in the briefing packets."

"There isn't any," Bates told him. "No one, and I mean no one, knows you're coming."

"No ground signals? How in hell are we supposed to know when we're over the DZ?"

"It'll be a blind jump, that's true," said Bates, "but not to worry. The C-123 you'll be using is packed with the latest electronics. Pinpoint navigation system confirmed by both an inertial platform and geosynchronous satellite nav-link. I'm told they can tell their exact position anywhere on the globe to an accuracy of plus or minus three meters."

Gerber's look plainly said he didn't believe it for a minute. "They'd better be. We come down in the wrong place, we could spend half the night just trying to figure out where in hell we are. Besides, I don't want to come down with a teak tree up my ass."

"If that happens," Bates said with a grin, "you won't have time to feel the goose. Not at the height you're jumping from."

"There's a whole lot of things we might not have time for on this one, Colonel," Gerber told him. "If just one little thing goes wrong, if any of our information is off by just a teeny little bit, the whole shooting match could be blown."

"In that case we'll miss our opportunity," said Bates. "All the intel we've got on this has been checked and rechecked. Nothing should go wrong."

"And if it does?"

"Then use your own judgment. You'll be the man on the spot, Mack. If you have problems, but feel you can still continue the mission, continue it. We want those Chinese bastards. We want Peking to know that if they're going to play rough, they're going to get their noses bloodied. But I don't want them bad enough to have eight dead men and one dead woman on my conscience. If you have to take some casualties to accomplish the mission, well, that's war. I don't have to tell you that. But I don't expect you or your people to commit suicide. If things go sour, get out fast and send the emergency pickup signal. The choppers will be standing by to come in and pick you up.''

"Weather permitting," Gerber reminded him.

"Weather permitting," Bates admitted. He was silent for a moment, then said, "Look, Mack, I know this whole mess really sucks. If I'd had any choice . . ."

"Skip it, Colonel," said Gerber. "A job has to be done and we drew the short straw, and that's all there is to it. I accepted that situation way back when I signed on the dotted line and held up my right hand for the oath. I just get cranky when my leave gets cut short. Proves I'm human, I guess."

"Well, when this one's over, you and the team can have two weeks wherever you want it, no recalls. I'll put that in writing if you like."

"Just don't put it in a telegram," said Gerber. "I'm really beginning to hate telegrams."

Bates knew what he meant. A lot of the more unsavory missions he'd been forced to send Gerber and Fetterman on had started with a telegram, either from Bates or to him from the Puzzle Palace. In fact, thinking it over, Bates decided that with very little effort he could learn to really hate telegrams, too.

"How's the team shaping up?" asked Bates, changing the subject. "Any problems?"

Gerber grinned. "Kind of late to be worrying about that now, isn't it, sir? It'll be okay. Some minor worries, but no real problems."

"Such as?" Bates wanted to know.

Gerber shrugged. "I guess it's mostly the unknown. I haven't worked with Yoon or Bunnell before, but, well, they seem all right. Fetterman, Bocker and Tyme are solid, of course. And Krung, well, he's Krung. There's really no understanding the man. You just have to accept him as he is. He'll do his job. He always does. I just wish sometimes he didn't put doing it on such a personal level. It's our other two teammates who have me just a little bit bugged."

"All right," said Bates, "let's take the easy one first. What's bothering you about Bhangsang Souphona-phouma besides the length of her name and the fact that she's a woman?"

"The fact that she's a woman would be enough," said Gerber, "but there's more to it than that. It just seems a little too convenient that she supposedly went through everything she did and still managed to escape and bring us the information in time to act on it, not to mention fak-ing her own death so that the Pathet Lao wouldn't be wise to the situation and move the meeting or call it off."

"The scars are real enough," said Bates. "You've seen what they did to her."

"I'm not questioning the authenticity of her injuries, Colonel, only how she got them."

"Come on," said Bates. "You don't seriously think someone would let somebody carve them up like that just to sell us a bill of goods?"

"It's been done before," said Gerber. "You going to sit there and tell me the Chinese aren't capable of it? Or the VC? This whole thing could be just one big sucker play to get us to walk into a trap in Laos. That would look just fine on the evening news, wouldn't it? American Special Forces team captured in Laos while attempting to assassinate visiting Chinese neutrals. U.S. expanding war of murder in Southeast Asia.''

''I'm relying on you guys not to get captured,'' said Bates. ''Besides, don't you think you're being just a little bit paranoid? Our little Mata Hari has been vouched for by the CIA.''

''She's been vouched for by Jerry Maxwell,'' said Gerber. ''That's not the same thing. Do you remember what happened with that female Kit Carson scout he saddled us with in Cambodia? I lost a good communications sergeant and a lot of indigenous troops on that one.''

''That wasn't exactly Maxwell's fault, as I recall,'' replied Bates mildly. ''In fact, I seem to recall that he stuck his neck out rather far in order to keep those B-52s from dumping a world of shit on top of you guys.''

''And was only partially successful,'' Gerber reminded him. ''Besides, if he'd known his agent better, we wouldn't have been in that mess in the first place.''

''It wasn't Maxwell's fault,'' insisted Bates. ''It was his CIA superior who was pulling the strings. The agent was just following what she believed to be valid orders.''

''Which only proves that an endorsement from the Agency isn't such a hot recommendation, either,'' said Gerber.

''You're overlooking one little thing, Mack. All the intel on this mission has been confirmed by other sources. Hell, we've got aerial photos of the camp.''

''We've got photos of a Pathet Lao camp, all right. That doesn't prove there's going to be a meeting between a bunch of Chinese and North Vietnamese big shots there.''

''The meeting's been confirmed by other sources,'' Bates said flatly.

''What other sources?'' demanded Gerber.

Bates was silent.

"Uh-huh, I thought so," said Gerber. "Our friendly spooks from the Agency again."

"That doesn't mean the information isn't good," said Bates.

Gerber shrugged. "All right. So the information's good and I'm just being paranoid. Let's say that Bhang's story is true, just for the sake of argument. How's she going to react if we bump into a Pathet Lao patrol after what they did to her?"

It was Bates's turn to shrug. "What's she say about it?"

"She says she'll kill herself first," said Gerber. "What she'll actually do if confronted by the situation is anybody's guess. If she panics at the wrong time, it could give away our position and the whole shooting match along with it. Killing herself could be just as bad as running away or getting caught."

"Nevertheless, you'll need a guide to get you through the Pathet Lao positions, and Bhang knows the area, so—"

"So she goes," said Gerber. "You asked me for my concerns, Colonel, and I'm giving them to you, that's all. We both know it's too late in the ball game to go changing the players now."

"What about Corbett?" asked Bates. "Any problems with him? He's the key to this whole operation, you know."

"He has dreams," said Gerber.

"Dreams? What the hell are you talking about? What sort of dreams?"

"He has dreams about the first VC he ever killed."

"So what's the big deal?" asked Bates. "A lot of guys have dreams about the first man they ever killed."

"The first VC Corbett ever killed wasn't a man," said Gerber. "It was a fifteen-year-old Co Cong pushing a bicycle loaded down with AKs and ammo. Almost every night he dreams about it. Only each time, when he turns the body over, the Co Cong has a different face. Sometimes it's Corbett's. Sometimes it doesn't have a face at all.''

''I don't like the sound of that,'' Bates told him. ''You think Corbett's tapped out? Think he's getting ready to crack?''

''I don't know what to think about him,'' Gerber confided. ''I'll tell you this, though, the son of a bitch can shoot. I just hope he can pull the trigger when the time comes.''

''He's got to,'' said Bates. ''Otherwise it's all a waste.''

''I'm sure Fetterman and Tyme will be glad to know you have so much faith in their marksmanship skills.''

''You tell them I said that and I'll shoot you,'' said Bates. ''But you know what I mean. Corbett's the primary shooter. That's why he's got the primary targets. If he freezes on the trigger, you'll have to figure out some other way to get the job done.''

''I'm open to suggestions.''

''Have the others shift targets or somebody else take over for him. Hell, Mack, I don't have to tell you what to do, surely. You have formulated a plan in case you lose one of your shooters, haven't you?''

''Yes. And Bocker, Bunnell and myself have put in a couple of practice sessions with the M-21s. So far, though, none of us have been able to suggest how we're going to hit the targets at a thousand yards. If the information's correct about the range we'll have to shoot from, I don't think we've got any alternative but to have Corbett do the shooting. What I really need is a suggestion about how to make sure he does it.''

"Right now I'd suggest you start getting your team ready for insertion," said Bates. "I've arranged to have some decent food brought in so that you can have a good meal before the plane gets here. Steak and lobster fresh from Nha Trang. I figured it might be a while before you get to eat anything that doesn't come out of an aluminum foil pouch."

"The condemned man ate a hardy last meal," Gerber intoned morosely.

"Let's hope not," said Bates with mock seriousness. "I'm weeks behind on my paperwork now. Just think of all the letters I'd have to write."

"To hell with writing letters," said Gerber. "Just think of the bill you'll run up at the officers' club without me around to buy all your drinks."

GERBER POURED each of them a carefully measured shot of bourbon before dinner, but advised them there would be no beer with the meal, or at any other time until their return. It was an announcement that almost brought tears to Bunnell's eyes, as he thought of all those poor lonely cans and bottles languishing in the dark refrigerator for their return. Gerber knew the brass would have frowned heavily upon the consumption of alcohol in any amount a few hours before a parachute drop, but he figured what the hell? After all, what could they do to them? Send them to Vietnam? Anyway, they were all in for a dry spell, it wasn't enough alcohol to seriously effect anybody, and besides, it afforded them an opportunity to drink a toast to the success of the mission.

After the surf and turf, washed down with copious amounts of iced tea and topped off with a half gallon of raspberry sherbet Bates had brought with him from Nha Trang in an insulated cooler, they checked their gear and weapons for the final time, readied their packs and suited up in their Belgian paratrooper jumpsuits.

"I suppose it's a bit late to think of this," Gerber said to Bhang, "but I presume you've had parachute training?"

"I train by CIA when recruit me," she told him, "but not jump in four year."

"Terrific," said Gerber. He exchanged glances with Bates, who shrugged.

"Maxwell said she was jump-rated," Bates said. "How was I to know she hadn't jumped in four years?"

"You could have asked," said Gerber.

"You, too," Bates reminded him, trying to share the blame.

"Would it have made any difference?"

"Probably not," Bates allowed. "On an operation put together this quickly, I doubt we could have found time to run her through a refresher course at the ARVN paratroop school."

"So what do we do now?" asked Gerber.

"We go as planned," said Bates. "She'll just have to jump and take her chances. It's a static line jump, anyway."

"It's also a low-altitude blind jump into a night DZ. She could wind up with a broken leg. Or a broken neck."

"Which puts her in the same boat as any other member of the team," said Bates. "Your actions in such an instance will be dictated by your assessment of the team's ability to continue the mission, the same as it would be in an incident involving any other member of the team."

Bhang had been staring at them, trying to follow their conversation. "Excuse please. I no understand. There is problem?"

"I suppose it's useless to hope you've ever made a night jump before," said Gerber. Then, seeing the blank look on her face, he translated the question into French. "Have you ever made a parachute jump at night?"

"No," Bhang responded. "Is there a difference between jumping at night and jumping during the daylight?"

Gerber rolled his eyes. "You won't be able to see the ground. Just keep your legs together, stay loose and remember to roll when your feet hit. It might be helpful if you can remember to hold your arms in front of your face once the parachute opens and keep your chin tucked in. That should give you some protection in case you come down in the brush." He carefully avoided any mention of coming down in the trees, figuring there was no point in scaring her any more than necessary. "We'll be jumping from quite low, so get ready to land as soon as the chute opens."

"I understand," said Bhang with apparent unconcern.

Gerber wasn't at all sure she understood. He couldn't imagine anyone being unconcerned about a night parachute jump from low altitude into an unmarked drop zone.

"Just out of curiosity, how many jumps have you made?" he asked.

"Altogether I make fifteen jumps," said Bhang. "Three from C-47, two from balloon and ten from training tower. I train in Thailand," she added proudly.

"Wonderful," Gerber said sourly. "Just remember what I told you. Get ready for the landing as soon as your chute opens. And stay close to me in the aircraft. I'll make sure you get out the door okay."

"That okay with me," Bhang told him. "You no worry. I do fine." She spoke as if she might have been agreeing to go for a short walk around the compound.

"Well," offered Bates, "look at the bright side. She can't weigh much more than a hundred pounds. That'll give her more time. She'll fall slower."

"You call that a bright side?" Gerber glared.

He looked at Bunnell. "And when did you last jump, Bush Hog?"

"About six months ago, Captain," Bunnell told him. "Not much opportunity to stay on jump status advising village militia. Not to worry, though. I've got more than fifty jumps, and at least a dozen are either night or low altitude."

"And how about our Marine Corps contingent?" Gerber asked Corbett.

"Uh, I guess about four months since I last jumped, sir," Corbett told him. "Of course, I've pretty much had the whole gamut during training. In recon we jump both static and free-fall. I've done HALO and HAHO for lateral insertions with a ram air canopy."

"What about low-altitude jumps?"

"Well, sir, how low are we talking about? In recon low altitude usually means stepping off the rear ramp of a helicopter and falling fifty feet into the water. I didn't do real good at that sort of thing. Kept getting too much water up my nose."

"We'll be doing a static line deploy from five hundred feet," said Gerber.

Corbett swallowed. "At that altitude we won't have much time to deploy a reserve if anything goes wrong."

"At that altitude we won't have *any* time, son," put in Fetterman. "That's why we don't wear a reserve. All it does is add extra weight and make you fall faster."

"Oh!" said Corbett, swallowing hard again. He didn't look at all pleased with that piece of news.

At 1930 hours Bates passed out the parachutes and Gerber and Fetterman made sure everybody was clear on their functioning. Actually, there wasn't a lot to memorize, provided they remembered to hook up their static lines and didn't foul them on anything on the way out of the plane. There was no point in conducting a review of emergency procedures. From five hundred feet there was no time to initiate any. The chutes had been recently inspected and packed by two master riggers, cross-checking each other as they did so, and the static line deployment system was as foolproof as possible. The only potential area of difficulty would come if someone hung up on the outside of the plane and the others weren't able to pull him back inside. There was no reason why that should happen, but if it did, they would have to either abort the mission or cut the man free and continue on without him. It wasn't a pleasant prospect.

When they all had been strapped into their parachute harnesses, had clipped on their equipment bags and buckled up the chin straps of their French paratrooper helmets, there was nothing to do but sit and wait.

At exactly 2000 hours a covered deuce-and-a-half driven by a Special Forces NCO from the local MACV-SOG detachment arrived to take them to the airstrip. The tailgate was let down and a small wooden step set next to it in order to make it easier for the team to climb into the back loaded down with their parachutes and equipment.

Bates climbed in, too, to ride out to the plane with them. It was already raining, and he glanced at his watch before pulling down the rear tarpaulin. "Rain's early," he said. "Shouldn't have been here for another twenty to thirty minutes."

Gerber nodded but said nothing. They'd gotten pretty wet just getting into the truck. He hoped the soaking they were sure to take moving from the truck to the airplane wouldn't affect the functioning of the parachutes.

As they passed through the gate and out into the main compound heading for the airstrip, Fetterman, sitting across from Gerber and Bates and looking out through a gap in the canvas tarps, could see about a dozen troops getting ready to go out on a night patrol. They were mostly Rengao tribesmen from the local area, and like the Nung, they had a reputation as superb fighters. The two American Special Forces advisers going out with them were conspicuous by their size. Fetterman had no idea what their mission was, but he silently wished them luck.

At ten minutes past the hour the airplane arrived and successfully landed on the perforated-steel-plate runway despite the storm. The C-123 was painted dull black and showed no nationality insignia or other markings. It taxied back to the end of the strip, turned around, stopped and lowered the tail ramp, its propellers turning over slowly.

The driver of the truck drove up from behind the plane, turned around and backed up the deuce-and-a-half as close to the ramp as he could. Then the tailgate of the truck was lowered, the wooden step set into place, and they climbed down from the bed of the truck and walked up the ramp into the aircraft as quickly as possible.

"Well, I guess this is it," said Bates, making the rounds and shaking hands with each member of the team. "From here on out you're on your own. Nothing left but to wish you good luck and good hunting. I'll be waiting when you get back to debrief you."

"Just be sure to have plenty of cold beer on hand," quipped Bunnell.

"Cases of it," Bates promised.

"Fine. Fine," said Bunnell. "But what's everybody else going to drink?"

Bates looked at the man uncertainly. He wasn't sure if Bunnell was joking or not. Shaking hands with Fetterman and Gerber last, Bates said, "I'd like to be able to say I wish I was going with you, but it would be a damn lie. I wouldn't wish this assignment on anyone, and I'm damn sorry it had to be you two. All I can promise you is an extended leave when you get back. Don't you old-timers go doing anything stupid out there, like getting hung out to dry trying to get this Rhee character. I meant what I said before. We want this meeting broken up, but I don't want it at the cost of eight good men and one good woman. If you get in there, and the setup doesn't smell right to you, send the emergency signal and get out fast."

"Not to worry, Colonel," Gerber told him. "We've done this sort of thing before, remember? Besides, I'm getting too damn senior to do anything stupid. One of these days, poof! I'm going to turn into a major right before your very eyes."

"It should have happened a long time ago," said Bates, meaning it. His own promotion to brigadier general was long overdue, as well. "You know the Army, though." He glanced around the interior of the aircraft, trying to think of any last-minute thing that needed to be done, any last-minute word that needed to be said. Finding nothing, he simply repeated, "Well, good luck and good hunting. Keep your heads down."

It suddenly occurred to him that he should have told them to keep their powder dry. The old military phrase struck him as funny, and he hurried down the ramp to the truck before he gave in to the temptation to use it.

Once Bates had made his exit, the jumpmaster, a thin Nationalist Chinese wearing a solid-black flight suit and a U.S. Air Force emergency parachute, raised the ramp and made sure everyone was properly seated in the jump seats along the sides of the fuselage. When he was finished, he disappeared forward, and almost at once the roar of the engines building up to full power for takeoff could be heard, the airframe vibrating slightly underfoot.

The pilot checked the magnetos on both engines, chopped power down while the checklist was completed, then throttled back up and released the brakes. The plane started to roll, slowly at first, then rapidly picked up speed as it clattered down the runway. Just when Gerber was starting to wonder how the pilot could possibly see well enough to keep the aircraft on the runway in the driving rain, the floor tilted back, stayed at an angle for a moment and then the plane seemed to leap into the air.

Back at the side of the airstrip, Bates sat in the cab of the deuce-and-a-half with the Special Forces NCO and watched the black C-123 roll down the runway, rise into the air and vanish into the stygian night. Gradually he became dimly aware of his wet clothes.

"Wish you were going with them, Colonel?" asked the Green Beret staff sergeant sitting behind the steering wheel. He had no idea where the people he had just delivered to the Fairchild Provider were headed, but he had seen enough clandestine operations mounted out of Kontum aboard black-painted aircraft to know that wherever they were bound for it was outside South Vietnam.

"No," said Bates. "I wish I was in some dry clothes and in bed. Run me over to the VOQ, will you?"

Knowing what lay ahead for Gerber and the others, Bates hoped he would be able to sleep.

12

ABOARD CLANDESTINE
OPS C-123 SOMEWHERE
OVER THE TRIBORDER
REGION CAMBODIA,
LAOS AND RVN

The cargo bay of the Fairchild C-123, designed to carry up to sixty-one troops, fifty stretcher patients when used in the Medevac role or twenty-four thousand pounds of freight, seemed like a vast, empty cavern. The combined weight of the nine members of MACV-SOG Special Action Team Chuck Connors and their equipment barely taxed the lift capabilities of the aircraft by one-twelfth and left more than enough room to park a truck in. The excess space served as a subtle and unwelcome reminder of just how few in number they were and of the awesome odds arrayed against them.

Gerber didn't know whether to be amused or annoyed by the code name selected for the team. He couldn't decide if it was someone's idea of a bad joke, or a very clever ploy designed to instantly identify the team to MACV-SOG radio operators while confusing the enemy. The American actor Chuck Connors had starred in a television series called *The Rifleman* about a Western hero who used a Winchester instead of a Colt six-shooter. It was unlikely that any NVA or VC radio operators who intercepted a message from the team would be familiar with the actor or the role he had played, while almost any American soldier who had grown up in a household with a television set would. And if there was any one word that seemed descriptive of the mission, it was rifleman. Corbett was a rifleman par excellence, and was going to be called upon to do what riflemen in armies the world over do best—kill the enemy long-distance.

Gerber just hoped that when the time came Corbett would live up to the name. For a rifleman whose job was that of sniper, of killing the enemy dispassionately, unsuspected, in cold blood, Corbett seemed to have a lot of funny ideas about the fine line that distinguished a military sniper from a common murderer.

Yet it was a very fine line, Gerber knew, the principal difference being that the sniper had to be able to turn the ability to kill in cold blood on and off. In wartime the skill was practically a necessity for personal survival, while in time of peace it produced the likes of Lee Harvey Oswald and Charles Whitman and could earn the man who possessed it and couldn't turn it off a life sentence in prison or a trip to the gas chamber, the electric chair or the gallows.

Gerber often wondered how many such men might be walking the streets of the United States today. Unlike professional soldiers such as himself, the average grunt rifleman in Vietnam was little more than a kid, trained to kill without any effort being put into teaching him when not to kill. Drafted at age eighteen, given six to eight weeks of basic training and then another twelve to twenty-four weeks of specialized training, the typical infantry soldier was carefully conditioned, both physically and psychologically, to perform one single task: kill the enemy in combat. Then, usually before his nineteenth birthday, he found himself shipped to Vietnam, where the enemy could be anyone from a fifteen-year-old girl to a seventy-five-year-old grandfather and combat could take place anywhere from a rice paddy to downtown Saigon. To make matters worse, the enemy didn't usually wear a uniform and was often a farmer, shopkeeper or even government employee whom you saw every day, but who at night became a Vietcong.

The result, of course, was that the teenage American soldier learned to trust no one outside his squad and to consider everyone, whether man, woman or child, a potential enemy. In Vietnam the only rule was stay alive any way you can, and if that meant sometimes killing women and children, so be it. Thus the American soldier learned to kill without regard to age, sex or apparent civilian status. Then, not as in other wars where you were in for the duration and had a period of occupation and a slow boat ride home to give you time to decompress, after twelve or thirteen months in Vietnam a nineteen-year-old killer was given a fast plane ride back to the States and turned loose on the streets of America without any thought having been given to how he was supposed to stop being the killer he had been so carefully conditioned to become. Miraculously most of them made the transition to civilian life successfully, but a few of them didn't. It was small wonder, then, that television and the movies portrayed the Vietnam veteran as a walking time bomb, waiting to explode, when they bothered to portray him at all.

Perhaps it wasn't such a bad thing that a young man like Corbett, who could kill with ease from a thousand yards, had doubts about the morality of his job. The prospect of a silent army of such men, walking the streets back home, men who had never fully been defused of their killer instincts, was to Gerber an unsettling one.

It was too bad the military hadn't found a way to surgically remove a man's conscience when he was drafted, then graft it back into place when he was discharged. Until then there would always be killers who didn't want to kill and killers who didn't know how to stop killing once they got started.

Gerber leaned forward in his seat and looked down the line at Corbett, sitting on the other side of Bhang. He was just a kid with the faint beginning of a mustache, who had already acquired the thousand-yard stare of men who had been too long in combat and seen too much death. He had at once the look of someone too green in-country to really understand what the war was all about and the tired, worn-out look of the experienced vet, counting down his short time until he was next. Perhaps being a sniper with twenty confirmed kills to his credit aged a man early.

The two of them, Corbett and Bhang, would have made a fine-looking couple in the library of some stateside college campus, yet they made an unlikely-looking pair sitting in the back of a cargo plane, waiting to jump out into the night sky over enemy-occupied Laos. Sitting there in their camouflage suits and helmets, their faces smeared with multihued face paint in bright green and dark earth tones, they might have been made up for some garish homecoming ritual or a Halloween parade. Even beneath the greasepaint and battle fatigues, their youth was obvious. But their eyes were those of the aged and the tired, of those who had seen too much and would never be able to forget.

Gerber felt a brief flare of anger. Why was it that old men persisted in starting wars for young people to lose either their lives or their innocence in? He pushed that thought quickly from his mind. If he dwelt on it too long, he might be tempted to stop killing enemy soldiers and start killing politicians.

He ran through the details of the mission once more in his head, then, satisfied that nothing had been overlooked, leaned back against the side of the airplane and closed his eyes, trying to clear his mind. It was all well and good to ponder, from the safety of an overstuffed armchair in some college professor's home, the relationships between those who started wars and those who were sent to die in them, but in combat there was only time for instincts and the will to survive. Gerber's team would be in enemy country soon enough. He wanted to be ready.

Across the aisle Bunnell sat nervously fingering his jump bag, which contained the RPD light machine gun, longing for a tall, cold bottle of Milwaukee's finest. It was hard for him to say exactly why he had volunteered for a second tour in Vietnam, except that when he had gone back to the States at the end of his first tour he had felt curiously adrift. The spit-shined, polished-brass Mickey Mouse shit of the stateside military had left him feeling out of sync with time and his surroundings. It had seemed an unreal world full of unimportant little people forever dreaming up unimportant little things for him to fill his days with. He had always been a heavy drinker, although only of beer, but the intense, unrelenting boredom he had experienced at Fort Benning, Georgia, as part of the training cadre at Airborne School, coupled with the confusion he'd felt over the antiwar protests and the flag burnings shown almost nightly on television, had pushed him to the point of alcoholism. When it was suggested that he either get his act together or consider resigning his commission while it was still possible to do so with an honorable discharge, he had opted instead to return to the only place where he really understood the operating rules, and to the only people he really understood and who understood him.

The MAT assignment to advise a village militia unit in Lam Dong Province had proven a lifesaver, to both his career and his sanity, although with his language skills and two clandestine operations under his belt from his first tour, he had expected an assignment to Prairie Fire. Perhaps the Army hadn't felt they could trust a drinking man in such a sensitive post, although they didn't seem particularly bothered by doing it now.

If Bunnell fidgeted nervously with the case containing his weapon, Tyme, sitting next to him, stroked the case holding his rifle almost lovingly. Even as a child he had been fascinated with all types of firearms. To him, there was nothing more beautiful than the burled walnut and cold steel of a truly fine-quality sporting arm, yet even something as functionally ugly as an AK-47 held its own variety of utilitarian beauty. Perhaps that was why he had opted to become a light-weapons specialist. It gave him a chance to know intimately weapons that other people could only read about. The M-21, he knew, was an excellent choice for the mission, although he was secretly just a little bit disappointed that they hadn't been able to come up with a Soviet Dragunov. He would have liked the opportunity to examine and fire one, although it was supposed to be a bit inferior to the M-21.

Seated next to Tyme, Bocker was erect but relaxed, placidly chewing his omnipresent wad of bubble gum. He didn't concern himself with thoughts of radios or codes or the mission ahead. Every problem that could be foreseen he had already dealt with, and those that couldn't, he would have to deal with as they arose. He thought only of his wife and their two young daughters, Melanie, age ten, and Jennifer, eight, and was glad that all three were safe back home in North Carolina.

As placidly as Bocker chewed his gum, Krung implacably sharpened his knife on a large whetstone placed on his right thigh. He tried never to think of his family, now all dead, but only of the enemy and of the trophies he would claim in the fight that lay ahead.

Yoon, the medical specialist, pawed continually through his bag of supplies as though afraid he had forgotten something they would have to go back for. He thought only of sucking chest wounds, shock and traumatic amputations, and the treatment modalities for each, and of the M-79 grenade launcher with which he could take life as quickly as he could save it.

Across the aisle from Yoon, Fetterman had only one thought: what it would be like to place the cross hairs of his rifle's telescopic sight on the face of Rhee Ming Wong and squeeze the trigger.

Corbett had seen Bhang fingering the zipper of her Belgian paratrooper jacket. ''Does it hurt much? The scars, I mean,'' he asked so softly that his words were barely audible above the drone of the aircraft's engines.

Bhang was so startled by the directness of his question that she almost jumped. She stared at him curiously for a moment, then said in broken English, ''It no the scars so much. It memory of how get there.''

''It must have been awful for you,'' said Corbett sympathetically.

Bhang shrugged. ''It no fun. I no care repeat same.''

Way to go, jerk, thought Corbett. What else could she say? ''I'm sorry,'' he told her seriously. ''I didn't mean to pry into a painful subject.'' He wanted to say more, but couldn't think of anything that wouldn't make the situation worse.

"What you do before you soldier, Corbett?" said Bhang after a while.

"Why, I went to high school," he said, surprised both by the question and by the fact that she had voluntarily chosen to continue their conversation. He didn't bother to explain that he was a Marine, not a soldier.

"What high school?" she asked.

"It was called Theodore Roosevelt High School."

She looked confused. "No understand. What mean high school?"

"Oh! Sorry. I thought you meant which high school. It's a kind of secondary school, sort of like that place you went to in France, I guess." He searched his rusty French vocabulary for the equivalent term, but couldn't come up with it. "Theodore Roosevelt was one of our presidents. The twenty-sixth, I think. He was a war hero, conservationist and sportsman. The school was named after him."

"What war he hero in? Vietnam? World War II?"

"The Spanish-American War. He led a group of men called the Rough Riders in a famous battle. The charge up San Juan Hill."

"Spanish-American War? Not know that war. Americans fight Spanish, too?"

"It was a long time ago. Way before I was born."

Bhang nodded. "That why they name school for him?"

"I guess so. I don't think he ever hunted around my home or established any parks there."

"What mean con-ser . . . con-ser-vation?"

"Conservationist," corrected Corbett. "It means somebody who loves the land and animals and tries to make sure that they'll always be there for future generations to enjoy. Roosevelt helped establish the National Park System in my country.''

Bhang looked thoughtful for a moment. ''I think it better be con-ser-va-tion-ist than be soldier. It better to love land than kill its people.''

Corbett agreed with that, but thought that it was necessary sometimes to be a soldier if the people were to have freedom. He said as much.

''Yes,'' agreed Bhang, ''but it also good to be alive. The dead have freedom, Corbett, but they no have life. Is it not better to live?''

Corbett was silent for a moment. ''It is better to live free,'' he said at last. ''For some people freedom is more important than life. I would have thought that you, of all people, would know that.''

''I know, Corbett. Just want to be sure you do.''

Corbett wondered what in hell she meant by that.

For perhaps the next fifteen minutes it was quiet in the dimly lit cargo bay of the C-123. Aside from the drone of the engines and the spatter and hiss of rain on the outside of the aircraft, the only sounds were Yoon's occasional rifflings through his bags, the chomp and pop of Bocker's bubble gum and the steady scraping of Krung's knife on the sharpening stone as he strove to perfect what was already a razor's edge. Just when Corbett thought she must have gone to sleep, Bhang spoke again.

''You no like your job, do you, Corbett? You good at it, but no like being sniper.''

''I like the job well enough. It's challenging and requires that you be able to think, to plan ahead and be clever, as well as be good with a rifle.''

''Okay. You like job. But you no like something about it, I think. I hear you talk in sleep, in barracks at Kontum. You no like to kill.''

She succeeded in surprising him. Corbett hadn't realized that he talked in his sleep. "I don't like killing people," he admitted, "although most of the time I don't give it much thought. When it comes to shooting the enemy, I think of the target as just that, a target, not a man."

"Yet it bother you afterward," persisted Bhang. "I hear you talk in sleep."

Corbett wasn't sure why, but he felt a need to try to explain it to her. "There's one time that bothers me. Once I had to shoot a Vietcong soldier from a long ways off. The light wasn't very good, either. I found out later the soldier was a fifteen-year-old girl."

"She civilian or VC?" asked Bhang.

"She was Vietcong all right. She was pushing a bicycle loaded down with guns and ammunition. I guess she was getting ready to deliver them to some local VC unit. But she was still only fifteen. To me, that was like shooting some girl in junior high school. She should have been in school, damn it, not out pushing some bike loaded down with rifles. She should have been going to parties and dances and dating the captain of the football team. She should have been loafing at the malt shop or going to drive-in movies, not smuggling arms. Damn it all, why did she have to be pushing *that* bicycle? Why couldn't she have just been hanging out with kids her own age?" Corbett stopped short. He hadn't intended to ramble on like that.

"Corbett, you must understand something. Vietnam not like your country. Laos not like your country. No have malt shop and football. Have war. All Indochina have war. Your VC still VC, no matter what age. Pathet Lao, VC, Khmer Communists, all same. All want take away freedom. To have life without freedom is no good. You know that. You say so self."

"The VC girl I shot was only fifteen," growled Corbett. "Do you expect me to believe she was trying to take away your freedom? Anybody's freedom? Hell, she wasn't even old enough to know what freedom is!"

Bhang sighed deeply. "I try make you understand, Corbett, but you no understand. Your country, my country, not same. America, all Indochina, not same. She VC, Corbett. She Communist. All Communist same. Better to shoot them. She old enough to know what do. She old enough to shoot."

"She was fifteen," said Corbett doggedly. "That's *not* old enough to shoot in anybody's war. That's not even old enough to know what war is."

Bhang shook her head hopelessly. "I try make you understand," she said after a moment, "so I can maybe talk to you, but you will not understand. Indochina not America. We have war here long time. Children here grow up in war. See war every day. Know war every day. Fifteen plenty old enough to know war. You think you know everything because you nineteen and American. You know nothing. Four year ago when I go work for CIA I fifteen. My brother, he become radio operator for Special Forces in Laos last year when he fourteen. Staff Sergeant Krung, how old you think his sister when VC kill whole family except her? They only rape her. She kill herself afterward. She not even thirteen. Fifteen plenty old enough to know too much war, Corbett. In Indochina fifteen old enough to fight for either side or be killed by either side. Indochina not America. Not land of big PX. This war, Corbett. Here only death. You better to learn, or you die here."

Any further discussion was cut off by the Nationalist Chinese jumpmaster returning from the pilot's cabin. "Team leader?" he asked. He had a clipped British accent that reminded Gerber of Captain Minh, an ARVN LLDB officer he had known from his first tour who had been educated at Sandhurst.

"Over here," said Gerber, holding up a hand.

The man walked down the aisle and leaned against the fuselage. "Right. Don't tell me your name, sport. Don't want to know it in case someone asks later. You know we're not flying in direct? Don't want to give the baddies a direct line on our flight path."

"Sure," said Gerber. "It was in the briefing packets. That sort of thing is fairly routine. I can't honestly remember the last time I flew anywhere direct."

"Right. Well, old chap, what you don't know is that the cover strikes have been delayed because of the weather. We're going to have to hang out a ways and orbit a bit."

"Terrific," said Gerber. "That ought to give them a really good radar plot on our position."

"Not to worry, sport. We'll be at least fifty kilometers away from the drop zone, so even if they do pick us up on radar, it won't jeopardize your show. If they see us at all, they're sure to figure we're command and control for the air strikes, or just out nosing around on our own. Anyway, as soon as we get word that the fighter-bombers are on their way in, we'll break orbit and fly an indirect dogleg to the drop zone. No worries at all, except you'll be jumping about thirty minutes late. Just thought you'd like to know. I'll be back to give you the five-minute warning and help you on your way."

Gerber merely nodded.

The jumpmaster clapped him on the shoulder and said, "Ta-ta for now." Then he went back up front.

When the Nationalist Chinese had left, Fetterman got up and shuffled down the aisle to speak with Gerber. "Trouble, Captain?" asked Fetterman.

"Air strikes are held up. It's the weather. We're going to jump half an hour late."

"Then we'll lose last light. No visual on the DZ at all. Won't be able to see the ground."

"Affirmative," said Gerber. "I'd hoped for some twilight for the inexperienced, but we'll be completely in the dark."

"Oh, well. We figured it would probably work out that way anyhow. I'll pass the word to the others." Fetterman ambled back to his seat, pausing as he went to give the others the news.

Waiting, Gerber knew, was always the worst part. The Army was full of it. Waiting in lines. Waiting for orders. Waiting for the word. Now, just at the moment when everyone's level of tension was at its highest, immediately prior to a combat jump, they would have to wait yet again. Last-minute delays like this put everyone's nerves on edge.

Even the minimal conversation, difficult at best because of the noise of the engines and the rain, dried up. Only the steady scraping of Krung sharpening his knife remained. The sound was beginning to get on Gerber's nerves when the aircraft hit a sudden updraft, causing Krung to miss a stroke and slice through the knee of his camouflage jumpsuit before he could stop his hand. He nicked his leg only slightly, but left a three-inch cut in the fabric of his trousers. As the bumpiness of the air continued to increase, he put away the knife and sat silently to wait like the rest.

As they held their slow orbit near the Laos-Cambodia border, waiting for the strike aircraft to solve their problems, Gerber was uncomfortably aware of the passage of time and checked his wristwatch frequently.

At last they broke their holding pattern, and a short time later the jumpmaster reappeared. "Strike aircraft will start hitting their targets in ten minutes. We'll be turning on our final approach to the drop zone at that time. You'll then have five minutes. Please be ready and exit the aircraft as quickly as possible once the jump signal's given. About four minutes out we'll descend to jump altitude. Once you're away, we'll change course again, climb back up a bit, change course and do it all again, except you won't be aboard. We'll run three empty drops in all. We hope it'll appear like an aircraft in trouble to any enemy radar, a reasonable enough assumption considering the weather. If it doesn't, the phony drops should keep them guessing as to who actually got off and where. The navigator has assured me he'll pinpoint the DZ, but timing will be rather critical, so when the jump signal comes on, don't wait for me. Is everything clear?"

Heads nodded on both sides of the aircraft.

"Right, then. Initial equipment check, everyone."

Each team member ran through the routine, checking first his own gear, then that of the persons in front of and behind him, making sure all gear bags were closed and all buckles on parachute harnesses were closed and locked.

Ten minutes later the aircraft banked sharply to the right. "Both sticks stand up," the jumpmaster called out. They rose to their feet, turned and faced the tail of the aircraft.

"Final equipment check," he said, and they ran through the procedure again, unclipping each static line hook as they finished the check and handing it to the jumper who wore it. "Sound off for equipment check."

Each team member reported that he was ready by giving his or her number in line and saying, "Okay," after it.

"Hook up static lines." There were nine distinct clicks as each jumper snapped his static line hook to the length of metal cable running down the center of the cargo bay above their heads. "Check static lines." Nine hooks rattled as they were tugged on to make sure the safety covers were fastened securely.

The pitch of the engines changed as the pilot throttled back and the aircraft settled into a slow descent. "Stand clear of the door," the jumpmaster said unnecessarily. He opened it, swinging it inward and to the side out of the way.

The interior of the C-123 was instantly filled with noise and a cool, damp breeze, a fine spray of rain entering the open doorway. Two minutes later a small red bulb in a little box above the open door began flashing the attention signal and then turned to steady red.

"Stand in the door!" bellowed the jumpmaster above the noise of the engines and the rain.

Bunnell stepped forward, and placing a hand on the outside edge of either side of the doorway, crouched slightly, ready to hurl himself into space. He looked directly at the jump indicator light above the door.

As the red light winked out and the green one next to it came on, the jumpmaster yelled, "Go!" and reached out to slap Bunnell on the seat of his pants, but he was too late and struck only air. The others followed as if being poured from a funnel.

Gerber got a face full of rain as soon as he reached the door, but there wasn't time to fully appreciate it. He shoved himself out and had a brief false impression of the airplane suddenly being lifted away from him. He automatically counted to three, heard the rustling as the static line pulled the sleeve from the container and knew the chute had deployed. Except for the instant when he could see the aircraft moving away, he had no idea which direction was down. Then he felt the opening shock and looked up to make sure he had a good canopy, not that there was anything he could have done if he hadn't, but because it had been ingrained in him through hundreds of practice sessions and previous jumps. He could have saved himself the effort. The canopy was black nylon, and in the near total darkness of the rain and night, almost impossible to see.

He reached for the looped straps that replaced the steering toggles on this particularly model of chute, but couldn't judge the wind well enough to know which direction to turn into it. The horizon was completely unreadable. A few seconds later he felt the bone-jarring shock of impact with the ground. He tried to roll, to lessen the effect, but had landed with the wind instead of into it and only made things worse. He hit like a sack of potatoes and was dragged along the ground on his face.

Since the parachute was a sport model, it lacked the chest release found on the Army T-10, and he had to roll over on his back, pop open the safety cover at his shoulder, get a thumb in the ring and pull down to trigger the quick release and shear away one side of the canopy. Once he had managed that the air spilled out of the nylon, and the canopy collapsed and quit dragging him across the ground. For a moment he could hear the dwindling sound of the C-123's engines, and then there was only the rain and the wind and the limp flapping of the canopy's nylon.

For a moment he lay there, wiggling his fingers and toes, making sure he hadn't broken anything important in the landing. Then he unclipped his equipment container and hauled out his pack and AK-47. That done, he got unsteadily to his feet, unbuckled the harness and let it drop, then began hauling in the chute and stuffing it into the jump bag. His back hurt like hell, but he didn't think he'd broken anything. Probably just pulled a muscle.

When he finished stuffing his parachute into the canvas bag that had held his pack during the jump, Gerber struggled into the heavy pack, and dug out his compass and took a reading. Then he picked up his rifle, heaved the jump bag holding his parachute up over one shoulder and staggered off in what he hoped was the direction of the southeast corner of the drop zone, feeling the rain in his face and hearing the faint squish of his rubber-soled boots amid the thudding of the raindrops.

The drop zone was a soggy mess covered with water-filled mud puddles, most of them just deep enough to lap over Gerber's boot tops. Twice he tripped in the darkness, once over a tree branch about four inches in diameter that had absolutely no reason to be lying in an open field, and once when he stubbed his toe against a rock. Both times he sprawled headlong into a puddle and struggled back to his feet, cursing under his breath through clenched teeth. Finally he got the idea to crouch low and wait for the lightning to flash. It made him less of a target for anyone watching the field and gave him a chance to look over the terrain ahead. He would then get up and move several yards after the lightning had died, then crouch down again and wait for another flash. The system was time-consuming, but not nearly as frustrating as trying to walk across the field in total darkness.

When Gerber finally reached the southeast corner of the DZ, which was the assigned RP for after the drop, he found Bunnell, Tyme and Bocker already waiting. A couple of minutes later Krung arrived, swaying under the heavy load of pack, weapon and chute-filled jump bag. About a minute after that Corbett showed up, and almost ten minutes more passed before Bhang put in an appearance, dragging her jump bag behind her.

When half an hour had passed with no sign of Fetterman or Yoon, Bocker and Tyme wanted to make a sweep along the sides of the DZ to see if they could pick them up, but Gerber vetoed that. He didn't want the men mistaking one another for Pathet Lao or VC in the darkness and getting into a firefight.

As the seconds ticked away on his wrist, Gerber agonized over whether to wait until morning when they could search for the others in daylight or to press on without them. If Fetterman and Yoon were lying hurt or dead somewhere out on the drop zone and they left them behind to be found by the enemy, the team's infiltration would be compromised and the mission jeopardized. On the other hand, if they waited until daylight, they would be considerably behind schedule, and any additional delays might cost them so much time that they wouldn't be able to make the target area in time for the ceremony. After a full hour had passed, Gerber finally decided they couldn't wait any longer and sent Bocker, Tyme and Krung a short distance into the woods to dig a hole and bury the parachutes in preparation for moving out. It was another half hour before they finished, and they were just returning when Gerber heard the last sound he had expected to hear in the jungles of Laos: the hooting of an owl.

Gerber responded with a turkey gobble, and a few moments later heard Fetterman utter a single word out of the darkness. "Three."

"Four," answered Gerber, the numbers adding up to the agreed-upon recognition signal of seven.

A moment later Fetterman dropped beside him.

Gerber was only dimly aware of the man's location by the faint sound of something heavy being lowered to the ground, and by the fact that the blackness of the night was slightly more opaque where Fetterman squatted, hardly surprising, since a man could barely see the outline of his own hand held up to the sky a few inches in front of his face.

"Where the hell have you been, Tony?" asked Gerber. "You're late."

"Burying Sergeant Yoon," said Fetterman. "We both came down in the trees just off the end of the DZ. Yoon didn't make it. Broke his neck somehow or other. It took me a while to cut him down and dig the hole. I guess we're going to be short a medic. I brought his weapon and most of his gear. Had to bury both our chutes with him. I couldn't carry it all."

"Christ!" whispered Gerber. "What a way to start a mission. If the Pathet Lao find the grave—"

"They won't. Not unless they're looking for it, *and* know where to look. I made it deep enough so that the scavengers can't unearth him. Dug it in underneath a thicket of thorns next to something resembling a locust tree, then camouflaged it. It's not the sort of place likely to invite the curious. He'll be safe enough there, sir."

It was hard to fathom a business where a dead man was thought of as safe, but Gerber understood what Fetterman meant. Yoon wouldn't be found by the enemy. The man was safe from discovery, and that meant the mission, and the rest of the team, was safe as well. At least they were safe for the moment.

"It's a hell of a line of work we've gotten ourselves into, isn't it, Tony?" said Gerber softly.

"Yes, sir."

"All right, then," said Gerber, "let's spread Yoon's gear around and get ready to move out. Krung, you know the route?"

"Affirmative, Captain Mack."

"Fine. You take the point. We'll follow five minutes behind. Stop every half hour and wait for us to catch up. We don't want to get separated and start losing track of people at this stage. When we get closer to the target area, I'll have Bhang join you to guide us through the Pathet Lao checkpoints and patrols. If we lose anybody, we'll rendezvous at the last stopping point and wait there for one hour. Don't dawdle, because we can't afford to get behind schedule. After an hour we'll have to move on, whether everybody's accounted for or not. Is everybody clear on that?"

There was a chorus of whispered "Yes, sirs" and affirmatives.

"Right. One more thing," said Gerber. "There's to be no shooting. If we encounter the enemy, we go around them or let them pass by if possible. If you have to take someone out, use your knife. Everybody check your weapon and make sure the safety's set. Nobody, and I mean nobody, is to fire unless the enemy fires first. If that happens, we'll have lost the element of surprise, so hit them with everything you've got. If the enemy's a squad or less, we'll assault. If the enemy's stronger than that, I'll fire two red flares. In that case immediately break contact. The RP will be our last stopping point. If you fail to make the RP, you'll have to continue on to the target area as best you can alone. The only way out will be the extraction team, so don't be late at the LZ or you'll miss your ride. Don't get careless and walk into a Pathet Lao patrol or step in a hole and break your leg, either. You should have plenty of time to make the pickup point as long as you don't waste it. Any questions?''

"Sir, what about recovery?" asked Corbett.

"Recovery? What recovery? You're clear on the exfiltration procedures, aren't you?"

"I meant, what about recovering Sergeant Yoon's body?"

Gerber sighed. "There'll be no recovery, Corbett. Oh, Master Sergeant Fetterman will duly report the location of the burial as best he can to the graves registration classified file, and some year, when the war's over, the Army might be able to recover the remains, but I wouldn't count on it. Yoon belongs to Laos now. He won't be going back to the land of the big PX. I thought you understood that." There was silence for a moment, then Gerber said, "Okay, that's it. Krung, you've got the point. Move out."

Krung got up and moved silently past them and was swallowed by the darkness before he had gone three feet. They were left with only the blackness of the night and the hiss and wetness of the rain, occasionally broken by a clap of thunder as a flash of lightning garishly but briefly illuminated their nightmarish, camouflaged features.

The seconds seemed to stretch into hours as the five minutes dragged by until at last Gerber gave the word. As they rose to leave, Corbett felt a hand lightly touch his shoulder. It was Fetterman's.

"I know what you're thinking, son," whispered the master sergeant. "Believe me, the captain doesn't like it any better than you do. Special Forces doesn't believe in leaving its men in the field any more than the Marines do. We also don't believe in sacrificing the living to save the dead. Short of dragging Yoon's body along with us, there's nothing else we can do for him, except write lies to his family when we get back. We can't even tell them where or how he died.''

"I know we can't take him with us," Corbett whispered back, "but just leaving him here still sucks.''

"There it is," said Fetterman. "Welcome to clandestine ops, Gyrine.''

13

JUNGLE WEST OF BAN TASSENG

Krung moved through the jungle with all the fanfare of a phantom, all the sound of a shadow. Every piece of his equipment had been padded or tied down so that it wouldn't shift or bounce, and every buckle or metal surface had been taped or wrapped with cloth so that it wouldn't rattle or clink. He had tied the sleeves and legs of his uniform tightly to his body with strips of cloth so that they couldn't scrape against branches or catch on thorns, and the sling of his AK-47 assault rifle had been wrapped around his weapon and secured with black electrical tape in such a fashion that it couldn't catch or rattle, yet kept the operating handle and bolt free so that the rifle could be brought instantly into use if needed.

The AK, Krung knew, was an excellent infantry weapon. Although the workmanship was somewhat crude at times, depending on the country of manufacture, it was a sturdy and reliable weapon. While both the rifle and its ammunitions were heavier than the M-16 and its rounds, it could take a great deal more abuse and still function, and the heavier bullets used in the AK had better brush-bucking characteristics, an important advantage when fighting in dense foliage.

Tonight, though, it wouldn't have been in his hands if there had been a convenient way of carrying it that was reasonably silent and still allowed for quick access. Unfortunately, tying it down securely alongside his pack would have made for a quiet but inaccessible carry, and slinging it afforded too great an opportunity for it to catch on things, so the only reasonable course was to keep it in his hands.

Still, it was on a night such as this that Krung most needed his hands free. There was rarely enough light to see by when the lightning broke the darkness, and that illumination was reduced to twilight by the overhead leaves of the double- and triple-canopy jungle.

He needed his hands to tell what was in front of him. The rain masked both the sounds and scents that would otherwise have provided a wealth of information to his peculiarly sensitive hearing and nose in the darkness, and if he should bump against the enemy in the wet, black world that surrounded him, he would need both hands to strike silently and swiftly before the enemy could call out a warning.

Three and a half hours into the march, the strain of playing what amounted to blindman's bluff in the rain forests of southeastern Laos began to take its toll. The entire team was battered and bruised from falling down and walking into trees, and they were covered with scratches from thorns. They were still ahead of schedule, but only because the mission planning had allowed them more time to reach the target area than should have normally been necessary. But that safety margin was rapidly dwindling, and Gerber was concerned that if they continued to lose time at the same rate, they wouldn't reach the objective until after sunup.

Gerber considered having Fetterman relieve Krung at point, figuring that even Daniel Boone would have been exhausted with trailblazing under such conditions, but when they halted for a rest stop it quickly became apparent that Krung was doing better than the rest of them. He only had to find his way over unfamiliar ground in an impossible situation while remaining alert for the enemy. The others not only had to do that, but had to stay together and find Krung each time they stopped for a break. Gerber considered the tiredness of his troops, and despite the press of time gave them an extra ten minutes of rest.

Twenty minutes later, just as Krung was preparing to halt again so that the others could catch up, he heard a rustling in the broad-leaved weeds ahead of him and froze, listening. Krung realized that he was straining his eyes uselessly, trying to see some movement. It was like being blindfolded with a velvet bag over your head. He put aside the natural human tendency to try to see, even in total darkness, and closed his eyes, concentrating wholly on hearing. At first there was nothing, and while Krung was positive that he had heard *something*, he was just about ready to mark it down to the passage of some night animal hunting its supper when the sound came again. This time there was no mistaking it: the sound of leaves scratching against heavy plastic and canvas, a poncho and rucksack, almost directly in front of him.

Moving with agonizing slowness dictated by caution and the need for absolute silence, Krung edged his way laterally toward the left until he came up against the trunk of a large tree and slowly lowered himself toward the ground. Squatting there, he felt along his left leg until he came to the thigh pocket of his Belgian jump pants and eased open the twin metal snaps.

He didn't take the small Japanese-made hand radio from his pocket, but merely slid the antenna out alongside his leg. He felt the top of the radio for the earplug jack, then followed the tiny black cord with his fingers until he came to the end of it. Sticking the minuscule earphone in his ear, he switched on the transceiver and was greeted with a burst of static that seemed deafening but was audible only to him. He felt along the side of the radio, found the transmit button and squeezed it three times—the danger signal.

It was answered almost at once by the sound in the earphone of squelch being broken twice. Bocker, not far behind with the others, had acknowledged the warning.

Krung switched off the set, telescoped the antenna and stuffed the earphone back into his pocket before buttoning the flap. Then he quietly unsnapped the retraining strap on the sheath of his big Muela knife and eased the heavy rubber-band safety retainer over the handle. Placing his rifle beside his feet and against the tree, Krung drew the knife silently and held it ready, blade upward.

The enemy soldier stopped moving, and Krung tensed, afraid that he had somehow been discovered. The beat of his heart was like a drum in his temples. Surely the enemy could hear it, too, or at least the sound of his breathing. But the steady hiss and drip of the rain made it impossible to hear sounds much louder than that, and after a moment the enemy moved on, the occasional swishing of a leafy stem, the creak of a buckle or the rubbing of canvas against poncho or tree marking his progress away from the area.

Krung stayed put. It wasn't reasonable to assume that an enemy soldier had decided to go for a walk in the forest at night and in the rain, without a light and on his own. There would be others who would follow. It was important to know their number and direction of march.

Less than five minutes later Krung was mildly surprised to see a faint light bobbing toward him through the woods. He recognized the illumination at once as being that of one of the tiny kerosene-fueled lamps used by the Vietcong and Pathet Lao. The fact that the enemy troops were using lamps, although their point man hadn't, indicated that, although cautious, they felt fairly secure here. That could work to Krung's and the team's advantage.

Silently Krung slipped around to the opposite side of his tree and pressed himself to the ground. Knife in one hand, AK-47 in the other, he waited. In daylight he would have tied leaves to his uniform and equipment to increase his camouflage, but in a parachute jump, or at night, the fewer loose ends one had hanging from one's uniform to catch and tangle on things, the better. He had tied strips of cloth and used patches of black electrical tape on the barrel, stock and magazine of his rifle to help break up its outline; in fact, the weapons of the entire team had been sprayed with green and gray paint in Kontum, as had their packs and webgear. He hoped their precautions would be enough. He hadn't counted on running into an enemy patrol using lights.

In a few moments the enemy came into view. They were dressed in black pajamas, like VC, but were NVA-issue olive-drab tennis shoes and equipment. They were well armed, each soldier carrying either an AK-47 or Chicom-type 54 submachine gun, the PLA's version of the Soviet PPS-43. Many of them were wearing rain gear, some the heavy plastic or waterproofed nylon ponchos used by the American and Royal Lao armies, others the hooded, rubberized capes issued by the PLA and NVA. The men's facial features however, marked them as Laotian. Pathet Lao.

It was a big patrol, twenty to twenty-five soldiers, although only every third or fourth man had a lamp. There was still too much light for Krung's liking, and he hugged the short, wet grass and muddy ground closer and practiced becoming part of the earth. He kept his head tilted back slightly so that he could still see the enemy, but closed one eye to protect its night vision and squinted the other down to a bare slit so that the reflected light from his eyeball wouldn't stand out against the camouflage makeup covering his face.

Less than two meters away, through the grass, he could see part of the body of a snake, presumably driven from its hole by the flooding rain. He couldn't positively identify it, but thought it was a boa of some type. Whatever it was, he hoped it wasn't venomous, and that it didn't decide to suddenly take an interest in him.

As the Pathet Lao approached, the snake decided to vacate the area and slithered away through the grass. Krung thought the snake's decision an excellent one, given the circumstances, but he was considerably larger than the snake, and it was too late for him to repeat the reptile's performance.

Krung forced himself to breathe shallowly as he counted the enemy and made note of their equipment. They passed through the area on a general line that should have taken them slightly to the right of the rest of the Special Forces team, the nearest of them passing within ten meters of Krung's tree without noticing him.

When the Pathet Lao patrol had passed and it had grown dark again, Krung dug his radio out, switched it on and squeezed the transmit button five times, the pre-

viously agreed-upon signal for ''Many.'' It was acknowledged by two clicks from Bocker, letting him know that
the team understood there was a large group of enemy
soldiers headed roughly in their direction.

Krung was just putting the radio away when he heard,
quite close by, the unmistakable squeak of a wet, rubber-
soled tennis shoe. He froze, the radio pocket half-
buttoned. Was it some sort of rear guard, or merely a
straggler who had gotten too far behind the main group
of Pathet Lao? He couldn't see the enemy, but knew that
he had to be close, no more than a couple of meters away.

Briefly Krung considered trying to capture the man. A
POW could prove to be an excellent source of information about local enemy troop strengths and checkpoints,
as well as patrolling schedules and movements in the area.
The nature of their mission, however, was such that once
the captive had been pumped dry of information, he
would become more of a liability than an asset. He would
have to be kept bound and gagged at all times and watched
closely in order to prevent his jeopardizing the mission.
He wouldn't have to escape to warn his enemy comrades,
or even yell out a warning. Simply stepping on a twig or
allowing a branch to snap at an inconvenient time could
be sufficient to alert nearby Pathet Lao troops to the
presence of the team. And having to drag along a reluc-
tant prisoner would be sure to both slow the team's progress and make it noisier. It might well be better to simply
let the man pass.

Abruptly the decision was made for the Nung scout.
There was a faint clank, followed by the soft scuffing of
fabric rubbing together, a muted rattling, and then, to his
absolute horror, the unmistakable scratching sound of a
wooden match being struck against the side of the box.

In the brief red-orange flare of light, Krung was mortified to see that the faint metallic clank he had heard had been caused by the enemy's olive-drab tennis shoe stepping directly on top of the barrel of Krung's AK-47, where the soldier's foot still rested. The Pathet Lao was no more than one meter away from Krung's head and was looking down at him. It was hard to say which soldier's face registered the greater shock.

Despite the startling situation, Krung reacted immediately and moved before the enemy did. Abandoning his rifle for the moment, the Nung shoved himself up with his hands, managed to get a foot beneath himself and launched his body at the enemy soldier, bringing the knife up as he came off the ground.

The Pathet Lao reacted a fraction of a second later, but instead of dropping the match and lining up his rifle for a shot, stepped backward and jerked up the hand holding the match in front of his face as though to ward off a blow.

Krung had the brief impression of a fairly young face with handsome features before his hand clamped tightly over his victim's mouth, pressing the match against the Pathet Lao's lips and extinguishing it as he bent the enemy's head backward.

Krung drove the blade in hard, edge uppermost as he had held it, and used the momentum of his body weight, combined with the enemy's backward step, to topple his opponent. As they fell together, he used all the strength in his forearm to rip upward, through viscera until he heard the splintering crunch that told him he had hit the sternum. As they struck the ground, he twisted the blade over with great difficulty and yanked outward and to his right, hearing the snap and crack as the blade bit through ribs on the outward stroke.

Krung lay atop the Pathet Lao, his hand covering the enemy's mouth, smelling the faintly coppery odor of warm blood mixed with the stench of open bowel for several minutes as his victim kicked, thrashed about and finally lay still. Then he sawed the blade of the bit knife across the soldier's throat, cutting carotid, jugular and larynx to be sure of the job. It was a professional but unnecessary act. He had gutted the enemy like a fish, lacerating both large and small intestines, liver, pancreas, stomach, diaphragm and heart, as well as collapsing one lung. As the Pathet Lao died and lost control of involuntary muscles, the bladder emptied and the scent of fresh urine was added to the air.

Krung relieved the enemy of an AK-47 like his own, and of ammunition, pack and pocket contents, then felt around for his own rifle. Finally he slit open the enemy's trousers and prepared to claim the trophy of his kill for the scoreboard he kept in honor of Lieutenant Bao. Something seemed odd, though, and he slid his hand under the shirt to confirm it.

The Pathet Lao, it seemed, like their comrades the Vietcong, were equal-opportunity employers.

Despite his abiding hatred of all Communists, Krung felt a grudging respect for this dead female who had had the courage to take up arms in support of the struggle she believed in. Lieutenant Bao's memory would have to wait for another day to be avenged.

There was no time to dig a proper grave, but Krung scraped out a shallow depression, packed mud over the corpse and camouflaged it as best he could. It might be found in a few days, or never.

He left the body unmutilated.

GERBER DEPLOYED the others in a tight defensive circle as soon as Bocker advised him of Krung's warning about the approaching Pathet Lao patrol. There was no time to put out mines or trip wire grenade traps, and little time and no light for finding a suitable defensive position. All they could do was go to ground within touching range of one another, arrayed so as to meet a threat from any direction and hope that the enemy bypassed them. If not, the plan was to break contact using white phosphorus grenades and cover their rear and flanks with CS grenades while they fell back to the last rally point, then reorganize and try a different route to the target area. No one was to fire a weapon unless absolutely necessary, because the muzzle-flash would give away their position in the darkness. If shooting had to be done, it should, if at all possible, be left up to those equipped with the M-21 sniper rifles, since the Sionics suppressors would reduce both noise and muzzle-flash.

They never did spot the enemy point, and presumably were unnoticed by him. When the soft yellow glow from the enemy's lamps revealed the path of the Pathet Lao patrol, there were some bad moments when it appeared the enemy were going to walk straight up to the team's position, but when they were still about thirty meters away the patrol suddenly halted. One of the Pathet Lao apparently consulted a compass, and the patrol marched off in a new direction that took them across the front of the team's position and out of sight.

SAT-team Chuck Connors remained motionless for ten minutes, waiting for the tail gunner of the enemy patrol. When none materialized, Gerber took a head count to make sure no one was missing, then they started forward again.

"They not regular patrol unless schedule changed. At least I not think so," Bhang told Gerber helpfully. "Must get closer to camp. I not know this area too well."

Gerber would have rolled his eyes, but realized the gesture would have been wasted in the dark. Besides, the woman was trying to be helpful. It wasn't her fault that she couldn't tell them what she didn't know about. He thanked her, and they moved on to the next RP, where they found Krung waiting for them.

"Any problems?" Gerber asked the Nung striker.

"No problems, Captain Mack," Krung assured him.

"I thought for sure they'd have a rear guard of some kind," said Gerber. "You didn't see or hear anyone?"

"I hear and see," replied Krung. "Our score one Pathet Lao KIA confirmed. No problems."

Gerber was silent for a moment. "You took out their rear guard?" he asked evenly.

"Maybe rear guard, maybe just straggler. Only one. I kill, Captain Mack. No problems."

"Tell me exactly what happened," said Gerber. "Exactly."

His voice was noticeably cool. So was Krung's response.

"Captain Mack, I know what you think. I no go hunting trophies. You say let enemy pass, so I try, but it no good. Pathet Lao Co Cong come along behind patrol. Walk right on top of me, so I kill, then hide body. I good soldier. No take trophies when Captain Mack say so. Mission come first. I no have choice. Anyway," added Krung, "I no take trophies from Co Cong. It enough to kill them."

"All right, Sergeant Krung. I believe you," said Gerber. "If it couldn't be helped, it couldn't be helped. We'll just have to hope they don't notice she's missing for a while. And please try not to get into that kind of situation again.''

"I try," said Krung dubiously. He couldn't imagine how anyone could avoid having someone accidentally walk into him in total darkness.

At two o'clock in the morning Gerber put Bhang on point with Krung, and everybody was roped together with parachute suspension cord at three-meter intervals. They were starting to get into the area Bhang was familiar with, and Gerber needed her forward to guide them around Pathet Lao checkpoints. He also needed to keep the team closer together in order to exercise tighter control over his troops as they worked their way through the enemy positions.

It worked a lot better in theory than in practice. It was still almost impossible to tell exactly where they were or where they were going. Landmarks that Bhang remembered were hidden by the darkness, and although they tried using one of the Starlite scopes, it wasn't much help. Most of the time it simply came down to walking a compass heading for a given distance, determined by averaging the counted pace, and then trying to find some identifiable feature that would confirm they were where they thought they were. The progress was agonizingly slow.

By 0430 it was obvious that they weren't going to reach the target area before sunup, and Gerber resigned himself to finding a spot where they could hole up during the day. They would, at least, have to rest for a few hours, then look things over and decide whether to risk movement during daylight or wait for the following evening to continue onward.

The weather had cost them the extra time and daylight he had planned to use for a thorough recon of the target area. He hoped the information about the date and time of the signing ceremony was accurate. If the enemy were a day early, Gerber's team could miss the whole show. That kind of thinking was useless, however, and he dismissed it. If their information wasn't accurate, the signing could have already taken place, or could take place a week or a month from now. They had to assume the information was good and that the ceremony would take place the day after tomorrow. Otherwise there was no point to the mission and Yoon had died for nothing, along with Bhang's friends and several other people.

A little after 0500 they found a likely spot, a small thicket near the top of a hill with a ravine on two sides, which Bhang had remembered, the first real landmark she'd had any luck locating. The rain had finally stopped, and there was enough moonlight filtering through the trees so that they could actually see a few feet in front of them, although not, of course, any detail.

They set up their perimeter with claymores, one of the few concessions mission sterility had been forced to make to practicality, and pulled into a circle in the thicket to eat and rest. Half an hour later Gerber was mortified to discover that they had movement *inside* their perimeter. Another Pathet Lao patrol had apparently walked through their mines with the intention of occupying the same thicket.

There was absolutely nothing they could do. The claymores were useless. They couldn't start shooting without risking hitting one another, and they were too damn close to the target area to risk getting involved in a firefight, anyway. All they could do was wait. Gerber passed the word to the others about their uninvited guests and told them to sit tight and keep cool.

The Pathet Lao walked right into the thicket, sat down, broke out their rations and started to eat. Gerber hoped the guerrillas weren't looking for a spot to spend the day in, as he had been. It was getting awfully close to morning, and as it started to get lighter, the situation would soon become apparent to everyone.

After a while Fetterman crawled over to Gerber and whispered in his ear. "Captain, this is starting to get really grim. Their patrol leader just told me I've got the point when they move out of here. How about we get the hell out of this place before we get our asses shot off?"

Gerber was considering doing just that—passing the word to the others and crawling away, leaving the claymores behind, before it got light enough to reveal the absurd situation to the enemy—when the patrol leader softly called out a few orders and the Pathet Lao got up and walked off.

As soon as it was light enough to see, Gerber gave the order to roll up the firing cords to the claymores. He figured that particular thicket was just a little too popular to be safe in.

"That's as close a shave as I ever want to have," he told Fetterman. "Just thinking about it is enough to take five years off my retirement."

Fetterman was philosophical about the whole affair. "Well, Captain," he said to Gerber, "it could have been worse."

"How do you figure that?"

"Simple. At least they didn't ask us to stand guard for them."

Gerber thought it over and decided he was thankful for that.

14

PATHET LAO BASE CAMP
BEN TASSENG

Senior Captain Rhee Ming Wong of the Personnel Security Section of the General Political Department of the Chinese People's Liberation Army helped himself to his second cup of tea and first Marlboro cigarette of the morning. It had rained again last night and the parade ground outside his window, running past the open-air assembly hall where tomorrow afternoon's historic signing would take place, was its usual sea of red mud. By late afternoon it would be baked dry, with only an occasional puddle of standing water, just enough for one of the visiting dignitaries to muddy his boots in. But then, Rhee reminded himself, such important persons were careful never to muddy their boots or dirty their hands. That was what they had people like himself for.

Rhee had been more than a little surprised that such men would inconvenience themselves by a trip to inspect the southern terminus of the Ho Chi Minh Trail, but that was a political decision, and political decisions weren't a part of Rhee's particular province. His concerns were strictly military and security, along with the limited amount of protocol necessitated by his job of protecting such stellar personages.

Beyond the parade ground Rhee could make out the lumpy, net-covered shapes of the motor pool, where two ZIL-157 trucks, six-wheel drive, two-and-a-half-ton monstrosities, waited for the Pathet Lao honor guard that would greet and protect the dignitaries during their visit. General Kang Mang's smaller GAZ-69 command car, along with two others for the visiting generals and Senior Colonel Chow, were parked beneath the trees at the edge of the grove just south of the grassy knoll, some five hundred meters distant, having completed their own perilous journey down the Ho Chi Minh Trail last week. Once the big shots had gone back north, all the vehicles, with the exception of General Kang's, would be returned to their duties hauling supplies on the Trail.

The high-ranking Chinese and NVA officers were due to arrive late that morning and would be taken on a guided tour of the Trail network in the immediate area, a tour Rhee considered madness since it was to be conducted in full daylight.

The tour would take most of the afternoon, and the visitors would then be driven into town where a short parade celebrating their arrival had been carefully staged so as to appear an almost spontaneous welcome by the local populace. After that they would be treated to a special banquet in their honor and spend the night in comfort in a pair of very nice concrete villas thoughtfully left behind by the French when they vacated Indochina.

In the morning the dignitaries would meet with a thoroughly screened group of businessmen and political leaders from Ban Tasseng, attend a brunch with members of General Kang's staff and then be driven to the camp to inspect its troops and training facilities. The inspection would conclude at four in the afternoon. At 5:00 p.m., in front of photographers, select members of the Chinese, NVA and Pathet Lao propaganda apparatus, and a few hundred Pathet Lao soldiers chosen to dress out the show and painstakingly coached on when to clap and cheer, the protocol document would be signed beneath the tin roof of the rustic assembly hall, a fitting location for an agreement between peoples involved in a military struggle to throw the capitalists out of all Southeast Asia.

Rhee finished his tea and stubbed out the remains of his cigarette in the bottom of the cup. It was going to be yet another long, hot, humid day, and he sighed deeply at the thought of having to spend it inside the stifling confines of the silk jacket of his summer service uniform. At least he wasn't expected to greet the generals wearing his dress uniform. He pulled on his tunic with its sky-blue collar tabs holding the gold wings and parachute of his airborne insignia, then fastened the Sam Browne belt that held his Tokarev pistol.

Rhee considered the Tokarev a miserable weapon for personal defense, its cartridges too weak to be counted on to reliably stop an assailant. He preferred, and normally carried in the field, one of the big American .45-caliber Colt semiautomatics. The .45 was a heavy weapon, too large for many Asian hands, but its 240-grain bullets spoke with the voice of authority in a serious social confrontation. Today and tomorrow would be as much an affair of state as of the military, however, and it was important to be correctly attired. For that reason alone he chose the Tokarev as he had his stiff-brimmed service cap, which unlike his sun helmet, did little to protect the wearer's head from the merciless Southeast Asian sun. At least he could compensate for the Tokarev by carrying his AK-47 with him in the command car.

Rhee tucked his cigarettes and the Zippo lighter that had once belonged to an American Special Forces sergeant first class, a medical specialist named Ian McMillan, into a pocket of his service blouse and took down his AK-47 rifle and webgear containing his spare ammunition and grenades from the wooden peg on the wall of his hut.

There were many who would have considered all the combat paraphernalia to be overdressing for what was essentially a political visit, but Rhee wasn't a man to allow security considerations to be outweighed by what others might think of as proper dress. He had made the necessary concessions to issue uniform and side arm, but he wasn't about to go chaperoning a senior colonel and a bunch of generals around the jungles of southern Laos on the eve of an important meeting without the necessary means to defend them, or himself, especially since the full responsibility for their safety once they set foot in Laos was his and his alone. True, there was the security detachment coming with them, which would be placed under his direct command immediately upon their arrival, and the Pathet Lao honor guard, but if anything untoward should happen to one of the high Party members, his head would be the first to be placed on the chopping block. Although he had never seen it, he knew that there was already a black mark in his personnel file from the Hong Kong affair. The Party would tolerate only so many errors of judgment, and allowing the death of a general he had been assigned to protect would constitute a very major error.

Rhee couldn't say why, but some sixth sense warned him that all was not as it should be. After his conversation with the NVA sniper, Duc Van Co, he had spent a fitful night, his sleep troubled by images of big-nosed, white devil Americans in funny green hats, their faces painted with green and black camouflage makeup, emerging out of the shadows and lush jungle foliage with knives held between their teeth like storybook pirates. They were ludicrous images, he knew. No one with any common sense would carry a knife that way, and the American Special Forces soldiers didn't wear their jaunty green berets in the field. Still, the images had unnerved him. They had all been of men he had known before.

Gerber, Fetterman, Tyme, the black medic they had called T. J., whose name was Washington. They were all Americans he had fought against while advising the Vietcong troops in South Vietnam's Kien Phong Province. And Fetterman and Gerber had nearly killed him in Hong Kong.

The worst had been McMillan, the man he had killed. In the dream he had had blank and staring eyes, dead man's eyes, but he had laughed mockingly and told Rhee that he had come for him.

Rhee didn't believe in avenging spirits, but he did believe that everything happened for a reason, and he believed now that there must be some reason for the dream. He had absolutely no reason for believing that the Americans had any knowledge of the visit by the high-ranking comrades, or the protocol document they would sign. It was hard to imagine anything they could do about it if they did.

He had doubled the number of patrols around the camp, planned for a heavily armed escort for the dignitaries, seen to it that an outpost was established in the grove of trees that Duc had expressed concern over and even had the cleared killing zone of the camp's perimeter pushed back an additional hundred meters. He had imported the best shot in the entire NVA to counter the threat of enemy snipers. Short of the impossibility of establishing an air cover umbrella over the camp itself, he couldn't imagine what else he might do to make the situation any more secure.

Yet there was always the possibility that he had overlooked something, some small detail; that the Americans, in fact, did know about the meeting, and that a small, well-led and highly motivated, skillful and resourceful team of men, men such as Green Berets, would somehow penetrate all the security arrangements and do the impossible.

He had taken every precaution he could think of. All he could do now was try to be ready for the unexpected and react quickly if it occurred.

Rhee glanced at his watch and saw that he still had time for breakfast if he hurried, then walked out the door and down the steps, angling toward the mess hall.

There was no point in facing an army of white devils on an empty stomach.

IT WAS LATE MORNING when Fetterman, attired in a new growth of daylight camouflage consisting of freshly cut plants tied on top of his camouflage cloth uniform and equipment, tapped Gerber lightly on the arm to awaken him.

Gerber opened his eyes instantly, but didn't move, waiting for some indication of what the trouble was. He heard it almost at once: the heavy growling of truck engines in low gear. They were fairly close and getting closer.

Gerber sat up and looked at Bhang, who was awake and, like all the team members, resembled an ambulatory bush. He raised a questioning eyebrow. The Laotian shook her head and whispered, "We not near any part of

Trail I aware of. I not know this area good, but main part of Trail is north and east of here. I sure.''

They woke up the sleeping members of the team and listened to the sound of the approaching trucks. After a few moments the trucks stopped somewhere nearby, close enough for them to hear the doors slam as the drivers got out.

Fetterman looked at Gerber. "What do you think, Captain? Want me to go have a look?"

Gerber considered it. They were there to shoot a few Chinese generals, not discover a new branch of the Ho Chi Minh Trail. But why had the trucks stopped?

"I think maybe we'd both better go have a look . . . in case they're looking for us," said Gerber. "Captain Bunnell, you're in command."

Gerber and Fetterman weren't anxious to walk into a trap. They took nearly an hour to cover five hundred yards, and did the last hundred on their bellies. When they finally pushed through the last bit of brush to where they had a good view of the big clearing ahead of them, neither man was quite prepared for the sight that greeted his eyes.

"It's a goddamn airfield," whispered Fetterman.

"Well, an airstrip, anyway," agreed Gerber. "Recently lengthened, too, from the raw look of some of those tree trunks. Probably started out with a natural clearing and enlarged it."

"I just don't believe it, Captain. The fucker must be a thousand yards long. How in hell can the Air Force photorecon boys miss something that big? Wait a minute. Over there by the trucks. See that small hill? Only it's not a hill.''

"Camouflage netting," Gerber whispered back. "Lots of it. And there's more on down the strip and again at the end. They must have had a hundred men up half the night readying the field.''

"Industrious little buggers, aren't they?" observed Fetterman. "I wonder what they're waiting for."

"Let's hope it's not heavy bombers," said Gerber. "Jesus! I didn't think the bad guys had this kind of air assets available to them."

"Listen," said Fetterman. "Hear it? Sounds big."

Gerber listened for a moment, then nodded. "Twin engines at least."

He took out his binoculars and studied the far side of the airstrip, but could only make out two trucks and three smaller vehicles that seemed to be a cross between jeeps and pickup trucks. There was one knot of about thirty men near the vehicles, and a couple of similar-sized groups lounging around the piles of camouflage material.

"You reckon they're waiting to unload supplies, or fixing to go for a plane ride?" asked Fetterman.

"I reckon we're about to find out," said Gerber. "Let's get down under a little better cover and wait to see what happens."

The two men slid back under the bushes where they could still see part of the airstrip but were shielded from overhead observation, and waited. Within a minute or two a big, high-tailed, twin-engine turboprop transport with North Vietnamese markings dropped in over the trees and landed on the grass runway with fat, low-pressure rubber tires.

"Recognize it?" asked Gerber.

"Looks like an Antonov An-8 Camp. Soviet rough-field assault transport. I didn't think the North Vietnamese Air Force had anything like that."

"They do now," said Gerber. "If memory serves, one of those things can haul about seven and a half tons of cargo, or carry fifty paratroops. Sort of like the ComBloc version of a Provider."

"I don't like the look of this," said Fetterman. "Let's get a little closer and have a look at what they're hauling."

"We'll move back up to the edge of the strip and have another peek through the binoculars, but that's it. Let's not forget why we came here. Okay?"

They slid out from under the brush and glassed the field. The transport came to a stop with plenty of runway to spare, turned slowly and taxied back to the trucks, where a group of soldiers were lining up in two ranks. Even before the plane had halted, soldiers were running out onto the runway at the far end of the field and beginning to erect camouflage nets with a system of poles, ropes and stakes. Gerber decided that his estimate of a hundred men and half the night had been a bit large. The hundred men was probably right, but it looked more like only a couple of hours. He had a hunch that by noon both the strip and the plane sitting on it would be invisible from the air.

The pilot lowered the tail ramp of the An-8 and shut down the engines. Gerber and Fetterman watched the whole process and were astounded to see a small armored scout car, equipped with a radio antenna and what appeared to be a Goryunov 7.62 mm machine gun, roll down the ramp. The half-dozen men riding in the back of the vehicle were easily identified by their uniforms as Communist Chinese paratroopers.

"Christ!" said Fetterman. "Now I really don't like the look of this."

"Shh," Gerber reminded him. "Look what else is coming out."

A group of Chinese officers walked down the ramp. Although the distance was too far for individual recognition, even with the binoculars, there was no mistaking their distinctive ivory-colored summer dress uniforms. Two men in NVA uniforms were with them, and as the group stepped to the ground, an incredible sound reached Fetterman's and Gerber's ears. Unbelievably the Pathet Lao had arranged for a military band, and it now broke into a somewhat tinny rendition of "The East is Red" as the black-clad honor guard snapped to attention.

"I do believe our guests of honor for the Bullet Surprise of the Year Award had arrived," said Gerber. "Whether it means the signing ceremony has been moved up a day, or they've just come early to have a look at the Trail, I don't know."

"Shit," said Fetterman. "Our big chance to end it all right here and now with a couple of well-placed shots and me with the wrong gun."

He had opted to take the AK-47 Krung had liberated from the now-deceased Pathet Lao straggler as a more convenient weapon for a recon, leaving his M-21 back with Bunnell and the others. It had seemed a good idea at the time, but now he regretted the decision. From here, with the M-21s, it would have been fairly easy shooting. With AK-47s there was hardly any point in trying.

"Take it easy, Tony," Gerber told him. "It probably saved us from having to make some tough choices. We stick with the original plan. You couldn't have gotten them all, anyway."

"I could have gotten enough of them," replied Fetterman bitterly.

"You will when the time's right. This isn't it, that's all. We're too damn far from the pickup point, anyway, with the camp between us and it. At least we know that our intelligence was right about the visit. We work on the assumption that they're right about the rest of it, too. These guys probably just came early to check out the local nightlife. We stay with the plan."

"Yes, sir," said Fetterman. "I just hope we aren't assuming too much."

"Don't worry, Tony. You'll get your chance. Now let's get the hell out of here. I think that right now, while everybody's busy greeting the brass at the airport, might be a good time for us to do a little traveling ourselves. They've got so many people out here putting out the red carpet that there can't be all that many people holding the fort. I think this might be an excellent time to grab ourselves a couple of box seats for the main event. That is if you're finished sight-seeing."

"I've seen enough," said Fetterman. "I never cared much for playing tourist, anyway."

15

JUNGLE WEST OF BAN TASSENG

"You'd never believe what we found. I'm not entirely sure *I* believe it, and I saw it," Fetterman told the others as he slid down next to them.

"Meaning what?" asked Bunnell.

"Meaning the Pathet Lao have carved themselves an airstrip at least a thousand yards long out of the jungle. It starts not more than half a klick from here," answered Gerber, dropping beside them.

"An airstrip? That's silly," said Bunnell. "It'd show on the aerial recon photos."

"Not the way they've got this baby camouflaged," said Gerber. "It would take a low-altitude flight and you'd have to know what you were looking for. I doubt if the place would even show on an IR scan, unless there were planes or vehicles parked on it at the time."

"So what in hell are the Pathet Lao doing with an airstrip?" Bunnell asked.

"Apparently," said Gerber, "they built it to receive the aircraft carrying their Chinese visitors, a nice, big, twin-engined Antonov-8 with North Vietnamese markings that just buzzed overhead. After all, they couldn't expect a bunch of important Chinese to come all the way from Hanoi by bus, could they?"

"I did," said Bunnell. "That is, at least by truck or jeep. Somehow it never occurred to me to think of aircraft. I guess I'm just not used to thinking of the VC as having an air force. We figured the airplane was one of ours."

"The VC per se don't have an air force, although Hanoi does. Those MiG-21 fighters they got from Ivan have been causing our flyboys as big a headache as the SAM missiles up north. I didn't realize they had any transport capability until now, though. I vaguely remember reading they had some light stuff, like the Colt biplane and a few Hound helicopters, but I can't recall ever seeing either one."

"The Chinese, they were on the plane?" asked Corbett.

Fetterman nodded. "We saw them. Complete with a half-dozen or so Chinese paratroopers for a personal bodyguard and a cute little armored car."

"Hey!" said Bunnell. "Nobody said anything about the enemy having armor."

"It's just a little one," Fetterman assured him. "Besides, it won't be able to travel very fast or far through the jungle. If we stay off the roads, it's not going to cause us any trouble."

"I still think it needs to be killed," said Bunnell. "Damn, I wish we'd brought a bazooka or some RPG rounds."

Corbett brought them back to the more immediate concerns of their mission. "Are the Chinese still on the airstrip, Captain? Are we going to try for them now?"

"Negative," said Gerber. "Now we move. We stick with the original plan and take them tomorrow afternoon on schedule. They've got 100 to 150 guys out there right now, and we're too far from the pickup point and a day early. I don't want to ding these guys and have a company of Pathet Lao chase us all the way to the LZ only to find out the choppers can't make it because they're tied up somewhere else hauling ash and trash. Besides, we don't know how many troops they've got left back at that camp, and it's between us and the LZ. I figure we get in close now while they're busy thinking about other things, make our reconnaissance before dark and then get into position for tomorrow's turkey shoot. Besides, I don't think they'll be hanging around long enough for us to go back and take a crack at them now." As if to emphasize Gerber's point, the sound of truck engines could be heard starting up again.

"Captain Gerber," said Tyme, "what was all that racket we heard earlier? It sounded almost like music."

Gerber laughed.

"You're getting to be quite a critic in your old age, Boom-Boom," said Fetterman, smiling. "That stuff that sounded almost like music to your trained ears was the Royal Pathet Lao Marine Corps Marching Band, conducted no doubt by John Philip Sousaphone Sihanouk. I think they were playing the Chinese national anthem, but I'm not entirely sure."

"No shit?" said Tyme, laughing.

"Not understand," said Bhang. "Pathet Lao no have Marine band."

"You can say that again," said Gerber. "Let's get moving. Bhang, you take the point with Krung. We'll follow along in five. You know the route?"

"Yes, Captain," both answered.

"Fine. You run into any problems, one of you drop back and let us know what's ahead. At all costs avoid any shooting. We're too close to the camp. We don't want the entire Pathet Lao army coming down on top of us."

As Bhang and Krung moved off, Gerber said to the others, "We should reach the camp in a few hours, depending on how many patrols and outposts we encounter. With luck we ought to be able to get a look at the target area before dark and get into position tonight."

"Taking kind of a big risk, aren't we, Captain?" asked Fetterman. "Moving in that close in daylight, I mean."

"It can't be helped, Tony. We're running too damn far behind schedule as it is. I want to get a look at that place while there's still some light left. Come tomorrow morning, I don't want anyone moving around until show time. In my judgment, waiting till morning to conduct the recon would be taking an even bigger risk. We don't know what changes they may have made at the last minute that could require us to adjust our plan. I don't want to find out about alterations in the morning, be pressed for time and have to change everything, move everybody around, in broad daylight on the opening day of Chinese officer season."

"Yes, sir. I see what you mean," said Fetterman. "The hostiles will likely be even more alert for somebody trying to interrupt their powwow tomorrow."

Gerber turned to the Marine sniper. "Corbett, once we get to the camp and have a chance to scope things out, it'll be up to you to pick the locations for the members of the shooting team. Within the limits of tactical common sense, of course. You've got more training and experience in that area than anyone else, and I figure you can probably pick the best spots. Keep in mind that not everyone can shoot as well as you can. We want to do this thing right. We've only got one shot at it."

"Don't you mean six shots, sir? One for each target?" said Corbett with a smile.

"Seven shots," said Fetterman. "Let's not forget our old friend, Comrade Rhee." He didn't smile at all.

"Right," said Gerber, checking his watch. "Let's roll up the claymores and boogie, gentlemen. Fetterman, you're tail gunner."

"Riding drag again." Fetterman sighed, but he grinned briefly as he rose. Next to walking point, the trail position was perhaps the most important in a unit formation. It was that man's job to hang back a little behind the others and make sure the enemy didn't sneak up on the team from the rear.

While the others were gathering up their mines and preparing to move out, Krung and Bhang slipped quietly ahead through the scattered waist-high ferns and weeds. Bhang walked only a few meters behind Krung, closer than they would ordinarily have been spaced for daylight movement, in order to facilitate communication between them. She would advise him of potential trouble spots as they neared areas where she could remember the Pathet Lao having established outposts.

They didn't hurry. They would walk forward for thirty seconds, then pause and listen for fifteen while watching the forest around them. Although the precise interval varied anywhere from fifteen seconds to a minute and a half, they were careful to listen for at least half the time they moved.

They had traveled that way for perhaps an hour when Bhang came forward and placed a restraining hand on Krung's shoulder. "I think we near first outpost," she whispered. "It better I go forward alone now. You wait. I come back when know for sure."

Krung didn't like the idea. He was the scout, and it was his job to walk the point. He had far more combat experience than the woman, and besides, he didn't entirely trust her. For one thing, she was Laotian, and Krung had learned the hard way to have a healthy distrust of people not of his own race, although he had learned that some Americans could be trusted. Some Americans, Green Berets, for instance, but not all Americans. As far as Laotians were concerned, he had little firsthand experience. He had seen the woman's scars, but that didn't make her trustworthy. He had only the word of others as to who had given her the scars, and aside from them, no way of knowing for certain where her loyalties lay. She could be a Pathet Lao agent sent to lure a team of American Special Forces soldiers into a trap inside Laos rather than a CIA agent sent to lead them through dangerous territory. Krung's experience with CIA agents had taught him that they weren't trustworthy individuals, either.

Yet if the woman was who she claimed to be, her arguments made sense. Krung had no illusions about war being man's work. The enemy, both here and in Vietnam, made use of female soldiers as well as males. Krung could see no reason why he should operate by a different set of rules than the enemy. He nodded his assent, then crouched down to wait.

Bhang eased slowly ahead until she was out of sight. She was so intent on finding the bunker she remembered that she almost missed the first booby trap. Its trip wire was stretched only a few centimeters above the ground and was difficult to see even in the sparse cover. At first glance it appeared to be only a vine, but closer examination showed a cleverly concealed trigger mechanism attached to the kind of mantrap called a rake, a large square of woven bamboo or boards studded with sharpened stakes. It was attached to a small sapling or piece of green bamboo bent back under tension and held by a carved wooden trigger. Hitting the wire and releasing the trigger caused the bamboo or sapling to propel the wooden square forward with great velocity, impaling the unsuspecting victim on the sharpened stakes.

Bhang carefully avoided the trap and began looking around for others. In the space of twenty minutes she found three punji pits and a whip, a trap similar in operation to the rake, but designed instead to hurl arrows or spears into the chest of the person unlucky enough to trigger it. She reported back to Krung, warning him about the traps, and then went forward again, still looking for the bunker.

Bhang considered the traps to be a good sign. The Pathet Lao wouldn't go to all the effort of placing so many traps in an area they could cover with machine gunfire. One or two, perhaps, to initiate an ambush, but not five. When she located the bunker, her suspicion was confirmed. It was empty. So were the next two bunkers she found.

Bhang returned to Krung and the others and explained the situation. "Pathet Lao pull back from outer perimeter to strengthen positions close to camp," she explained. "They set out many traps and are sure to increase patrols. We must be very careful."

With Bhang and Krung both on point again, the team continued slowly forward. Bhang took them past the traps she had found, with Krung spotting and pointing out two others she had missed.

It was hard work, slow and miserable going, and in the hottest part of the day. Their bodies were covered with sweat and their clothing soaked with it. The mosquitoes feasted on them unmercifully until it was too hot even for the mosquitoes. The muddy ground from last night's rain covered their uniforms with a red-brown slime that hardened into a carapacelike second skin that cracked and flaked away as the heat slowly dried it out. The land seemed to slope steadily upward, but at times gave way to deep ravines that couldn't be circled, requiring them to clamber down steep banks and then struggle back up the other side. Inside of three hours they were all exhausted, and Gerber called a twenty-minute halt, which he let stretch into forty before continuing onward.

The fourth bunker they encountered, part of an inner ring, was occupied, but they managed to circle behind it. The fifth bunker was a new one Bhang hadn't known about, and they almost walked in front of it before Krung spotted the slightly domed earthen mound.

It was a well-camouflaged structure, with firing ports cut almost at ground level, and two others like it were nearby, sited so that each could provide mutual supporting fire. The team lost an hour finding a way around them and then ran into one of the most heavily booby-trapped areas they had yet encountered. All were thankful that the traps were crude constructions of native materials and not modern antipersonnel mines that would have been even more difficult to detect.

The most dangerous moment, however, came when they encountered an outgoing Pathet Lao patrol. There was simply no decent cover to be found, and all that Gerber's team could do was go to ground and practice becoming plants. The simple ruse worked, and the enemy passed some forty yards away without spotting anyone.

"This place is more crowded than Times Square on New Year's Eve," observed Fetterman after the patrol had passed.

"I wish it were Times Square," offered Tyme. "Then we'd only have muggers, prostitutes and pickpockets to contend with."

"What would you do, Boom-Boom, shoot them all?" asked Fetterman.

"Nah," said Bocker. "He wouldn't do that. Boom-Boom would just beat hell out of the muggers, lay the prostitutes and rob the pickpockets. Thieves need a dose of their own medicine, but you can't blame a working girl for trying to turn a buck."

"I tell you what I wish," said Bunnell. "To hell with Times Square. I wish we were in the East Village. Then we could stop in at McSorley's and have ourselves a couple of cold ones."

"And I wish you guys would shut the fuck up before somebody hears us, comes over here and shoots our asses off," said Gerber. "Jesus. You'd think you guys have never been in enemy territory before. What do you think this is, some kind of Boy Scout picnic?"

Gerber's criticism was a bit harsh. None of the men had spoken above a whisper. But the chastisement did serve as a reminder of the seriousness of the situation they were now in. None of the men took it personally, but all were quiet after that.

They waited until they were sure no one was following the Pathet Lao patrol and then moved on. Ten minutes later Bhang touched Krung lightly on the arm and held up a hand, then motioned the others forward.

"What is it?" Gerber asked anxiously. "Another patrol?"

"No, Captain," said Bhang. "It end of journey. Camp lie over next ridge. We arrive."

16

JUNGLE NORTH OF
PATHET LAO BASE CAMP
BAN TASSENG

"Well, what do you think?" asked Gerber softly.

"It's an interesting problem," answered Corbett, lowering his binoculars. "In some ways the action area works to our disadvantage, and in others it makes the job easier."

"Such as?" asked Gerber.

It was late afternoon and they were conducting a long-distance reconnaissance of the enemy camp, having successfully infiltrated through the outlying Pathet Lao patrols and outposts.

"As you can see," Corbett replied quietly, "our action area is fairly clear and free of obstructions, assuming intel was right about the signing taking place in that open-sided structure near the center of the camp. The whole place is laid out like a shallow punch bowl, giving us a slight height advantage from almost anywhere around the perimeter of the camp and allowing for unobstructed gun target lines. You'd have thought these guys would have picked higher ground. It's a pretty basic tenet of infantry operations to always take the higher ground.''

Fetterman frowned. ''Probably built it the lazy man's way—just started with a natural clearing and let things develop from there, like they did with the airstrip. It's easier to camouflage something from aerial observation if it lies below the level of the surrounding terrain, and it isn't quite as likely to show up on photo recon because the interpreters don't expect the enemy to build a camp at the bottom of a bowl. Either that or maybe these guys studied the same handbook as the French.'' Then, seeing the blank look on Corbett's face, he said, ''Dien Bien Phu.''

Corbett smiled, understanding both the geographical analogy and the tactical one. ''Let's hope it works as well for these guys as it did for the French.''

''It true what you say about camouflage,'' offered Bhang, who had guided them up to their little observation point. ''Mr. Maxwell tell me CIA not know camp here until my people get word out to them. Nearly all structures covered with nets and leaves. From up high just big clearing dotted with trees and brush. Not until American jet take low-altitude pictures you see in briefing do any details show.''

''That's right,'' continued Corbett. ''It's by no means a perfect job of concealment, but from up high it's probably good enough. Fortunately our angle isn't so great that we have to look down through all the nets, and we're close enough to pick out some pretty good detail beneath the ones we have to look through. If you don't mind, I'd like to get out one of the spotting scopes and have a better look at some of the structures down there.''

''I was just about to do that myself,'' said Gerber. ''Go ahead. You first.''

''Thanks.''

Corbett took one of the powerful Zeiss spotting scopes out of his pack and set it up on the little camouflage spray-painted tripod. He spent several minutes fiddling with the focus, changed eyepieces, then refocused before speaking.

"It's a good thing we're going to do this job long-distance," said Corbett. "It looks like they aren't entirely relying on camouflage to protect themselves from the air. I can see at least two 12.7 mm Degtyarev Shapagin heavy machine guns down there, a twin-mount ZU-23 automatic cannon and what looks like a 14.5 mm ZPU-4 quad-mount. That kind of hardware could cause us a lot of grief if they can bring it to bear on our positions once the shooting starts. All of them have an effective range of more than a thousand meters. The ZU-23 is probably twice that."

"You're suddenly awfully well informed about ComBloc antiaircraft weapons for a Marine NCO," said Gerber.

"I'm awfully well informed about what can kill me," replied Corbett, unruffled. "A sniper who doesn't know what can shoot farther than his rifle is liable to wind up dead, and then he'll be in a world of shit because Marines aren't allowed to die without permission—thus saith Gunny Anderson. This is serious shit, Captain. Those guns can outshoot us by a country mile, and the gunners don't even have to be particularly good at what they're doing to do it."

"Then I guess we'd better shoot fast and accurate and run like hell."

"That's pretty much the way I see it, too, sir."

"So how do we play this?" asked Gerber.

"Well, I don't think you're going to like this very much, but as I see it, we're going to have to split the team."

"Damn right I don't like it," said Gerber. "Weren't you the one who was just talking about basic military tenets? One of them, in case you've forgotten, is never divide your forces in enemy territory."

"I was hoping you would be unconventional enough in your thinking not to feel you had to abide by that particular maxim."

"Failing to abide by that maxim is what got Custer wiped out at the Little Bighorn. I don't intend that the same should happen to us."

"Custer didn't have the advantages we've got, sir."

"What advantages? We're outnumbered at least fifty to one, and that doesn't count whatever troops they may be able to mobilize off the Trail, or have garrisoned in town. You just told me they've got at least four guns down there with more range than we've got. They've probably got mortars and rockets, too. And they obviously expect some kind of trouble because they've tightened up security and pushed the tree lines back another hundred yards."

"I figure we've got surprise, stealth, mobility and accuracy on our side," said Corbett. "First, just because they've tightened security doesn't mean they're expecting trouble. It just means they're trying to be prepared for it, the same as we would. They don't know what form the trouble's going to take and they don't know where it's coming from. The Sioux knew Custer was coming. Those jokers down there don't even know we're here.

"Second, at this range, and with the Sionics suppressors, they won't be able to see our muzzle-flashes or hear our weapons. By the time they know they're being shot at, half the targets will be dead. By the time they get a reaction force organized to come looking for us, we'll be long gone. That's where the mobility comes in. We've got helicopters coming to pick us up and fly us out of Laos to safety. Custer could only stand, fight and die.

"And, finally, we've got good rifles with good marksmen behind them. Better than anything that lot down there has. Sure, they can hurt us with those heavy machine guns, but they haven't got the pinpoint accuracy we have. Those are area-fire weapons, and they've got to know what area to fire in. If we do this right, they aren't going to see or hear us, and even if they do, we can make it tough on them by giving them three different areas to deal with. Besides, it's just as easy to shoot an enemy gunner from nine hundred yards as it is to shoot an enemy general."

Corbett paused, then continued. "Anyway, Captain, putting shooters in different locations is the only way to be sure that one of us will have a clear shot when the time comes. Any little thing could queer it. A truck could be parked in the wrong spot, or a camouflage netting pole could get in the way, or somebody could step in front of the targets just as we start shooting. The enemy could find us at the last moment, and we'd have to move, losing our chance. It could rain and the wind could be blowing so hard that they might drape tarpaulins around the sides of that giant hootch, blocking our view. There's a thousand things that could go wrong. If we put shooting teams in each of three locations, one of them will be in position to do some damage. We might not get all the targets, but we'll get some of them, enough to disrupt the meeting, maybe enough to prevent the signing."

Gerber thought it over, Corbett seemed calm, self-assured. There was no indication that he was still having any second thoughts about being able to pull the trigger.

"You know," Gerber said slowly, "part of the idea of having the rest of us along was to provide security for the shooting team. If we have to split up, we won't be much help in that respect."

Corbett shrugged. "Someone's going to have to spot for each of the shooters, anyway. We'll just have to take our chances. Once we make the touch, we can fall back and regroup somewhere, then go on from there together. I know it's not a very elegant plan, but it's the best I can offer."

"Captain," Fetterman put in, "we need to think about making a recon of the exfiltration route, too. We're going to be in a big hurry when we leave this place. We go rushing headlong through the jungle without knowing what's in front of us, we could wind up running straight into an enemy bunker complex. Someone's going to have to scout things out beforehand."

"That true," continued Bhang. "Pathet Lao build *beaucoup* new bunkers, set *beaucoup* traps. You see it take us long time to come through on way in. We no have so very much time when leave, I think. We must know where bunkers and traps hidden so we can avoid, no waste time looking for same. I know where old bunkers will be, so it best I make recon."

"Not alone," said Gerber. "I won't risk that. Krung will go with you."

He turned back to Corbett. "Where do you want the shooting teams?"

"If I could put them where I wanted them, I'd put one on top of that small knoll about five hundred meters to the west of the assembly hall, another in that little grove of trees just south of the knoll and the third in that tree line at the edge of those vegetable fields on the south side of the camp. However, since we want this to work, I don't think any of those would be good places to be."

"Meaning?" asked Gerber.

"Meaning they're all obvious places for a sniper. They're the best places to shoot from, which means, assuming the enemy isn't completely stupid, that the Pathet Lao will either have established outposts there or will have registered their heavy weapons on them to ensure a quick response. Besides, they're too damn close to that ZU-23 for my liking."

"So where do we put the shooters?"

"Well," said Corbett, "somebody can shoot from right here. The range is only about eight hundred meters and it's a clear shot across the parade ground, although you might have to shoot over a few heads on those benches."

"That's a pretty long shot," said Gerber. "More than eight hundred and fifty yards."

"It's as close as we're going to get if you want to do this job and get out alive."

"All right. We know *you* can shoot from here. But what about Fetterman and Tyme? They're not as good shots as you are."

"Fetterman or Tyme can shoot from here. There's nothing closer. The other one can shoot from that first hill to the east of the camp. There's a little outcropping about two-thirds of the way up that you can see through the scope. A small group of boulders. Again, I make the range just about eight hundred meters. Whoever takes that spot will have to be careful because he'll be within range of that one 12.7 mm. The boulders ought to cover him, though. Once he shoots, he'll have to withdraw around the north side of the hill and come down the east side. That small stand of trees near the bottom would screen him from the machine gun for most of the way until he can put the second hill between it and himself. After that he's got about a hundred meters of open ground to cross to make it into the jungle, which should cover him as he finishes his climb up out of the punch bowl.''

"What's going to keep him safe where the trees don't screen him?'' asked Gerber.

"I will,'' said Corbett. "Once I've taken out my targets. I'll have plenty of time to make life miserable for the gunners on that 12.7. It's an antiair mounting, so they won't be particularly well protected from rifle fire from above. I won't even have to kill them. Just hit one or two so the others will want to keep their heads down.''

"I'll take the hill, Captain,'' said Fetterman. "I make a much smaller target than Boom-Boom does.''

"I'll spot for him, sir,'' said Bocker.

"There goes my size advantage,'' moaned Fetterman.

"Don't worry, Master Sergeant. I'll run bent over and duck a lot,'' said Bocker, placidly blowing a big gum bubble.

"And where will you be?'' Gerber asked Corbett.

"Right at the corner, where the tree line on the south butts against the jungle. I'll have to shoot across the mortar pits, but it shouldn't pose any serious problems.''

"And what if there *are* Pathet Lao in the tree line?''

"Like I said, I'll be at the very end of it. They shouldn't see or hear me, and if they do, I'm sure Captain Bunnell can keep them off me with that RPD of his long enough for me to make a couple of shots.''

"The range has got to be eleven or twelve hundred yards. Can you hit the target at that range?''

"Captain, you know I can. I'm not saying we'll get all the targets, but we'll get some of them. We may not kill them all, but it'll be enough to disrupt the meeting. That's what we came here for, isn't it? And it'll give us half a chance to get out of here alive. There's just one catch.''

"What's that?''

"From any of the positions I talked about, the angle's going to be high enough that we won't have good, clear shots at them seated at any sort of table down there. There's too much of an overhang to the roof. Since I don't see any of those trucks or jeeps, or that little armored car you and Master Sergeant Fetterman talked about, I'm assuming the Chinese will arrive by vehicle transport sometime before the ceremony. We'll shoot them before they get out of the cars."

"What if it's raining and the tops are up, or they don't park near the hall? What if they decide to walk?"

"Then we'll shoot them after they get out. We've got to take them before they get under the roof. It might not produce the same psychological effect as splattering the chief general's brains all over the document just at the moment of signing, but they'll be just as dead, and dead men don't sign documents."

Gerber looked at Fetterman. "What do you think?"

"I think a thousand-meter kill on a moving target is one hell of a long shot. I also think we haven't got any choice."

Gerber checked his watch. "All right. That's the way we'll do it. There isn't time to recon everything before dark, and I don't want anybody hitting a trip wire in the night, so we'll split now. I'll stay with Tyme. Krung, you and Bhang recon the route out, then establish an RP two hundred meters east of the second hill near the top of the ridge line. We'll meet you there when it's over. I'll signal you on the radio as soon as we've made the shots, although there'll probably be enough commotion in the camp for you to hear it. If we aren't there in thirty minutes, pull out. Don't wait for us any longer than that, or you might not be able to get out yourselves. Understood?"

"We'll use LZ Alpha Sierra Foxtrot Alpha Tango for the primary pickup site. LZ Charlie Indian Delta Golf Sierra will be the primary alternate, and India Mike Foxtrot Charlie Charlie will be the secondary alternate. If things turn to shit and you can't make the RP, try to make it to one of those and radio your position so we can pick you up. Does everyone have their HTs? Good.

"One last thing. We'll try to wait for Corbett to shoot first. Timing our fire together should give us the best chance of getting the most Chinese for our money. But each man is responsible for his own targets. If it looks like you're going to lose yours, like he's going to make it under the roof or step behind a truck or something, go ahead and take your shot. I don't want to lose them all because everybody's waiting for somebody else to shoot first. Questions?"

There were none.

"We'll see everyone tomorrow afternoon, then. Good luck and shoot straight. Now move out."

Corbett gathered up his spotting scope and the three teams headed out. When they were gone, Tyme set up his scope and readied his M-21 sniper's rifle.

"How about it, Justin? Think you can do it?" asked Gerber.

"It's pretty long, sir, but this is one hell of a good rifle. A lot better than what Charlie has. I'll be able to hit someone with it. Whether or not it's the right person, or I kill him, remains to be seen."

"You think we're trying this from too far out?"

"Fetterman and me maybe. Not Corbett. You've seen how he can shoot, Captain."

"Yeah," muttered Gerber to himself. "I just hope he does."

THE THREE TEAMS MOVED as a group until they reached the drop-off point for Fetterman and Bocker, Krung and Bhang heading away from the camp to the east to scout the escape route, Corbett and Bunnell continuing southward.

Corbett had expected Gerber to protest the personnel arrangements and had been a bit surprised when he hadn't. He had expected that Gerber would want to remain with him, since Corbett had the primary targets and Bunnell, although competent at normal combat distances, wasn't that great a long-range rifle shot. Gerber wasn't either, for that matter, but he was better than Bunnell and had a lot more experience with the M-21. If anything had happened to Corbett on the way in, Gerber would have been expected to take his place in the firing lineup, with the primary targets being shifted to Fetterman. Still, Bunnell was an officer and presumably capable of taking charge if something went wrong. The burden of taking out the primaries was now clearly in Corbett's hands.

Corbett thought of what lay ahead and was annoyed to find that his hands shook a little. This was the most important job of his young life. He would probably never again have to make a shot under such difficult conditions and would certainly never have such an important target as the two men he would kill tomorrow. It was no time to develop a nervous tremor.

He tried to cope with it by concentrating on how he would do the job. The range tomorrow would be more than a kilometer, the longest at which he had ever killed a man, though he had hit targets at even longer range. There was no reason for this to be any different. He just had to remember to think of them as targets and not as human beings. They were the enemy and he had his orders.

There would be only seconds for him to identify and shoot his targets. Bunnell would have to make the actual recognition. There wouldn't be time to shift from the spotting scope to the ART on the rifle, and at a thousand meters the magnification of the rifle's scope wouldn't be great enough for a positive identification of the target's facial features. He would have to depend on Bunnell to tell him who to shoot. Then he would pick one of the targets the Special Forces captain pointed out to him, regulate his breathing and squeeze the trigger until he felt the recoil of the weapon. He would shoot until the first target went down and then, without rushing, shoot the second if it was still visible. Worrying too much about hitting them both might cause him to miss altogether. Like shooting quail, it was better to single one out and take your time with the first shot, then try for a double once you were sure of the first kill.

It is not the rifle that kills. It is the heart of stone of the man who squeezes the trigger, Gunny Anderson had said.

Corbett wished he could turn his heart to stone, wished he could find some reason for hating the men he would kill tomorrow. It would make the job more palatable. It was difficult to kill people you had nothing against personally. The United States wasn't even at war with Red China, at least not officially, although he knew the Chinese supplied war matériel and advisers to the VC and NVA, as did the Russians, Cubans and East Germans, while the Czechs supplied assault rifles and ammunition.

All those war supplies were used to take American, South Vietnamese, Cambodian and Laotian lives. He knew that, and knew also that the situation would worsen if the protocol agreement for Chinese intervention to protect the Ho Chi Minh Trail was signed. He told himself that by taking a handful of lives tomorrow the team might prevent the deaths of thousands in the future, but it was a cold, military expedience kind of logic that didn't set well with his personal values and moral code.

The Communists, whatever their nationality, might indeed be hell-bent on world domination, but so was the West in its quieter, capitalistic sort of way. Did it really matter if you imposed your way of life on other cultures with economics instead of bullets?

The enemy did terrible things, but he had killed a fifteen-year-old girl. Wasn't that a terrible thing also? Was he really very much different from the people he had been sent here to kill? Maybe that was what war was all about—doing terrible things to other people. But why? Why do them at all? Because some people needed to be killed, as Bunnell was fond of saying? Did anyone really *need* to be killed?

Bhang thought so, and so did Krung. They both agreed that Communists, of any variety, needed killing. Was it right to exterminate people simply because they held different views than you did?

No, it wasn't. And it wasn't right for them to kill and maim others for the same reason, either. To kill to impose your views was one thing; to kill to defend yourself or others from such imposition was something else. Corbett wasn't quite clear on precisely how it was different, but his gut instinct told him it was.

Corbett thought of the Vietcong who were trying to impose their particular brand of world order on South Vietnam, of the Khmer Rouge who were trying the same thing in Cambodia and of the Pathet Lao who had managed to do the job on half of Laos, Bhang's homeland.

It is better to have freedom, Corbett, she had told him. The freedom to choose your own government and not have one rammed down your throat at the point of a gun.

Corbett thought about the kind of People's Freedom the Pathet Lao had brought to Bhang's people—the freedom to be tortured and mutilated in the name of extracting information. There was a difference, he decided, between himself and the enemy. He might be able to shoot a fifteen-year-old Co Cong smuggling guns to guerrillas, but he could never bring himself to do to a young woman what the Pathet Lao interrogators had done to Bhang.

She, Krung and Bunnell were right.

Some people needed to be killed.

17

**PATHET LAO BASE CAMP
BAN TASSENG**

Duc Van Co lay in the narrow confines of the shooting box on the second hill east of the camp, his body awash in a small sea of mud and cold rainwater, and silently cursed his stupidity for not having put an elevated floor in the structure. He had spent a wet, miserable night there in order to be in position before daylight, a precaution he considered an exercise in futility since he didn't believe the Americans were coming, but one which prudence and his orders from Comrade Rhee dictated.

He had eaten breakfast at eight—a couple of rice balls and a few sips of water from his canteen. The rice balls had been soggy, as was nearly everything else in the small three-sided bunker. Only his precious Dragunov rifle, carefully wrapped in his poncho and suspended from the ceiling's thin bamboo beams, had remained dry.

The rain had started a little past midnight and had continued unabated ever since. By his watch he saw that it was nearly noon and wondered if the ceremony would be postponed or moved to a less exposed location if the weather didn't let up soon. Surely the visiting Chinese comrades wouldn't want to get their important papers wet.

Duc could see with any clarity only a few meters beyond the firing port of his position, so heavy was the rain. The neighboring lower hill, which he was expected to keep free of mythical, suicidal American snipers, was only an indistinct gray blur. It gave him some small comfort to know that if he couldn't see an enemy on the hill, neither could such an enemy see well enough to make the eight-hundred-meter shot to the assembly hall at the edge of the muddy parade ground. That was why he hadn't yet bothered to unwrap the Dragunov.

Duc shivered and pulled his thin, waterlogged blanket closer around him. It did little to warm him. He was thankful that the broad leaves of his carefully constructed camouflage had produced a fairly waterproof roof. At least it had saved him the additional insult of being dripped on. There were a few leaks, but for the most part he could avoid them. All the water on the floor of the bunker, and there was a lot of it, had come as runoff from the slope of the hill behind him, filling the shooting box from its open rear side.

The rice balls hadn't agreed with his stomach, and his bowels churned agonizingly. He closed his eyes momentarily and tried to ignore the sensation, but the pain wouldn't go away. A sudden spasm warned him of the impending event, and he just managed to slide backward in the muck, crouch near the end of the bunker and pull down his trousers before his sphincter muscles gave way to the inexorable pressure and he let fly a very liquid stream of excrement. He wondered briefly if he might have food poisoning, or if he had contracted amoebic dysentery again. Emptied, he leaned weakly against the side of the bunker for a moment, then, because he had no dry paper or cloth, he washed himself with the muddy water covering the dirt floor of the bunker. Unsteadily he pulled his trousers back up and crawled forward into position once more.

Feeling slightly better, he lay down in the filth to continue his senseless vigil. This was Laos. There were no Americans to kill here. He should be back in A Shau, where targets were plentiful. In the A Shau Valley he need wait only long enough for the Americans to come to him. The possibility of any action on this cold and dreary day seemed remote.

Yet Duc knew he had chiefly his own expertise to blame for his discomfort. The Chinese comrade in charge of security had feared a sniper threat, and so had sent for the best man available as a countersniper. Being in this miserable excuse of a bunker was, in a way, a high compliment. Rhee had needed the experience, judgment and skill of the best sniper in the NVA and had sent for Duc. Still, surely comrade Rhee could have dealt with the situation just as easily by putting a squad of soldiers on the hilltop below. Why he hadn't done this, but instead had chosen to give Duc the responsibility for its security, Duc couldn't say. It was, he felt, perhaps some sort of test—the Party was always testing its members—but what sort of test, and why, he couldn't imagine. His instincts told him it was, in some way, connected with the visit of the Chinese generals and their ceremony scheduled for this afternoon, connected in some way other than the obvious one that he was there to help protect them.

Duc knew he might never have the answer to his unspoken questions, but after this afternoon the test, whatever it was for, would be over. The Chinese officers would be gone.

He put his face up near the firing port and checked the view outside, but there was still nothing to be seen. He sighed and consoled himself with the thought that he had only a few more hours to wait.

FETTERMAN AND BOCKER huddled beneath their tiger-striped Portuguese army ponchos, trying to keep their radios dry and heat enough water in a canteen cup placed over a tiny bit of burning plastic explosive to rehydrate and warm a couple of chili and macaroni camp dinners. With the rain falling, their efforts weren't going all that well, but then they didn't have to worry much about someone hearing or seeing them and interrupting their meal, either.

They were crouched among the boulders, well back from the edge of the rock shelf where Fetterman would actually do his shooting when the time came. There was no point in being out there now, because there was nothing to see. The rain was falling so hard that the camp below was barely visible, and anyway, it was too early. The Chinese delegates weren't expected until late afternoon. Besides, Fetterman had already noted that a man lying out there could be seen by someone near the top of the second hill, and he had no intention of exposing himself until he had to, just in case the Pathet Lao had been clever enough to put an observer up there. When the time came, he and Bocker would have to crawl out on the shelf and take their chances doing the job, but until then they were going to continue practicing being invisible.

"What do you think the odds are of really pulling this thing off?" asked Bocker, munching on a mouthful of chili and macaroni that wasn't quite warm enough yet to taste like anything other than cardboard and rubber. The rain kept trying to wash the food out of his plastic spoon before he could get it to his mouth.

"It's hard to say, Galvin," answered Fetterman. "The range is awfully far. We were all hitting the targets during practice, but not necessarily with a killing shot. That was eight hundred yards, too. This is well over eight hundred fifty. Those cardboard targets weren't moving, either. The real ones probably will be, and after the first volley's fired, you can bet on it.

"With a bit of luck I'll probably be able to hit my first man. With a bit more luck, Tyme might get one of his. I wouldn't count on either of us getting the second. Corbett's got nearly three hundred yards farther to shoot, but I wouldn't be too surprised if our young Marine lad actually gets both his men. The kid's really good.

"Of course, if they come up on the wrong side, we might miss everybody. On the other hand, if we get all the breaks, we could get them all. It may take them a couple of minutes to figure out where the shots are coming from. That could be all we need. Realistically I figure we might get two to four of them between the three of us. It all depends on exactly where the targets are located and what they can find to hide behind once they figure out what's happening to them. Naturally," he added with a smile, "the odds will be better if you do a good job of spotting for me."

"And what about the seventh man—Rhee?" asked Bocker.

"You heard the colonel. We've got permission to take him out if we can."

"That's not exactly what I meant. What if he shows his face first? Suppose he steps out of the car before anyone else?"

"Damn it, Galvin, I want the man dead. You know that. But this is too important even for him. If we have to let him get away in order to get the main targets, then he takes a walk. Of course, if he happens to get in the way of a bullet after the first volley's fired, I don't think anyone's going to blame us for that, so long as we hit one of the big shots first.''

"It would be nice to finally end it with this guy," said Bocker. "We owe him a lot of payback."

"Yeah," agreed Fetterman. "And when we finally do even accounts with Comrade Rhee, I want to make sure that in his case payback is *no* Medevac."

RHEE PACED back and forth in the lobby of the Hotel Coronet. His manner was agitated, and he realized that he was chain-smoking his precious Marlboros at an alarming rate, but couldn't seem to force himself to slow down. Things were beginning to fall apart, and he didn't like the smell of it.

It wasn't anything major, or even anything specific that he could put his finger on, just a bunch of little things that by themselves meant nothing. Nevertheless, Rhee was a man who firmly believed that things happened for a reason, and looking at the whole picture, he found it unsettling.

First there had been the affair of Bhangsang Souphonaphouma, General Kang Mang's mistress, who had turned out to be a spy for the American CIA. Then had come a low-level pass by a jet, presumably an American fighter, which had overflown the base several days ago, perhaps a reconnaissance plane looking for the camp, and perhaps only some off-course jet jockey.

After that had come the brief, apparently stray bursts of RF transmissions picked up by the com-sec radio operator at the camp, little more than a transmitter breaking squelch and too short in duration to triangulate a position fix on. They had been noted the night before last and could have come from a hundred kilometers away or a hundred meters outside the camp's perimeter.

Late yesterday he had been informed that a Pathet Lao soldier, a female comrade, was missing from her patrol of the previous evening. She had apparently lagged behind her unit and became lost in the dark and rain. There was as yet no clue to her whereabouts. It was possible that she was simply lost, or that she had decided to desert. It wasn't uncommon for Pathet Lao soldiers grown tired of the fighting to simply walk away from their unit and return to their home village. It was also possible that something less benign had occurred.

And then there was the business of the delegates' aircraft. The pilot had reported some trouble in flight with one of the engines, and an examination made after the landing had shown a defective part. Rhee was forced to ask himself it it could be sabotage. In any event the aircrew mechanic had been unable to repair the problem, effectively stranding the delegates. A new apparatus to replace the broken part was to be flown in from the military airfield at Dong Hoi as soon as the weather permitted.

These were just a collection of little events, individually without meaning. Yet to a paranoid individual they could be seen as the first brush strokes of a sinister portrait, and as chief of security for the meeting, it was Rhee's job to be paranoid. Had they occurred at any time other than in close proximity to the meeting, he would have thought little of them, but he wouldn't even have been here to be aware of them were it not for the delegates' visit.

Rhee couldn't imagine what more precautions he could take than he already had. The patrols had been increased, as had the number of outposts close to the camp. He had arranged for Pathet Lao troops to occupy any potential trouble spots and had arranged for Duc Van Co as a countermeasure to the sniper threat. Yet with all that he still felt ill at ease. He had attempted to discuss his feelings, both with General Kang Mang and with Senior Colonel Chow Ping Lai after the delegation arrived, but he had had only suspicions and hunches and feelings, and without some form of proof they wouldn't listen to him. The political issues were too important, the propaganda value too great. They wouldn't consider canceling the ceremony. The signing must take place as scheduled, regardless of the weather or Rhee's feelings. Nothing must be allowed to disrupt the protocol process. It was more than just a piece of paper; it would change the entire face of the war in Indochina.

Rhee had listened to their arguments and wondered why they wouldn't listen to his. It was precisely because the document was so important, precisely because nothing must be allowed to interfere with its signing, that the ceremony should be moved to a new location and time, he had pleaded. He might as well have been trying to persuade the Great Wall to get up and move a few hundred meters. They simply didn't hear him. Colonel Chow had informed him that the delegates had no time for the silly little fears of a paranoid.

So while the dignitaries of three countries enjoyed their excellent brunch and chatted amiably with local businessmen and politicians about matters largely unrelated to the true purpose of their visit, Rhee paced the hallways and worried about the small detail that had been overlooked, the unsubstantiated threat that lurked in the jungle waiting to strike and destroy everything, the phantom Green Beret raiders who just might ruin it all.

KRUNG WOULD HAVE LIKED to pace, but didn't want to risk any more movement than was absolutely necessary. Twice now, once last night and again early this morning, Pathet Lao patrols had passed near his position. He had no desire to attract their attention again. A single AK-47, no matter how skillfully employed, was no match for a well-armed enemy patrol.

Krung was alone on the RP. The high-profile enemy presence, coupled with an abundance of traps and bunkers and rapidly diminishing light, had forced Bhang and him to explore separate escape routes for the team last night, and Bhang hadn't returned.

The Nung tribesman was at his wit's end with worry, for fear she had been captured by the Pathet Lao, but there was nothing he could do about it. He wanted to inform Captain Gerber of the disturbing situation, but there was no way for him to do it. The simple patterns of broken squelch they had worked out were insufficient to convey the message, and he didn't dare risk a voice transmission on his little radio. Nor could he chance daylight movement to go tell him personally. He could only wait and hope for the best. If Bhang was a prisoner, there was nothing anyone could do about it, anyway.

Krung's job after scouting a withdrawal route was to establish an RP and secure it for the others. He had done that, insofar as it was possible for one man to do. To move from the RP now, however important the news he might be carrying, could easily make matters worse.

While Krung waited he heard a faint rustling in the brush, and a moment later Bhang appeared. She was walking along in a crouched posture, moving slowly with frequent pauses and obviously searching for something, presumably him.

Krung remained silent and waited until he was sure no one else was with her. When she was almost past him, he whistled softly, and when she looked in his direction, he moved slightly so that she would be able to spot him. She didn't acknowledge his signal but came directly to him and knelt beside him.

"What happened?" Krung asked. "Where have you been?"

"I have some trouble," she told him. "It take longer than I expect and it dark before I could start back. The rain not yet started and I making good progress when meet two Pathet Lao. It too dark they see me good, but still see each other outline. I almost walk into them."

"You kill them?" asked Krung with growing apprehension. One man wandering alone through the dark might not be missed for some time, but two soldiers traveling together would surely be missed. If the enemy started looking for them, they might find the team before they could shoot the Chinese.

"Not kill them," answered Bhang. "They look for woman you kill night before. They say they think maybe she run away because tired of being soldier. In the dark they no can see face, so think maybe I her. I tell them no, but they no believe. They say must take me back to camp for reeducation. I not want go. I think maybe to kill them, but worry others come to look if they not return camp. I have to..." She hesitated. "I have to make deal with them."

Krung was instantly alert, suspecting she had led the enemy to him. "What kind of deal you make?" he asked, his voice low and threatening.

"I no can kill them without risk mission," insisted Bhang. "They think I missing woman, so I tell not want to go back to camp. Tell want to go home to family instead. I tell if not take me back, I make deal.''

"What kind of deal?" Krung asked again, trying to inconspicuously ease the safety off his AK-47.

Bhang hung her head and wouldn't look at him. "I make deal," she said. "I tell if no take me back, I entertain them."

Krung was puzzled. "What you mean, entertain?"

Bhang suddenly glared at him defiantly. "I entertain them. Man to woman. Entertain. You understand. Make the boom-boom."

Krung was taken aback. It wasn't at all what he had expected. "Both of them?"

"Yes, both. Of course. You think maybe only one want to make boom-boom?"

Krung shook his head. "Just surprised they not make you go to camp after boom-boom."

Bhang looked disgusted. "Make much boom-boom. Boom-boom for long time. First one, then other one, then first one again, then his friend again. They make much boom-boom long time."

Krung shook his head again. "When they let you go?"

"Not let go. Make much boom-boom long time. They get tired. Finally I sneak off after boom-boom both same time. They not want to go back to camp then. Only want sleep."

"I understand," said Krung. "Just hard to believe. I think maybe one would stay awake so you not slip away."

"They no care about that when finish," asserted Bhang. "Just want sleep. I make very good boom-boom. Last long time."

"Not doubt that," said Krung.

Bhang looked as though she were going to hit him.

Krung held up a hand. "Not be mad," he said. "No insult. You do right thing."

"I do what must for sake of mission," replied Bhang. "That is all. You think maybe they come look for me, anyway? Maybe tell others about find?"

"No," said Krung. "I not think they tell others find missing Co Cong and make boom-boom with her, then fall asleep and let get away. Not look good to officers. I think they keep mouths shut."

"Then what I do right?"

Krung nodded once. "It right. You do good. Keep team safe, mission secret. You brave soldier. I fight Communists with you anytime."

Bhang stared at him for a moment, and then her face softened. He thought that perhaps she would cry. "Make me feel unclean," she said. "I need to know did right thing."

"You do right thing," he said. "Do not worry. They not come look for you. They not tell anyone. I not tell anyone, either. You have no reason for feel bad. You do only thing possible."

She did cry then, and Krung, in a gesture of sympathy and affection unusual for him to display, reached out and held her gently against his shoulder with one arm. "Do not worry," he repeated. "You do right thing. And do not cry. You feel better after we kill a few Communists."

"Yes," agreed Bhang. "Feel much better then."

18

PATHET LAO BASE CAMP
BAN TASSENG

The rain had stopped an hour earlier, and with its ceasing, the wind had died and the air had grown oppressively hot. Overhead, gunmetal-colored clouds continued to hang, threatening a repeated downpour, but there were a few scattered patches of clear sky beginning to show to the northeast. Gerber pressed the soft rubber eyecups of the binoculars to his eyes and scanned the ground below.

The Pathet Lao camp was laid out in a more or less circular pattern, necessitated by the surrounding terrain. It reminded Gerber vaguely of the Barringer Meteorite Crater near Winslow, Arizona, although on a less rugged and shallower scale, and he wondered briefly if the two landforms might be of similar origin.

Looking southward from his position, he saw a number of longhouses, presumably serving as barracks, then the flat parade ground, and beyond it the large, tin-roofed, open-sided assembly hall with its dozen rows of rough-hewn bench seats between it and the parade ground. There were smaller huts scattered around, including what was obviously a generator shed, and one with several pole and long-wire antennae outside it, suggesting a radio shack. Beyond the assembly hall were more huts, a sort of obstacle course, three mortar pits that he could see and what might be a kitchen and mess hall, judging from the traffic in and out of it. There were some bunkers, and several items he couldn't positively identify because of their camouflaged coverings. Light antiaircraft guns sat in sandbagged, circular revetments in several locations. Then there were a couple of larger hootches, similar to the barracks, and some fields, apparently used to grow vegetables for the camp's food supply, running on down to the tree line that cut between the fields at the extreme southern edge of the depression.

Although there were no roads as such through the camp, dark openings in the surrounding tree lines suggested that at least three roads approached the camp's perimeter and had been screened from aerial observation by having the branches of trees growing along either side tied together over the roadway itself.

"It looks like the party's still on," said Gerber, offering Tyme the binoculars. "Here. Have a look."

Tyme passed on the binoculars with a shake of his head and rolled over to have a look through the more powerful spotting scope.

"A lot of activity going on down there at the assembly hall," Gerber continued.

"Yeah," agreed Tyme. "They're putting up banners and posters and stuff and setting up chairs. Where do you suppose they got all those folding chairs, anyway?"

"Who knows?" said Gerber. "Maybe they ordered them from Sears, Roebuck."

Like Tyme, he was used to encountering the enemy chiefly on patrols, or in bunker and tunnel complexes in Vietnam. It was always something of a surprise when the mission took them into Laos, Cambodia or North Vietnam and they discovered the other guys had large, well-organized camps, often of a permanent or semipermanent nature, established in the sanctuary countries or home territory.

"I wish they'd get on with it," said Tyme. "There's nothing I hate worse than dragging things out."

"Patience, Justin. At least we know they're coming. Otherwise they wouldn't be hanging out all the decorations."

"Maybe they're already down there."

"I don't think so," said Gerber. "Not just yet anyhow. I didn't see any vehicles. There were two trucks full of soldiers, three command jeeps and that little Chinese armored car at the airstrip yesterday. I don't see any of them down there now. They probably spent the night in town."

"The roads all stop at the edge of the perimeter, Captain. You think they'll walk from there?"

"I wouldn't bet on it," Gerber told him. "They're generals, and generals, no matter what army they're generals in, don't like to walk. They'll probably pull up right next to the hall, roads or not."

"That's going to cut down on the amount of time we've got to shoot. Once they get beneath that overhanging roof, we won't have a clear shot any longer." Tyme wasn't offering a protest or an alibi, just an observation.

"Don't worry about it, Justin. We'll have plenty of warning. There's no need to get excited about it before they start lining up the audience. You don't think they'd pick this spot, this location, unless they wanted a crowd, do you? It's a big event for them. When they start filling up those benches down there, then it'll be time to start getting ready. If it's like most public appearances, the crowd will be ready at least an hour before the guests arrive. These clowns have traveled a long way for this. They'll want to play to a local audience.''

"Yes, sir. It's just that—listen! Hear it?''

Gerber strained his ears. "Helicopter," he said. "Sounds as though it's headed our way. That's just terrific. All we need is some Air America cowboy picking today to buzz this place. It'll spoil everything if he spooks them.''

"There it is.'' Tyme pointed to a speck in the sky west of the camp. It seemed to be coming from the north-northwest and was headed pretty much toward them.

Gerber trained the binoculars on it. "It looks like a Sikorsky. I wonder what the— Wait a minute. It isn't an S-55. It's a Hound. I'll be dipped in shit if it isn't a Commie helicopter. I'll bet it's headed for that airstrip we found.''

"Jesus!'' said Tyme. "First an Antonov An-8 and now a helicopter. Why the hell doesn't the Royal Lao Air Force do something about all this shitbird air traffic?''

"They probably aren't even aware of it,'' said Gerber. "I wonder what it's doing here?''

"I wonder if they've got any more surprises?'' said Tyme sourly. "The next thing you know they'll start air-dropping tanks.''

"Just so long as they don't start dropping bombs. If I remember right, some of those things can, and they all carry a machine gun pod under the forward fuselage,'' said Gerber.

"Great. Now they've got helicopter gunships.''

"Well,'' allowed Gerber, "it's not really a gunship, but I wouldn't want it shooting at me.''

The sound of the helicopter's engine increased, and the aircraft began a slow descent toward the spot west of the camp where the airstrip was hidden. They watched it descend until it vanished among the trees, then turned their attention back to the camp below.

"Better begin getting ready," said Gerber. "They've started filling up the benches down there. Our pigeons must be on their way."

RHEE RODE in General Kang Mang's radio jeep at the head of the column. The general himself was two vehicles back with Lieutenant General Fan, Colonel General Quai and General Nguyen. A truck carrying several Pathet Lao honor guards was between the two GAZ-69s. Major General Le, Major General Phan and Senior Colonel Chow followed in the third command car, with a truck full of troops behind them and the armored car bringing up the rear. Kang's aide-de-camp and the propaganda ministry camera team rode with Rhee. He did his best to ignore them.

Rhee was glad to have finally gotten things moving. He'd feel better once he had the dignitaries safely inside the camp. There were just too many places along the road from town where ambushers could be lying in wait. He wouldn't feel completely safe, though, until the delegates were on their way back to the north. Once they boarded their airplane, they were the responsibility of the pilot and the lieutenant in charge of the airborne security squad. Then, and only then, could Rhee relax.

Before they left the Hotel Coronet the radio operator in the command car with him had informed Rhee that a helicopter had arrived with the replacement part for the transport aircraft and that repairs were proceeding and should be completed by the time the ceremony was over. Rhee had been surprised that they'd used a helicopter. He had expected them to fly the part in in an An-2 like the one that had brought Duc Van Co. It was unusual for the

North Vietnamese to risk one of their helicopters outside
their country. But then there was much about this whole
affair that was highly unusual. At least it had been decided to dispense with the inspection of the camp and
proceed directly to the protocol signing. The rain had
lasted into the afternoon and put things behind schedule,
and the delegates were anxious to conclude their business
with the protocol and be on their way home.

There was the usual gauntlet to be run of a carefully
prepared throng of flag-wavers and hand-clappers, small
but enthusiastic and politically correct, to ensure that all
the generals felt suitably important. Then they were out
of town and following the main road until they turned off
on the hidden route to the camp.

This was the part that Rhee dreaded the most, despite
the fact that the area had been swept for mines early this
morning and continuously patrolled by foot and bicycle
troops since. The cover was close in to the sides of the road
in order to hide the road from the air, and from practical
experience Rhee was familiar with just how devastating
an ambush with automatic weapons could be from close
range.

There was a bad moment when the convoy, struggling
along the muddy route, had to stop for a limb that had
fallen across the way, but it was only a limb and there was
no accompanying ambush. It was quickly moved out of
the way and they continued onward, lurching through
ruts and standing puddles that splattered them with dirty
water until they came to the camp.

Cutting deep ruts, which would take some labor to fill
but which it would be up to somebody else to fix, they
drove down the hill and out of the jungle, crossed the perimeter of the camp and headed straight for the assembly
hall, where a crowd of by now no doubt extremely bored

soldiers waited to finally find out what all the fuss and hoopla of the past few days was all about.

CORBETT WATCHED the little column of vehicles pull into view to the north of him between his position and the hill on which Fetterman waited. Two trucks, an armored car and the three open-topped GAZ-69s. That was a good sign. It made the job easier. He had been worried that they might still have the canvas tops up because of the recent rain, which would make it difficult, if not impossible, to tell who was in which car. With the tops down he might be lucky enough to get both his targets before the men ever stepped out of the cars.

The route took them close to the base of Fetterman's hill, and he hoped that the master sergeant wouldn't get antsy and fire too soon. Timing was everything if they were to get all the targets, and if Fetterman decided to take the easy shot as they were passing by, the range would be too great for Tyme to add his firepower to the assassination attempt.

Corbett needed time to set his shots up as well. Not much, but it would take a few seconds. He'd had to place Bunnell where he could cover the tree line with the RPD after they'd heard voices, indicating there were Pathet Lao perhaps only a hundred meters away. That meant he would have to do his own spotting before he shot.

Corbett swung the spotting scope over to check Fetterman's position. Knowing exactly where he would shoot from, he expected to be able to see Bocker and the master sergeant, but found only boulders and the empty rock shelf in his eyepiece. Panicked, he moved the scope to glass the second hill, fearing they had misunderstood him. The range to the assembly hall from the second hill was nearly thirteen hundred meters, and he was afraid that would be too far for Fetterman to handle.

At first he saw nothing, then, as he swung the scope back, he saw the thin line of a rifle barrel poking out of a clump of bushes on the wrong hill. The shape told him that it didn't have a Sionics suppressor on the muzzle. For perhaps two seconds he was puzzled, and then he understood with sickening clarity. He glanced back toward the camp. The convoy was almost to the hall. Without hesitation he moved his rifle barrel away from the center of the camp, dragged his pack around and rested the rifle across it. He found the spot near the top of the second hill and dialed in the maximum range, estimating the additional holdover he would need. It was a bit more than twelve hundred meters. In the scope the rifle barrel looked like a toothpick. Corbett welded his cheek to the stock, steadied it against his shoulder with his left hand and snapped off the safety. He regulated his breathing and took up the slack in the trigger.

FETTERMAN AND BOCKER had waited until the last possible instant to crawl out onto the rock shelf. The lead vehicle had halted by the time they were set and both men had their eyes pressed to scopes, Fetterman's to the rifle's and Bocker's to the spotting scope, when dirt suddenly flew up near Fetterman's elbow, sprinkling his face with rock chips. The bullet glanced off the flat rock, whizzed past Fetterman's head, missing it by less than an inch, struck the boulder farthest out to his left and ricocheted back, tearing into the backpack strapped to Bocker's shoulders and plowing through the HF radio inside.

"He's above us," yelled Fetterman, rolling for the additional cover at the back of the rock shelf. It was only then that he was aware of hearing the report of the rifle.

Bocker lay without moving, fully exposed on the shelf, an odd, tingling sensation coursing through his body. He tried to open his mouth experimentally a few times and finally managed to get the words out, "Tony," he said softly. "I'm hit."

Fetterman reached out and grabbed Bocker by the ankles, hauling him to cover as a second bullet screamed off the rocks where Bocker's head had been only moments before. The radio was protruding through a rent in the pack, a mess of splintered glass and twisted wire. It looked as if a miniature bomb had gone off inside it. Fetterman yanked out his knife and cut the shoulder straps, then ripped open the back of Bocker's camouflage jacket. There were bits of glass, wire, sheet metal and blood all over the place. Bocker was bleeding from the side of his head, too.

"Jesus Christ," hissed Fetterman, knowing it would be better to say nothing, but unable to keep the words from slipping from his lips.

A third bullet screamed past them, flaking off bits of rock, but it was farther away, almost clear out to the end of the shelf.

"Tony, is it bad?" asked Bocker, a pounding, rushing sound in his ears. And then the curtain of gray descended and Bocker closed his eyes.

DUC VAN CO HAD WATCHED as the convoy from town drove out of the trees and into the camp, and still there was no sign of any enemy. Then, when the vehicles were almost to their destination, he had seen the movement he had been looking for but never really expected to see. Two very well-camouflaged men, one of them with a long-barreled rifle, appeared exactly where he had predicted on the boulder-surrounded rock shelf. An enemy sniper team.

Duc didn't hesitate. He shouldered his Dragunov SVD, which he had unwrapped an hour and a half earlier, chambered a round from the 10-shot magazine, sighted and squeezed the trigger.

He intended his first round to take the man with the rifle in the upper back and thought for a moment that it had as the target jerked suddenly sideways, but it appeared the man had only rolled away. The second man hadn't moved, however, and Duc fired again quickly, aiming for the head. He couldn't tell if he had hit the man or not, as his partner suddenly yanked him backward among the boulders at the rear of the shelf.

Duc corrected his aim, still able to see part of the man, and was squeezing the trigger a third time when a force like a swinging two-by-four slapped him across his face and his rifle flew from his suddenly numb hands. Momentarily stunned, he didn't realize that he had been struck by the butt of his own rifle as the weapon was shot from his hands, and he lurched upward, trying to grab the Dragunov. As he did so, he staggered too far upright, punching through the thin overhead camouflage of his shooting box and above the safety of its thick timber walls.

Corbett's second and third rounds took Duc in the chest.

The greatest sniper in the North Vietnamese Army looked down with curiosity to see what had struck him. He could see two dark stains beginning to spread around the two neat little holes in his shirt, but he couldn't see the two large wet patches on his back or feel the blood beginning to fill his lungs. There was surprisingly little pain, but it was suddenly very hard to breathe. He coughed to clear his throat, coughed again and managed to eject a wad of bloody sputum, then slowly toppled over the side of his carefully constructed shooting box.

Duc Van Co's last thought was that now that he had finished his job perhaps he would finally get the parade he deserved.

TYME HAD BEEN CAREFULLY tracking his targets in the third command car ever since Gerber had identified them for him as the convoy pulled into view. When he heard the first shot ring out, he adjusted the scope to frame the target between the stadia wire of the ART and fired immediately. It was only with the muffled report of his own rifle that he realized he had fired early. He was supposed to wait for Corbett, and Corbett was using a suppressor like his own. Tyme shouldn't have heard him fire, only seen the results.

The bullet missed and bored into the seat between Major General Phan Van Phouc of the North Vietnamese Army and Senior Colonel Chow Ping Lai of the PLA. Knowing that the attempt was now no longer a secret, Tyme fired again, missing his mark completely as a second rifle report echoed across the dish-shaped valley. Incredibly the GAZ jeep came to a full stop, providing a stationary target.

Tyme put the cross hairs of the scope on Phan's head and tried again, shooting him through his good left eye. The back of the man's skull exploded outward in a shower of gray and white brain tissue, and he slumped on the seat as though he had suddenly grown tired.

Tyme's fourth and fifth shots struck Senior Colonel Chow in the region of the right collarbone and the lower left abdomen. The man was slammed back against his seat, twisted out of it and fell over the side of the little four-wheel-drive truck, landing on his face.

"There's one more," said Gerber. "In the front seat. Take him."

Tyme adjusted his aim and fired three more rounds, two of the bullets striking Major General Le Shao Quan in the hand and arm.

For reasons known only to General Le, he attempted to crawl over the windshield of the command truck, and a final bullet from Tyme's shattered both it and the general's spine.

It had taken him nine rounds to do the job, but Tyme had just shot three men from a range of more than 860 yards, killing one of them outright and mortally wounding the other two. It was the best long-distance shooting he would ever do in his life.

"Three down," said Tyme.

"Come on, Justin, let's get the hell out of here. We've done our bit for world peace. There's no point in getting greedy about it," said Gerber.

"Sir, what about Rhee?" Tyme reminded him.

Gerber shifted the scope back to the lead vehicle, but it was empty. He could see someone trying to hide on the other side of it, but couldn't tell who it was. It wasn't Rhee, though, because the man was wearing black pajamas.

"To hell with it," said Gerber. "He's gone."

"Gone where?" demanded Tyme.

"How the hell should I know, Boom-Boom? I can't see him any longer. Now pick up your pack and let's get out of here before they figure out we're up here and start dropping mortar shells on our heads."

Tyme found the prospect of being mortared sufficient motivation for leaving and pulled on his pack. "We're out of here," he said.

As soon as he had killed the enemy sniper, Corbett shifted his sights back toward the column of vehicles. There was no time for the spotting scope now. He would simply take targets of opportunity. He checked the nearest command car, saw that there were already at least three bodies in or near it and went on to the second car. He aimed only for the light-colored uniforms, figuring them to be the Chinese.

Corbett left the range finder dial at its maximum setting but still had to adjust his holdover point. The distance was about 1150 meters. He sighted on the back of the head of a man in an ivory-colored uniform trying to climb over the side of the truck, did his breathing routine and took in the slack with his finger. When the weapon went off, he put the round through the left lung and left ventricle of the heart of Colonel General Quai Chi Lim.

Corbett looked but couldn't see any more ivory uniforms or khaki and green ones. There was an abundance of black ones, however, so he took his time and shot three of them, using one round apiece. Although Corbett didn't know it, the second one was a fifty-seven-year-old general of the Pathet Lao who had once had a young mistress who turned out to be a spy for the CIA. The bullet struck Kang in the groin, and he bled to death holding his mutilated manhood before the camp doctor could get to him. His aide-de-camp died a bit more quickly at his side.

Corbett was considering whom to shoot next when a flash of something white near the rear wheel of the lead truck caught his eye. He sighted carefully, breathed, squeezed and shot Lieutenant General Fan Song Huynh in the chest. The bullet severed the descending aorta, punctured the pancreas and lacerated the liver. General Fan lived for almost five minutes.

For good measure Corbett adjusted the bullet drop compensator on the ART down to six hundred meters and shot the five-member gun crew of the nearest 12.7 mm machine gun as they rushed toward their weapon pit.

BOCKER WOKE to a stinging slap in the face, felt another one land and put up a hand to ward off any follow-up blows. Vaguely he was aware of the sound of Fetterman's voice shouting at him.

"Galvin! Galvin, wake up!"

Bocker didn't want to wake up, but he didn't want Fetterman to hit him again, either. He said as much.

"Come on, Galvin, you're alive. Damn it, wake up! You're too goddamn big for me to carry you!" shouted Fetterman.

Bocker slowly opened his eyes and tried to focus them. There were two Fettermans leaning over him. One of them in the world was enough, he thought. He had the worst headache he'd ever had in his life.

"Listen to me," Fetterman was shouting at him. "You're going to make it. A rock chip hit you on the ear and knocked you out. That's all. Your back is a mess, but it doesn't seem to have any real holes in it. The round was pretty well spent when it hit the radio and drove part of it into your back. Galvin, they know where we are. We've got to get out of here. Can you walk?"

Bocker thought it over for a moment before answering. His tongue felt thick in his mouth, and the words were a little bit slurred, but he got them out. "Walk, hell!" he said. "Get my feet under me and I can run."

Fetterman pulled him upright and held him there for a moment to make sure he wouldn't fall over.

"What the hell happened?" asked Bocker.

"There was a sniper on the hill behind us. He damn near got us both, but somebody got him first. I can see him up there, hanging partway out of some kind of bunker. I think we're going to owe Corbett a case of Beam's Choice when we get back to Kontum. Can you stand yet?"

"Give me a second or two," said Bocker. "I can't see too well yet. Jesus, I feel like shit."

"You'll live," said Fetterman. "That's all that counts." The master sergeant took his rifle and cautiously ducked out onto the shelf to retrieve the Zeiss spotting scope. He jammed it under the flap of his pack and cinched the straps, then pulled on the rucksack. He slung Bocker's AK-47, took his own M-21 in his right hand, stuck out his left and pulled Bocker to his feet. "You okay now, Galvin?" he asked.

"Hell, no," said Bocker, picking up the cut straps of his own pack. "But I'm up and I'm functioning. Let's get the fuck out of here."

ONCE HE REALIZED that people were no longer dying all around him, Rhee lost no time in organizing a response. He had gambled and lost and his career was probably in the toilet, but he could still make those responsible pay.

He saw to it that General Nguyen Chi Thon, the only dignitary who had escaped the massacre, was safely ensconced in a bunker ringed by a company of armed soldiers and that the hillsides surrounding the camp were pounded by mortar and heavy machine gunfire. He had the mortar crews pay special attention to the two hills east of the camp at the bottom of the valley. He assumed that since he hadn't fired again after the third shot, Duc was dead, and in any event, the man was now considered expendable. After that he sent out patrols with trackers to try to pick up the enemy's trail, and then called the Chinese paratroopers over to him.

"Lieutenant Wu," he said, addressing the paratrooper commander. "Take your five men to the airstrip and prepare the helicopter for immediate flight. I'll personally select an additional five men from our Pathet Lao allies and follow you as soon as possible. When word is received from the patrols as to the enemy's direction of movement, we'll use the helicopter to get in front of them and kill or capture them."

Lieutenant Wu looked uncertain. This was more than he had bargained for. Nobody had said anything about getting directly involved in a war. He was just supposed to protect the generals.

"Lieutenant, in case it has escaped your powers of observation, your charges are dead. You may consider your obligations to them discharged. Your orders place you under my direct command. You'll prepare the helicopter for flight and stand by to pursue the enemy. You may consider that a direct order."

"Certainly, Comrade Captain," replied Wu. He'd had enough experience, both with the Party and the military, to know when it was and wasn't wise to try to buck the system. He and his small detachment of men piled into their little armored car and took off for the airstrip.

Within an hour Rhee had the report from one of his patrols that Duc Van Co was dead and that blood had been found on the rocky shelf of the first hill east of the camp, indicating that the enemy had been wounded. Additional patrols were dispatched to look for the enemy's trail. Forty-five minutes later they found it, and a twenty-man patrol equipped with a radio and a team of trackers was in pursuit.

Rhee received the news with a surprising amount of cheer for a man who had just seen five generals and a senior colonel, whose safety he was responsible for, have their lives snuffed out before his eyes.

"Now, my mysterious silent killers," he said to himself. "Now we shall find out just exactly who you are and what kind of men you are to be able to kill the best sniper in the North Vietnamese Army as well as five generals and a colonel. And we shall also," he added, "find out if you're fast enough to outrun a helicopter."

19

JUNGLE EAST OF BAN TASSENG

Bhang and Krung were waiting at the RP when Fetterman arrived with Bocker, the slight team sergeant supporting the massive communications specialist on one shoulder. Bocker didn't really need help holding himself upright, but he was still suffering double vision and kept walking into trees without Fetterman to guide him.

Fetterman gave his and Bocker's claymores to Krung to set out, adding to their limited defensive capability, then dragged out the late Sergeant Yoon's medical bag and grenade launcher.

He handed the M-79 to Bhang and asked, "You know how to use this?"

"Of course," she said, taking the weapon and the four bandoliers of 40 mm grenade rounds that went with it. "I not expert, but have used before."

"Swell. The woods will probably be crawling with people looking to kill us in a little bit. There's no point in secrecy if they find us."

"Understand," she said. "Do not worry, Master Sergeant. We take many with us before we go."

"I hope the only place we're going is the pickup point," replied Fetterman. "Just be ready in case trouble shows up." He turned to Bocker. "How's the head?"

"Hurts like hell and I'm still seeing two of everything, but they're a little closer together, whatever that means."

"That's a good sign," Fetterman replied. "At least I think it is. I'm going to have a go at cleaning up that back of yours while we wait for the captain and the others. You want something for pain before I start?"

Bocker shook his head, then stopped because he didn't want it to fall off. "I'm having a hard enough time seeing what I'm doing now. You shoot me up with morphine and I'm liable just to lie down and go to sleep until the Pathet Lao come and find me. Just get out your forceps and dig away, Dr. Mengele. I'll bite on a bullet like they do in the Westerns or something."

"Right, Hoss."

Fetterman set about the business of picking slivers of glass, metal and wire out of Bocker's back and cleaning it up with hydrogen peroxide. When he finished, he covered the injured area with a large sterile dressing and secured it with roller gauze, then fastened the jacket back together with safety pins. After that he went to work on the cut on the communications sergeant's ear and the side of his head.

"I think you're probably going to need a couple of stitches in the ear," Fetterman told Bocker. "It'll look a whole lot prettier if I don't try to do it. I've put a couple of butterfly closures on it, which seems to work fairly well, and covered it with a dressing and bandage. Try not to mess with it, or it could start bleeding again."

"I'll try not to get hit in the head with any more rocks," Bocker promised. "What about the back? I thought I was a goner for sure when he hit me. Everything felt all tingly and I couldn't move for a little bit."

"Near as I can figure," said Fetterman, "the sniper's first round hit on my right, glanced off the rocks and whizzed past my head, struck one of the boulders and rebounded into your pack, where it wrecked the radio. The bullet must have been flattened out the size of a golf ball by then, and moving at about the same speed. It smashed up the radio and the impact drove a bunch of the little pieces into your back. Probably just stunned you. It looked a lot worse initially than it turned out to be. I've got a feeling you won't be sleeping on your back for a few days, though."

"I'm not complaining," said Bocker. "And I'll never gripe about carrying one of the damn heavy things on my back again. I know a lot of guys don't like lugging a radio because RTOs tend to draw enemy fire, but this makes the second time that having a radio strapped to my back kept me from going home with a Congressional Medal of Honor. You remember what happened in North Vietnam?"

Fetterman nodded. "I remember. You didn't exactly get away lucky on that one, Galvin. You were hurt pretty bad."

"I'd have been pretty dead if the radio hadn't slowed down the slug."

In the distance they could hear a lot of heavy automatic weapons opening up.

"You think they found some of our guys?" asked Bocker.

Fetterman listened for a minute, then shook his head. "Sounds as though it's all outgoing from the camp. General suppressive fire. They're probably just trying to blanket the area, hoping to hit somebody or at least keep their heads down until they can get a reaction force into the field. Pretty much standard countermeasures for a sniper threat.''

"We wouldn't be able to hear any return fire from an M-21 with a suppressor,'' Bocker pointed out.

"True, but we would from an AK-47 or an RPD. Besides, the firing's general, not concentrated.''

Bocker listened for a minute, then nodded very carefully. ''Let me have my rifle back, will you?''

Fetterman unslung the AK and passed it over. ''You feeling better?''

"I'm still seeing double, if that's what you mean. I figure if I bump into a Pathet Lao, I can just shoot both of him.''

"Maybe you ought to shoot between them instead,'' said Fetterman.

"Whatever. At least I can put out rounds in their general direction.''

Gerber and Tyme arrived a few minutes later, breathing as though they had just run a mile carrying all their equipment, which wasn't far from the truth.

"Where's Corbett and Bunnell?'' Gerber asked, breathing heavily as he dropped beside Fetterman.

"Not here yet,'' answered Fetterman. ''Captain, Bocker and I ran into a little bit of trouble. Seems the enemy had a sniper of their own looking for guys like us. We didn't get to fire a shot.''

Gerber noticed Bocker's bandaged ear and asked, ''You okay.''

"Got some double vision and one hell of a headache, but I'll be okay. Radio got shot to hell. Saved me from taking a bad one in the back, though.''

Gerber glanced at the safety-pinned jacket and raised a questioning eyebrow.

"Nothing to worry about Captain," Fetterman put in. "Just a lot of little pieces of glass and metal from the radio. I got most of them dug out just before you got here."

"When the bullet hit the radio, the impact sort of stunned me," Bocker continued. "Couldn't move for a minute. Fetterman was pulling me out of the line of fire when their boy got off a second round and almost caught me in the head. The master sergeant says a rock chip banged me in the ear and knocked me out for a couple of minutes."

"What happened to the enemy sniper?" asked Gerber.

"Somebody took him out before he could get a good bead on us again," said Fetterman. "I figure it must have been Corbett. We just got the hell out of there. Like I said, we didn't get a chance to shoot."

"I did," said Tyme.

"Do any good?" asked Fetterman.

"I hit three of them. I got Phan and Le for sure, and I definitely hit Chow. I think I killed all three."

"Attaboy, Boom-Boom," said Fetterman. "That ought to screw up their little ceremony. Did you see Rhee? He was in the first car."

"We saw him on the way in," said Gerber, "but he disappeared when the shooting started. We never saw him again after that."

"Damn it!" swore Fetterman. "That son of a bitch is slipperier than an eel. I really thought we had him this time."

"Maybe it just isn't the man's time," said Gerber. "It'll come, though. He can't live a charmed life forever."

"The bastard's done okay so far," Fetterman reminded him.

"Captain, if you don't mind, I'd like to check out the backup radio you're carrying while we wait," said Bocker.

"There's some good trees here for a long-wire antenna, and I might be able to get a signal out before Corbett and Bunnell get here. It would save us having to stop later on, and if they've got an RDF capability, I'd rather they got a fix on us now than later."

"Do it," said Gerber, shucking his pack.

Bocker quickly set up, tuned the radio and strung an inverted V antenna with the help of the others. He dialed in the primary frequency and used a knee pad bug to transmit the team's call sign and attention signal. On his third attempt he got a reply and sent the appropriate coded message. The unknown operator in the MACV-SOG TOC acknowledged receipt and repeated the message. Bocker confirmed its correctness and signed off. The whole exchange took less than three minutes.

"They've got it," said Bocker, switching off his set.

Just then they heard the concussion of a couple of fragmentation grenades, followed by the sustained *brrrupp, brrrupp, brrrupp* of an RPD light machine gun, a sporadic crackling of rifle fire, a very long burst from the RPD, two more grenades, more rifle fire, a pause followed by two more explosions, three additional burst from the RPD, the last of which was cut off short, what sounded like two pistol shots, and then silence.

"Sounds like Bunnell and Corbett are coming and they've got company with them," observed Gerber. "Galvin, break down that radio. Krung, Fetterman, start rolling up the claymores. I think we're going to want to leave in a hurry."

CORBETT HAD BEEN POTSHOOTING occasional Pathet Lao in the camp whenever one of them was foolish enough to show himself. It wasn't hard to find targets. The camp was full of them. He had just dinged either an officer or an NCO, apparently trying to rally the panic-stricken troops, when he heard Bunnell open up with grenades and the RPD and knew it was time to go.

He gathered up the spotting scope and stuffed it into his pack, struggled into the harness, slung his binoculars around his neck and used the butt of his rifle to shove himself up off the ground. He turned to give Bunnell a hand and was horrified by what he saw.

The Special Forces adviser was doing a John Wayne, assaulting all by himself an enemy patrol that had come up the tree line. He was screaming like a banshee, firing the RPD from the hip and hurling grenades in front of him. A couple of the Pathet Lao were shooting back, and Bunnell suddenly went down. Corbett snap-shot the two nearest enemy soldiers, hitting both men in the chest. Bunnell then threw two more grenades, got back up and charged again, still firing. The RPD suddenly jammed, and Bunnell ran headlong into the remaining two Pathet Lao who had been stunned by the grenades, knocking them over before they could react. He drew his Browning pistol from its holster and shot both men in the face at point-blank range.

"What the hell are you trying to do, get yourself killed?" yelled Corbett, running over to him. "I thought Green Berets were supposed to be smarter than that, uh, Captain."

Bunnell was bent over, breathing hard. He still had the pistol in his hand and the machine gun slung around his neck so that it hung in front of him. With his left hand he was trying to stop the blood flowing from his leg. "Fuck, I'm getting too old for this shit. Didn't want any of the bastards to get away and bring back help."

"Does it matter?" asked Corbett. "The whole jungle has heard where we are now."

"In a general way only. These guys could have led them to the exact spot."

"Here, let me take a look at that leg for you," said Corbett, kneeling.

Bunnell waved him away. "Later. I can walk on it. That's all that counts. Let's get the fuck out of here. We don't want to miss the others at the RP." Bunnell turned and started to limp off, grimacing every time he put weight on the hurt leg. "Christ!" he said. "The fucker hurts. I sure as hell wish I had a beer."

IN THE TOC at the MACV-SOG compound in Kontum, a radio operator pulled the yellow flimsy sheet from his mill and handed it to the duty signals officer, a young lieutenant, who took it down the short hallway to the tiny office where Colonel Alan Bates had waited anxiously since early morning, drinking too many cups of GI coffee and fouling the air with an endless chain of cigars. The signals officer knocked twice and waited for permission to enter.

"Come in," said Bates. "Yes? What is it?"

"Message from SAT-team Chuck Connors, Colonel," the signals officer told him.

Bates paused with his cigar halfway to his mouth and said, "Read it to me."

"Yes, sir. The message reads as follows: 'Personal to Crystal Ball. On secondary transceiver. Confirm three kills. Others unknown this time. Full hunting party hasn't reported in yet. One friendly remaining behind.'"

"Is that it?" asked Bates.

"Yes, sir. That's the whole message."

"How's it signed."

"Just with the team's code name, Colonel. Chuck Connors."

Bates let out a sigh that was half relief and half concern. The team had gotten at least three of their targets, but which three? Furthermore, what did it mean that the others were unknown? Had they not shown, or was Gerber unsure if they had been hit? And what did it mean that the entire hunting party hadn't reported in yet? Had the team members been forced to separate for some reason? And why were they using the backup transceiver?

The only thing he was sure about was the last part about one friendly remaining behind. Either one of the team had been killed or he had been too badly wounded to continue or be carried out, in which case Gerber would have followed his orders and completed the unpleasant task of finishing off one of his own people. There could be no living prisoners left behind for the enemy to stage a show trial with.

"All right," said Bates. "Make a signal to Green Hornet Operations at Air Studies Group in Nha Trang. Tell them the extraction team for Chuck Connors is now on standby status. I want the air assets forwarded to here immediately in case we have to pull those boys out early. And tell them to be damn sure to bring the McGuire rigs and the rope ladders. I don't want our boys left standing on the ground looking stupid if the LZs are compromised or the team can't make it that far."

"Yes, sir. Signal to Air Studies Group in Nha Trang. Extraction team for Chuck Connors is now on standby status. Air assets are ordered forwarded to Kontum and are to be sure to bring McGuire rigs and rope ladders," repeated the signals officer.

"I said they're to be damn sure. Send it priority one," added Bates.

"Yes, sir. Damn sure to bring McGuire rigs and rope ladders. Priority one." The signals officer started out the door, then paused.

"Is there something else?" asked Bates.

"Well, not really, sir," said the signals officer. "The radio operator who handled the traffic wanted me to tell you something. I don't think it was important."

"I'll judge what's important if you don't mind, son," said Bates. "What was it?"

"Sir, he wanted me to tell you that the originating operator had a fine business fist, despite the Lake Erie Swing, and he wondered who it was if it wouldn't be violating security. Do you understand what that means?"

Bates smiled. "Yes, I do. Tell your man the originating operator's name is Bocker, and if I ever hear him mention it again, I'll have him shipped to Alaska until he's ready to retire."

The signals officer smiled back. "Funny you should mention it, sir. He's talked about nothing else except retiring to Alaska ever since he came to Vietnam."

"In that case tell him Panama," said Bates.

"Yes, sir. I'll tell him what you said."

Bates checked his watch after the signals officer left and saw that it was nearly 1800 hours. It was going to be a long night and he hadn't eaten lunch. He got up and went down the hallway to stick his head into the radio room and let the duty officer know where he could be found, then walked over to the mess hall to see what was for dinner.

The cook had done a pretty fair job on a beef Stroganoff, but for all the attention Bates paid to it, he might just as well have been eating C-rations. He kept wondering which member of the team wouldn't be coming home and how he or she had died.

CORBETT AND BUNNELL arrived at the RP, with Bunnell limping badly.

"We had a little trouble with a Pathet Lao patrol," Bunnell reported.

"Did they follow you?" Gerber immediately asked.

"They won't be following anybody except angels," said Bunnell, "assuming they don't go the other way, of course."

"You got them all?"

"Corbett got two of them. I got the rest."

Gerber looked at Corbett. "What about the mission targets?"

"I got two of them also, Captain. Both Chinese. I couldn't get a positive ID, so I just had to shoot guys in ivory uniforms."

"What do you mean, you couldn't get a positive ID?"

"After I took out the sniper who was shooting at Fetterman and Bocker, I didn't have time to positively ID the targets through the spotting scope. They were already going for cover and I couldn't see well enough through the ART to identify faces. I saw two guys in ivory uniforms, like you said the Chinese big shots were wearing, and I shot them. I'm sorry, but I can't tell you which Chinese they were."

"I can," said Tyme. "Colonel General Quai Chi Lim, and Lieutenant General Fan Song Huynh. You got your targets."

"How do you know?" asked Corbett.

"Because I got Chow, Le and Phan."

"Nice shooting," said Corbett. "If they ever kick you out of Special Forces, we'll give you a job as a Marine sniper."

"Me a Gyrine?" said Tyme. "No thanks. I heard they beat you guys with chains and feed you raw meat in boot camp."

"Not really," said Corbett. "The meat's usually cooked."

Fetterman was busy bandaging Bunnell's leg. "Did either of you see Rhee?" he asked without looking up.

"Negative," said Corbett. "Like I said, after I got the sniper off your back, I couldn't get a positive ID on anybody. I shot a lot of other people, though. Maybe one of them was Rhee."

Fetterman shook his head. "Nope. The bastard's still alive. I can feel it." He looked up hopefully at Bunnell.

"Sorry. I was busy with the Pathet Lao patrol. I couldn't spot for Corbett. That's why we've got no positive ID on the Chinese. Maybe he was one of the other guys Corbett hit."

"Not this guy," said Fetterman as he finished tying the bandage. "He's bulletproof."

"Nobody's bulletproof one hundred percent of the time," said Corbett.

"Gentlemen, this is neither the time nor the place for this," said Gerber. "We got five out of seven. That's pretty damn good shooting in anyone's book. If we got Rhee, fine. If not, there's not a hell of a lot we can do about it."

"We could go back and make sure," said Fetterman.

"You can't be serious."

"Not really, I guess. It was just a thought."

"Well, stop thinking like that. Just give it a rest, will you?"

"No, sir," said Fetterman. "Not ever. Not until I know for sure the SOB is history."

"All right, fine, Master Sergeant," said Gerber irritably. "Have it your own way. But not here and not now. As far as I'm concerned, the mission was a success. We did our part, got five out of the six intended targets, Rhee being only a bonus. We're definitely not going back looking for him."

As if to punctuate Gerber's comments, mortar shells started to rain down on the hill behind them. "I vote we put a little more distance between us and those mortars," said Gerber, "and nobody else gets a vote. Now let's get out of here. Krung, you and Bhang take the point. Stay ten meters in front until it gets dark, then drop back so we won't lose you. Everybody else at five-meter intervals. Tony, you've got the rear, and I expect you to keep up. Let's book it."

20

PATHET LAO BASE CAMP
BAN TASSENG

"Comrade Rhee, we have evidence of two separate blood trails," reported the Pathet Lao captain whose name was so long that Rhee could never remember it, let alone pronounce it properly. "Apparently the enemy was in at least two separate groups, and one of them ran into one of our patrols before joining up with the other group. All nine men of our patrol are dead. Two of them were shot in the face, execution style. The enemy evidently then rejoined their unit and the two groups traveled on together. I have a large patrol with trackers and a radio following them, and more men on the way, but it will be some time before they can catch up. I'm afraid we may lose their trail in the approaching darkness."

Rhee's interpreter translated both sides of the conversation between the two men.

"That you must not do, Captain," said Rhee. "Put every available man into the pursuit. We must not allow the enemy to slip through our fingers."

"I've already given the necessary orders, Comrade. However, you must realize that the enemy has a considerable head start. We may not be able to catch up."

"Then we must delay them," said Rhee. "What's their direction of travel?"

"Almost due east. They'll cross the Trail in an hour or two at most."

"Then signal our comrades on the Trail to intercept them."

"Comrade," said the Pathet Lao officer, "you know that's not possible. Many of our units lack adequate communications capability, particularly those units moving supplies down the Trail. I've alerted what guard posts I can to watch out for the enemy and asked those that can spare the men to send out patrols. That's all I can do."

"It's not enough," said Rhee. "And it's not all I can do. Show me their last reported position on the map."

The two men consulted the map laid out on Rhee's desk. "It appears their route will take them toward this area," said the Pathet Lao.

Rhee studied the map a moment and nodded. "Yes. They undoubtedly hope to reach one of these open areas by morning, where they can be picked up by helicopter, but we won't allow that to happen. By a stroke of luck we have our own helicopter. I'll take the men I have selected and use the helicopter to land here first at the nearest of the possible landing fields. Then we'll be in front of them. It'll be up to you to push them toward us."

"I understand, Comrade. But it's nearly dark. We may lose the trail, and anyway, will the pilot of the helicopter be able to see the landing field?"

"He'll have to," said Rhee. "I'll have him drop us off ahead of the enemy. You must arrange to have the airstrip lighted for his safe return."

"Won't that expose the airfield to enemy planes?"

"The enemy may already know of its existence. You'll have the fires lighted when you hear the helicopter return and extinguish them as soon as it lands. I also want General Nguyen escorted to the airstrip under heavy guard as soon as the transport plane is repaired. He must leave at once before another tragedy occurs."

"I'll make the necessary arrangements, Comrade."

"Good. Then do so now. I'll leave at once for the helicopter. You must also have ready an additional squad of men to reinforce us. Have the pilot of the helicopter fly them out to this position at first light," said Rhee, pointing to the spot on the map. "We'll meet them there."

When the Pathet Lao officer left, Rhee gathered up his five handpicked Pathet Lao soldiers and his interpreter and headed for the nearby airstrip in the late General Kang's command car. Upon his arrival he encountered an unexpected problem. The North Vietnamese pilot refused to make the flight.

"It's already too dark," he argued. "We won't be able to see the landing field and will crash into the ground. We'll all be killed. My crew and I won't be part of any foolish suicidal scheme to chase some mythical enemy into the night."

Rhee took the man aside and spoke with him in Vietnamese. "I have no time to argue with you," he said in a very low, calm voice. "You'll take us where we wish to go, or you'll die right here. If your helicopter isn't ready for flight in five minutes' time, I'll shoot you myself." To emphasize the point he pulled out his Tokarev and pointed it at the Vietnamese's head.

The pilot blanched. "You're bluffing, Comrade. You wouldn't shoot me. If you kill me, who'll fly the helicopter for you?"

"Perhaps your copilot will be more tractable once he's witnessed your lifeless form," said Rhee.

"And if he isn't?"

"Then I'll shoot your mechanic. If he still doesn't wish to take us after that, I'll shoot him."

"If you kill both of us, there'll be no one to fly you," the pilot told him. "The crew of the transport isn't qualified to do so. You'll simply ensure that you go nowhere."

"Perhaps that's true," Rhee replied softly. "But you and your crew will be dead."

"Don't be ridiculous. If you shoot us, the repercussions from Hanoi—"

"Would be as nothing compared to the repercussions I already face from Peking. I have allowed a senior colonel and four generals for whose safety I was responsible to be killed. I'm already a dead man, Comrade Pilot. It's of no consequence to me if I have to kill a few people to get what I want. Unless you have a strong desire to join me in the afterlife, I suggest you cooperate."

"You wouldn't dare," the pilot almost screamed.

"Yes, Comrade. You're right," Rhee told him sedately. "I wouldn't dare. After all, I have too much to lose." He cocked the hammer of the Tokarev. "You now have two minutes."

The pilot looked at Rhee and then at the pistol the Chinese held. The open mouth of the muzzle was pointed directly at his right eye, and Rhee's hand was absolutely rock steady. He considered trying for his own side arm, but under the circumstances that was certain to be the last act of a fool. Slowly he raised his hand and swung it in a circular motion over his head. Behind him he heard first the whirring of the electric starter as his copilot cranked over the engine, and then the engine itself as the Mi-4 coughed to life.

"CAPTAIN, we're definitely being followed," said Fetterman.

He had dropped back a bit to check their trail and had caught up with the others again only moments before.

"Numbers. How far?"

"A pretty big patrol. Maybe twenty or thirty men. They're making a lot of noise. Can't be more than ten minutes behind us. Fifteen at the most. Distance-wise, they could probably spit twice and hit us, but they're having trouble following our trail, even with lights."

"They're using lights?" Gerber asked incredulously.

"It's their home turf, Captain. I reckon they figure they can use lights if they want to. Who's going to see them but us? And we aren't likely to want to hang around and meet them."

"They'll follow us right to the LZ," said Gerber. "We've got to come up with something to slow them down."

"How about we take a couple of minutes to rig a mechanical ambush? Nothing fancy. Just a couple of claymores on some trip wires. Even with the lamps they're using, they ought to be pretty hard to spot in the dark."

Gerber did some fast thinking. "How far do you figure we are from the Trail?" he asked Bhang.

"Maybe thirty, maybe forty minutes."

"Okay. We can't afford to get caught between these clowns and the troops on the Trail. If they have a radio, they've probably already radioed ahead for someone to meet us. We'll rig the ambush right here. We'll lay a false trail to the southeast beyond the ambush, then swing northeast and cross the Trail just below the town. Once we're across, we'll swing back southeast again and head for the pickup point."

"Captain, do you think that's wise? Crossing so close to town, I mean?" asked Fetterman.

"It's not something I'd try normally," Gerber admitted. "Let's hope the bad guys think the same way. What do you think, Bhang, can we do it?"

Bhang considered for a second, then nodded. "It possible, I think. Know place were guard posts far apart. We cross there okay if no traffic on Trail."

"Right, then. Let's set it up. Tyme, Krung, one claymore apiece. Set them about fifty meters apart."

"Captain, if I may suggest a slight refinement?" said Fetterman.

"Let's hear it."

"Tie the first one to a tree, angled to fire up the trail and run the trip wire well ahead. Place the second up the trail angled to fire back down it. If they trip them both, they'll get hit from the front *and* the rear. It ought to confuse hell out of them. I'd also like to tie a CS grenade into the trip wire for the first claymore. It'll only take about a minute longer to do, and when the grenade pops, it'll panic them, hopefully into the second mine."

"Go. Do it."

In five minutes the trap was ready and they hurried along the trail. They had gone six or seven hundred meters when they were rewarded by a metallic-sounding explosion, followed by wild bursts of firing, and a short time later by a second shattering blast, followed by lots of firing.

"I think that's going to take them a little while to sort out," said Fetterman, bringing up the rear of the column. "Sounds like they're shooting the hell out of one another back there."

For good measure he paused briefly to wire a second CS grenade and a WP grenade to a small tree along the side of the trail, then stretched a trip wire from the pins across the trail at about throat height. He was gambling that after hitting the claymores and the first CS grenade, the enemy would proceed slowly, carefully searching the ground ahead for the almost impossible-to-spot trip wires. A man with a lamp looking for trip wires close to the ground would walk in a bent-over posture. He might not see a thin, camouflage-painted wire at head height and walk right underneath it. The men following along behind him wouldn't be so lucky, and the combination of CS and WP was intended to produce the maximum psychological effect.

By angling to the northeast they didn't intercept the Ho Chi Minh Trail as quickly as they would otherwise have done. The Trail was actually a collection of footpaths and roads running throughout the area, but it was only crossing the roads that was a major problem. They carried the heaviest volume of traffic, especially at night, and large convoys, sometimes made up of several dozen trucks and hundreds of men could be encountered. Groups of bicycle porters might pass down the roads every fifteen or twenty minutes on a moderately busy night. There were also roving patrols to be considered, and guard posts every few hundred yards. The Ho Chi Minh Trail was one of the most heavily defended pieces of real estate in all of Southeast Asia, and if the Chinese did come in under the terms of the protocol agreement, the situation would be compounded considerably.

Enemy defensive measures along the Ho Chi Minh Trail were geared chiefly toward protecting it from the FWMF aircraft, mostly American, that bombed and strafed traffic moving along it day and night. Every half mile or mile there was an antiaircraft machine gun or automatic cannon. The enemy felt fairly secure from ground attack here, though, so while there was a preponderance of AAA, there were very few mines or booby traps. The greatest danger was from air-dropped antidisturbance mines and de-layed-action bombs, which the United States Air Force sowed in great numbers on the roads and surrounding areas. The region south of Ban Tasseng had been left alone for the past few weeks in preparation for the raid by Gerber's team, but it was conceivable that there were still some such devices lying around.

The team crossed three heavily rutted mud roads without incident, being delayed only once while a group of about twenty porters pushing bicycles, each of which must have carried loads close to three hundred pounds, struggle down the dirt road in front of them. It was tempting to stop and rig a claymore, or leave behind a couple of antipersonnel mines in each case, but Gerber was far more interested in putting as much distance as possible between the team and the pursuing enemy than he was in harassing traffic on the Trail in a fairly minor way.

When they reached the main branch of the Trail coming south out of Ban Tasseng, a fairly well-graded and maintained all-weather route covered with pea gravel, they were held up for fifteen minutes while a convoy of thirty-two trucks growled slowly along the road with their lights out. For men used to seeing the Vietcong on foot in squad- or platoon-sized units, it was something of a shock to see nearly eighty tons of supplies being trucked along a good road. Gerber did his best to locate the position of each road as accurately as possible on his maps for later use by the Air Force.

Once across the main trail, they walked steadily for two hours, then paused for a fifteen-minute break. After that they would move for fifty minutes and rest for ten. Fetterman, still covering their rear, had seen no sign of pursuit for several hours, although experience told him that the enemy hadn't given up the chase but were merely being more cautious after losing a few of their number to the traps the team had left behind. The team walked throughout the night and by morning were near the pickup point.

In the gray half-light of predawn Krung moved forward to scout the landing zone. As he neared the edge of the clearing, the air was suddenly filled with the rattle of AK-47s and the exaggerated burping of an RPD. The Chinese paratroops had been waiting for them, and an overeager young private, tense from a terror-filled night of waiting for his first combat, had fired the moment Krung stepped into view, springing the ambush too early. Krung was hit in the thigh and abdomen and went down, but immediately pushed himself back up into a semisitting position and returned fire with his AK-47.

Gerber immediately moved the team on-line, and all began firing back at the enemy, each side directing their fire toward the muzzle-flashes of the other.

Krung was hit again and fell back into the grass. Before anyone else could react, Tyme ran forward and snatched the little Nung tribesman by his shoulder harness and dragged him behind a tree trunk. As the others continued to lay down covering fire, Tyme then low-crawled fifty yards through the brush, pulling Krung behind him.

When he reached the others, Tyme quickly checked Krung and found that he was still alive, although having trouble breathing. He yanked off Krung's pack and webgear, opened the Nung's jacket and found an entrance wound in the lower left chest, but no accompanying exit wound. Tyme quickly covered the wound with his hand and dug out a field dressing, tearing open the plastic wrapper with his teeth. He opened out the plastic and placed it over the bullet hole, using tape from the first-aid kit on his belt to fasten down three sides of the plastic. He then tied the field dressing, actually a combination bandage and compress, over the upper two-thirds of the plastic to act as a flutter valve in case a tension pneumothorax developed. The improvised occlusive dressing in place, Tyme used another of Krung's field dressings and one of his own to bandage the scout's other wounds.

"How is he?" yelled Gerber, firing his AK in short, controlled bursts. The last was marked by three green tracers, letting him know that his weapon was empty, and he hit the magazine release forward of the trigger guard, letting the empty magazine fall to the ground as he dug a full one out of one of the pouches on his chest webbing. He snapped the loaded magazine into the AK, drew back the operating handle and let the bolt slam home, chambering a round. He sighted again and continued firing.

"Not good!" Tyme shouted back. "He's alive, but just barely."

"You know the drill," Gerber shouted back, feeling sick as he said it. He had known Krung a long time and considered him a good friend.

"To hell with that shit, sir. We didn't come this far to start shooting our own people. He'll make it. I'll carry him."

"Justin!" Gerber started to protest.

"Damn it, Captain, I said I'll carry him!"

Gerber let it go. There was no time for an argument, and he wasn't too keen on killing Krung, anyway. The green tracers, the last three rounds in each of his magazines, ripped their way out of the barrel once again, and he switched magazines a second time.

"We're breaking contact!" yelled Gerber. "Bhang! Get some grenades on those sons of bitches now! Everybody fall back a hundred meters and make for the secondary pickup point on my signal."

Bhang fired quickly, using the M-79. The range was only about a hundred and fifty meters, but her first round was short and her second shot too long. She got the next four on the tree line at the far side of the LZ where the enemy was, however, and suddenly the Chinese became temporarily disinterested in continuing the battle.

"Now!" yelled Gerber.

Tyme threw Krung over his shoulder, and moving as one, the team got up and ran.

They ran for almost forty-five minutes solid, at first panting, then gasping and finally staggering under the weight of their equipment, Tyme burdened with the extra load of Krung and both their weapons. By the end of it Bunnell's wound was bleeding again, his trouser leg soaked with blood, and he was hobbling along using his machine gun as a walking stick.

They were almost to the second LZ when machine gunfire from two RPDs pinned them down. The enemy had once again beaten them to the LZ.

Gerber had no way of knowing it, but they had just run into Rhee, his interpreter and five very good, combat-experienced Pathet Lao soldiers. Rhee had guessed correctly the team's intended destination.

For perhaps fifteen minutes the two groups exchanged fire. Gerber's team couldn't maneuver, and indeed could hardly stick their heads up far enough to return accurate fire. SAT-team Chuck Connors had suddenly gone from a fairly well-executed mission to a fight for its life.

And then things got worse. In the distance a helicopter could be heard approaching, and Bocker began trying to contact the extraction team on the small UHF transceiver but could get no response. The sound of the helicopter got louder, and abruptly they could see it through the trees as it passed overhead and settled onto the LZ beyond the enemy. It was the North Vietnamese Mi-4 Hound, bringing the reinforcements Rhee had ordered.

Being on the other end of an air assault, even if it was only from a single helicopter, was so unusual that for a moment Gerber and the others were stunned. It was obvious that the enemy could simply keep ferrying troops until the team was overcome by the weight of sheer numbers. They were already beginning to run low on ammunition and were so well pinned down by the cross fire from the two RPDs that they couldn't disengage. The troops were too beat for another marathon run, anyway. Something had to be done, and fast.

The break came when Corbett managed to hit one of the RPD gunners and the machine gun fell silent. It wasn't much, but it gave them some room to maneuver. They took it.

As Rhee realized what was happening, he knew he couldn't wait for his reinforcements. Using his remaining machine gunner to cover his flank, he took his interpreter and the three remaining Pathet Lao and swung around in a wide circle to cut off the escaping team. The two opposing forces clashed almost head-on.

Fetterman and Corbett, now on the far flank of Gerber's team, pivoted around in a wide arc to try to get behind Rhee's group. If they couldn't break up the blocking force quickly, the fresh Pathet Lao from the helicopter would come up behind the team and chop them to pieces.

Fetterman and Corbett pushed through a thicket and came out not behind the enemy as they had intended, but on the enemy's flank. The range was too close to use grenades.

"Rush 'em!" yelled Fetterman. He charged forward, firing his AK in short bursts.

Corbett, thinking a direct assault a silly thing for a sniper to do, threw the rifle up to his shoulder to shoot, but Fetterman stepped into the line of fire. Unable to see his target, Corbett ran toward the enemy as well, his mouth open in the war yell he hadn't used since boot camp. As they ran down the slope toward the enemy, Fetterman's AK emptied, and he pulled out a pistol and shot the nearest Pathet Lao three times in the back.

They were almost on top of the enemy when a loud explosion knocked both men to the ground. The Pathet Lao had been preparing to throw a grenade toward Gerber's group when the three rounds from Fetterman's pistol had caught him in the back. He dropped the grenade, which detonated after the normal three-second delay, killing his two comrades lying next to him. The blast swept both Corbett and Fetterman off their feet, injured Rhee and ruptured the eardrums of his interpreter. For a moment the jungle became eerily silent.

Gradually Corbett became aware of the sound of the North Vietnamese helicopter in the distance. There was blood streaming from a cut above his right eye. It had gotten into the eye and he could barely see. His right arm refused to function, and he thought it might be broken.

Slowly he looked around and found his rifle lying a few feet away, the ART scope atop it smashed. He crawled painfully to it, picked the rifle up with his left hand and steadied it across his knee. He bent his head over, sighted along the top of the barrel and shot the now-screaming interpreter who held both hands pressed over his ears.

It was no way to sight or hold a rifle, and it took Corbett six rounds to hit the man, even thought he distance was less than thirty feet. As the Vietnamese toppled over, the bolt locked back on the M-21, telling Corbett that his weapon was empty. Feeling suddenly very tired, he let the rifle slip from his knee.

Dazed, Fetterman sat up and looked around for a weapon, but there were none within easy reach. He had lost his pistol when the grenade exploded and it was no-where to be found. With an effort he pushed himself up on one knee. His empty AK lay about a yard away. All he had to do was pick it up and put a fresh magazine in it, then chamber a round and go forward to check the bod-ies.

As Fetterman started toward the rifle, Rhee rose out of the grass and the two men stared each other directly in the face. "You?" said Rhee with a look of utter disbelief.

"You!" replied Fetterman. "I might have known."

Rhee stooped slowly to pick up his own AK-47. There was no way for Fetterman to get to his rifle, load it, cham-ber a round and fire in time.

Corbett, with an empty rifle himself and a broken arm, suddenly remembered that he wasn't completely un-armed. With his left hand he pulled up his trouser leg, ripped free the Velcro and pulled out the little PPK the master sergeant had given him in Kontum.

"Fetterman! Catch!" he yelled as he tossed the pistol.

The Green Beret master sergeant moved with the speed of a cobra, caught the small German-made semiauto-matic in midair, threw his hand out forward, as though he intended to toss the pistol underhanded, and pumped five rounds into Rhee's face, just as the Chinese was lining up the AK-47 on him. The soft-nosed hollowpoint bullets chewed into Rhee's head and bored out the back of his skull as he toppled over backward.

Pistol in hand, Fetterman walked over and knelt beside Rhee Ming Wong to feel for a carotid pulse.

"Is he dead?" asked Corbett.

"He's dead," Fetterman answered, picking up Rhee's AK. "This time the SOB is really dead."

"See," said Corbett. "I told you no one's bulletproof one hundred percent of the time."

Fetterman started to rise. As he did so, something bright and shiny lying next to the Chinese officer caught his eye, and he picked it up, slowly turning it over in his hand. It was a cigarette lighter—Ian McMillan's Zippo. "At last you're avenged, old friend," he said too softly for Corbett to hear.

Fetterman pocketed the lighter and straightened. He checked the bodies of the other four men, then checked the magazine in Rhee's AK to make sure it was loaded. Finally he picked up his own rifle and walked over to help Corbett up.

"Told you I'd get that thing back to you in one piece," said Corbett, nodding at the Walther.

"You got a great sense of timing, kid. That was a nice toss."

"Yeah," Corbett agreed. "Left-handed, too. My old man would have been proud."

"So why didn't you just shoot him yourself?"

"Christ, Fetterman, I'm right-handed. I'd have likely as not hit you instead of him. Besides, I'm a rifleman. I never was all that hot with a handgun, anyway."

"In that case, Rifleman Corbett, you'd better have this," said Fetterman, handing him Rhee's AK-47. "It's not really a rifleman's rifle like the M-21, but it looks like your weapon is pretty well fucked up.''

"Thanks, now how about helping me up? Careful of the right arm. I think I broke it."

As Fetterman helped Corbett to his feet, the North Vietnamese helicopter lifted and flew off. "Come on, Gyrine, we got work to do. We're not out of the woods yet."

They started back toward the rest of the team, but met Gerber and the others coming toward them.

"You guys okay?" asked Gerber.

"Corbett says he thinks he's got a busted arm," Fetterman told him. "Other than that, just a loud ringing in our ears. Rhee's over there." He nodded in the general direction.

"Rhee?"

"This time he's dead for sure," said Fetterman. "I found this lying next to him." He showed Gerber the lighter.

Gerber read the inscription and merely nodded. "We got the other machine gunner," Gerber told him. "And Bocker finally managed to raise the extraction team. Green Hornet One-Seven is inbound with gunship support. I think that's why the NVAF left in such a big hurry. Must have spotted our boy's outriders coming in with their fangs out. We may still have unfriendlies on the ground to worry about, however, so I'm not going to risk the LZ or try for another. Bhang says there's a small clearing about five hundred yards from here. We'll use that."

The team walked the distance, and Gerber popped smoke to mark the location for the helicopters. A few minutes later one hovered overhead, while two gunships buzzed back and forth like angry bees, looking for a target.

"He'll never be able to set that thing down in here," said Corbett.

"He's not going to," replied Fetterman as twin rope ladders dropped from either side of the helicopter.

"Oh, shit. I was afraid this was going to happen," said Corbett. "We used to practice it in recon training."

They clipped themselves onto rungs of the rope ladders, thoughtfully dropped in a bundle from above, and secured the unconscious Krung in a similar fashion. As the helicopter lifted them up out of the jungle and swung around to point its nose toward the southeast and Kontum, trailing its passengers underneath on the swaying ladders, Fetterman heard Corbett say something but couldn't quite make it out.

It sounded like, "God, I hate heights."

EPILOGUE

The debriefing was over and Bates had produced a box of cigars and a bottle of Beam's Choice as they sat on folding steel chairs outside the bunker, feeling the cooling breeze of the first evening in weeks without rain. When the first bottle was empty, he had brought out a second, and with that gone, finally pulled the cork on a third, but everyone was feeling pretty mellow now, and the level of liquor had hardly gone down in the bottle.

"I want to congratulate you boys again," said Bates, slurring his words. "You did a hell of a job. It was a good mission."

Tyme and Bocker were nearly asleep in their chairs. Corbett, his arm in a cast, had been there for a while earlier, but had finally gone off looking for Bhang. "To discuss the finer points of Indochinese politics and learn a bit more about the war in Southeast Asia," he had claimed.

"*Was* it a good mission?" asked Gerber. "We lost Yoon almost before it got started. Krung's in the hospital with three bullet holes in him. Corbett broke his shooting arm.

Fetterman and Bocker almost got killed. And Bunnell has a hole in his leg and the nurses won't give him any beer. You call that a good mission? To me, a good mission is one where everybody comes home in one piece. We couldn't even bring Yoon home. He's buried beneath some brush pile at the edge of a field in Laos.''

"I call it a successful mission," said Bates. "You got six out of seven targets, including all of the Chinese."

"But I wonder, did we really make any difference?" said Gerber. "If the Chinese are hell-bent on coming into the war, this won't stop them."

"No," agreed Bates, "but it may slow them down a little. If that happens, and they get to thinking things over, they may decide they don't want to play at all. Quit being so hard on yourself, Mack. You couldn't have done anything about Yoon or the rest of it. Rule number one is, people die in wars. You know that."

"And rule number two is, you and I can't change rule number one," said Gerber.

"There it is," replied Bates.

"You're awfully quiet this evening, Master Sergeant," said Gerber. "Got something on your mind?"

"Just thinking things over a bit, sir. Running through the mission again. Trying to figure what, if anything, should have been done differently."

"And the way you see it is?"

"I'd have to call it very successful, despite the cost, sir. We did what we set out to do and we evened an old score. Sort of like killing two birds with one stone. And now, sir, if you and Colonel Bates will excuse me, I think I'll turn in. I'm rather tired and I'm looking forward to a good night's sleep."

"No more ghost of Rhee Ming Wong to haunt your dreams, Tony?" asked Gerber.

"No, sir. This time I got to touch the body, Captain. This time the kill is confirmed."

GLOSSARY

AAA—Antiaircraft artillery. Machine guns, cannon or guided missiles. Also called Triple A.

A-CAMP—Fortresslike base, often triangular or star-shaped, built by Special Forces as a base of operations in Vietnam. Such camps were often designated by the alphanumeric designation of the team that constructed or used it, as in Camp A-102.

ACTION AREA—Immediate terrain in which a raid, assault, air strike or other military action will occur.

AFVN—American Armed Forces radio network in Vietnam.

AIR AMERICA—Airline and air freight service actually owned and operated by the CIA in Southeast Asia. It served as a useful cover for clandestine air ops and supply flights to covert Green Beret teams in Laos and Cambodia.

AIR STUDIES GROUP—Air operating arm of MACV-SOG. It was composed of the Ninetieth Special Operations Wing and included a squadron of U.S. Air Force UH-1F Green Hornet helicopters, a squadron of USAF C-130 transports, a covert-operations squadron of C-123s flown by Nationalist Chinese pilots and the South Vietnamese 219th Sikorsky H-34 helicopter squadron. It was headquartered at Nha Trang.

AO—Area of Operations. Geographic area in which a military unit conducts its activities.

ART—Automatic Ranging Telescope. A telescopic sight used by snipers that utilizes a system of stadia wire linked to camps to automatically calculate the range to a target and adjust the cross hairs in the scope to compensate for bullet drop at the point of intended impact.

ARVN—Army of the Republic of Vietnam. The South Vietnamese Army. Often disparagingly referred to as Marvin Arvin.

ASH AND TRASH—Routine supply mission.

A-TEAM—Basic ten-to-twelve-man operational detachment of Special Forces advisers.

BDA—Bomb Damage Assessment. Ground reconnaissance to determine the effectiveness of an air strike.

BOOM-BOOM—Term used by Vietnamese prostitutes to sell their product.

BOONDOGGLE—Any operation that hasn't been thoroughly thought out.

BROWNING P-35—Last pistol designed by American firearms inventor John Moses Browning. A 9 mm parabellum semiautomatic pistol with a 13-round magazine, it is probably the most widely issued military side arm in the non-Communist world and was popular with Special Forces troops.

BUG—Adaptation of the radiotelegraph straight key, allowing greater ease of operation and transmission of Morse code at a higher speed. Also any electronic eavesdropping device.

C-47—U.S. World War II-vintage twin-engined transport aircraft. An attack version, the AC-47, equipped with miniguns and parachute flares for night operations, was known as Puff the Magic Dragon.

C-123—Fairchild Provider. A twin-engined cargo plane developed from the design of a World War II glider. It could carry sixty-one troops or twenty-four thousand pounds of freight and operate from short, unimproved airfields. Later versions were augmented with two J-85 turbojet pods under the wings. The C-123 was used extensively in Vietnam.

C-130—Lockheed Hercules. A four-engined turboprop transport aircraft. It could fly at 368 miles per hour, could carry 92 troops or 64 paratroops and had a maximum range of more than 4,000 miles. It was probably the most commonly used cargo plane of the Vietnam war. An attack version, the AC-130 gunship, armed with miniguns, 20 mm Vulcan cannon and sometimes 40 mm automatic cannon or even a 105 mm howitzer, was known as Specter.

C-141—Lockheed StarLifter. Heavy cargo aircraft. A four- to six-man crewed strategic transport powered by four-jet turbofan engines. It can carry 154 troops or 127 paratroops or more than 50,000 pounds of cargo and has a range of more than 6,000 miles and a maximum cruising speed exceeding 500 miles per hour.

CHARLIE—From the phonetic alphabet Victor Charles for the letters *VC*. The Vietcong. Used generically for both the VC and the NVA. Also known as Mr. Charles and Luke the Gook.

CHICOM—Chinese Communist.

CHINOOK—U.S. Army CH-47 twin-rotor helicopter. Called a shit hook by the troops because of all the ''shit'' stirred up by the rotors during takeoff and landing. The Navy and Marine Corps used the similar CH-46 Sea Knight.

CLAYMORE—U.S.-made directional mine. It can be either command-detonated by a small hand-held generator or other electrical device, or mechanically detonated by a trip wire. It weighs about 3.5 pounds and fires 750 steel pellets in a deadly, fan-shaped pattern. It is considered lethal out to fifty meters but can produce casualties out to 250 meters.

CO CONG—Female Vietcong.

COLT—American arms manufacturer that produced both the model 1911A1 .45-caliber semiautomatic pistol and the M-16A1 assault rifle. Also the NATO code name for the Antonov An-2 biplane, a light Soviet cargo and transport aircraft designed to operate from short, rough airfields.

COM-SEC—Communications Security. Refers either to using codes or special equipment to prevent enemy intercepts of RF transmissions, or to efforts to locate enemy transmitters.

CO VAN—Vietnamese for *adviser*. A title of address used by the Vietnamese when referring to the U.S. military personnel assigned as advisers to the local militia and the district and province forces and administrators.

C-RATIONS—U.S. military canned combat rations, designed to be eaten either hot or cold right from the can.

CW—Continuous Wave. Morse code radio transmissions.

DEROS—Date Estimated Return from Overseas Service.

DEUCE-AND-A-HALF—Six-wheel drive, two-and-a-half-ton truck used by U.S. military.

DI—Drill Instructor. An NCO in charge of the basic training of soldiers or Marines.

DISTRICT MOBILE COMPANY—Major Vietcong guerrilla fighting unit organized within an administrative district. It carried out offensive operations, sabotage and terrorism.

DZ—Drop Zone. A landing field for parachutists or supplies dropped by parachute.

FINE BUSINESS FIST—Said of a Morse code operator who transmits clearly and is pleasing to listen to with very few errors.

FRONT—National Liberation Front. The North Vietnamese and Vietcong effort to "liberate" South Vietnam and unify the country under Communist rule.

FWMF—Free World Military Forces. Term used to describe the South Vietnamese, Australian, New Zealand, Filipino and Thai forces in Vietnam. U.S.

forces were sometimes included in this term and sometimes spoken of separately.

GI COFFEE—Strongest and worst-tasting coffee in the world, with the possible exception of Marine Corps coffee.

GREEN BERETS—U.S. Army Special Forces soldiers trained in counterinsurgency and unconventional warfare. They were frequently "loaned" to the CIA for special operations and conducted raids and reconnaissance deep behind enemy lines or clandestinely into Laos and Cambodia.

GUNNY—U.S. Marine Corps slang for a gunnery sergeant, roughly the equivalent of an Army sergeant first class.

GYRINE—Slang for a Marine. May be used either affectionately, or in an insulting manner.

HAHO—High Altitude, High Opening. A high-altitude exit, chute-opening parachute jump, usually used in conjunction with lateral insertions.

HALO—High Altitude, Low Opening parachute drop. To make sure an extended free-fall parachute jump from high altitude, waiting to open the chute until close to the ground. Militarily the technique is used to avoid observation or when for other reasons it is not desirable to deploy the chute at high altitude, but it is desirable to leave the aircraft at high altitude.

HAT—Green Beret. Special Forces men referred to themselves as Hats and reminded non-Special Forces personnel who used them that they weren't Hats.

HF—High Frequency. That portion of the radio spectrum used for long-range transmissions, usually CW rather than voice.

HOOTCH—Almost any structure, from a bamboo-and-thatch hut to a permanent building.

HOUND—NATO code name for the MIL Mi-4 helicopter, an eight- to fourteen-passenger piston-engine helicopter resembling the Sikorsky S-55. The Mi-4 has been used by the Soviet Union since 1953. Equipped with clamshell rear doors, it can carry a GAZ-69 command car or a 76 mm antitank gun instead of troops and is normally armed with a machine gun pod under the forward fuselage.

HT—Hand radio. Small radio transceiver used for short-range voice communications.

HUEY—Any of the series of Bell UH-1 helicopters. Perhaps the best-known helicopter of the Vietnam War.

IN-COUNTRY—Said of troops serving in Vietnam. They were all in-country.

IR—Infrared. A portion of the electromagnetic spectrum not visible to the naked eye. Night vision devices work either by amplifying existing light, as in the Starlite scope, or by using a filter over a spotlamp light source to send out a beam of infrared light visible only through a special image tube attached to a telescopic sight, as with the active IR weapons sight. IR systems also detect heat emissions invisible to the naked eye and can be used to track a jet or missile exhaust, or locate the heat from the engines of camouflaged vehicles.

IRT—Infantry Regiment Training. The Marine infantry counterpart to the Army's AIT (Advanced Individual Training) for foot soldiers. A course following boot camp that teaches patrolling, orienteering and other specialized skills for the infantryman beyond those learned in boot camp or basic training.

JUMPMASTER—One who acts as the person in charge of a parachute drop and makes sure the first man in a stick of jumpers exits at the proper moment. He also makes sure everyone and all equipment get out of the aircraft safely and on time.

KHA—Killed in Hostile Action. See *KIA*.

KIA—Killed in Action. Since Vietnam wasn't a declared war, use of the term KIA wasn't authorized for U.S. casualties. The term KHA was used instead. KIA was used to refer to enemy dead only.

LAKE ERIE SWING—The swing is a unique "accent" representing the exaggeration of dits and dahs when using a bug, developed by some telegraphers. The Lake Erie Swing is a peculiar type, named for the region of the country in which it developed with old-time railroad telegraphers.

LATERAL INSERTION—Technique of using a steerable, ram-air or square-rigged parachute canopy in conjunction with a HAHO jump in order to maneuver laterally for several kilometers after exiting the aircraft. Thus the airplane doesn't pass directly over the drop zone, making anticipation of the landing site by the enemy much more difficult. Lateral insertion is a frequently used method of inserting troops for covert or clandestine operations.

LEG—Derogatory term for military personnel who aren't airborne-qualified.

LIMITED WARFARE LABORATORY—Established in 1962 in Maryland, it was supposed to develop counterinsurgency weapons and hardware for the U.S. Army to employ in limited war situations. It did develop some useful products, such as a leech repellent and lighter, high-calorie meals to replace the old C-rations, but many of the inventions it came up with were characterized by a lack of common sense and proved useless in combat.

LLDB—Lac Luong Dac Biet. The South Vietnamese Special Forces. Early in the war LLDB troops were little more than an elite political guard and were sometimes referred to as Lousy Little Dirty Bug-outs because of their tendency to run away from combat. The LLDB Training Center was at Dong Ba Thin. After October 1969 it was known as the National Training Center. U.S. Army SF Detachment B-51 served as advisers to the RVN staff at the center and were successful in transforming the LLDB into an effective elite fighting unit.

LZ—Landing Zone. A landing field or clearing for helicopters.

M-14—U.S. 7.62 mm assault rifle. A 20-round magazine-fed rifle normally firing in the semiautomatic mode but capable of being fitted with a selector permitting fully automatic fire. It replaced the M-1 Garand rifle and M-1 carbine as the standard U.S. shoulder arm and was itself replaced by the M-16. It was widely used during the early U.S. involvement in Vietnam and didn't begin to be generally supplanted by the M-16 until about early 1968, although some units, such as Special Forces, were equipped with the M-16 as early as 1964.

M-16—Any of a series of lightweight selective-fire assault rifles chambered for the 5.56 mm round. The M-16 replaced the M-14, becoming the U.S. military's standard infantry rifle of the Vietnam War.

M-21 SNIPER SYSTEM—Specially modified M-14 rifle fitted with a Sionics sound suppressor and a quick-change mount for either a three- to nine-power variable Leatherwood/Redfield Automatic Ranging Telescope or the Starlite passive night vision device. It was used by U.S. Army snipers in Vietnam.

M-79—Shoulder-fired 40 mm grenade launcher resembling a single-shot shotgun with an overgrown sawed-off barrel.

MAC—Military Airlift Command. The USAF air transport service.

MACV—Military Assistance Command, Vietnam. The U.S. advisory effort in South Vietnam.

MARKER ROUND—White phosphorus (WP) artillery shell set to explode above the trees and fired at a known map location in order to aid patrols in the jungle in locating their exact position. Also such a round used to mark the position of an enemy target.

MASTER RIGGER—Person highly experienced in packing parachutes so that they will deploy properly.

MAT—Mobile Advisory Team. Small five- or six-man teams, often Special Forces, that worked with village militia units scattered throughout the districts of a province in South Vietnam.

MAT-49—Compact 9 mm parabellum submachine gun of French manufacture.

MCGUIRE RIG—Harness and rope assembly that could be used to jerk the wearer off the ground and up from the jungle when a helicopter couldn't land to pick him up because of dense trees. Using a McGuire rig meant a long and exciting ride back to base, hanging suspended beneath the helicopter, but was preferable to falling into enemy hands.

MEDEVAC—Medical evacuation of casualties. Said of helicopters and fixed-wing aircraft used as flying ambulances.

MI-4—Soviet helicopter. See *HOUND*.

MIG-21—Single-seat, short-range jet interceptor with limited all-weather capability. The MiG-21 carries one or two 30 mm automatic cannon and usually two Atoll infrared homing missiles similar to the U.S. Sidewinder. The MiG-21 is widely used throughout the Communist or Eastern-aligned world and was the mainstay fighter of the North Vietnamese Air Force.

NCO—Noncommissioned Officer. A corporal or any of the various ranks of sergeant.

NUNG—Member of the Nung Tai ethnic group of Chinese origin. Nung were often employed as mercenary soldiers by the Special Forces and CIA in Indochina.

NVA—North Vietnamese Army, as distinct from the Vietcong. Also known as the PAVN (People's Army of Vietnam).

OD—Olive Drab. A dark grayish-green color.

OP—Operation. A military mission. Also an observation post.

ORIGINATING OPERATION—Radio operator who originates a contact, i.e., the person who is calling with a message.

P-38—Small folding can opener of sheet metal issued with C-rations. Called a John Wayne can opener by the Marine Corps. Also the Lockheed Lightning, a twin-engine long-range fighter aircraft of World War II vintage.

PLA—People's Liberation Army. The Chinese Communist military, including naval and air forces.

POW—Prisoner Of War.

PRAIRIE FIRE—Cover name for U.S. Special Forces covert operations in Laos.

PSP—Perforated Steel Plate. Steel or aluminum planking with holes bored in it used to surface runways and occasionally roads in Vietnam. It was also sometimes laid down as sidewalk.

PUNJI PIT—Booby trap consisting of a small hole lined with sharpened bamboo stakes designed to penetrate the foot and covered over with sod or other camouflage. The stakes are sometimes dipped in water buffalo urine or covered with excrement to induce infection in the victim, which can be very difficult to treat even with modern antibiotics.

PUZZLE PALACE—The Pentagon.

PUZZLE PALACE EAST—MACV Headquarters, Saigon.

RDF—Radio Direction Finding or Range and Direction Finding. Electronic equipment or the use of such equipment for "fixing" or triangulating the position of a radio transmitter. Depending upon the sophistication of the equipment, it can also tell the range or distance to the transmitter.

RDM—Reported Direction of March. The route of travel followed by a military unit as reported by an observer.

RF—Radio Frequency. Electronic emissions in the radio portion of the electromagnetic spectrum. Also Reconnaissance Fighter, a prefix denoting a fighter aircraft modified to carry cameras or other intelligence-gathering equipment.

RF-4—Photo-reconnaissance version of the F-4 Phantom II jet fighter. The F-4 in all its various configurations was perhaps the most widely used American fighter of the Vietnam War and served as an air superiority fighter, reconnaissance aircraft and close air support fighter-bomber, as well as being used to bomb North Vietnam.

RF-101—Although obsolescent by the time of major U.S. involvement in the Vietnam War, this photo-reconnaissance version of the F-101 Voodoo jet interceptor saw extensive use in Southeast Asia.

ROA—Radius of Action. The fan-shaped area described by a line drawn from a sniper team's position in an arc around it. This is the area in which the team will engage enemy targets.

RP—Rally Point or Rendezvous Point. A previously agreed-upon meeting place, particularly one where troops will regroup immediately following an assault or raid.

RPD—Soviet Bloc squad light machine gun firing the same 7.62 mm round as the AK-47 but fed from a 100-round, nondisintegrating metal link belt housed in a drum-type carrier beneath the weapon.

RPG-7—Soviet-made rocket-propelled grenade launcher similar in appearance to a bazooka.

RTO—Radio Telephone Operator. The radioman of a military unit. Also, but less often, Radio Telegraph Operator. A Morse code radio operator.

RUFF-PUFFS—Regional Forces-Popular Forces. South Vietnamese district and village militia units. A sort of paramilitary home guard.

RUOU NEP—Alcoholic drink made from fermented glutinous rice.

RVN—Republic of Vietnam. South Vietnam.

SAM—Surface-to-Air Missile. Often redundantly called a SAM missile. It can be any surface-to-air guided missile, but in Vietnam usually referred to the SA-2 Guideline, a Soviet missile used for air defense by North Vietnam.

SANDY—A-1D Skyraider. Developed as a U.S. Navy attack aircraft at the end of World War II, it was flown extensively by Air Force pilots in Vietnam in the counterinsurgency role. It was well armored with self-sealing gas tanks and very heavily armed.

Although not fast, it could loiter over a target for a long time and carry an impressive amount of bombs, napalm and rockets.

SAT—Special Action Team. A MACV-SOG clandestine operations team assembled for a specific, onetime-only mission. Usually redundantly referred to as a SAT-team.

SECTION EIGHT—Military discharge for being mentally incompetent.

SF—Special Forces. Elite U.S. troops trained in counterinsurgency and unconventional warfare. Sometimes referred to as Science Fiction because they were so fantastic.

SFOB—Special Forces Operating Base. The headquarters for a Special Forces C-Detachment, which coordinates the activities of the various B-Detachments and their subordinate A-Detachments.

SHORT TIME—Marine Corps slang in Vietnam for a quickie. Also the days remaining on one's tour of duty. See *Short-Timer*.

SHORT-TIMER—One whose tour of duty is nearly over. A soldier with less than ten days remaining in-country was said to be a single-digit midget, while whichever man in a unit had the least amount of time remaining before he could go home was said to be next.

SKY PILOT—Derogatory slang for a military chaplain. Derived from the hit song by the musical group known as the Animals.

SMOKE ROUNDS—See *Marker Round* and *WP*.

SNUFFIE—From Snuffie Smith. Marine slang for lower-ranking enlisted personnel.

SOG—Studies and Observations Group. Cover name for MACV special operations group that conducted covert and clandestine operations in Vietnam, Laos, Cambodia, North Vietnam and even China. Mostly made up of U.S. Army Special Forces personnel, MACV-SOG also employed Navy SEALs and Marine recon personnel and had its own air assets (Air Studies Group).

SOI—Signal Operating Instructions. Small booklet containing radio frequencies, code words and authentication tables to be used for radio communications.

SOP—Standard Operating Procedure. The way things are normally done.

SPOOKY—World War II-vintage C-47 cargo aircraft fitted with three miniguns—a type of modern Gatling gun—and used for aerial fire support. Also known as Puff the Magic Dragon because the tracers from the miniguns were said to resemble the breath of a fire-breathing dragon when seen at night.

SR-71—From Strategic Reconnaissance. A large, very high-speed aircraft that replaced the U-2 spy plane in the 1960s. It carries a two-man crew who wear astronaut-type pressure suits and can fly at more than a hundred thousand feet altitude. Fast enough to outrun enemy fighters and missiles, it remains the current U.S. high-altitude reconnaissance aircraft.

STARLITE SCOPE—Passive night vision device that works by amplification of existing light, hence the name. The technology used in these scopes was considered secret in Vietnam and users had orders to destroy them to prevent their capture by the enemy.

STRIKE FORCE—CIDG (Civilian Irregular Defense Group) mercenaries hired by Special Forces and organized into company- or battalion-sized groups for camp defense or offensive operations.

STRIKER—Member of a CIDG strike force. Trained, equipped and led by Special Forces personnel, the CIDG strike force was usually composed of ethnic tribesmen who often hated the South Vietnamese as much as they did the Vietcong but were fiercely loyal to the Green Berets who trained them and led them in combat. They received better pay and equipment than the Ruff-Puffs and were exempt from the ARVN as long as they remained in the Strike Force.

TAIL GUNNER—Rear guard of a unit. The last man in a patrol formation. Opposite of point. Also called drag or trail.

TEAM HOUSE—Building or bunker in which members of a Special Forces team or a MACV-SOG special action/special mission team was housed. It was often a combination barracks, briefing room, chow hall and recreation room. Officers and NCOs alike share the same quarters, a situation unique to Special Forces.

TENTH—U.S. Army's Tenth Special Forces Group stationed at Bad Tolz, West Germany.

TOC—Tactical Operations Center. A radio-equipped bunker or command post from which an ongoing mission is monitored and directed.

TWO-OH-ONE (201) FILE—Soldier's personal records, listing his training, accomplishments and awards. The 201 file is sent with a soldier reporting to a new assignment so that the receiving commander may know something about his new trooper.

U-2—Slow-moving, high-flying reconnaissance aircraft used by the United States in the fifties and sixties. It had very long range, could fly at more than eighty-thousand feet altitude and carried sophisticated cameras and electronic and radiologic sensors.

UMZ—Ultramilitarized Zone. GI and Marine slang for the DMZ or Demilitarized Zone, which divided North Vietnam from South Vietnam at roughly the Seventeenth Parallel. So called because of all the military forces built up on both sides of it by the opposing armies.

WHA—Wounded in Hostile Action. See *WIA*.

WIA—Wounded In Action. Term in common use but not officially authorized for referring to U.S. soldiers wounded in action during Vietnam. WHA was the official term. See *KIA* for explanation.

WP—White Phosphorus. Also called smoke rounds, marker rounds, willie pete or wilson pickett—the latter particularly in predominantly black units. White phosphorus chemical used in grenades, artillery and mortar shells and bombs. It is an incendiary mixture producing dense white smoke and causes terrible burns on contact with flesh. Used to mark targets, destroy flammable materials, produce casualties and for psychological effects.

ZU-23—Soviet 23 mm twin automatic cannons on a towable chassis, used for low-altitude air defense. A quad (four cannon) mount on a tracked, self-propelled chassis with integral targeting radar is known as the ZSU-23.

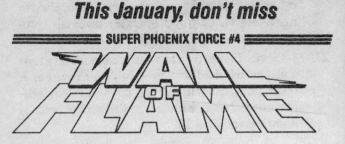

Phoenix Force—bonded in secrecy to avenge the acts of terrorists everywhere

SEARCH AND DESTROY $3.95 ☐

American "killer" mercenaries are involved in a KGB plot to
overthrow the government of a South Pacific island. The
American President, anxious to preserve his country's image and
not disturb the precarious position of the island nation's
government, sends in the experts—Phoenix Force—to prevent a
coup.

FIRE STORM $3.95 ☐

An international peace conference turns into open warfare when
terrorists kidnap the American President and the premier of the
USSR at a summit meeting. As a last desperate measure Phoenix
Force is brought in—for if demands are not met, a plutonium
core device is set to explode.

Total Amount	$ _____
Plus 75¢ Postage	___.75
Payment enclosed	$ _____

Please send a check or money order payable to Gold Eagle Books.

In the U.S.	In Canada
Gold Eagle Books	Gold Eagle Books
3010 Walden Ave.	P.O. Box 609
Box 1325	Fort Erie, Ontario
Buffalo, NY 14269-1325	L2A 5X3

Please Print

Name: _____

Address: _____

City: _____

State/Prov: _____

Zip/Postal Code: _____

SPF-AR

DON PENDLETON's
MACK BOLAN.

The line between good and evil is a tightrope no man should walk. Unless that man is the Executioner.

TIGHTROPE	$3.95	☐
When top officials of international Intelligence agencies are murdered, Mack Bolan pits his skill against an alliance of renegade agents and uncovers a deadly scheme to murder the U.S. President.		
MOVING TARGET	$3.95	☐
America's most powerful corporations are reaping huge profits by dealing in arms with anyone who can pay the price. Dogged by assassins, Mack Bolan becomes caught in a power struggle that might be his last.		
FLESH & BLOOD	$3.95	☐
When Asian communities are victimized by predators among their own—thriving gangs of smugglers, extortionists and pimps—they turn to Mack Bolan for help.		

Total Amount	$ _____
Plus 75¢ Postage	.75
Payment enclosed	$ _____